A FINE PLACE FOR DEATH

Also by Ann Granger

Say It With Poison
A Season for Murder
Cold In The Earth
Murder Among Us
Where Old Bones Lie

A FINE PLACE FOR DEATH

Ann Granger

St. Martin's Press
New York

A FINE PLACE FOR DEATH. Copyright © 1994 by Ann Granger. All
rights reserved. Printed in the United States of America. No part
of this book may be used or reproduced in any manner
whatsoever without written permission except in the case of brief
quotations embodied in critical articles or reviews. For
information, address St. Martin's Press, 175 Fifth Avenue,
New York, N.Y. 10010.

Library of Congress Cataloging-in-Publication Data

Granger, Ann.
A fine place for death : a Mitchell and Markby village whodunit /
Ann Granger.
p.   cm.
ISBN 0-312-11787-6
I. Title.
PR6057.R259F56   1995
823'.914—dc20   94-34238   CIP

First published in Great Britain by Headline Book Publishing

First U.S. Edition: January 1995
10 9 8 7 6 5 4 3 2 1

'The grave's a fine and private place,
But none, I think, do there embrace.'

Andrew Marvell

Chapter One

HUNGRY AND alert, the fox emerged from the maze of old tunnels which ran down beside the foundations of the abandoned building. In the deepest reaches of this animal-excavated catacomb the air was poisoned by a miasma of decay which made him uneasy, so that he never entered the lowest level.

Recently he'd been made uneasy above ground, too, by a new scent which had begun to pollute the copse, even up here where the air was fresh. Man had returned to this deserted spot. Man who, like the fox, moved by darkness about his purpose, and whose approach was signalled by the low roar of a car engine. The fox had learned to recognise the sound and slink away.

Tonight he trotted across the frost-crisped ground on his slender, black-stockinged legs. Pointed nose held low and bushy tail drooping, he urgently sought the scent of a meal, some refuse he could scavenge or creature weaker or more foolish than himself on which to prey. Then his sharp ears caught the distant mechanical growl. The fox paused, glancing back at the copse and the twin pepperpot turrets, touched with silver by the moon, which showed above the trees. A sudden beam of light swept over him, making his eyes gleam fiercely. Man had come again and, just briefly, the two prowlers of the night glimpsed one another before parting, each about his own mischief.

Adeline Conway stood by the window and stared fearfully into the darkened grounds. Her thin white fingers on which the loose rings had swivelled so that the precious stones were turned inwards, clutched a velvet curtain, crushing the pile. Her husband knew she was afraid of the dark. But he didn't call her to come away because he also knew that it held her fascinated. He

1

watched her twitch at the heavy drape, pulling it across to hide the silhouetted trees bowing and dancing against the night sky. As she turned back towards her chair by the fire, she rubbed chilled fingers together and he saw that the nails were bluish-white and that surreptitiously she twisted the rings back to their proper place.

'It's cold!' Her voice had a mewling, insistent plaintiveness like a lost kitten's. It was impossible to ignore it or to be angry with it.

Pity mingled with his exasperation. He sighed and got up to add a small log to the open fire in the wide Adam hearth.

The blaze spattered up with crackle of sparks and sent a pattern of shadows flickering round the room, disturbing a large black Persian cat which slumbered on the hearthrug. The cat raised its head and fixed Matthew with hostile emerald eyes. It knew he had caused the spit of embers and besides, being Adeline's pet, it reflected her moods and feeling towards him. If he ever attempted to smooth its fur, it bit him. Now its heavy head sank back on its paws and its eyes narrowed to mistrustful green slits, watching him.

Matthew's irritation redoubled. He would be going out shortly into the cold winter air and in here the warmth was unbearable. He'd very likely catch a chill and all because Adeline insisted on this room being heated up of an evening like a Kew Gardens hothouse. It was in marked contrast to the hallway and bedrooms which were left icy.

He stared rebelliously about him. The drawing room's eighteenth-century elegance still conveyed an aura of gracious living, though the paintwork was faded, furniture now a mish-mash of styles and the discarded sheets of his evening paper ill-disguised worn patches on the carpet.

Adeline fitted the surroundings well with her thin, aristocratic features and that slightly dishevelled air. As well she might, for she'd grown up here in this old house, her family home. Incapable she might be of many things, but not of deciding matters regarding Park House which was so indisputably hers, literally and morally. Hence the erratic heating. Hence the refusal to have the painters in, or other strangers to measure up for new curtains or carpets. Hence the impossibility of getting her out of the place, no matter what ...

His gaze moved to a nearby table scattered with photographs

and an early picture of his daughter as a baby, sitting on her mother's knee. He had only to look from that to the portrait hanging on the wall above, to see how soon the physical and mental disintegration in his wife had begun. In the oil painting Adeline was a lovely, laughing girl of eighteen, with curling chestnut hair and warm brown eyes. The young mother in the studio portrait stared out at the photographer with a haunted gaze and clutched nervously at the plump infant on her lap. Whenever he compared these two, as he often did despite himself, the old, guilt-ridden question came back. 'Has all this been my fault? Did I destroy her?' And with the guilt came the resentment, that he should be made to feel this way.

Matthew began to study his wife surreptitiously. She'd lost even more weight over this past year. She must be nothing but skin and bone without her clothes. But it was a long time since he'd seen her as anything but fully dressed.

Aloud he said, 'I'm going out to fetch Katie in about five minutes. Shall I call Prue?'

Adeline's face twitched. 'She ought not to be out there, after dark. It's dangerous! I wish Katie wouldn't go to that youth club. I wish she wouldn't go into Bamford at all. She meets the wrong sort of young person there! She's no idea ... she's such an innocent child! Those other youngsters, they're like – like young savages!'

'I'm sure Father Holland keeps a strict eye on his youth club!'

'I never had so much independence at her age! My parents would never have allowed me to mix with riff-raff!'

Despite himself, he nearly laughed aloud. They hadn't managed to stop her marrying what they'd probably thought riff-raff, had they?

'Times change, Addy. At least give Katie the chance to live some normal life. You'll get your way next summer when she goes to France, to Mireille.'

He tried but was unable to keep the bitterness from his voice. His wife, given her way, would have kept the child cocooned in a rarefied atmosphere which she could not see held its own dangers. Let Katie go out and enjoy herself like other kids! Let her learn about the real world. That had been his wish. Anything rather than have her grow up like her mother! That she had to grow up at all was almost too painful to contemplate.

3

Adeline had returned to her seat by the fire. Sam, the cat, sat up, craning his neck to see if there was space on her lap, but she'd picked up her embroidery in its round frame and was plucking nervously at the half-finished work. Matthew wondered vaguely what it was destined to be, a tray cloth or some other useless object. But she was an expert needlewoman and the mauve daisies and leaves in shades of green were beautifully worked.

She broke the awkward silence, saying, 'Yes, she must go to Mireille!'

He didn't want to start an argument. Anyway, there wasn't time just now.

'You're tired, Addy. I'll call Prue on my way out.' She didn't answer and he got up and stooped over her. 'You'll be in bed by the time I get back with Katie, so I'll say goodnight now.' He kissed her forehead.

She flinched before his touch. 'I want to see Katie when you come back! Tell her to look in my room and say goodnight!'

'Yes, of course.' He never received any invitation to her room these days. But he no longer cared. He'd long since made other arrangements in that regard. He squeezed her hand briefly in farewell but although he was sweating, her touch was still as cold as a corpse.

Matthew went out of the stuffy drawing room. Stepping into the hall was like stepping into a fridge but he drew a deep breath of relief. For a moment he stood there alone, enveloped by the quietness and emptiness of the big house. A long-case clock ticked softly in a corner. The time it told the world was wrong. It could have stood as a symbol for the whole place, out of its time, wrong and never to be put right. Not as far as he could see at any rate.

Matthew glanced to his left. In fact the house was subdivided nowadays. The corridor down there was blocked by a baize door. Getting that put in had meant weeks of argument with Addy, punctuated by bouts of her hysteria. But she'd agreed in the end because beyond it lay the office suite from which he ran his business affairs. The constant ringing of the telephone and clatter of the printer had disturbed her, but most of all the obtrusive nearness of his workaday business world, a breath of reality. She'd agreed to the door out of fear.

But he too hid. He hid behind that door from his domestic problems, immersing himself in work with the help of his personal assistant, Marla Lewis. Marla lived on the second floor in a self-contained flat. She never came anywhere near Adeline.

Matthew ran up the broad staircase and stopped before the first door at the top. Behind that lay another suite of private rooms, though less isolated from the house than Marla's. The accessibility of these rooms to those lived in by the family was necessary. From behind the door now came the faint sound of a television game show, laughter and applause. He tapped.

'Prue? Mrs Conway will go to bed now!'

The game show was abruptly silenced. He heard someone stirring on the other side and a no-nonsense voice called back, 'Right you are!'

'I'm going out now, over to Bamford to pick up my daughter!'

The door opened before his nose and he moved back with a start. A stocky capable-looking woman in a hand-knitted cardigan and tweed skirt appeared.

'Off you go then,' she said. 'Don't worry, I can manage.'

'Thank you, Prue.' He paused then added, 'I really do thank you. Without you, I couldn't, we couldn't . . .'

'Yes, yes, go along!' She cut him short briskly.

As he went out of the front door, pulling on his overcoat and revelling in the cold crisp night air on his sweating face, he heard Prue Wilcox open the drawing-room door behind him and say, 'Ready to go up the wooden hill, are we, dear?' as if she addressed a child.

He pulled the front door to and set off towards his car, fumbling for his keys. Things couldn't go on as they were. He couldn't take it much longer.

The sweat was cooling unpleasantly on his skin in the night breeze. He rubbed his broad hands over his face and all at once felt old, although he was only forty-eight. In his prime, damn it all. Yet if things went on in their inexorable, predictable way, his life held nothing, his past successes reminders only of the optimism he'd lost, his future inescapably shackled to Adeline.

He'd grown up in a three-bed terraced row in a London suburb and made his way in the world by his own efforts, his brain and his talents. He was proud of that. He'd met Adeline quite by chance at someone's party, a gathering at which he'd been a rank outsider, awkward and belligerent with shyness. Adeline too had been shy, even though she'd belonged there and had been among friends. They'd been drawn together. Perhaps she'd felt sorry for him. He'd simply thought her quite the most beautiful creature he'd ever seen. Their marriage had appeared to him a culmination of all his ambitions. And when Katie was born that, of course, had been the icing on the cake.

From that time on, however, it had all been downhill.

Like many unhappy couples, they'd long been linked only by their child. But even about Katie they couldn't agree. Adeline's idea of preparing Katie for adult life was to send her to Paris for a year when she finished school in the summer. He loathed the stupid plan hatched by his wife and her French girlfriend, Mireille, hating the notion of his little girl in the care of that predatory Frenchwoman who saw in Katie, no doubt, a suitable match for her ne'er-do-well son. But no objection could he get into Adeline's head. Katie would be packed off against her own wishes and his. And he? He'd be left alone with Adeline. The prospect was nightmarish, intolerable.

Why not just leave? he asked himself. Why not divorce her or let her divorce him? She wouldn't. She was a clinging vine, or poison-ivy, more like it! Nor could he abandon her in the state she was. She'd hovered on the edge for years now. It wouldn't take much to push her over into mental chaos. He was trapped.

As if to give a prod to his jangled nerves, a burst of squealing broke out in the darkness behind him.

Matthew scowled. If he could just get rid of the wretched pigs! Brooding, he sent the powerful car roaring down the drive towards the road into the market town of Bamford to collect his only child.

'All right, settle down, everyone!' yelled Father Holland.

The noise in the church hall continued unabated. During the illustrated talk they'd been kept in check. Now that the lights had gone on again the audience was released from its unaccustomed immobility. Chairs scraped and voices competed shrilly. There was a scrummage over at the table where Mrs Pride in a pink-checked overall tried to dispense orange squash in polystyrene tubs with a semblance of order. The assortment of homemade cake contributed by her ladies' circle had already disappeared, whisked away in seconds by eager hands.

'Shut up!' roared Father Holland.

Quiet almost fell. The mob turned towards him presenting, so Meredith Mitchell thought, few endearing qualities. She found their youthfulness at once arrogant and ignorant, throwing down an insolent challenge to authority of any kind. They'd sniggered, fidgeted and crackled sweet wrappers throughout her talk. But perhaps she was being unfair. She dredged up a hazy memory of her own pubescent years with all their agonies of body and soul. Such a miserable business, growing up. Your hormones gave you hell and you didn't know what you wanted only, with a passionate certainty, what you didn't.

'Now then!' The vicar was growing hoarse. 'I'm sure we're all very grateful to Meredith for giving her valuable time to the youth club tonight and bringing along her interesting slides of her travels. How about a round of applause to show our appreciation?'

Applause dutifully broke out and a ragged cheer or two, faintly ironic, from the rear of the hall.

'Thank you!' yelled Meredith above the hubbub. 'It's – It's been a pleasure.' Privately she had already resolved, 'Never again!'

Two youngsters approached, both aged about sixteen which made them a year or two older than the rest of the audience. One of them, an earnest, bookish-looking youth with steel-rimmed spectacles, began carefully to roll the projector flex. Catching her eye he smiled diffidently at her and then blurted, 'They liked your talk!'

'I'm not sure about that!' Meredith said and then, because she knew how easily the young feel slighted and had no wish to seem abrupt, she pushed back her thick dark brown hair and added, 'Thank you both for your help. I couldn't have managed otherwise.'

He blushed an unattractive dull red which made his ears glow and the girl beside him burst out, 'Oh, yes! It was great, Meredith! I'd love a really interesting career like yours!'

In truth, Meredith, busy with the effort of keeping the audience's attention, had paid little attention to the appearance of her helpers in the darkened hall, grateful to them though she'd been. So now it came as quite a shock to realise that this girl, perhaps barely sixteen, was one of those beings at whose birth, surely, some Olympian deity must have smiled. There was more than mere prettiness, even carrying the promise of a future real beauty, there was a kind of luminosity about her, an almost palpable freshness and spontaneity.

Meredith heard herself say, 'The foreign service really is a large civil service department. It's just located occasionally in interesting places, together with a whole lot of pretty awful ones. But I don't get so much chance to travel these days. I work in London and it's all very routine.'

The girl leaned towards her confidentially. 'But at least when you travelled you did it because you wanted to – and it had some proper purpose! It's not like my mother's idea of sending me to this friend of hers—'

The youth interrupted, blurting out, 'She can't make you go!'

'Yes, she can. You don't understand, Josh, it's not her fault!'

Meredith, suspecting some complicated source of dispute and not wanting to become involved in their squabble, indicated the audience slithering like quicksilver through the exit into the chill November night. They could be heard shouting raucously to one another outside, their voices fading into the distance. 'Perhaps they were all bored stiff,' she said to the pair, trying to sound reasonably lighthearted. 'They seem to be leaving as fast as they can!'

The vicar loomed up mopping his brow. 'It's not easy keeping their attention. You did well, Meredith! It's not easy persuading them to come to the Youth Club. Of course, in just a year or two's time, they'll want to mix in quite different company and we'll lose them to the pubs. The problem is that, in a small town like this, there's so little else to do.'

'Those here tonight will be under age as regards pubs for some time, surely?'

Father Holland's beard bristled. 'I must say most of the pubs in town are very good about refusing under-age customers. The local police keep them up to scratch. But late in the day when the bar staff are harrassed, they don't always have time to notice the person placing the order, and kids think it's clever and grown-up to outwit them.' He heaved a sigh. 'And there are still a few rogue publicans to whom money in the till is more important than strict enforcement of the law!'

He transferred his attention. 'All right there, Katie? How are you getting home?'

'My father's coming out to pick me up.'

'Fair enough. How about you, Josh? If you wait a tick I can take you on the back of my bike.'

'Room in the car,' offered Meredith.

Josh pushed his spectacles up the bridge of his nose and smiled nervously. 'Honestly. I don't mind walking. It's not far.'

'Well, many thanks to both of you! Just leave everything. I'll see to it. Get yourself some squash and a cake if there's any left.'

'Nice kids,' said Father Holland briefly as they moved off. 'Pity there aren't more like them. I shall miss Katie's help if she goes away, but I suppose she will do eventually. Her people live at Park House, it's a little way out of town and someone always has to come and fetch her home. Josh's parents live overseas and he lodges with an aunt. He's a bit inhibited as you've probably noticed and helping at the club has brought him out of his shell. Ah, Mrs Pride!'

Mrs Pride surged forward, red-faced and shining from her exertions. Her silvery curls had been disarranged in the scrum round the cakes and the front of her overall was damp with spilled squash but she was unperturbed.

'I've got the kettle on out in the kitchenette. Now I'm sure you'd both like a cup of tea!'

'Bless you!' said the vicar.

'And a macaroon? I saved some for you. Those children are like gannets. They swoop on everything! So now I've learned to hide away a few for us afterwards. You could eat a macaroon, couldn't you, Meredith dear?'

'Thank you for your efforts tonight, dear lady,' said Father Holland a few minutes later when the tea had been produced. 'You know, I often think it would be a good idea to have two helpers on the snacks instead of just one every time. The kids don't have much in the way of party manners.'

'Mavis Farthing might have come with me but she's got a touch of flu,' said Mrs Pride, dusting a macaroon crumb off her ample bosom. 'I must pop over and see her tomorrow. And Miss Rissington has to be careful in the cold weather on account of her chest. There's always Cissy, of course. But she doesn't like being out late of an evening, not at dark times of the year. I can manage, don't you fret! Little Katie came across and gave me a hand.'

The three of them finished their tea. Meredith helped Mrs Pride clear away the cups and plates and tidy the kitchenette whilst Father Holland toured the hall, closing windows and flushing toilets.

'All correct!' he said returning with his bunch of keys. 'I can lock up and we can all go home! Many thanks again, Meredith. Are you taking Mrs P with you?'

'That's right, we're neighbours,' Meredith smiled.

'Nice for me to get a lift,' said Mrs Pride, stowing plates in a box. 'I usually have to manage on my old bike! And it means I can take this box with me now and don't have to come over tomorrow and collect it. Now then, whose plate is this? The sticky label's come off. I fancy this one belongs to Mavis. She's lent it before. I'll take it over tomorrow when I go.'

'Oh yes, Mrs Farthing,' muttered Father Holland, scribbling in a notebook. 'If she's sick, I'll try and look in on her tomorrow.'

Outside the hall Katie and Josh were standing close together apparently in heated argument. They broke off as Meredith was silhoutted in the brightly lit doorway and watched in silence as she went to unlock her car. The vicar and Mrs Pride emerged, the vicar switching off the light and locking the main door behind him.

'You sure your father's on his way, Katie?'

'Yes, he'll only be a few minutes and Josh is waiting with me.' Katie, who had donned white nylon fur earmuffs, tucked her hands under her armpits and began to jump up and down to keep warm. She looked like a child's plush rabbit come to life.

The adults dispersed. Father Holland donned his motorcycle helmet and roared away on his powerful Yamaha. Mrs Pride wedged her box on the back seat of the car and puffing with effort, squeezed herself into the front. They set off homeward.

'Spooning!' said Mrs Pride unexpectedly.

'Sorry?' Meredith assimilated the old-fashioned phrase and tried to apply it to present circumstances.

'Young Josh and little Katie!'

'Were they? I thought they were falling out about something.'

'Oh no!' said Mrs Pride firmly. 'He stands out there with her every Thursday night till her dad comes to collect her. But he's too backward when it comes to going forward! I told him, faint heart never won fair lady! But he blushed beetroot, right up to his hair.'

They traversed the town centre, passing the brightly lit shop fronts, the town's Indian restaurant, lights glowing behind its orange shutters, and the kebab van and the late-night chippie, and plunged into the gloom of the ill-lit streets beyond.

'Of course,' continued Mrs Pride thoughtfully, 'I suppose Mr and Mrs Conway, Katie's mum and dad, would fancy someone better for their daughter.'

'Better?' Meredith asked, startled.

'You know what I mean, dear. He's a nice lad, young Josh, and I know times have changed since I was a girl. But not everything. Mrs Conway, she was a Devaux. They were the big family around here once. Still got a pretty penny or two. They own Park House. It was kind of you to bring along your pictures,' went on Mrs Pride, changing the subject firmly. 'It's nice to see newcomers to the town joining in and lending a hand, you being such a busy career woman too! I must say I enjoyed your little talk no end! I'd no idea you'd been in so many exotic places! Will you go away again?'

'Doubt it.' Meredith slowed at an intersection. 'There are always more people wanting overseas postings than postings available. All the travelling I do these days is by train up to London and back every day. I didn't want to discourage Katie who seemed interested in a career like mine, but that's the way of it, I'm afraid. As for lending a hand in the community, there's not much I can do. Unlike your ladies circle. You seem to help out in everything!'

'What else should I do with my time?' asked Mrs Pride simply.

They had arrived at the row of terraced cottages which provided homes for both of them, Meredith in the end cottage and Mrs Pride as her next-door neighbour.

Mrs Pride peered through the windscreen. 'Besides, young folk like you have always got lots of other things to do. You'll be working away on that house again this weekend, I suppose?'

'I'm about to tackle the kitchen. I've been looking out for a Welsh dresser, a nice old one, antique if possible. Old, anyway. But there aren't any house sales going on at the moment around here and the antique shops so far haven't had anything remotely suitable.'

Her companion shook her head disbelievingly. 'I can never

understand why people nowadays want to buy up all that old junk we threw out years ago. You can get lovely fitted kitchens now with the formica tops and everything. If you must have antique, why don't you go up to the DIY superstore? They've got antique units that come flat-packed in boxes with the screws and everything, all you got to do is put them together. I dare say,' here Mrs Pride threw Meredith a skittish look, 'that nice policeman friend of yours would lend you a hand.'

'He's pretty busy, too,' said Meredith, squashing the implication.

'Ooh!' persisted Mrs Pride with elephantine playfulness. 'Let's hope it's nothing serious! We don't want any nasty murders and such in Bamford!'

Chapter Two

'WHERE'S YOUR friend tonight?' asked the man with the moustache.

He rested one elbow on the bar and imperceptibly straightened the lapel of his green checked tweed jacket with his free hand. To his visible annoyance someone else, worried that closing time approached and the round hadn't been got in, chose that moment to lean across him and shout an order. His view of the girl he'd addressed was interrupted and he missed her answer.

Luckily she repeated it. 'She had something else to do!'

'Got a boyfriend, has she? I thought you were always together.'

The girl pushed back her long frizzy fair hair and stared at him. 'Might've. I don't know. We're not Siamese twins, her and me.'

'You couldn't be twins. You're prettier than her!' he said gallantly. 'Can I buy you a drink?'

She glanced across the room but a younger man she had been eyeing earlier was now talking to another girl. 'All right,' she said. 'I'll have a lager and lime.'

He signalled down the bar. 'Over here, barman!'

As Terry Reeves, landlord of The Silver Bells, edged along the bar to serve the customer, he heard his wife hiss, 'Ask that girl how old she is!'

Reeves, whose own taste ran to buxom women, cast an eye over the youngster in question and dismissed her as having 'no bum and no tits'. Her short black skirt was wrapped round a stomach as flat as a washboard and her low-cut blouse revealed only an immature bosom on which a gold chain hung flat. In contrast, her cheeks had a youthful roundness and her lips a full pout. The effect was of a child who had dressed herself up in clothes borrowed from an elder sister.

13

Reeves quelled a twinge of unease and glanced at the clock above the bar. In five minutes he'd be calling closing time and there was little point in making a fuss now. The girl had been in the pub for at least an hour. He served the drinks and took the five-pound note the man with the moustache handed him.

'There you go, squire!' he said, passing over the change.

When he'd returned to his wife she muttered, 'Well?'

'Give over, Daph. It's nearly time. She must be eighteen.'

'I had a copper in here the other day giving me a pep talk about under-age drinkers! He left a poster to go up in the bar. I wish I'd stuck it up now. I will, tomorrow!'

'Give over, will you?' Her husband glanced up to the clock and shouted, 'Last orders, ladies and gentlemen, please! Last orders!'

There was a flurry of activity at the bar. The man with the moustache and the girl with the frizzy hair moved away from the crush to a far corner.

They weren't quite alone there. An elderly man, unremarkable in appearance, was slumped apparently asleep in the corner of an oak settle. He was unshaven, his grey hair too long and his clothes crumpled and unmended, although they'd once been good quality. As the pair approached, his eyelids flickered. He gave a snort which might have been a snore and shifted his position slightly.

Someone nearby raised an argumentative voice. The people sitting with him tried to quieten him. Reeves took another glance at the clock. It might be advisable to bring forward the closing call by a minute or two.

'Time!' he bellowed above the general hubbub. 'Time to go home, folks!'

There were a few protests at his promptitude, but the bar began to empty, people drifting towards the doors, calling to one another, laughing. Daphne Reeves came to stand by her husband.

'You should've asked that girl how old she was!'

''S all right! She wasn't buying, anyway. He was. I can't stop him buying drinks for her.'

'He was twice her age and chatting her up! You know I don't like that sort of thing!'

'That's what people come to pubs for, half the time, isn't it? Find a friend?'

'We said when we took this on, Terry, that we were going to go up-market!'

'And we will! But first we gotta build up a bit of capital! I'll turn out anyone rowdy, otherwise, their money's all good!'

'Even his?' Daphne retorted.

The bar had emptied except for one corner still occupied. 'Barney Crouch!' said Terry resignedly. 'As ever the last!'

'Gone to sleep, has he?' Daphne picked up a tray of glasses and moved into the kitchens.

Terry walked heavy-footed across to the corner and stooped over the recumbent figure. 'Can you hear me, Barney?' He grasped a shoulder of the threadbare jacket. 'Do you hear me, you daft old git? Wake up! You gotta go home.'

The figure stirred and opened one eye. 'I hear you, Terence! You don't have to yell down my ear. I wasn't asleep. I was contemplating human folly. Reflecting on the frailty of man and of woman, too.'

'Well, go and do it somewhere else! The pub's empty. Everyone's gone and Daphne and I want to close up. We need our beauty sleep.'

'Speak for yourself!' called a female voice from regions unseen.

Barney stirred and sat up. 'Then I shall take myself off, Terence my lad! I shall go . . . home.' He frowned.

'You can remember where it is, can you?' asked the landlord sarcastically.

'I can! Don't you take that tone with me!' Barney struggled to his feet and stood there swaying. Then he pulled his disreputable cap over his unkempt mass of grey curls and lurched towards the door.

Daphne appeared from the recesses of the bar. 'Terry? Are you sure the poor old chap is all right? Perhaps you ought to get the car out and give him a lift home. He lives miles out and it's bitter cold out there.'

'Not a chance!' said her husband brusquely. 'A couple of people have brought me drinks tonight. Suppose I was stopped and Breathylised? I'd probably read positive and how would that look? You can drive him home if you like.'

She bridled. 'Me? I should think so! Drive with that old devil beside me? I wouldn't trust his hand not to wander, even in his condition! Anyway, it's late and I'd have to come back on my own. I don't like driving alone through the country at this time of night. We could call him a mini-cab.'

'Who's going to pay for it? He'll get home all right,' said her husband. 'He's been walking home every night from this pub for years. Nothing's happened to him yet.'

Barney Crouch made his way slowly and unsteadily along the open road, the lights of the town now well behind him, and with no company but the sound of his own feet and the coughing of the wind in the boughs of the horse chestnut trees lining the verge.

The Silver Bells was situated on the extreme eastern edge of the market town of Bamford and had long been Barney's local. He lived about two miles out into the country, a long walk for anyone at the best of times and at his age and at this time of night – to say nothing of the time of year – it was considerable. Advancing years and general alcoholic decrepitude meant that nowadays it took him longer than it once had and, indeed, he sometimes felt it took him just a little longer every time. But he wasn't yet ready to give up what he saw as the social part of his day.

For the last quarter-mile the narrow road descended a steep hill. His house was a red brick Edwardian double-front situated at the bottom of the slope. It had been built in this isolated spot by a local farmer for a married son who hadn't wished to bring his bride home to the parental roof. Barney had moved into the house over twenty years ago. At that time he and the house had both been quite presentable. The drink hadn't yet become a problem and he'd made a living writing musical scores. He'd thought himself, and generally been seen by others, as a gentlemanly Bohemian figure, a man of talent and education with a few acceptable eccentricities. These had been twin weaknesses, understandable if mildly scandalous, for young actresses and mature whisky.

Before the whisky became more important than the sex, he'd brought girls down to his house. But none had stayed around long. In those days it had been even more isolated. The housing estates which had mushroomed around the town in recent years had yet to be built and the pub, once a halt on the route of the packtrains carrying the wool on which so many fortunes hereabouts had been founded, had stood alone on the roadside. All the girls, some of them quite pretty though he couldn't recall any of their names, had fancied the idea of a country cottage. But the red brick house wasn't quaint or old-world. It was just lonely and inconvenient and, after a few days, they'd had enough. As far as Barney was concerned, the whisky more than made up for their loss.

Headlights split the gloom and a large car swept by him. Barney was forced to jump to the side and nearly fell into the ditch. He swore vigorously. One of these days they'd find him dead on this road in the morning, mown down! Though it was pitch dark along here, no driver ever made allowances for it.

He set off again and when he'd calmed his indignation found himself thinking again about the girl in the pub and the half-forgotten memories she'd stirred. Unlike the landlord, Barney hadn't been misled as to her probable age. Sixteen and not a year more. Truth to tell she might only be fifteen or even less. They all frizzed and coloured their hair and painted their faces these days. Schoolgirls wore the sort of outfits only seen in Soho when he'd been young.

Why was it, wondered Barney with some curiosity, that little girls of about ten or twelve suddenly turned into women, just like that, overnight? Years ago there was an in-between stage when they were leggy and awkward and giggly. When they experimented with pale pink lipstick which they washed off before they went home; when they grew scarlet in the face if a boy looked at them. Now they went from childish innocence to astonishing sophistication in one jump and the boys, as far as Barney could judge, went in terror of them!

He stopped to get his breath and sat down on a stile. Besides the annoying breathlessness there were sometimes gripping pains in his chest which he put down to too much gas in the beer. But very soon now, he wouldn't be able to make the long walk any more. He put off thinking what that would mean. It was cold sitting here, his blood thinned by alcohol. He shivered and rubbed his hands together. As he did, his ear caught a distant porcine squeal and he grimaced.

Across the road from where he sat was a break in the trees and he could see through it straight across the open ground behind. On this frosty November night stars glittered like crystal drops in the sky and a bold moon threw a bright bleaching light over everything. He could see hedges, gates and trees all sharply delineated like a paper frieze.

They all comprised the grounds of Park House. Right over there in the distance he could even see the house itself, a Palladian miniature with a pillared portico like pale asparagus stems in the silver light. The whole house looked other-worldly as if it had been lifted up whole from somewhere else by a magic hand and deposited here in its rural surroundings. The moon provided the tricks of *son et lumière*. It reflected off the upper windows and made it look as if they were lit but if there were lights, they were hidden behind heavy curtains.

Barney had been interested in local history when he first came to the area. He'd contemplated writing a radio play about the Devaux family who'd built the place so he knew a bit about them. Grown rich like others from the wool trade, by the eighteenth century they'd felt secure enough to copy the ways of gentry. Having built Park House, they'd made the Grand Tour in order to fill it with Roman vases and broken bits of Greek statues. They furnished the park with follies long since collapsed from neglect and with a little chapel which still stood. The chapel had a practical purpose. It was their mausoleum, a fitting home for them in death. It was built on the extreme boundary of the park here, behind those trees, down a hundred yards or so of track and accessible from the road since the wrought-iron gates had been taken for scrap during the Second World War and never replaced. But no Devaux had been buried there for many years.

Entering his line of sight, a small dark shape trotted across the open ground before the house, something half-dragged and half-carried in its jaws. A fox taking home his supper.

'Nature red in tooth and claw!' said Barney aloud to the cold night air. 'Come on, you silly old sod, time for you to get home too!'

Having admonished himself, he stood up and prepared to walk on, but just then he fancied he saw a light glimmer through the trees across the road. Just down the track there where the mausoleum stood.

At first he thought it was the moon playing her tricks again, shining on the mausoleum's glass as on the house windows. But as he squinted towards it, he saw it flicker again, a moving light not a pale frozen reflection. 'Now then!' he said aloud. 'This isn't right, this isn't!'

He moved swiftly across the empty road and paused again at

the top of the rough track leading to the mausoleum. It was cold and very late and the warmth induced by whisky and the over-heated bar room had been dissipated by sitting on that stile in the freezing air. Niggling pains shot up and down his legs. He ought to keep going, still a long way to his house. He'd make a cup of tea when he got in.

Despite this self-lecture, he remained where he was, listening. Someone was down at the old chapel and had lit a light in there. It glowed through the leaded panes. A tramp, perhaps?

Barney began to walk decisively down the track. As he neared it the bulk of the building detached itself from the surrounding trees. He could see the two little pointed turrets which stood above the main door reaching up into the night sky.

Suddenly the light which had shimmered against the lattice-work was extinguished. Barney found himself in darkness beneath the surrounding trees. He slowed his step and treading with extra care crept towards the door.

Then he heard it, a low grating noise and the clank of a chain. Barney stopped dead, appalled. He pressed himself back against the chapel's outer wall, his former practical curiosity replaced instantly by a far more ancient fear.

He fought it, telling himself that he wasn't a superstitious man. He didn't believe in ghosts. The whisky hadn't addled his brain to the extent where he saw things which weren't there nor heard them! The wind blowing through a crack in the masonry or dislodged tiles on the dilapidated roof gave rise to the noises. It was that simple.

He'd hardly consoled himself with this eminently reasonable explanation, when there was another loud creak and more scrap-ing, as if something rubbed on stone. To his horror he realised that the door of the chapel was opening. Reason gave way to an instinct to run. But his feet seemed glued to the spot and he could only watch the slowly widening crack with awful fasci-nation. From behind it came a horrid hoarse breathing and a dragging sound as if something hauled itself painfully along towards the open air. An odour seeped out into his nostrils compounded of damp and decay, ancient tombs and the undis-turbed dust of years.

The graveyard smell served to dissolve the paralysis in his legs. Shaking in every limb and with sweat pouring down his face despite the cold air, he turned and fled. The chest pains returned in agonising spasms as he ran as he hadn't done for twenty years or more and kept going, plunging recklessly down the hillside until panting and pain-racked, he tumbled through his own front door.

He locked it. Then he hurried round the house, checking windows with nervous fingers, peering out through the dusty panes into the night, thinking he saw things and then reassuring himself that he didn't, couldn't! When he was sure all was fast he went to the cupboard and pulled out a bottle. It wasn't a night for tea. It was a night for a good stiff drink!

Chapter Three

KATIE CONWAY eased open the door to her mother's bedroom with her shoulder and sidled in carrying a breakfast tray. 'Morning, Mums! How are you feeling today? Shall I open the window?'

She set the tray down and without waiting for an answer went to draw back the heavy drapes. Pale bright winter sun flooded the room. It picked up the layer of dust veiling the mid-Victorian furniture and the brown varnish on the oils of children whose adult bones mouldered together now in the mausoleum on the park edge.

Adeline Conway, struggling to a sitting position, disturbed the cushion of black fur curled up at the foot of the bed. Sam the cat sat up and yawned, displaying sharp white teeth and a curling pink tongue. He stretched first his front half and then his back legs, digging needle claws into the sprigged coverlet. Finally he slid to the floor with a thud and trotted off to the kitchen.

'Really, darling, you know I can't stand a draught!'

'Okay, then.' Katie left the window shut, plumped up the pillow behind her mother, placed the tray over her lap and finally kissed her pale cheek. The skin felt like fine tissue paper against her lips. 'Sleep okay?'

'I do wish,' Adeline said pettishly, 'you wouldn't keep saying "okay"!'

'Okay, I mean, all right.'

'Sit down.' Adeline patted the coverlet. 'I want to talk to you.'

Katie obediently perched herself on the edge of her mother's bed and ran a fingertip over the snagged threads. 'Sam's doing an awful lot of damage to this! Can we talk after breakfast? I haven't had mine yet and I'll have to dash off soon.'

21

'You can have my toast. And yes, it has to be now. I've already waited. I didn't say anything last night when you came home from that awful youth club!'

'It's not awful at all! You'd have enjoyed yesterday evening. A Meredith Mitchell came to talk to us about her travels. She'd brought slides. She was very nice and funny and it was great!'

'Travel, yes!' Adeline seized on the word and her daughter gave her a hunted look and bit her lip ruefully as if aware she'd made a false move. 'About Paris—!'

'We've been over and over this! I don't want to go!' Katie interrupted. 'I've told you. Why don't you listen? Daddy doesn't want me to go either.'

'What your father wants doesn't matter! What does he know about it?' Adeline's voice rose on its familiar mewling note. Her hand trembled and her coffee cup rattled in the saucer. 'I blame your father for it all!'

'What all, Mums? What's poor old Daddy done?'

'Don't be flippant!' Adeline sighed and pushed irritably at the tray. 'Do take this thing away! I don't want it!'

'You should eat something.' Katie's face clouded with concern. 'You're fading away.'

'I'm perfectly all right! Just pass me my pills.'

'I wish you wouldn't keep taking those. They're addictive.'

'Nonsense. I need something for my nerves with all I have to put up with.' Adeline suddenly leaned forward and gripped her daughter's hand with surprising strength. Her eyes held a feverish glow and two spots of scarlet colour had appeared on her prominent cheekbones.

'Darling, of course I don't want you to go away, either! Your presence is the only thing which makes my life worthwhile. But for your sake, you must get away! I should have insisted you went to boarding school. But your father wouldn't have it. I know I didn't go away to school, but things were different then and other arrangements were made for me.' She plucked disconsolately at the coverlet, as if recalling a different world. 'I suppose St Faith's is all right in its way and you've been happy there. But if you'd gone away you'd have met an entirely different set of people. That's why I want you to go to Paris. It's very kind of Mireille to offer to have you for a whole year. She lives in a lovely house at Neuilly and you'll be able to ride in the Bois de Boulogne!'

Adeline's grip on her daughter's hand relaxed, she leaned back, her gaze drifting to the windows and became wistful. 'When I was your age I was sent to Paris for a summer. That's when I met Mireille. I think those were the happiest months of my entire life. We were seventeen-year-old girls together and we had a wonderful time! I know you will, too. And your French will come on by leaps and bounds!'

'Look, Mums,' Katie leaned forward and Adeline turned her absent gaze back to her daughter almost fearfully. 'I know you don't want to hear this, but it's what I think and it's me we're talking about! I'm not really keen on Mireille. I know she's your old friend but whenever she's visited us here she's been rather horrid, not to me but to Daddy and Prue, sort of critical and sneery. I didn't like that. She does it to me too, in a different sort of way. "Zees cloth do nozzing for you!" ' Katie's voice took on an exaggerated nasal accent. "We should find you somzing *bon chic, bon genre*, wiz the brass bootons and ze look *militaire!*" '

'How dare you be so rude about Mireille, Katie!' Adeline almost upset the tray. 'I certainly didn't bring you up to be like this! I know what it is, it's going to that youth club and picking up their uncouth ways! Well, young lady! It just goes to prove that it's high time you got away from such bad influences! Mireille is just the person to help you gain poise and – and yes, she's right! It is time you stopped running round dressing like – like one of those homeless people one sees on television! If I were strong enough, I'd take you shopping—'

Katie looked horrified. 'No, listen, please! I don't need anyone to choose my clothes! I wouldn't dream of letting Mireille do it! The way I dress is the way everyone does now! If you ever went out of the house you'd see it for yourself!' Her voice stumbled. 'I wouldn't mind going to Paris for a couple of weeks or even a month, if you like, but a year with Mireille? It would be like being in prison and brain-washed at the same time! And as for that creepy son of hers—'

'Jean-Louis is a very nice boy! Sensitive and well-educated. And there's the title – Don't laugh, Katie! It's certainly not funny!' Adeline's voice cracked.

'I'm sorry. I know it isn't funny, but it is silly and snobby! I don't want to be Comtesse anything!'

'Then you're a very silly girl!'

She had never heard her mother's voice so angry or so forceful.

Katie was silenced, staring in amazement as the shrill cracked tones echoed about the room.

Adeline seized her advantage. 'You think these things don't matter because you're young. But they do, as you'll find out! When I die, this house will be yours—'

'Don't talk about dying! It frightens me! You're not ill, not in that way—' Katie broke off and turned scarlet.

But Adeline was too intent on her own speech to have paid any attention to the words her daughter had let slip. 'Be quiet and listen! It's in my will. I've left the house to you outright and all the furniture and things which are mine, which means most of it!'

'What about Daddy?' Katie whispered.

'What about him? If I die first I'll tell you what your father will do. He'll marry someone else! Well, let him. But he's not bringing her here as mistress of Park House! This house belongs to the Devaux! I'm a Devaux and so are you!'

'I'm a Conway, actually.'

Bewilderment crossed her mother's thin face before comprehension dawned and anger flared up in her eyes. 'Don't talk nonsense! You're my daughter, you're a Devaux! If your father were to remarry after my death and if I hadn't left the house to you, well, his new wife could have a son and the house could pass out of the family all together! I've seen these things happen! Leaving things in trust doesn't always work. Clever lawyers get around it! Or else the money's badly invested and the trust turns out to have nothing left in it! That's why it matters so much how you marry. Don't make my mistake!'

Her daughter had paled. 'I don't think you ought to speak that way about Daddy. He's not a cheat! I love you both. Can't you see that? Why can't we just all, all be like other families?'

'Because,' said her mother fiercely, 'we're not any other family! We're Devaux! If you loved me as you say you do, you wouldn't continually work with your father to thwart me in this! He's the one who's turned you against Paris!'

Her eyes were glittering and she had begun to perspire. Katie knew the moment had come to abandon argument or her mother might fall into one of her nervous crises. But youthful rebellion bubbled up.

'You're blackmailing me! Emotional blackmail, that's what it is! I hate it! I get all tight inside and sick when you go on like this. I don't want to go to Paris.! I like it here. I go out with my friends and have fun here! And I'm going to stay here, so there!'

She leapt up and flung out of the room.

'Katie, come back!' screamed Adeline, her voice echoing along the upper landing after her daughter's fleeing form.

'Now then, dear!' said a firm and comforting voice. Prue Wilcox's cardigan-clad figure entered the room. 'We're not getting all worked up, are we?'

'Of course I am!' Adeline screeched. 'Haven't I got cause?' She flung back the bedclothes and began to scrabble with her emaciated limbs to get out of bed.

'Now, now, you just stay there for a bit.' Prue gently pushed Adeline back. 'I'll run your bath and help you get up in a moment or two when you're calmer.'

'But I must talk to Katie, make her see—'

'Later. Katie has to leave now if she's going to catch the school bus. If you're going to get yourself into a state, I'll have to call Dr Barnes.'

Adeline seemed to shrink. 'I don't want a doctor!' she whispered.

'Then you must do as I say, mustn't you, dear? Come along, just relax. You'll feel much better in a while.'

Adeline sank back on the pillows, trembling and resentful.

Her daughter had continued her precipitous course down the staircase into the hall and only came panting to a halt when a voice shouted, 'Hey, mind out, kid!'

Katie's flushed little face grew even redder. 'I'm not a kid!'

'Sor-ry . . .' said Marla Lewis drily. She jangled a bunch of keys in her hand. 'I was looking for you, as it happens. Your father has just asked me to drive you into Bamford to catch the school bus.'

Katie stared at the slender figure before her with increased resentment. 'Why can't Daddy take me?' she demanded belligerently.

'He has important calls to make. He has a busy day. Come to that, so do I! So why don't you get together whatever you need for school and make it snappy, huh?'

The girl's eyes blazed and she tossed back her auburn hair in a defiant gesture. Very clearly she said, 'I don't like you, Marla!'

Her father's personal assistant sighed. 'When you get a little older, sweetheart, you'll find out that half of this old world hates the other half. We all just have to get along somehow.'

'I don't have to get along with you!'

Marla paused, her red lips pressed together. Then she gave a shake of her head. 'You are one spoiled brat, do you know it? Personally I can't wait for you to go to Paris next year. Right now, between you and your basket case of a mother, I don't know how much longer I can stand it here.'

'So go!' Katie challenged her. 'And you don't have any right to talk that way about my mother!'

'You may not like this, and I dare say your sainted mama doesn't like it either, but your father needs me!' The steel in the woman's voice silenced Katie. Pressing home her advantage, Marla added, 'So let's move, all right? I have work to do and you, for what it's worth, are in school until the summer!'

Katie turned and marched head high down the hallway. Behind Marla a voice said calmly, 'That was unkind of you, Mrs Lewis. She's a very unhappy little girl.'

Marla turned her head to see Prue Wilcox standing just above her on the staircase.

'You think I'm unkind to her? There's a world out there which is going to be a whole lot more unkind to her one day. It's about time she learned to handle it and realise it won't turn round her as it does here!'

She walked briskly after Katie towards the front door.

Behind her, Prue muttered, 'If I had time to worry about you, I would!' Adeline's voice could be heard calling. Prue turned to go back upstairs, heaving a sigh. 'But I haven't . . .'

Alan Markby, detective chief inspector in charge of Bamford CID, sat in his car and stared resentfully through the windscreen at the denuded hedge which overhung the low brick wall running down the side of the station carpark. Shrub potentilla. Each spring he pruned that hedge out himself and carefully shaped it. Over a period of time he'd doubled its length by striking cuttings from it and extending it the whole length of the wall. It rewarded him with its smiling-faced primrose-yellow flowers throughout the summer.

Now look at it! Few leaves graced its wintry twigs. In their place it had gained a collection of potato crisp and cigarette packets stuffed in among its twisting spikes. Late night revellers had even jammed empty lager cans in there as well.

This small, domestic source of irritation was replaced by deeper gloom occasioned by a recent dispiriting interview with his new immediate superior, Superintendent Norris. Supt McVeigh, with whom he'd always got along well, had gone from the scene, retired to Bournemouth, to glare at the sea and drive Mrs McVeigh mildly insane.

Norris, the replacement, was a grey, competent man. One couldn't dislike him. One couldn't take to him. He put Markby in mind of a steel filing cabinet, tough, practical, unlovely and useful, blending with the background. But a filing cabinet, if you treated it unwarily, could give you a very nasty bruised shin or trapped finger. Markby suspected it wouldn't do to approach Norris wrongly, either.

One of Norris's first acts had been to move all the furniture around in McVeigh's old office. It had been disconcerting. Markby, remembering, frowned. Every time he went in there nowadays he found his gaze constantly directed to where things used to be and weren't now. It wrong-footed him and he hoped it hadn't been done with this intent. With Norris it was impossible to tell.

Further disruption to his routine was caused by Pearce, Markby's indefatigable sergeant, having gone on a course. As yet, he hadn't been replaced. Norris had promised a temporary officer seconded from elsewhere in the division. Markby hoped nothing cataclysmic broke before the new man turned up.

He sighed. When things started to get him down he turned his mind to Meredith Mitchell to cheer himself up. That was one situation which had changed for the better. Meredith was living in Bamford now and commuting daily to London. It was time-consuming and an effort for her but he could only view it with entirely selfish feelings of glee. Perhaps now that she was here permanently and they could see a little more of each other their relationship, which lurched along in a disorganized fashion, might be put on a more regular basis. He began to wonder now whether she'd like to drive out somewhere pleasant this weekend, weather permitting, or whether she'd insist on painting her kitchen.

She'd got Do-It-Yourself mania these days since she'd bought herself that run-down end of terrace cottage. Whenever he went to see her she was up a ladder or crawling about on the floor with a hammer and a mouthful of tacks. Before he knew it, there he was, scraping ancient wallpaper from the back bedroom or pulling up floorboards.

Markby roused himself, got out of the car and locked the door. As he turned towards the station he heard himself hailed.

'Excuse me! I say, over there! Excuse me!'

A figure was striding towards him across the carpark. He supposed it female but it was difficult to tell. It wore a knitted hat pulled down to the eyebrows and a woollen muffler wrapped round its neck and the lower half of its face. Beneath this it wore a quilted coat, thick cotton jogging-pants and fur-lined boots. One mittened hand clasped a lead at the end of which bounded a small hairy dog, well bundled up, like his owner, in a tartan coat. The other mitten gestured urgently at him to wait.

The newcomer puffed to a halt. 'Are you a policeman?' The voice was indistinct through layers of wool, contralto in pitch, but indisputably female.

'Yes, madam!' said Markby politely.

She pulled the muffler from her mouth. She was red of face and a faint moustache decorated her upper lip. It was difficult to tell her age, perhaps in her sixties.

'I'm Miss Rissington,' she announced. She scooped up the little dog which perched in her arms, pink tongue lolling. 'And this is Tiger!'

The dog with its button-bright eyes, and its owner with her protuberant blue ones, fixed him expectantly. He smiled down at them both. There were Miss Rissingtons in every country town. They were generally daughters of a long-dead vicar, local doctor or retired colonel. No one would have dreamt of addressing them familiarly by their first names. They remained 'Miss' to their dying days. It was a symbol, not of their unwed state, but of their old-fashioned, middle-class upbringing.

Whatever response he was supposed to have made, he obviously hadn't done it. Effortlessly she took it upon herself to organise him.

'Look here!' she said briskly. 'You've got to come at once. Tiger's made a dreadful discovery!'

Markby had a weakness for eccentrics, but they could be a

nuisance. However, he realised that it would be useless to attempt to usher her into the station and hand her over to someone else. Resigned, he waited for details of Tiger's adventures.

'I have to be careful of my chest,' she informed him in a manner which brooked no argument. 'Tiger takes chill rather easily too. In this cold weather we just take one good long walk a day, nice and early before there are too many people about. Today we went round the playing field. Only when I let him off his lead, he ran away. He can be naughty. I had to chase after him. He ran behind some nettles and rubbish in the far corner and started barking. Absolutely refused to come when I called! So I had to scramble in there and get him.' She paused. 'And there it was!'

'What was, Miss Rissington?'

'A body! I've come to report it.'

He began to suspect she was slightly more than eccentric and possibly given to fantasy. Markby considered how best to handle this one. 'You actually saw a body, an entire human body?'

'No, not all of it. Just the legs.'

Macabre pictures were thrown up in Markby's mind. 'Only the legs? On their own? Cut off? A dismembered body?'

'I don't know about that! Most of it is under some flattened packing boxes. I could see the legs sticking out. To the best of my knowledge the rest of it was under the cardboard.'

'Ah, cardboard! Was it possibly a tramp asleep?'

'No! Absolutely not! They were thin white bare legs!' she said indignantly. 'Not trousered ones with boots! Anyway, I called out to it and it didn't reply or move. Nor had Tiger's barks disturbed it. It's dead, I tell you!'

'All right, Miss Rissington! Now, Fireworks Night was only a couple of weeks ago and several of the local schools held competitions to find the best Guy. You're sure this wasn't a rag and straw Guy Fawkes, thrown away?'

'My dear man!' exclaimed Mis Rissington with scorn. 'Tiger and I would have recognised a cloth dummy!'

'Okay!' Markby gave way in the face of such adamant denial. 'Let's go and look at it, shall we?'

It took quite a time to load Miss Rissington and her dog into his car.

'He associates cars with going to the vet!' she explained above Tiger's protesting yelps.

Fortunately it was only a short drive to the playing field. The sun had not yet thawed the frost from the tree-sheltered sides and round the edge ran a line of dark footprints and scraped tracks where the silvered grass had been trampled underfoot destroying its tinsel sheen.

Tiger leapt out of the car as if propelled from a cannon and his owner shot out nearly as quickly, urging, 'This way!'

'Hold on!' Markby was now convinced she was barmy and her story the product of a disordered imagination, but he'd better take elementary precautions. 'Don't step in those marks. Come this way with me.'

'Ah, footprints! Quite right!' said Miss Rissington approvingly. 'Only I'm afraid Tiger and I have already spoiled the trail earlier. But we were not to know, were we?'

They set off briskly together, Tiger on his lead bobbing along in his tartan overcoat beside them. They were heading towards a far corner where frost-blackened nettles and weeds grew over a pile of rubble.

'Behind there!' She stopped and pointed, adding with a sudden and belated discretion, 'If you don't mind, Tiger and I will wait here while you look.'

Markby advanced alone. He rounded the pile of rubbish, cautiously parting long wet grass and thistle stalks. It smelled bad round here, of damp earth, animal faeces and decay. There were the sheets of sodden cardboard she'd mentioned. A large box of some kind had been broken up and spread on the ground. Sun beamed into this corner and had melted the frost to all-pervasive wetness. The cardboard lay not flat, but humped. The printed words 'This Way Up' were still legible but a snail had passed across them leaving a silver trail.

For the first time Markby felt a trickle of unease run up his spine. Surely she couldn't be right?

'Have you found it?' bellowed Miss Rissington unseen from the other side of the rubbish heap. Tiger barked shrilly.

'Not yet! I can see the cardboard.'

'Shall I come and—'

'No, stay where you are!'

He edged forward then gave an exclamation quickly stifled

by a sharp intake of breath.

Lying amidst crushed wet dock leaves and coarse grasses, a pair of human legs sprawled pathetically from beneath the cardboard sheets. They looked young, coltish, lacking the roundness of maturity, and were female. The toenails were painted a garish blood red. Cheap high-heeled shoes had fallen off and lay to one side.

Markby hunkered down and carefully lifted a corner of sodden card with the tip of one finger.

Against all the odds she was right. Tiger had found a body.

Chapter Four

DR FULLER bawled, 'Hang on a jiff! I'll be with you directly!'

Markby muttered, 'Right!' and gazed gloomily at the sparkling tiles and glittering steel around him. Despite a conscious wish to find something else to look at, or perhaps because of the lack of anything else, his gaze was dawn back to the white sheet and the tell-tale outline beneath it.

He put out his hand and reluctantly turned back the sheet. Fuller had only made a preliminary examination and had yet to begin his grisly task in earnest. She was very young. She might have looked a little older last night before her death, lipsticked, mascara-ed, teetering on the high-heeled shoes. But now she looked no more than a child. A half-matured body midway between that of a woman and of a schoolgirl. A pretty little face with the rounded contours of youth. The paint on it seemed incongruous, as if a child had plundered its mother's dressing table.

Any charm she'd exerted in life had been destroyed by a great dark hole in her left temple, filled with congealed blood, splintered bone and matter. Some force had caved in the skull as efficiently as a spoon mashing into a soft-boiled egg. Glued around the wound and caught in the dark sticky muck were strands of frizzy tangled hair. More blood had trickled down the side of her face and into her ear. Bits of grass were stuck to it. The photographer, when taking his pictures of the body, had put a cloth over all that when taking one of her face for purposes of identification, should no one come forward to claim her.

But even this horrifying mutilation would pale into insignificance beside the painstaking butchery of the post-morten soon to be inflicted on the pathetic remains. Dead bodies in various stages of decomposition were a part of Markby's life. Hideously

33

battered and disfigured bodies, mutilated limbs, bits of bodies. People who'd died of natural causes in their homes and not been found for weeks. None of them, however ghastly, filled him with as much repugnance as a neatly and skilfully dissected cadaver on a marble slab. There was at least a kind of passion in murder. The meticulous poking and prying of autopsy was different, an act of official curiosity, both prurient and inhumane. It reduced the dead person to an item of anatomical and forensic interest, a mere specimen.

Fuller had returned, holding his spectacles in one hand and a sheet of paper in the other. 'Young female aged between fourteen and sixteen. Probably nearer the lower age limit. Know who she is?'

'Not yet. When did she die?'

'From the outward signs between ten yesterday evening and one o'clock this morning. Let's say, between eleven and midnight. You know I can't be more precise that. You'd think,' added Fuller who had daughters, 'someone would have missed a girl of that age if she hadn't come home or rung in last night. I would.'

'You'd be surprised. Some parents scarcely ask where their kids have been.'

Markby felt a familiar dull anger burning in him as he spoke. It was a jungle out there, didn't any of them realise it? Neither the young nor their parents? Whoever she'd been and whatever the circumstances of her death, she'd stood no chance, that kid on the slab. But then cool commonsense argued that Bamford was a country town not a teeming inner-city ghetto. Most families living there still had local roots. Why should they fear danger in such familiar surroundings? Why should their children not grow up as they had in comparative safety? Had the town and the world outside changed so much?

Fuller was clearly anxious to get on with business. 'Really? You'll have seen,' he went on, 'she suffered a blow to the temple, a pretty hefty knock which split the skin and quite made a hole in the skull. That's clear even from preliminary examination.' He gestured dispassionately at the smashed bone with his pen. 'Some fairly large object did that.'

'Yes, I did notice!' Markby muttered sourly. 'Seems as though unnecessary force was used. Half the effort would have done for her.' He leaned forward. 'What's that?'

Fuller stooped over the corpse and put on his spectacles to peer at the red line on the girl's throat. 'It's not from a ligature, if that's what you're thinking. It's just a graze caused by something like a necklace, a thin chain, perhaps.'

'There was nothing like that amongst her clothing.'

Fuller turned back the sheet at the other end and revealed the girl's bare feet. He lifted one so that Markby could see the heel and then the other. The skin had been rubbed from both heels. Silently he redraped the sheet over the toes.

'Oh, damn,' said Markby wearily. 'That complicates it good and proper!'

The injury suggested vigorous manhandling of the body. That in turn suggested that she'd been killed elsewhere and the body dumped where Miss Rissington had found it. A great pity indeed that she and Tiger had trampled all over the marks on the frosty grass. Anything untrodden would have melted by now in the sun. Would any of it have survived long enough for the photographers?

'Want to go into my office?' asked Fuller kindly.

Provided with a rather nasty cup of instant coffee, Markby felt no better. He hated the all-pervasive sweet smell overlaid with the tang of antiseptic, the gleam of white tile and stainless steel, the unnatural cleanliness of his surroundings, to say nothing of the chance of suddenly alighting upon something horrid in a jar.

'I think,' said Fuller delicately, 'there was some recent sexual activity, within the last twenty-four hours.'

'Rape?'

'So far I've found no sign of unnecessary force, but post-mortem might reveal a great deal outer examination can't.'

'Just as a matter of interest,' Markby asked him, 'does this job ever get you down?'

'All jobs do that,' Fuller pointed out. 'Doesn't yours?'

'I try to dwell on our successes rather than our failures.'

'Same here. Look at it this way,' Fuller beamed at him, 'No one actually expects me to cure any of my patients. They're all dead.'

Markby abandoned congealing coffee and conversation. 'Right! I'll be back when you open her up. I'm due at divisional head-quarters in ten minutes.'

'We'll keep her cold,' Fuller, still cheerful, added unexpectedly, 'I'm glad my daughters—' He broke off.

'Glad your girls what?' Markby eyed him curiously. Fuller seldom displayed any emotion with regard to a corpse or even seemed to consider the deceased as an individual. But this one had got to him.

'Glad they're decent girls,' said Fuller awkwardly. 'Not little tramps as that one obviously was!'

'It's not always possible to put people into categories like that,' Markby said moodily.

He could have pointed out to Fuller that all too often the innocent fell victim, not the tarnished. Sometimes it helped to know the score. Though sometimes it just led to a fatal over-confidence.

In any case, he'd met Fuller's daughters who were alarmingly intellectual and poised and had always struck him as formidably capable for their years. It wouldn't surprise him if one of them finished up running the country.

Fuller walked with him to the door of the pathology unit, passing by the slab and its tenant. As they did, there was a sinister rustling sound. Markby turned his head in time to see the sheet twitch as the feet, which Fuller had handled, moved on their own.

'Rigor's setting in,' said Fuller. 'Muscular spasm. She is, as the popular phrase has it, turning up her toes! Don't look so green, Chief Inspector. She isn't going to get up and walk away!'

This minor but grisly experience had succeeded in unsettling him. Markby entered divisional headquarters' austere building prey to a feeling that somehow things were beginning to go wrong in a big way.

A dead body can never be an auspicious omen but this one seemed to be announcing a period of bad fortune. Not that he was a believer in the 'stars' or the future foretold by any system of divination. He'd had an aunt who'd sworn by the teacup method. But he'd lost confidence in that at an early age when she'd informed him that it only worked 'when you had the large tea leaves'. Any system which purported to work only within such narrow perimeters was no system at all, only a particular set of circumstances.

Nevertheless he sometimes got this feeling that events were about to take him on a bumpy ride. It almost tempted him to review his dismissal of the stars. He sensed a definite lack of harmony in the atmosphere. The wrong sort of leaves.

He began to climb the staircase but before he reached the superintendent's office he heard himself hailed. Looking up, he saw Norris standing above him on the landing. Behind him stood a young woman with very short cropped hair and a tense expression.

'Any news?' Norris asked crisply when Markby had acknowledged his greeting and joined him. His mouth moved but not a muscle of the rest of his face. A bit, thought Markby, like those toes on the slab.

'I've just come from the mortuary. There's a mark on her neck I can't quite account for, and the skin's scraped from both heels indicating the body was dragged along over some abrasive surface, probably by someone gripping it by the shoulders or by the upper arms.'

Norris's eyes glinted. 'That puts the place of death away from that playing field!'

'Almost certainly. When she was found, her shoes were lying about eighteen inches from the body. Possibly the killer just threw them down beside her because he wanted to get rid of them and didn't know what else to do ... or wanted to obscure the fact that they'd come off earlier. In the boot of his car perhaps? I'm speculating, of course. The men searching the field right now might turn up something.'

Norris looked dissatisfied. 'Look here, we've got to get moving on this. A young girl ... the press will make a lot of it and parents of other youngsters will be frightened.'

'I'm aware of that!' Markby said crossly.

'Nothing else Fuller can tell us now?'

'Not until he does his p.m. Oh, she'd had recent sex but as yet there's no indication of rape.'

He'd forgotten the woman's presence but he remembered her now, too late. He glanced surreptitiously at her. She looked unshocked though still tense. She was wearing a black skirt and jacket in black, white and grey check over a red polo-neck sweater. He wondered if she were a member of the public, or even, could it be Mrs Norris? If so, no wonder she looked tense.

Markby went on quickly, 'As you know, I don't have Pearce at the moment and now I've got this on my hands I need—'

Norris interrupted. 'It's taken care of.' He indicated the woman. 'This is Detective Sergeant Helen Turner. She'll be with you on a temporary basis until Pearce gets back.'

'Good . . .' Markby realised his voice sounded disembodied. He pulled himself together. 'Glad to have you aboard—' Rephrase that! 'Glad to have you working with us, Turner.'

'Thank you, sir!'

There was an alarming zeal in her voice. Norris's protégée, this one! The wrong leaves, all right!

'I'll leave you to get on with it and remember, we need results! This is a particularly unpleasant and brutal attack on a young girl. Our streets must be made safe for our young people. I want no stone left unturned to get to the bottom of this very nasty crime.' The ease with which Norris assembled the required clichés, and the Napoleonic gesture of one arm, foreshadowed an eagerness to get to the microphone of the press conference podium which Markby felt might be less than helpful.

'If young people are concerned, we'll have to be careful not to frighten potential informants off,' he said mildly. 'After all, we all want results.'

Left alone with his new sergeant, Markby found himself scrutinising her and being scrutinised back in return. He broke the eye contact.

'I could use a cup of coffee to smother the taste of the one I had over at the mortuary. Why don't you join me? Not in the canteen here, there's a place across the road.'

'Better coffee?' she asked

'No coppers breathing down my neck!' he told her.

She looked about to smile. It didn't happen, but the tense expression relaxed marginally. He wondered whether she was always as wound up as this and hoped not.

The café to which they went was functional but served good coffee. It had never, at any time he'd been in there, been very busy but this didn't appear to bother the management. Sometimes the policeman in Markby speculated idly about the café. At other times he just told himself to stop imagining duplicity everywhere.

'Double lives!' he said aloud.

Helen Turner looked startled. 'Sir?'

'There are all kinds of double lives. Have you had a chance to view the body?'

She hesitated. 'Yes, I did. As Superintendent Norris said, there's going to be a lot of public concern, isn't there? With the girl being so young, I mean.'

'Young but not necessarily innocent. She looks young enough still to be attending school. But in her spare time she was making acquaintances, or going places, or doing things – we don't yet know which – that led to her being murdered.'

She didn't answer this, but stirred her coffee despite it being black and without sugar.

I hope she's going to relax! he thought again, slightly irritated. He looked up and met her eyes which were grey with dark lashes. Quite nice eyes. He thought she'd cut her hair too short, though. She looked half-scalped. All of this was blatant sexist thinking, he realised. The hair style was probably fashionable. Maybe she didn't like *his* haircut, or anything about him, come to that! Perhaps, indeed, it wasn't nerves which led to that frozen attitude. It was dislike.

'Is it me?' he asked.

'Is what you?' she exclaimed adding belated, 'Sir!'

'You don't have to call me "Sir" all the time. I mean, do I make you nervous?'

She put down her cup. 'I hadn't realised it was so obvious. I'm not nervous, well, a little, I suppose.' She struggled. 'New case, new place, new gaffer . . .'

'When you get out to Bamford you'll find it's a fairly small, quiet place.' Markby tried to move on quickly. 'It's seen a lot of building in recent years but it's still basically a market town.'

'Thursday,' she said, 'is market day.'

It was his turn to be surprised. 'You've done your homework.'

She flushed. 'I always try to. And people have told me—'

'Go on!' She hardly needed to. The grey eyes were too expressive. He could see her working out how to answer prudently. 'Told you about me?' he asked.

'A little,' she confessed. 'Oh, nothing much. Only that – that you rather consider Bamford your patch and like to do things in your own way.'

'Really? I wouldn't have said – well, perhaps I do. If that gives you any problem, tell me. I do mean, tell me!'

She turned a nice shade of clashing red to her sweater. 'Perhaps you don't like being assigned a woman sergeant. But I hope you're not going to doubt my loyalty – sir!'

Markby's eyebrows shot up. Why did she have to raise the issue of her sex so bluntly? 'It doesn't worry me that you're a woman if it doesn't worry you!' he told her. 'All I ask of any officer, male or female, is that they do their job. Their loyalty, I hope, I can take for granted!'

That probably sounded a bit sharp, but if she was keen on being given equal treatment with male colleagues, then she had to accept he'd speak as directly to her as he would to a man.

'Anyway,' he went on more mildly. 'First things first. We'll have to find you somewhere to stay in Bamford.'

'They've already fixed me digs with someone called Mrs Pride.'

'Fine. Get yourself settled in and then report to me. We should get this girl identified quickly and then we'll have the pleasant task of standing by while Fuller opens her up.'

It was Friday, of course, and all weekend plans were ruined. He wondered if Turner had made any for this weekend, plans irrevocably disappeared in a puff of dust. Good job he hadn't settled anything with Meredith.

Meredith! He might have assured Turner he had no objection to working with a woman, but he wasn't sure how Meredith would take the news. On the other hand, she was a successful career woman herself, and would probably approve of Helen Turner. All the same, there was something else niggling at him, something to do with Meredith . . .

'What's the address of these digs where you'll be living?'

'Station Approach. I understand Mrs Pride has lodged police personnel before. Do you know it?'

'Yes,' said Markby faintly. 'I know it.'

That was going to help his relationship with Meredith along! She mightn't object to Helen Turner working with him. But also living next door to Meredith herself? That she most definitely wasn't going to like!

Chapter Five

MEREDITH STUMBLED through her front door, her briefcase clasped in her arms, and kicked off her shoes. Friday night travel was always fraught but tonight an earlier train had been taken off 'owing to staff shortages' and the following one consequently crammed with disgruntled commuters.

She scooped up a handful of letters from the mat, pulled off her coat awkwardly and then the phone rang. She tucked the receiver under her chin and riffled through the mail as she muttered, 'Hullo? Oh, Alan, hi!'

His voice sounded slightly apprehensive. Before she had time to wonder why, she found out. Meredith's protesting yelp echoed in the tiny hallway.

'Do you mean to say that she's going to be living next door to me, a mere party wall away, logging you in and out?'

'I can't do anything about it! I've got a new case of murder on my hands! I need Turner. However, I've got time for a drink this evening if you can meet me in The Bunch of Grapes at around eight. No, hang on! Better choose a pub out of the town centre.'

'This is ridiculous, Alan!'

'Better safe than sorry. Look, it's only until I get a chance to explain to Turner—'

'Do stop calling her "Turner"! You make it sound as if you're talking about the man who painted storms at sea! Hasn't she got a Christian name?'

'Look,' he said. 'Can we just fix a place to meet and discuss all this when we get there? Do you know The Silver Bells? It's right on the outskirts by the new housing estate. It's an old pub.'

'I know it but I refuse to hide from Sergeant Turner or anyone else! How long do you propose we skulk round Bamford with our coat-collars turned up pretending we're strangers?'

'You're being unreasonable, Meredith!'

'What d'you mean, I am?' demanded Meredith pugnaciously. 'And anyway, I've just got in after a lousy journey and I don't have to be reasonable!'

It wasn't as if he'd offered any good reason why she should turn out again on a cold evening to sit in a public house on the other side of town. Why not just take a long hot bath and collapse on the sofa in front of the fire and television?

'Are you going to be at The Silver Bells or not?' his voice demanded impatiently.

The chance was that in half an hour she'd have recovered enough to feel differently about going out. Meredith glanced at her wristwatch. 'All right! Make it eight-thirty. I know where it is. See you later!' She hung up.

Why was it they always seemed to be meeting in pubs? Because this was a small country town, that was why. It had a pub-based culture. They were the only meeting places left which required no qualifications of entry and offered neutral ground. On the continent there were cafés. Here the multitude of public houses offered a curiously comforting anonymity. As the gunslingers of the Old West had checked in their weapons at the doors of the classier saloons, so in modern English pubs up and down the land patrons checked in their inhibitions and worries. They hung them up with the dripping raincoats to be reassumed on leaving.

Meredith climbed the narrow stair to take an abbreviated bath. As she sat in it she heard water running through the pipes of the bathroom on the other side of the party wall, Mrs Pride's. Probably the newly installed Sergeant Turner climbing out of the tub. Meredith resisted an impulse to thump on the tiles for the hell of it.

Why she decided to walk to The Silver Bells she wasn't sure. Perhaps memory of the stuffy train journey lingered and fed a suppressed longing to move her limbs and take some exercise in the fresh air. Alan would have his car and could bring her back. It was only ten past eight and she had twenty minutes, ample time.

But what she had not done before was walk alone in town at this time of the year, after dark, when most people were keeping warm indoors. If necessary, as on the previous evening, she'd always taken her car and sped, safely insulated, to her destination. It had not occurred to her that the short brisk walk would take her through anything but now familiar landmarks across Bamford's ramshackle, friendly streets. She knew this town.

Now, with shock, Meredith realised she didn't know it at all, or at least, she didn't know what it became after dark for those on foot. With night came a different world, one in which she found herself a stranger, and to her astonishment, uncomfortably vulnerable. The centre of London, which she knew well, offered thronged streets and bright lights. Bamford was a deserted and sinister backwater. Windows were tightly curtained against outside eyes. The wind whistled sharply about her ears causing her to hunch her shoulders and scurry along over wet, cracked treacherous pavements.

She sought the High Street, hopeful of finding life and company there. But some shops were rendered bleak fortresses by heavy metal shutters, others sought security by keeping interiors dimly lit, which only made it the more obvious that the human element had fled. In locked, deserted and darkened entries rubbish rustled and fluttered up as she passed, making her jump and imagine muggers. Few cars swept past and of those several were taxis. There were no buses after early evening.

Yet there were people. She was not alone. But who were they? Through this altered world moved a strange population, young and noisy, roaming the town centre in little gangs, kicking along cans, shouting across the street to other gangs. A couple of years older than her audience at the church hall, they were clearly vastly more experienced. Where did they all come from? Where were they all going? Their pinched faces in the fluorescent glow of the street lights looked livid and unhealthy but alive with a kind of simmering animal vigour. They stared at her as they passed with a mocking curiosity so that she felt ridiculously out of place and angry.

Suddenly she walked straight into two youngsters who emerged unexpectedly from a side street. Her unsettled mood caused her to snap, 'Watch out!' and then she was even more startled to hear her name.

'Meredith? It's us, Katie and Josh.'

Meredith peered into the gloom. 'What are you two doing out?'

'We're going to hear a band.' They sounded eager and optimistic, unaware of their dreary surroundings.

'In Bamford? What sort of band?'

'Rock. At the Social Club. They've got a room at the back where they have live music on a Friday night. They're only local groups but they're pretty good – for Bamford anyway!' Josh pushed his glasses up the bridge of his nose.

'I see.' Meredith realised despondently that even they, so pleasant and normal, were part of that alien youth culture she found so disturbing. In the sulphurous yellow glow of the High Street lights their faces showed only an innocent happiness at being out and about enjoying their freedom. But remembering that Katie lived well out of town, Meredith asked the girl, 'How will you get home?'

'I phone and Dad comes out, like he did to the church hall after your talk. He doesn't mind. Or if he can't, I call a taxi or mini-cab. There are plenty.'

The streetwiseness of her assurance sat uneasily on her fresh young face.

'Are you going somewhere nice?' they asked her in their turn.

'Me?' Meredith said sheepishly. 'I'm going to meet a friend.'

'Oh, great. Cheers, then!' They waved and trotted off happily towards the source of their 'live music'.

Meredith scurried the rest of the way to The Silver Bells. The public house was strung about outside with red and yellow lightbulbs. It was an old building, straggling over a long uneven frontage suggesting that part of it might once have housed animals and been converted into extra human accommodation later. Its upper windows were obscured by overhanging eaves and its painted sign creaked in the night breeze. It showed not a simple bell or bells but a packpony with bells on its harness. The exterior of the building looked as if it had been restored recently. It did not look very busy yet, with few cars parked outside, but Alan's was among them.

Meredith pushed open the door and a blast of warm, beery air struck her. Alan was in a far corner by a crackling log fire in the huge open hearth. He rose to greet her.

'I walked,' she said. 'Hope I'm not late.'

'What on earth did you do that for? I could have called by and picked you up.'

'I know. I just thought I'd walk. Daft idea, really.'

A little later when he'd fetched her a drink he said, 'I'm sorry about asking you to come all the way out here. We could have gone to the usual place. I just didn't feel like running into anyone I know – I didn't just mean to avoid Turner. Her name's Helen, by the way.'

'That's okay, sorry I snapped. It makes a change to go somewhere different. Having a woman sergeant must make a change too.'

He fiddled with his glass. 'I'll have to explain to her about us. It's just bad luck someone decided to lodge her next door to you. I had nothing to do with it. It's not that I harbour some kind of Victorian fear of scandal, it's that, like you, I feel I'm entitled to my private life. Nor is it Turner's fault. It's just one of those things that happen.'

'What's she like?'

The last words slipped out as frankly curious. Meredith reproached herself. It was good for Helen Turner to be making her career in a branch of the police service not famous for its welcome to the female sex. But she couldn't deny a purely human curiosity.

Markby sipped at his pint and irritatingly took his time before answering. 'About your age. Smartly dressed. I haven't had time to talk to her much.'

'Oh well, I'll just have to keep watch from behind my curtains! She'll be okay with Mrs Pride, anyway. I've been in that house and it's very comfortable. Mrs Pride will love having someone to look after. I think she's lonely. She does a lot of work for the church.'

'Oh yes, how did the talk go? Last night, wasn't it?'

'They tell me it went very well. All I know is, I'm never doing anything like that again! Those kids are indescribable! They terrified me. Well, except for a couple of them.' The thought of Josh and Katie made her frown. 'Alan, would you say Bamford was a rough sort of town after dark?'

He took his time before answering. She saw his eyes grow sombre and he put up a hand and absently pushed his fair hair straight back so that it stood up in an untidy crest.

'If you'd asked me that last night or even first thing this morning I'd have answered, "No". I thought we had a fairly law-abiding community. Certainly, we had our ruffians and crooks, our Saturday night rowdies and our more unreliable citizens. But I reckoned we weren't a vicious community. I can't say that to you now. It's the new case, a very young girl. Such a mindless and unnecessary act of violence. She couldn't have been a threat to anyone. After seeing her lying on the frosty ground at the playing field with the side of her head bashed in I have to ask myself if I've mistaken some aspect of Bamford.' He looked glum. 'Maybe it's become rougher and I haven't noticed it! I hope we haven't become complacent out at Bamford station. Maybe society is altogether nastier.'

'I'm sorry. I haven't heard about it. But then I haven't seen anyone to talk to since I got back from work.'

'It'll be all over the town tomorrow. Norris is foaming about immediate results and public concern. We haven't even identified the kid yet.'

An idea seemed to strike him. He put down his glass and began to hunt in his wallet. 'Hang on, you were at the youth club last night. There's always a slight chance...' He pulled a photograph from his wallet and handed it to her. 'Know that face? Was she in your audience?'

Meredith took the photo and suppressed a shiver. The eyes were half-closed, lids drooping over sightless pupils and there was some kind of cloth over her left temple. The face did, indeed, look very young and an image of Katie's fresh young countenance, so alive, so assured, came into her head.

He had taken a risk in showing the photo, Alan knew, and it had perhaps been a mistake.

She handed the photo back, shaking her head. 'No one I recognise. But surely such a young girl must have family?'

'You'd think so. With luck they'll come forward any minute. They must be worried by now and they've had time to check her friends. I'm carrying the picture round with me because I thought I might ask around the pubs. I mean, she shouldn't have been drinking in pubs, she was almost certainly too young! But she might have been. She was all dressed and painted up as if she'd been out in some social group.'

Markby glanced towards the bar where the landlord was idly wiping over the surface and waiting for custom. 'If you'll excuse me, I'll just go over and ask mine host if he'd object to me showing this picture round his bar later.'

'He'll probably have every objection!' Meredith thought as he made his way across the room. 'A spectre at the feast!'

A charred log fell in on the hearth sending up a shower of crimson sparks amid the tongues of orange flame. But the cold hand of mortality had touched the warm bar-room.

Terry Reeves watched Markby approach warily. 'Yes, squire?'

'It's Mr Reeves, isn't it? I'm DCI Markby.' He leaned on the polished surface carefully avoiding the glass belljar into which customers were encouraged to drop coins in aid of charity.

'I know. Something wrong?' Reeves was a thickset man with close-trimmed hair and a somewhat bulldog look about him, especially at the moment with his square jaw stuck out and his thin lips pursed.

'No, no. I just wondered if you and your wife have a moment to look at a photograph.'

The landlord cast a beseeching glance down the bar but no new customer hove into sight demanding his attention. He sighed, put away his cloth and called, 'Daph! Come out here a minute, can you?'

'You're not a local man,' Markby observed with a smile.

'Me?' The landlord looked horrified. 'No, Londoner born and bred. The wife's a Bamford girl.'

'That's why you took over the pub?'

'Sort of. I was in the army. My time was up and I needed something in Civvy Street. It's not easy these days and Daph, her uncle had run a pub, so she thought, why not? The freehold of this place was going. The breweries weren't interested. It needed too much work on it to smarten it up and it was getting almost no custom. We reckoned it could do well. All the people in the new houses, they don't want to walk right into town for a pub.' Reeves glanced round him. 'It still needs a lot doing but without a brewery behind us, we've had to borrow from the banks. We started with the kitchens to bring them up to hygiene regulations, so's we could do the food. You got to offer food these days. You should've seen the ancient junk we took out of the old kitchens! Kept expecting Oliver Twist to fall out of a cupboard!'

Mrs Reeves, a neat blonde, appeared and took her place beside her stocky husband. Markby produced the photograph he'd shown Meredith. The photographer had done his best to make it look reasonable within limits and the dim lighting in the bar helped to disguise its drawbacks. But he'd seen from Meredith's reaction that these were still all too obvious. He put it down, right way round for the Reeves.

The landlord paled immediately with something more than simple distaste and Markby knew he'd hit the jackpot. Daphne Reeves burst out, 'She was in here last night! She—'

Her husband interrupted her with an unchivalrous, 'Shut up, Daph!' He fixed his small brown eyes pugnaciously on Markby. 'What is this? If you're going to tell me she's not eighteen, all I can say is, she looked eighteen to me!'

Daphne opened her mouth and then thought better of it.

'I can't go round checking them all!' went on the aggrieved landlord. 'Come in here all tarted up, what am I supposed to think? The bar was full, we was rushed off our feet, wasn't we, Daph?'

'Yes,' said Mrs Reeves dutifully.

They both stood looking at him, side by side, defensive, against a background of gleaming glasses. Markby waited a moment. His silence flummoxed them. Daphne looked frightened.

'We don't know nothing about her!' said Terry Reeves at last.

'Seen her in here before last night?'

'Might've. Couldn't swear to it. This town is full of youngsters. All look the same. Black leather jackets, jeans, mini-skirts, purple hair.'

'How was this one dressed?'

Daphne Reeves answered. 'She was smart in a flashy way. Short skirt and sort of little fitted top with buttons down the front, cut a bit low.' Defiantly she added, 'I had seen her in here before, once or twice. But like Terry said, you can't check all their ages. We've always been careful, as careful as we've got time to be!'

'What time did she leave?'

For some reason this question worried them. They exchanged furtive looks.

'Can't say,' said Reeves, beginning to wipe the bar again with slow methodical strokes, his eyes ostentatiously avoiding the photo which still lay on it.

'Just before we called time,' said his wife and her husband glared at her.

'Alone?'

'Daph—' muttered Mr Reeves.

'I'm, I'm not sure.' A rosy flush crept up her throat and into her cheeks.

Markby wondered why this question should worry them. But obviously they knew something they weren't prepared to tell at the moment.

Terry Reeves leaned on the counter. 'Look, why don't you have a word with old Barney Crouch? He might have noticed.'

'Oh, where can I find Mr Crouch?'

'Find him here if you wait a bit. He comes in every evening, never misses. One of the few old regulars. We took him on with the pub! If you buy him a scotch, he'll tell you everything you want to know.'

That didn't make Mr Crouch sound like an ideal witness. Markby's misgivings must have shown on his face because Reeves added, 'You can believe him. He's a bit of an old soak but still a sharp old bird. Educated man, old Barney!'

A small group of people entered the bar. ''Scuse me!' said the landlord firmly and moved off with some alacrity to serve the newcomers.

'I see you're busy, Mrs Reeves, I'm sorry to have taken up your time,' said Markby with a smile.

She relaxed, smiling back. 'That's all right. Don't mind Terry. He gets upset about the kids coming in. It is hard to tell, you know, but we do try. We've put everything into this pub.'

'Yes, I wonder, perhaps I could call and have a word with you tomorrow morning? I'll make sure and come early before you open up. In the meantime, if you can try and remember anything you can about this girl and anyone she spoke to last night.'

She put her head on one side. 'This isn't about under-age drinking is it? This girl's in some other kind of bother.'

'You could say that.'

'Me and Terry, we don't want any trouble, Mr Markby.'

'There's no reason why you should have any. I'll see you tomorrow. Thank you.'

Meredith had watched as he went to the bar and spoke to the landlord. She saw him show the photo. From where she sat the reaction on the landlord's face was almost comical. His mouth dropped open and dismay crossed his blunt features. Meredith picked up her cider with resignation. She and Alan were not even to have a quiet drink. Obviously the face had been recognised.

He was coming back. 'She was in here last night! What a break!' He sat down beside her, incredulity on his face. 'They're quite sure. Reeves, the landlord there, is very unhappy about it, mind you! Keeps saying he was sure she was eighteen! But under-age drinking's not what I'm investigating at the moment.'

'So what are you going to do?'

'Wait here for a while and talk to the regulars. They might know her. And there's an old chap called Barney Crouch comes in here most nights, it seems. Due any minute now. Reeves thinks Crouch might have noticed the girl, although, I understand, Crouch's brains are pickled in alcohol so he might not remember. I'll call back here tomorrow morning and see if Reeves and his wife have decided to tell me anything else.' He glanced at Meredith. 'Sorry.'

'Don't apologise. I was going to spend the weekend painting the kitchen, anyway. And I want to try that new antiques place. They might have a Welsh dresser. Old ones are more difficult to find than I thought they'd be.'

'Buy a new one.'

'Alan! I don't want a new one. I want an old one. I can see it in my mind's eye. It'll have wood smoothed by use and a lovely patina of age, the colour of honey.'

Markby shook his head doubtfully and took another sip of his beer.

Crouch didn't appear that evening. No one else in the bar recognised the photograph. Markby drove her home and before her door took a hunted look up at the front of Mrs Pride's house.

'Your sergeant will be in the back bedroom,' Meredith said. 'I know Mrs Pride sleeps in the front, she throws open all the windows every morning! No one's spying on us!'

'I'll have to go into work tomorrow,' he said gloomily. 'We've got to get that girl identified.'

'No point in asking you in for coffee then.' Meredith opened the door and swung her legs out on to the pavement. 'I suppose it's been a long day for both of us. I'll see you – well, give me a call if you've got time to come over on Sunday.'

'Fine, I'll do that.'

They exchanged a sedate kiss.

'She isn't watching!' hissed Meredith.

'I just feel as if she is!'

'Alan, you're getting a complex about this!'

'You should have told him, Terry,' Daphne Reeves said as they locked up that night. 'He is the police. I'm sure that girl went out of here with that chap in the tweed jacket.'

'We don't know that, Daph. Okay? We just saw them chatting.' Reeves put his hands on his wife's shoulders. 'Look, gal, blokes pick up girls every night of the week. It's not a crime! You don't need to bend that copper's ear with things like that. Nor with anything else, come to that. When the Old Bill comes asking questions, you just answer them straight yes and no. You don't volunteer a thing, right?'

'Why on earth not?'

'Because every little thing you say pulls you deeper in, love. We've put all we've got into this place. I don't want coppers crawling round it.'

'Was that why you sent him after poor old Barney Crouch?'

'Sure, get him off our back! Barney'll say he doesn't remember anything and the copper will call it a day, see? He'll have made his inquiries here and drawn a blank and he'll go on somewhere else.'

His confidence didn't impress her. She continued to stand in front of him, frowning and twisting a strand of blonde hair round her finger. 'But why was this Markby asking questions? And there's another thing worrying me, Terry, and don't just brush it off!'

'What?' asked the harassed Reeves with some exasperation.

'That was a funny sort of photo. Why'd she have that cloth or hankie or whatever it was over one side of her head?'

'Yeah, I know, I've been thinking about that, too,' he confessed.

'It was really weird. Made me feel peculiar. Her face looked odd, the eyes especially. No expression. Sort of dead.' She caught her breath. 'Terry? You don't think – I mean, Markby didn't say—'

'No, he didn't, love, because he's not volunteering anything either! And that's the way we play it, Daph, right?'

Chapter Six

He was a striking young man, Roman-nosed and olive-skinned, with long, crimped locks tied at the nape of his neck in a bunch. He wore one gold earring and a suit which wasn't quite Armani. Meredith indulged in a brief fantasy of Nineveh and Tyre.

'Welsh dresser?' he repeated with exaggerated lip movement. Visions of Ur of the Chaldees vanished. His voice was disappointingly Bermondsey. 'Do you mean a kitchen dresser or the real Welsh article?'

Meredith took up the challenge. 'I mean a piece of kitchen furniture with shelves above and drawers below, either standing on legs or on a cupboard base.'

His eyebrows twitched. 'They're sought after. I could sell as many as I got my hands on! But a popular item like that – hard to find. Prices reflect that, naturally.'

It was the sort of shop which indicated its status by putting just a few selected items on display, in this case a Victorian desk and two oils of dead birds. Things didn't look promising.

'Have you got anything like that?' she asked crisply.

His voice lowered to a conspiratorial whisper. 'Follow me!'

He led the way through to a further, larger, and better stocked room and indicated a piece of furniture in one corner. It was a dresser all right, the ugliest she'd ever seen. Meredith's heart sank and her dismay must have been visible.

'That,' he said loftily, 'is a genuine piece, dating from the 1880s. My partner found it on a Welsh hill farm.'

'How much?' inquired Meredith out of curiosity rather than true interest. 'How much!' she repeated incredulously on being told.

'It's rare!' he said defensively.

Meredith thought its rarity was no bad thing, and if he imagined she accepted the hill farm story... 'It's not what I'm looking for – and it's unsteady.' She demonstrated by rocking it.

He rushed to shield it from her impious touch. 'That's because it was previously standing on stone flags! Look—' His tone grew barbed. 'If you want something spanking-new looking, you can buy modern ones in Scandinavian pine!'

'I don't want a modern one. I want an old one, only not that one, thanks.'

She was taller than he was and equally determined. 'Well, good luck!' he said waspishly, 'sorry I can't help you!'

Well, if she couldn't find a dresser, she could at least get on with painting the kitchen.

'Right!' said Meredith aloud later by way of psyching herself up. Ready for action in an old shirt of Alan's, she seized a soup spoon converted into all-purpose DIY tool and used it to prise the lid off a tin labelled Sunburst Yellow. She peered into it doubtfully and then surveyed the surfaces she'd laboriously washed and rubbed down. Slap a bit of paint up there, that was the thing, see how it looked. She dragged the steps into position and had begun to climb them, brush and tin in hand when the front doorbell buzzed loudly.

It wouldn't be Alan, who was busy on his new case, so she ignored it. It buzzed again. Muttering, she descended.

'Hullo, Meredith!' said the visitor awkwardly. 'I don't want to disturb you or anything, but if you've got five minutes...'

'Katie?' Surprised, Meredith hesitated, conscious of Sunburst Yellow awaiting her attentions in the kitchen. On the doorstep, Katie fixed beseeching eyes on her. Her young face, above an outsize fisherman's knit pullover, looked apprehensive.

'Sure, come in!' Meredith gave way before the look and the endearing appearance of the floppy sweater.

Katie squeezed into the narrow hall. 'Are you very busy?' She could hardly ignore the smell of paint and was taking close note of Meredith's clothes.

'Just about to do a spot of decorating. Don't worry. I haven't actually started.'

'I can help if you like!' Katie brightened. 'This is old gear I'm wearing, honestly. It doesn't matter what happens to it. All I

54

need is an apron or something!' She looked eager.

'Okay, I'm not one to turn down an offer. I'll find you something to put over your pullover!'

A little later, Meredith stood atop the steps painting the higher reaches while Katie, enveloped in an old pink overall donated by Mrs Pride, tackled the lower level.

'I like doing this!' she said enthusiastically, sloshing paint liberally over the wall.

'How was the rock concert?' Meredith asked.

'Fine. Josh enjoyed it. He's got a guitar and he'd like to play with a group. He's pretty good. Too many people play guitar, though.'

They worked on for a while before Meredith climbed down, 'I'm getting a crick in my neck. Coffee? It'll have to be instant.'

Katie straightened up. She wiped her brow with the back of her hand, decorating her hairline yellow. 'I'll make it if you like.'

Meredith put the brushes to soak and the lid on the tin as Katie boiled the kettle. 'I'm glad of this,' she said gratefully, as Katie handed over a steaming mug.

Katie smiled wistfully. 'It must be nice to be independent. To have your own house and fix it up with the things you want.'

'I want a Welsh dresser,' said Meredith. 'But old ones are as rare as hen's teeth, it seems! But yes, I like my little house. It's a bit smaller than yours from what I hear!'

Katie's face clouded. 'Park House has always been in the Devaux family. I'd give it up tomorrow for something like this! Comfortable little house, a proper ordinary home and ordinary parents!'

Aha! thought Meredith. Has she been told off? What don't they like? The boy, Josh? Or her going out at night to hear rock bands?

'Did you get on well with your parents, Meredith? ' The question was put so ingenuously, it couldn't be offensive. Besides, Katie had now smeared yellow on the end of her nose.

'I got on fairly well with them, but they were elderly parents. In some ways it helped. I got a lot of attention. But they died when I was in my early twenties and that wasn't so good.'

'Were they still alive when you started working overseas? Did they mind?'

Meredith hesitated. 'Perhaps they did mind, but it was what

I'd decided and they went along with it.'

'That's it!' Katie burst out. 'It was your choice! They respected your decision. I never get the chance to make any decisions!'

Oh dear, teenage rebellion! Meredith thought wryly and with a little alarm. She didn't want to be dragged into the Conways' family row. 'Give them time to adjust to the idea you're growing up, Katie. It's difficult for them, too.'

'But they're not like other parents! How can they be, living in a place like Park House, all of it falling down! Except for the bit Daddy runs his business from. Mummy being ill all the time and Dad—' Katie paused. 'Daddy having found someone else.'

Dangerous ground and getting more so by the minute. 'Look, Katie, this isn't my business!' Meredith said firmly. 'I'm prepared to discuss generalities, but not your parents' private lives!'

'If you'd met the horrible Marla, you'd understand! The atmosphere at home is awful these days. I couldn't describe it.' Katie put down her mug. 'I think my mother is trying to deal with it in her own way. Her solution is to send me to Paris for a year, to stay with a French friend of hers.'

'Sounds fun.'

'Not with Mireille, it couldn't be. Anyway, I'm not a parcel, just to be posted off out of the way. Marla's the one who ought to go! She's caused all the trouble. Sometimes I wish she'd just drop dead!'

'It sounds a difficult situation,' Meredith interrupted. 'But you say your mother's trying to cope with it in her own way. So why not help her out? Go to Paris. You might like it.'

'I'm not going!' Katie said obstinately. 'Of course I'd love to travel like you. But in my own way!'

Meredith decided that beneath that troubled young exterior lay an iron will. Matthew Conway was a successful businessman. Perhaps his daughter had inherited a tough streak from him. There was certainly trouble brewing in the Conway household. But it was nothing to do with her and she wasn't sure she wanted to be an agony aunt. She did want to paint her kitchen. Meredith glanced up at the drying paint line.

'Try and avoid shouting matches,' she advised. 'Just stick to your guns quietly and logically. That's really all I can say to you.'

'It doesn't work!' Katie returned passionately. 'So what am I

56

to do? All I can do is try and shock them into listening to me! I've done things, too, which would shock them, if they knew!'

Unease touched Meredith. 'What kind of things?'

'Oh, things!' Katie was suddenly shy. 'But they don't know about them.'

'So not much point in doing them.'

'I couldn't help it! I just wanted to – to break out and be outrageous, so I – I did them. But I can't hurt my parents, even though I want to shock them. I love them. It's such a muddle.'

'Katie,' Meredith said slowly. 'You haven't been tempted to try anything silly, have you? Like drugs?'

Katie looked obstinate and didn't reply.

'If so, stop now. You may think you've got problems, but believe me, they're nothing to the problems you'll find you have it you get a drug habit.'

'I know.' The girl's pretty little face had a mulish look.

'So long as you do.' Meredith took the mugs to the sink and rinsed them out. Upending them on the draining board, she said, 'I'm sorry, Katie. It does sound as if life at home is difficult for you, but there's nothing else I can say or do.'

Katie said hesitantly, 'I thought, if you went and talked to my parents?'

'Me?' Meredith spun round. 'They don't even know me!'

'I've told them about you. They'd listen to you, I'm sure.'

'No, Katie, I can't do it!' Meredith told her firmly.

The girl had produced a scrap of paper. 'Look, I've written down our telephone number and my parents' first names. Adeline and Matthew. My father calls my mother "Addy". Adeline is an awful name, a family name. I was lucky I didn't get stuck with it. Daddy put his foot down. Katherine is a family name too, so I got that, thank goodness. But I think Mummy still wishes I were Adeline.'

'Katie, I can't do it!'

But her visitor was tucking the slip of paper under the jamjar. 'I'll leave it here. I've got to go now. Thanks for letting me help you paint. About six o'clock is a good time to get in touch with my parents. My mother has a nap in the afternoons.'

'No, Katie!'

The kid was obstinate, all right. Looked such a harmless little innocent, too! She was taking off the pink overall and hanging it neatly behind the door. 'Bye, Meredith!' The front door clicked shut behind her.

Alone, Meredith picked the scrap of paper from beneath the jamjar and, for want of anywhere else, put it in a pocket of the pink overall. She wasn't going to do it. Katie had to learn she couldn't manoeuvre people like that.

But Meredith's peace of mind was disturbed and concentrating on work was impossible now. She couldn't help speculating on what Katie had said. Who was Marla and did she live at Park House, too? Was Matthew Conway maintaining a *menage à trois*, blatantly under his daughter's nose?

At twelve her head was aching. She put the lid on the tin, took off the painting shirt, put on a sweater, brushed her hair and went to the front door.

As she stepped outside, someone closed Mrs Pride's door and emerged from the tiny porch. It was a young woman with short hair and a tense expression. She stopped and stared at Meredith who stared back.

'Helen Turner?' Meredith ventured at last, breaking a silence which threatened to become embarrassing.

'Yes, you're Meredith Mitchell. Mrs Price—' Helen broke off and turned slightly pink.

'Mrs Pride told you about me and Alan.'

Helen pulled a face. 'Sorry. She's a lovely lady but a bit of a gossip.'

The awkward silence returned while they looked shiftily at one another. This is silly, thought Meredith. Helen is a stranger in Bamford and a neighbour. I can at least try and be friendly!

'Are you going over to the police station now?' she asked.

'I'm headed there eventually, but I thought I'd stop off in the town and see if there are any small cafés. Mrs Pride provides me with breakfast and evening meal and I get my own lunch. The police canteen at Bamford station is a bit basic.'

'I'm going out for lunch too,' Meredith told her. 'I'm painting my kitchen and the smell is getting to me. Perhaps we could eat somewhere together? Do you like fish and chips?'

Alan Markby had been out and about early that morning, paying his announced call at The Silver Bells. At eight-fifteen, when he got out of his car, he saw the door of the pub wedged open. Stale beer and tobacco smells wafted towards him as he approached, explaining why.

He walked in. Chairs were upended on tables; a vacuum cleaner was abandoned in the middle of the floor. There was no one about. He shouted, 'Anyone home?'

From the rear came a crash and a woman's voice, cursing. Daphne Reeves appeared through a door behind the bar, wiping her hands on a tea-towel. When she saw him, she looked frightened.

'Oh, Mr Markby! You're early. Terry's gone in the van to fetch some stuff. He'll be back in about twenty minutes.'

'That's all right,' said Markby cheerfully. 'I'll wait, if I may.' He took a seat on a bar stool, propped his elbows on the damp bar surface and smiled at her.

In criminal investigations every little bit of luck helped. Like finding Daphne alone. Of the Reeves duo, she was unquestionably the less resolute, or at least, the more vulnerable to the promptings of conscience.

She was eyeing him nervously. 'Like a drink, Mr Markby?'

He looked along the bar to where a coffee machine burbled gently. The installation of that must have shocked some of the old regulars. He imagined the grumbles. Coffee in a pub? Yuppie nonsense! 'I'll have a cup of that,' he said. 'Thank you.'

She was surprised, but moved along the bar with alacrity, glad of something to do. 'I was just making it for when Terry gets back.' She brought it to him, a small plastic tub perched in the saucer.

'Aren't you having coffee?' asked Markby, stirring the cream into his cup. He added, 'Lot of hard work, running a pub!'

'You'd better believe it!' Daphne said with feeling. She fetched a cup and joined him. 'Terry won't be long.' She still wished Terry were there, but she no longer looked nervous.

'Business seemed fairly brisk last night. It's taking you a while to build up a trade, I suppose?' He sipped cautiously at the coffee. It wasn't too bad.

'It's getting better. Weekends we're generally full. Mondays and Tuesdays are slow. That's why we needed to get the food side of it going. If you can offer a decent bar meal at reasonable prices, word soon gets round. You get a decent class of customer, too. You know, dress nice.'

'But you still get a lot of youngsters, so you said last night.'

Her face muscles tightened again. 'We do ask their age if we've got doubts about them, Mr Markby. But it's really hard to tell these days, and if we're busy—'

'Yes, yes, I understand.' He picked up a menu card. The selection was limited and predictable but adequate. 'You do all the cooking, Mrs Reeves?'

'Yes, Terry's no good with saucepans!' A brief smile lit up her round, pretty face. 'He's a practical man! Mind you, he's worked like a beaver fixing up the kitchen.'

The kitchen had been mentioned by Reeves the previous evening. It was obviously a subject well to the fore in their minds.

'My – a friend of mine,' said Markby guilelessly, 'is busy pulling out an old kitchen and fixing up a house generally.'

As he spoke he felt a twinge of annoyance mixed with regret which had nothing to do with matters in hand. He had almost said 'my girlfriend', then jibbed at the term. He was in his early forties and Meredith in her thirties. 'Girlfriend' or 'boyfriend' appeared to him adolescent and inappropriate expressions. He wasn't a boy, nor Meredith a girl. What was wrong with 'man' and 'woman'? Did experience and maturity count for nothing these days? Must everyone be presumed to hanker after a callow youthfulness?

What he'd really like to be able to say was 'my wife'. Not much chance of that. He sighed.

Daphne sighed in sympathy. 'I know what it's like.'

'You do?' he asked, surprised.

'Yes. Trying to take out some grotty old kitchen is a nightmare. You wouldn't credit what we found behind old cupboards and work tops! If you see it now, you wouldn't believe – here, come and have a look!' She turned back a flap in the bar.

He followed her obediently.

'There!' declared Daphne a few moments later, indicating their surroundings with a proud gesture. 'What do you think of that?'

Markby gazed at a shining expanse of formica, chrome and ceramic tiles. He thought it looked like Fuller's autopsy theatre. 'It's very, er, smart. Actually, she, my friend, isn't trying for such a modern look. I mean, she's got a modern cooker and fridge and so on. But here is an old house and she'd like a – a period look.'

'Stripped pine?' asked Daphne knowledgeably. 'That's nice but no use for a commercial kitchen like this. We've gotta have tiled walls. Hygiene regulations.'

'I don't know about stripped pine. She'd like a Welsh dresser, an old one in good condition, if she could get one.'

'Would she?' Daphne's brow furrowed in thought. She stared at him, chewing her full lower lip.

'But I'm not here about kitchens!' said Markby, dragging the conversation back to business. 'Barney Crouch didn't come in last night. Know where I can find him?'

'Barney? Just follow the road towards Cherton, the back road. You go past Park House on your left, down the hill and there's his place on your right. You can't miss it. It sticks out like a sore thumb. It's red-brick, really out of place amongst all those fields.' She frowned again. 'I don't know why he didn't come in last night. I hope he isn't ill.'

'I'll check it out,' said Markby.

'Oh, good!' She beamed at him. She was a kind girl, Daphne. No, woman! He too had fallen into the word trap. Daphne was a young woman in full bloom. The body on Fuller's slab, that was a girl, young, immature, given no chance to blossom.

'I really do want every possible bit of information about that girl,' he said quietly. 'It's important or I wouldn't bother you.'

'She's dead, isn't she?' Daphne cast a look round her new kitchen but it failed to reassure her. 'I heard it on the local radio early this morning. They said a body had been found but not yet identified. We don't know her name, that's the truth!'

'But you do know something, don't you, Daphne?'

She looked miserable. 'Terry said— Terry doesn't want any trouble, neither do I!'

'Obstructing the police is trouble.' He felt cruel but her last defence collapsed.

'We wouldn't do that! Last night, when you came, you didn't say it was—' She balked at the word 'murder'. 'It was serious. I know I'll have to tell you or I won't rest easy. And we do want to help! But it's not much.' She told her tale.

'I see,' said Markby when she'd finished. 'But you don't know who this man in the greenish tweed jacket is?'

She shook her head.

'And you're sure he hasn't been back here since Thursday?'

Her blond curls shook vigorously in a nod.

It was a possible lead, tenuous, but it had to be followed up.

An engine roared, coughed and fell silent outside. The door slammed. Reeves stomped in, whistling. At the sight of Markby he stopped and gave his wife a worried look.

'I told him!' Daphne said defiantly. 'I told him about that chap with the green jacket. I had to. It's, it's—'

'It's a murder inquiry, Mr Reeves,' Markby broke in.

Reeves hunched his shoulders so that his neck seemed to disappear and his heavy jaw to rest on his collarbone. 'Reckoned it was, after we heard the radio this morning.'

Markby didn't ask whether Reeves had planned to come forward in the light of the new information. He'd dealt with the type many times and they never volunteered anything. Neither did they take their troubles to the police. They sorted it out themselves, generally with the help of a 'few of the boys'.

'You have no idea who this man was, no clue to his identity?' He asked – in vain he knew.

'Sorry, squire!' said Reeves firmly. He saw a warning glint in the chief inspector's eyes and his voice rose in protest. 'God's truth! Go and ask old Barney. He saw him too!'

'But he won't remember,' said Daphne. 'He was past noticing.'

'He didn't have too much to drink here!' Terry shouted at her.

Markby decided it was time to extricate himself from the atmosphere of growing marital discord. 'Thanks for all your help and for the coffee, Mrs Reeves. I hope I don't have to trouble you again But if either of you think of anything else, or you see the man you described again, call Bamford station right away!'

They promised, Daphne fervently, Terry insincerely.

'I'll go and see if Mr Crouch is around this morning, then,' said Markby. 'Since you're so keen I talk to him, Mr Reeves!'

'You know it's a waste of time, sending him along to old Barney!' said Daphne, removing the used cups to the kitchen.

'I told you before, I don't want the law hanging round here! By sending him to the old man, I get rid of that copper here and at the same time, it looks like I'm trying to help, see? The Old Bill likes that. It makes me a good citizen and it don't cost me nothing!'

'If you start messing Mr Markby about, he'll know it, Terry!'

'Go on,' said her husband loftily. 'He's just a country copper!'

Chapter Seven

'I LIKE this,' said Helen approvingly. 'Thanks for bringing me. What do you say it's called, The Dover Sole?'

They both laughed and Meredith, with a grin across the turquoise-checked tablecloth, warned, 'You won't be thanking me when you turn up for work reeking of frying oil! You might get some funny remarks!'

'Too bad!' was the robust reply. But Helen glanced at her watch. 'I'll have to eat pretty quickly. I've got to be over there by one, and I can't afford to be late, not right at the beginning of my time here!' She cut into golden crisp batter and plunged her fork into clean white flakes of cod.

'Two haddock, one saveloy!' cried a voice and the fryer hissed and sent up a wave of heat.

Meredith shook the vinegar dispenser generously over her fish. 'Why is it that chip shop vinegar tastes different to any you can buy?'

'I asked once. They said it was because it isn't ordinary vinegar, it's some sort of reconstituted stuff.' Helen put down her fork. 'Look, Meredith, I do understand that it's awkward for you, having me right there next door to you. It's awkward for me, too, if that's any consolation! He is, when all's said and done, my boss!'

'Come on, it's not your fault! Nor does it really matter. We're all being hyper-sensitive. We're three adults and ought to be able to respect one another's private lives! Anyway, I don't know how Mrs Pride has described it to you, but the – friendship between Alan and myself, it hasn't robbed either of us of our independence. He's got his career and I've got mine. We don't plan any changes to that. If Mrs Pride is describing it any other way, Mrs Pride has it wrong!'

Helen's grey eyes were studying her thoughtfully over the thick pottery rim of her teacup. 'I see . . .' But quite what she saw, she didn't explain.

'Two cod and chips!' cried the voice from the fryer. 'There you go, love!'

The customer took his package of fried fish and turned away from the till. The move led him to look straight at Meredith. He hesitated and then came up the table.

'Hullo, Josh!' said Meredith, surprised. 'Fish for lunch?'

'Yes, we always, my aunt and I, have fish on Saturday. She sends me out for it . . .' The youngster shuffled his feet and glanced awkwardly at Helen whom he didn't know. 'I don't want to interrupt your meal or anything, Meredith, but did Katie come to see you this morning?'

'Yes, she did.' Meredith eyed him curiously.

He reddened. 'Did she say anything about going to France? She doesn't want to go, you know, and they're trying to make her. That is, her mother is trying to make her go.'

'She did say something about it and Josh, I can only say to you what I said to her. It's really nothing to do with me. It's something she has to sort out with her family. So if you and she have hatched some plot to involve me, then that's, well, it's really out of order, you know.'

'You don't know her family!' Josh said stubbornly.

'No, I don't, and that's only one of the many reasons why I can't interfere. I take it you don't want her to go on this French visit, either. Is that because she doesn't want it, or is it just on your own account?'

'I'm not being selfish!' he raised his voice, caught Helen's interested gaze, and set his mouth tightly. Then he straightened up, clutching the warm package of fish. 'I've got to go or this will be cold! I'm sorry I bothered you! Like you say, you can't do anything! But someone ought to!'

He bolted out of the café. Helen twitched an eyebrow. 'What was all that about?'

'I'm not sure I know. What I do begin to suspect is that there are a lot of troubled young people in this town!' Meredith shook her head. 'But I can't help them. Why do they come to me, for goodness sake?'

'The important thing', Helen Turner said, 'is that they come to someone if they have a problem, before it's too late.' She glanced at her watch again. 'Meredith, I've got to dash. Sorry it's been such a rush. I've really enjoyed talking to you.'

'Call round my place any time you're free,' said Meredith. 'But be warned, you might be handed a paintbrush!'

Alan Markby, following the instructions given him by Daphne Reeves, had found Crouch's home without difficulty.

It was now mid-morning and he wasn't altogether sure he hadn't been sent on a wild goose chase, not by the comely landlady but by her husband. Perhaps Reeves, accustomed to the hard-bitten minions of the Met, thought he could get rid of a provincial Mr Plod with ease. If so, thought Markby with a grim smile, Reeves was due a surprise.

Daphne, however, was more reliable and her description of the house spot on. With its town style of architecture and red brick, it did stick out like a sore thumb against its farmland background.

The slam of his car door sent rooks cawing up into bare branches, but elicited no twitch of a curtain. Perhaps Barney was round the back. Markby walked down the side of the house along a weed-strewn gravel path. Moss covered the lower reaches of the brickwork and the mortar had crumbled. The place badly needed doing up. But Barney, from what he'd been told, didn't sound the sort of man to let such things trouble him. Markby hoped he'd find Crouch sober, not stretched out, sleeping off some monumental binge.

Someone was up and about. As Markby turned the corner he smelled frying sausages. Through the open back door came sound of sizzling fat and a mellow baritone warbled, 'A wandering minstrel, I, a thing of shreds and patches, Of ballads, songs and snatches . . .!'

Markby grinned. 'Hullo, the house!'

'Of dream—' The song broke off. An elderly man appeared in the doorway, holding a heavy cast-iron skillet. The sausages, dark brown and glistening, spat in their coating of fat. Barney obviously wasn't impressed by modern ideas regarding calories or cholesterol.

He leaned forward to squint at the identification Markby held out, the pan tilting and threatening to decant the sausages on to the visitor's shoes. 'A fine occupation!' he said. 'And to what do I owe the honour?'

'I'm trying to trace the movements of someone who was in The Silver Bells last Thursday night, Mr Crouch. If you could spare me a few minutes? Sorry it's so early and I'm disturbing your breakfast.' Hunger gnawed at his stomach as he spoke. Apart from coffee at the pub, he'd only had a cup of tea and a digestive biscuit that morning so far.

'I'm called Barney,' said Crouch. 'Come in, Chief Inspector. Perhaps you'd care to join me at table? Coupla sausages, a tomato or two? Fried potato? Eggs? I'm out of bacon, for which I apologise, but I might be able to find something in the fridge to make up for it.'

'Yes, please!' said Markby.

Barney's kitchen was surprisingly cosy and clean. Even more surprisingly, it contained a piano, which suggested he lived mainly in this room. He was a meticulous host, seating Markby at the table and giving him an enamel mug of tea laced with whisky, 'to be going on with!' Clearly, he didn't like talking and cooking at the same time, so Markby let him get on with the culinary side of things while he sipped cautiously at his tea and read a month-old copy of *The Stage*.

'I like to know what's going on!' said Barney, his muffled voice coming from inside his ancient refrigerator. 'Although I'm not actively employed in the business any more. Kidneys? I like 'em devilled with plenty of mustard and Worcestershire sauce!'

He was a man whose ideas on food lay in a distant age. By the time everything was to his satisfaction, the table groaned beneath a Dickensian breakfast spread. The sausages, tomatoes, eggs and fried potatoes were there as promised. So were the kidneys, appetising in a savoury-smelling sauce. There was a loaf of bread, a dish of butter, a pot of Frank Cooper's Oxford Marmalade, a pound of fiercely odiferous cheese, two bottles of Guinness and a fruit cake.

'That', said Barney, pointing a stubby finger at the cake, 'was given to me by one of those church women, always baking! A widow by the name of Pride. She cycles out here from time to time to see if I'm looking after myself!' Barney growled the last words. 'I fear the worst. Beware of good women, Markby. They stick like burrs.'

He spooned kidneys on to their plates, poured the sauce over, and opened the Guinness. Then he sat down.

Watching the dark brown liquid glug into his glass and the thick creamy head foam up to the brim, Markby wondered apprehensively how his stomach was going to react to this rich diet.

'You see,' confided Barney. 'Although I like to cook, I can't be messing about with meals three times a day. So I just have the one bloody good one, about this time, and perhaps some bread and cheese and pickle before I go out of an evening. Would you like a pickled onion with that?' He rose from his chair.

'No, thanks!' Markby said hastily. 'This is ample! My brother-in-law is a keen cook and writes about food. Did a little TV series once.'

'*Nouvelle cuisine*?' demanded Crouch, mouthing the words as if they represented the worst form of degeneracy.

'Oh, Lord, no. Making the most of your garden veg and dinner parties on a budget.'

'You can't give a dinner party on a budget!' said Crouch disapprovingly. 'Still, if he thinks he can ... Cheers!' He raised his glass.

'Cheers. Mrs Reeves, the landlady, was afraid you might be ill, as you didn't come to the pub last night.'

He was curious to see a tide of red surge over Barney's weathered cheeks. 'Didn't fancy it,' he mumbled unconvincingly. He hacked a slice of bread from the loaf and began to mop his plate. After a moment, he appeared to regain composure and observed, 'Comely woman, Daphne. Right shape.'

'Er, yes. You're a regular at The Silver Bells, I understand.'

'I am not a drunk!' said Crouch with dignity. 'I am a philosopher. The odd glass helps thought and clarifies many a muddy problem. *In vino veritas*, Chief Inspector!'

'I dare say you're an observer, too'

Crouch's small bright eyes fixed Markby. 'Whassup?' he asked.

'Heard about the local murder?' Markby glanced at the small radio on a dresser.

He had successfully shocked Crouch. 'No!' He'd seen Markby's look at the radio. 'Got no batteries for that damn thing at the moment! When was this? What's it to do with the pub?'

'The victim is a young girl. We haven't an identity for her yet.' Markby hesitated. This was hardly the moment to produce a grisly picture, after a gargantuan breakfast. Now the murder had been announced, it was easy to guess it was of a dead body. Crouch, as if to underline the inappropriateness of such an action, burped discreetly behind his hand.

'We believe she was in The Silver Bells on Thursday last. We're also interested in a man you may have seen there. Perhaps talking to her?'

'Like that, is it?' said Barney. He opened another bottle of stout. His fingers, though gnarled, were still well-shaped, slightly spatulate, and strong. 'I see.'

'The question is, did you see that couple on Thursday night?'

There was a silence while Barney drank deeply of his glass. He wiped foam from his mouth. 'I saw some very odd things last Thursday night, Markby, to tell you the truth.'

'Yes?' Markby leaned across the table. The movement told him him stomach was uncomfortably full.

'But I'm a little embarrassed to tell anyone about it. I fancy it makes me look a fool, or you might think I was drunk. I wasn't! Mellow possibly, but not to the point where I had started imagining things!'

'Tell me,' Markby invited. 'I'll believe you saw whatever it was.'

'Very well. But first of all, your couple in the pub. I fancy I may have seen the girl – and the fellow. Not that I would describe them as a couple in the ordinary sense. They didn't arrive together. But they left that way.'

Markby sighed and produced his photo, handing it to Crouch.

'Oh, yes,' said Crouch, returning it. 'That's the one. Can't tell you her name. She's a local, must be. Usually comes – came – in with friends. All about the same business.'

'Business?'

'Oh, yes,' said Crouch again. 'You'd have had to pay her.'

'She was very young, a schoolgirl, perhaps only fourteen!' Markby heard himself protest.

'I don't judge, I watch,' said Crouch. 'Take my word for it, on the game!' He pushed back his chair. 'I can't tell you her name or anything about her. Nor about the man. I'd maybe seen him once before. A loner. Bit of a fantasiser, perhaps? Sad sort of case.'

'Murder isn't sad, it's vicious!' said Markby sharply. 'What else did you see, Barney?'

Crouch's face took on a mixture of awkwardness and cunning.

'That wasn't at the pub. That was on my way home. Come along. I'll show you. A walk helps digestion.'

He led them back towards town, climbing the hill nimbly despite his age. He must be, Markby supposed, about seventy. Just how steep the gradient was, Markby hadn't realised, but his legs ached by the time they reached the top and the kidneys, sausages and stout lurched about uneasily in his stomach. He was rather glad of the stiff breeze which cooled his sweating brow.

'Here,' Crouch said, pointing, it seemed, towards the middle of nowhere. 'Over there. Know what that is?'

Markby looked. He saw lichen-grown gateposts without a gate between them, a muddy leaf-covered path between trees and a building, difficult to make out in the dark recess. It looked a little like a chapel.

'The Devaux mausoleum,' said Barney. 'They liked being buried in style in those days. Didn't want to slum it in the town cemetery. They preferred to stay close by the ancestral acres where they could keep an eye on their heirs. That little number was erected in 1778. Grand old days, Markby. No one begrudged a gentleman spending his money as he saw fit. If I'd been around then and had the cash, I'd have built myself a splendid monument. And look at it this way, think of the work it provided for labourers, stone-masons, sculptors and the poet who could turn an honest guinea writing mortuary verses! There was a fine pair of wrought-iron gates there before the war, according to old photographs. Before my time here.'

Markby took his bearings. Park House was just over there, to the left. The mausoleum, if that was really what it was, lay on the extreme edge of the grounds. It looked completely abandoned. But Barney was crossing the road and he followed.

'I wouldn't be showing you this or telling you,' Barney went on, 'if I hadn't come back here yesterday, just to satisfy my own curiosity, and seen those.' He pointed to where deep tyre tracks had scored the carpet of leafmould. 'Those told me I hadn't dreamed it – and it wasn't spooks!'

'Okay,' Markby said. 'Don't tread in them.'

Barney turned. 'I was sitting there on that stile, see? Looking over here, I saw a light. Hullo, I thought, someone in the chapel! That was odd because it ought to be locked up. It certainly was locked about six months ago, because I tried to get in. Just curious, again. So I came down here and sure enough, there was a light at the windows.'

They had approached the chapel. Markby took a good look at it. It was an ornate structure reflecting eighteenth-century obsessions, one with death and the other with classical architecture. The date was engraved on a triangular pediment above the door, supported by four Ionic pillars. But the clean lines of the façade were spoiled by small towers on either corner. It certainly bore witness to the desire to display a wealth which, as Barney said, bought you a thoroughly private burial place.

'So as I came up,' Barney was saying, 'I began to wonder who it could be in there. I'm not superstitious but I did think about Black Masses, I admit. But I thought it more likely to be a tramp. Any shelter on a cold night. He could have broken the lock.' He paused. 'If you can imagine it, Markby, it was late, cold, very dark. The trees rustled and there were other odd noises. I was very conscious of being alone and well, though not superstitious as I said, you lose a bit of confidence at times like that. Then I heard it.'

Despite himself, Markby felt an uncomfortable tingle run along his spine. There were more things in heaven and earth . . . 'What, Barney?'

'Something groaning, panting, struggling, for all the world – I'm sorry – for all the world as if it tried to get out of its tomb. And a scraping noise. Then the door began to open. There was a smell. Damp, dirt, decay, something mouldering and – dead . . .' Barney sighed. 'So I turned and ran. I admit it. I panicked. I ran home and locked myself in. Yesterday morning, I came back and had a look round. I saw the car tracks and knew I'd been a fool. Whatever I'd heard, it had been human. But last night, when it got dark, my courage failed me again. I decided to give the pub a miss.'

Markby had gone up to the door. He put out his hand and turned the latch. It opened with a faint, protesting creak. 'This lock isn't broken. It's been opened with a key and left like that.'

'Yes, I saw that. Lock's been oiled after a fashion. Amateurish job.'

Markby looked at his hand. There was a dark oily smear on it. He took out his handkerchief and wiped it. 'We'll take a look inside then, shall we?'

So this was what a past generation had thought a fitting place for their bones. The pillars were of different kinds of monumental stone or marble, varying in colour. Perhaps it reflected the Greek culture of Byzantium rather than that of the Acropolis. Curled acanthus leaves, thick with dust, formed the capitals. The floor was of stone slabs. At the far end was a rudimentary altar. But it was a plain affair, a token, compared to the rest, because this wasn't a place of worship but a self-glorifying claim to immortality in men's minds. The spirit it exuded was both arrogant and unrepentantly pagan.

To either side in the aisles lay the Devaux in a series of stone tombs. The lids were engraved with name, age, sex, date of death and any biographical detail deemed worth of record. Markby, stooping curiously over the inscription 'Member of Parliament', noticed that the dust had been swept from it recently. He frowned and raised his eyes.

Above the tombs, in a long niche running along each wall, were rows of busts, these covered in dust and for the most part indifferently carved. It was all incredibly depressing and anachronistic. The fresh air wafting in from the doorway was doing little to dispel the stale atmosphere. Markby sniffed. He could identify dust and damp, crumbling mortar and decay, all the odours associated with crypts. And in addition, something else. Candlewax.

Barney, who had been watching him, pointed upwards. 'Up there.'

On one of the ledges a stub of candle had been fixed. Looking round again Markby saw another, in a saucer atop a tomb.

'What do you think?' asked Barney hoarsely. 'Black magic?'

Markby walked down to the far end of the altar. The dust lying on that hadn't been disturbed in years. 'No. Something else.'

He moved back towards one of the tombs, then stopped and peered. On the sharply right-angled marble corner was a dark smear and caught in a single bright beam of light from the open door, two or three long, fair hairs moved in the draught. Delicately he touched the dark smear with the tip of his index finger. It was sticky. He put it to his nose and sniffed. Blood.

Markby straightened up and stepped back. As he did so, his eye caught a glitter in a crack between the paving slabs just to the rear of the tomb. He moved carefully round to the spot and using a penknife blade, managed to gain purchase on the object in its dusty retreat. He held up a cheap gilt chain, broken, with a charm in the shape of the letter 'L' attached.

Behind him, Barney said abruptly, 'I don't like this!'

Markby spun round. 'You didn't see the car? There must have been one, parked under the trees!'

'It was dark!' Crouch protested. 'I wasn't looking for a car. I didn't expect to see anything so ordinary! It could have been under those trees. If so, it was showing no lights. How should I see it?'

'All right, Barney, take it easy!' Markby was busy slipping the chain into a small plastic bag.

Barney watched, frowning. 'What's gone on here, then?'

'Something very nasty. You'd better stay around, Barney. You'll have to tell your story again and get it written up and signed. Don't talk to anyone but the police about this. No gossiping with the ubiquitous Mrs Pride!'

'Gossip with Doris Pride!' Barney exclaimed. 'I hardly speak to her and it still doesn't put her off!'

Markby called from his car for the scene of crime team and then sat reflecting on what to do next. He'd have to go up to Park House and tell them their mausoleum was about to be cordoned off and no one allowed near it. He'd have to ask about the unlocked door and where the keys were kept. He'd have to get hold of Turner. He looked at his watch and saw with dismay it was after one o'clock. But at least Turner ought to be at Bamford station.

'I'm glad you've called in, sir!' her voice came distorted. 'When I got here this afternoon a Mr and Mrs Wills had just arrived. Their daughter, Lynne, is missing. They heard the radio broadcast this morning and they're afraid the body could be hers. The general description they give of her does seem to match up.'

Lynne. A gilt chain with the letter 'L'.

'Right, you'd better get the Wills over to view the body. Then, if it's a positive ID, take them back to the station and wait for me. I'll be there directly!'

'Yes, sir,' she said in a flat voice. He'd handed her a rotten job. Asking relatives to identify a body was always a bad business. Asking parents to identify a child, by far the worst.

Markby drove his car back up the hill and parked opposite the mausoleum. He walked over and made his way cautiously through the straggling coppice until he found himself at the edge. He was looking over a low stone wall across open grassy parkland toward the east wing of the big house, clearly seen in the distance. But what could be seen from there? Unless someone had been looking out on Thursday night, no one would have noticed the headlights of the car which had parked under the trees, lights which had been turned off by the time Barney arrived on the scene. And the candlelight in the chapel? No, far too faint and disguised by the trees. Over there at Park House, they were blissfully unaware of the use to which their family resting place had been put. Or were they?

An oiled lock means a key, in this case a large, old-fashioned key. Had someone over there, at Park House, unlocked the chapel? If so, for what purpose? He reviewed what he knew of the Conways and was surprised to find it was very little. Matthew Conway ran a successful business from Park House, but it didn't involve the town and Matthew was seldom seen there. Mrs Conway? She must be a Devaux. Hmn . . . thought Markby. She was the sort of woman whose position in local society ought to have meant she sat on every charitable committee for miles around. But she didn't. He didn't think he'd ever heard her mentioned. That was very odd.

He was distracted by an unpleasant burning sensation in the pit of his stomach signalling the onset of horrendous indigestion. He'd have to call by the chemist on his way back to the station.

He turned away and stopped, frowning. In the distance something had squealed. It sounded like a pig.

'Couldn't be,' he muttered. 'They don't farm at Park House.'

Chapter Eight

'GOT ENOUGH fellows on the job, by the looks of it!' observed Barney.

It was some time later and they were driving past the newly arrived team busily unpacking their paraphernalia. In addition, two constables were struggling to hammer iron stakes into the hard soil to take the plastic tape which would cordon off the area.

'All of 'em from Bamford station?'

'Lord, no!' said Markby, startled. 'Mostly from the area serious crime squad. We don't have that kind of permanent staff at Bamford.'

'But you're running the show, are you? This murder investigation?'

'I've been asked to.' Markby thought of Norris. The image made his indigestion worse.

'I wrote the score for a detective film once, in the old days when they had "B" movies. Routine stuff but a lot of fun. The inspector in that wore a gabardine raincoat and a slouch hat.' Barney glanced at Markby's well-worn Barbour. 'And even the petty crooks called him "sir!" You don't look much like him.'

Markby resisted the impulse to apologise for his appearance and to explain that, nowadays, it was difficult to get rookie recruits to call him 'sir'. He wondered how many people's idea of police work, like Barney's, was rooted firmly in the procedures of the black-and-white film era, despite the amount of gritty realism depicted in much TV drama these days. Perhaps the public longed for the return of the man with the slouch hat, clipped moustache and clipped accent to match. He at least had inspired boundless confidence in his incorruptibility, and terror in wrong-doers. He hoped the public still believed most policemen honest. But when it came to detection, he had a horrible feeling that most people would have had more confidence in the chap with the 'little grey cells'.

At the station he handed Barney over to a constable so that his statement could be put on record. Then he smoothed his hair, steeled himself, and went to find Turner and Mr and Mrs Wills.

They were all in his office. Undrunk cups of tea stood on the desk and Turner looked pale and shaken, but was doing her stuff well. He awarded her an involuntary accolade. Clearly, the ID had been positive. He ought to be pleased, because that was a considerable step forward in the investigation and Norris would stop pestering for a bit. But, looking at the Wills duo, he only felt deep depression.

They sat side by side, holding hands awkwardly, something they probably hadn't done for twenty years. They were not the sort of people who went in for public displays of affection. Now, in their distress, they sought the reassurance of touch.

Mr Wills was a thin man, with sparse wiry grey hair, and wore a navy council-issue donkey jacket. His plump wife, made plumper by the quilted nylon car coat she wore, gazed at her surroundings with ill-suppressed fury and a fiery face. Wills himself, however, seemed bewildered. As Markby came in, he looked up with dull eyes and said, 'It was our Lynne!'

He'd obviously said that several times and addressed it not to the newcomer, but to himself, as if repetition could finally force the incredible awfulness of what had happened into his brain. He was clearly in shock.

Markby introduced himself and expressed his sorrow at their loss, and regret that they'd been put through the ordeal of identification. He meant what he said. But he still felt as though he deceived them, because he had learned more about Lynne, things they obviously didn't know, and he was going to have to tell them. Their agony was to be made worse.

Perhaps Mrs Wills sensed it. She leaned forward combatively. 'She was a good girl, our Lynne! She was never in no trouble! She was high-spirited, but girls are at that age! She liked to go out with her friends, dress up in those funny clothes they all wear nowadays. I sometimes used to tell her she wore too much make-up, but they all do, don't they? She was never no trouble!'

'Can you tell us about Thursday night, Mrs Wills? What time did she go out? Did she go with a friend?'

'She went, oh, just after half past seven. Nikki'd just rung up.'

Wills stirred and a measure of awareness entered his eyes. 'I never liked that Nikki!' He blinked.

'Do you know Nikki's other name? It's a girl we're talking of, or a boy?'

'Girl. I don't know her other name. But she lives in those flats built where they pulled down the old Gospel Hall. But she didn't go out with Nikki that Thursday. That's what I'm telling you! Usually Nikki calls for her, but that Thursday she rung Lynne to say she couldn't go, so Lynne went off on her own. But I expect she met some friends later. They do, don't they?' She glared at Markby. Her way of dealing with the situation was to go on the attack and woe to anyone, police officer or not, who would dare besmirch her daughter's name.

Wills said in a puzzled voice, 'I don't know why anyone would want to harm our Lynne!' He looked up suddenly. 'She won a prize in tap-dancing class, when she was only eight, didn't she, Rita?'

This simple appeal to joint memory shook Mrs Wills's entrenched self-defence. Her hand gripped her husband's more tightly. 'Yes!' she said briefly and turned her head aside to look out of the window.

Markby moved across to Helen Turner and said quietly. 'Arrange for a car to take them home if they've no transport. They're in no condition to talk now.'

'She was fourteen, by the way,' Turner murmured.

A schoolgirl. Markby's niece, Emma, was twelve and still very much a child but growing up fast. How fast? What would she be like at fourteen? Time went past so quickly. For the Wills, sitting there, Lynne was still in their minds a bright, tap-dancing prodigy. Could Barney really have been right in his claim that Lynne had been 'on the game'?

'See if you can find this Nikki. Anyone in the station will tell you where those flats are. I'm going out to Park House to see the Conways. We have to let them know what we're doing on their property and there's the matter of the key to – to that place.'

He glanced at the Wills but they weren't listening. Mrs Wills was struggling to button her coat and her husband was watching her wrestling fingers as if he couldn't understand why she was having so much trouble.

Turner nodded again and got up to escort the pair out. In the doorway, Mrs Wills turned back to fix Markby with a look of startling malevolence. 'You find him!' she ordered hoarsely. 'You find him quick! Because if you don't, I will, so help me! And there won't be much of him left when I've done with him!'

'We'll find him, Mrs Wills,' he assured her, hoping it was true.

Unexpectedly Wills spoke. 'It's all right, Rita!' he said quietly and put his arm round his wife's shoulders.

When Markby got downstairs again, Barney Crouch was standing in the front entrance, as if undecided.

'Someone taking you home?' he asked him.

'They kindly offered,' Crouch looked a little embarrassed. 'But since I'm in Bamford, I thought I might just walk round and see Doris Pride. Oh, it's all right!' he added hastily. 'I'm well aware I'm not to talk about this. But by calling round now I might save her a journey out to my place. The trouble is, you understand, that she's apt to turn up unexpectedly. I'll just go and see. You never know, she might be out!' he finished optimistically.

Markby left him and drove to the nearest chemist where he bought two packets of indigestion tablets and, chewing them one after the other, set off for Park House.

Matthew Conway sat at his desk in a ray of pale November sunlight. The room was warm because when the ground floor of this wing had been adapted for office use, he'd had basic central heating installed. It had not been extended to the rest of the building because Adeline had refused point blank to allow workmen in, so that in the coldest months the main house offered the home comforts of a medieval abbey. Katie, poor kid, brought her homework in here of an evening when her fingers froze in her own room despite the electric convector heater.

Matthew rubbed a hand over his eyes. He was tired and he was worried. Before him lay a stack of letters, all neatly docketed and cross-referenced. Marla was nothing if not efficient and she'd be in here shortly to ask if he'd been through it all. He sometimes thought she was a bit too efficient and would have been glad of an occasional lapse, nothing too serious, of course! Not that she wasn't satisfyingly human in other ways and not slow to let him know her inclinations and her intentions. But her intentions were a worry too, because she wanted far more than he could offer her, certainly at the present time.

It wasn't just Adeline, there was Katie. He would never do anything to distress his little girl, and his little girl plainly hated Marla's guts. Marla said Katie was spoiled which was nonsense. Marla didn't understand children, one of the areas where he might have wished her to show an indication of vulnerability. But she didn't, and anyway, too much vulnerability and you ended up with Adeline. He was caught in a three-way trap between the women in his life, and he was becoming increasingly desperate.

Adeline. How could he concentrate here today, when he'd witnessed such a peculiar thing last night? He'd gone to bed and to sleep as usual. Then, around two, he'd awoken with that feeling of something amiss which makes the hair bristle on the nape of the neck and the tongue dry. He'd sat up. The house was as quiet as any very old building ever is. There were the usual creaks and groans of ancient woodwork and inefficient Victorian plumbing; the sough of the wind against the panes and the rustle of a curtain in the many draughts. And then, a louder creak, from the main stair.

Matthew had got out of bed, pulled on his dressing-gown, and cautiously opened his door. They were well protected by a basic burglar-alarm system and it was probably only a tread, warping in the night temperature. He listened. No, someone certainly seemed to be moving stealthily in the hall below.

He moved out and leaned over the balustrade which ran round the upper landing. He couldn't see anyone, but the drawing-room door was ajar and a faint beam of light shone across the hall floor. Some one was definitely down there and had switched on a table lamp. The beam wasn't moving about like a torch.

Matthew became aware of how cold it was and that he'd neglected to put on his slippers. He couldn't go back for them now. He crept downstairs, keeping to one side to minimise the creaks, and moved barefoot to the drawing-room door. He put his face to the crack.

As he'd guessed, one of the table lamps was on, and gave the room poor illumination, heavy with shadows and dark spots behind furniture. He could see the remains of the fire, glowing dull amber behind the mesh safety-guard put across it at night. He took the risk of pushing the door open a little further.

An emaciated figure stood on the far side at the window, holding aside the long drapes with one white hand and staring out into the night. It was a woman enswathed in a white garment, with untidy long hair curling down her back. With shock, he realised it was his wife, her hair unpinned, wearing a lightweight satin wrap over her nightdress.

He opened his mouth to ask what on earth she was going, but then remembered that it was dangerous to awake sleepwalkers. If that was what she was. He recalled that lately she'd taken to standing there of an evening, staring out like that, although there wasn't a thing she could see except the empty grounds in the moonlight. Knowing her fear of the dark, he was astonished to see her here now, and it reinforced his idea that this was somnambulism. But what was she looking at, consciously or unconsciously?

The fire rustled and threw up a spurt of flame and he saw her face more clearly, profiled against the dark curtain. It made him catch his breath, because she was so beautiful for all her thin frame. Her face was pared to the basic fine bone structure and, immobile as she was, she resembled a classical statue. Then, in the most surprising development of all, he'd realised he was crying, the tears rolling silently down his face. He was weeping for all the happiness once promised and now lost, for the girl he'd married and the young man he'd been, and wishing that it could all have been different.

He rubbed his face dry and she must have heard something, because she turned her head and looked straight towards him. In the nick of time, he dodged back and pressed himself into the dark stairwell. He heard her move across the room and a click as the lamp was switched off. Did somnambulists do that? Remember to switch lights on and off? She came out, walked across the hall without seeing him in his hiding place, and up the stairs.

After a moment, he heard her bedroom door. He'd ventured out then, with feet like blocks of ice, gone into the drawing room and stared out of the window to see, if he could, what fascinated her. But he saw only moonlight on the park, a distant silhouette of trees and a funny pepperpot shape sticking up through them which must be a turret of that grisly mausoleum the Devaux – batty to the last man Jack of 'em – had built. Nothing, in short.

Something soft and warm had brushed against his bare leg, making him start and swear. As he instinctively kicked out, there was an answering hiss. Sam the cat, following Adeline as he always did. In days gone by, he'd thought bitterly, superstition would have dubbed the cat Adeline's 'familiar' and burned the pair of them!

He had gone back to bed resolved to tell Prue in the morning and the doctor when he next called. But today, after spending the rest of the night awake, he hadn't told Prue. He wasn't sure why. Instead, he'd persuaded Marla to work that Saturday, promising compensatory time off at some later date. He wanted to be busy here in his office, not sitting on the other side of that dividing door. He was hiding, of course, not facing up to the mess that was his domestic life. Marla had agreed amiably enough but she always knew when something was wrong. He'd caught her looking at him speculatively when she came in just now to find he wasn't working, just sitting there brooding.

Matthew started at the sound of Marla's voice on the other side of the door. He began guiltily to shuffle the letters about. Then he heard a man's voice, an authoritative tone, and he wondered who on earth it could be. No one on business, not today.

Marla opened the door, her face flushed. She said crisply, 'It's the police!'

Chapter Nine

'WELL, I'M sorry I haven't been out to see you, Barney!' said Mrs Pride vigorously. 'But I'm very busy just now. I've got this young police lady lodging with me, and the flu's gone through the Ladies Circle like the Assyrian.'

'Good grief!' said Barney. 'Some foreign chap breaking the hearts of your ladies?'

'Don't talk nonsense. You know very well I mean the poem.'

'Yes, I do. Lord Byron. "The Assyrian came down like the wolf on the fold, And his cohorts were gleaming in purple and gold!" Ah, Doris, they don't write them like it any more. What a genius and what a perfectly splendid chap to go out on the town with!'

'I don't know why I bother with you,' said Mrs Pride without rancour. 'I recited that at our school Christmas concert, 1943, the night a German bomber crashed in Marsh Hollow. We all traipsed out to see it the next day, and paid the farmer sixpence to climb in the cockpit. More tea? What's brought you into Bamford, anyway? Don't tell me it was just to call here, because I shan't believe it.'

'To be frank, Doris, the police brought me in, and before you hit the ceiling, I volunteered information and I was asked to make a statement. I can't tell you what about or any more than that. Sorry.'

She glared at him. 'You're the most aggravating man I ever knew. And look at you! Do you mean you went to the police station in that grubby old shirt and dirty shoes? I wonder they didn't put you in a cell!'

There was a pause while the gas fire hissed agreeably and they both drank their tea. Barney mopped up crumbs from his plate with a damp forefinger.

'Terrible manners you've got,' said Mrs Pride resignedly. 'Are you staying here for your supper? If so, behave, the young lady will be here.'

'I ate earlier, Doris. I ought to be going.' Barney pushed himself laboriously from the comfortable depths of his armchair, with a regretful look at the fire.

'Baked pork chops and parsnips, with sage stuffing balls, mashed potatoes and apple crumble,' said Mrs Pride carelessly.

He sank back. 'Doris . . .' he said in deep admiration. 'What man could refuse?'

Markby had arrived at Park House to find its gates standing open. But the gap between the posts presented a barrier in the shape of a cattle grid, a series of parallel poles set in a shallow pit, to prevent livestock straying. His car bumped and rattled over them on to the long, none too well-kept, gravel drive. To either side the once-ornamental box hedging was unclipped and, to his gardener's eye, a disgrace. Some of it must have been topiary work but it was almost impossible now to tell what the distorted overgrown shapes had represented. They lined the drive like a guard of mutants.

Ahead of him, the house looked sombre despite the grace of its façade. As he drew nearer, he could see that, like the drive, the building had not been particularly well maintained. He tried to estimate the annual running costs of the place. They must be horrendous. On the other hand, Matthew Conway was reputed to be a wealthy man and he used this house at his business base. For both reasons, he might have been expected to keep it neat.

It was a good thing Markby was driving slowly. Without warning, a gangling, wild-haired man darted out from between the hedges and stood in front of his car, waving his arms dementedly and mouthing 'Stop!'

Markby slammed on the brakes and halted in a flurry of gravel. He wound down the window and stuck out his head. 'What's up?' he demanded sharply.

He had no idea who this was. His first impression had been that one of the misshapen pieces of topiary had taken on life and left its hedge. The man's face was ageless, a sort of elderly child's. He wore a grimy sweater, filthy sleeveless body-warmer and corduroy trousers tucked into muddy gumboots. As he lurched towards Markby, arms still flailing as though he couldn't quite control them, a distinctive odour preceded him. It smelled like—

'Pigs!' the man yelled full in Markby's face.

It certainly wasn't outside Markby's experience to have abuse hurled at him. And the epithet 'pigs' for the police was current usage in some circles. But he was taken aback, because in an unmarked car and wearing ordinary clothes, he didn't know how this half-mad looking creature had identified him, or his profession, nor what he'd done anyway to provoke such a personal attack.

Before he could express any of this, the man yelled, 'The pigs is coming through! You gotta stop or you'll run the buggers down!'

At that, a burst of infuriated squeals split the air. Before Markby's astonished gaze, a small herd of pigs rushed through the hole in the box hedging and milled about the car in a frenzy. Markby's idea of a pig was based on the domestic Large White, slumped in its sty hoping someone would scratch its back. These pigs had gingery-brown hair and were extremely agile. They also appeared belligerent. Perhaps they were hungry.

'You stay there, sir!' howled the pigman. 'I'll bring 'em away!'

He began to dodge about, rounding up his vociferous charges, until, still waving his disorganised arms, pigman and pigs stampeded through the box hedging on the other side of the drive and were lost to view. Angry squeals and war-whoops drifted back on the air.

'Curiouser and curiouser . . .' Markby murmured, restarting his car. 'What else I wonder?' At least it explained the cattle grid.

The façade was in need of total renovation. Getting out of his car, he could see that lumps of plaster had fallen from the Corinthian pillars of the portico and moss covered the bases and the steps which led up to them. He tugged the old-fashioned bell-pull but nothing happened. There was a small wooden notice affixed to the wall which read 'Entrance to office at the side', accompanied by an arrow. It was Saturday, but he could try. There seemed no alternative. He rounded the corner of the building, and found a small, black-painted door with a modern bell-push. And he was in luck. He could hear a typewriter.

The door was opened by a vision as unlikely in its way as that of the pigman had been. Before him stood a sophisticated young woman in a purplish-coloured suit made up of a jacket trimmed with braid and gilt buttons and a very short skirt, displaying long shapely legs in black stockings, legs that terminated in shoes with heels like stilts. Her white-blonde hair was long and brushed back, secured with a black velvet Alice band. She wore a lot of make-up and enormous and elaborate earrings. She looked as if she'd stepped straight from the pages of one of the more aggressive glossy magazines for today's woman. He supposed her thirty-something.

As he stared at her, her sharp, pale grey eyes studied him. 'Can I help you?' she inquired in a transatlantic drawl.

He produced his ID and asked if it were possible to see Mr or Mrs Conway.

She took the little card in her purple-lacquered nails. 'What about? I'm Mr Conway's personal assistant. Mrs Conway doesn't see anyone.'

'Police business!' said Markby firmly, deciding that the time had come to regain the initiative.

From behind them, some piece of office machinery buzzed into action. She glanced over her shoulder. 'He's busy right now.'

'So am I!' said Markby with even more determination.

Their eyes met in a silent battle of wills.

'Come in,' she conceded. 'I'll go and see if he can spare you five minutes.'

'Thank you,' said Markby, resisting the desire to add, 'You do that!'

In sharp contrast to the exterior aspect of the house, the office was ultra modern. Its total inappropriateness in this gem of a building was enough to set the Devaux who had created the original spinning in their elaborate tombs over there in the mausoleum. To set it all up like this, mused Markby as he peered at tell-tale bumps in plaster and unevenness in ceiling cornices, must have entailed a certain amount of internal structural alteration to this wing. He was surprised that Conway had obtained the necessary planning permission. This must be a listed historic building. On the other hand, men like Conway had a way of getting what they wanted.

'What line of business is Mr Conway in?' he asked Marla Lewis.

'Computer technology, import and export!' she informed him crisply. She didn't like the way he was openly looking around.

'Really? I've often thought I ought to get myself one of those little lap-top machines. Useful.'

'The sort of technology we handle,' she said in crushing tones, 'is mostly destined for large educational foundations or hospitals. If you'll wait one moment, I'll see if Mr Conway is free.'

She clattered away on the spike heels. Despite himself, his eyes were fixed on those long, black-clad legs, and he knew that she knew they were.

She was back a moment later. 'He'll see you. This way please.'

'Can I have my ID back?' he held out his hand.

'Oh, sure!' Purple talons dropped it casually into his palm as if it had been some piece of litter destined for the waste bin.

Conway was rising from his desk in welcome as Markby entered. He was a handsome, slightly overweight man, hair greying at the temples. He looked, Markby thought, tired, but greeted the visitor affably.

'Thank you, Marla! Come in, Chief Inspector. What can I do for you? Bring us some coffee, Marla, will you? Or would you prefer tea?'

'Tea, please.' Markby was aware of his still-uneasy stomach and that his breath probably smelled of peppermint. Better than pigs though. 'I'm sorry to bother you. I'm afraid we've descended on a corner of your property. I'd have called earlier but I had to return to Bamford. We'll try not to make a nuisance of ourselves. Unfortunately, it does seem likely a serious crime was committed on Thursday night in the Devaux mausoleum. We've cordoned it off, so you won't be able to go there for a while. I trust that isn't inconvenient?'

Matthew blinked rapidly. 'That's impossible! I mean, what sort of crime? That ghastly vault is locked up, has been for years. We certainly don't need to go there. No one ever goes there!'

'Someone uses it. The door's unlocked and the mechanism oiled.'

Matthew was still shaking his head. 'I can't believe it. You don't mean—' he fidgeted with papers on his desk, 'Mumbo-jumbo? Satanic rites? Pentacles and that sort of thing?'

'No,' Markby eyed him curiously. 'What makes you ask that?'

'Why, the very nature of the place! One reads in the papers . . .'

'I see. No, rather worse, I'm afraid. Resulting in a death.'

'Oh, my God!' whispered Matthew. 'You don't mean murder?'

From behind them came a tinkle of porcelain. Markby turned his head. Marla stood in the doorway, holding a tray with the teacups. She had obviously heard. She didn't look shocked. Markby fancied it would take a lot to rattle that lady's iron composure. But she looked wary – and inquisitive at the same time.

Seeing they both stared at her, she walked briskly across and put down the tray. He guessed the cups were Coalport but there was no teapot. Instead, little bits of string with labels attached dangled from the cups and, in them, teabags were doing their best to colour hot water a pale gold. There was milk, also slices of lemon on a saucer, and some little paper packets which appeared to contain sugar-substitute tablets.

Markby, a firm believer in one spoonful for each person, one for the pot, and let it brew, cast a gloomy eye on it all.

'Thank you, Marla,' said Conway heavily.

She started to leave, but Markby exclaimed, 'Hold on! Perhaps your assistant could stay a moment? I just have a couple of questions and either of you might be able to help. To begin with, have either of you, or anyone else in this house, noticed any activity recently in the area of the mausoleum, or on the road going by it? Especially in the evenings, after dark? Lights, say, or car noise?'

'I haven't!' Matthew shook his head. But it seemed to Markby he hesitated. 'You, Marla?'

'Not a thing!' she said crisply. Her eyes met Markby's and defied him to query her reply.

'Well, how about the keys to the mausoleum? Where are they kept?'

'I don't know', Matthew looked helplessly at his p.a. 'I didn't even know there were any around still. It's years since anyone opened up the place. Oh, no, of course, you're telling us differently. But see here, Chief Inspector! No one in this house has reason to open up that ghastly monument. None of us ever goes near it!'

'If anyone knows about keys, Prue does,' said Marla with a touch of malice.

'Oh, yes ... Our housekeeper,' Conway explained. 'She might – she's in the house somewhere.'

'I rang at the front door earlier and no one came,' Markby told him.

'She was probably with my wife – or in the kitchen.' Conway looked unhappy.

'Shall I go find her?' Marla was already moving towards the door.

Conway glanced at Markby and nodded. 'Please do.'

When she'd gone, Conway handed over Markby's tea. 'I hope this unpleasantness can be kept from my wife. She's very nervous and not at all well. I wouldn't like her to be upset quite need-lessly. There's no way she could help you. The idea of strangers in the grounds, it's difficult to explain, but she'd be terrified. I couldn't possibly mention murder to her.'

Markby sipped his tea. Though weak, it seemed to settle his queasy stomach. 'I shall have to ask her if she's noticed anything unusual in the area of the family vault.'

'No, no, I've just told you, you can't!' Matthew almost shouted. 'She hasn't seen anything! She can't help you! You can't question her!' He fell silent, his voice ringing in the room. He pressed his hands to his temples. 'I'm sorry. It's just that she's ill, and being interviewed by the police is out of the question. If you wish, I'll get her doctor to write a certificate to that effect. I don't mean to obstruct inquiries. I realise that murder . . .' He set down his cup with a rattle. 'Look, suppose I ask Adeline for you, at a suitable moment? I'll tell you what she says.'

'All right,' said Markby slowly. He wanted cooperation from the Conways, but it seemed it wasn't to come without strings. 'That'll do for the time being. But I may still have to insist on talking to her later. The same applies to your daughter. Is she at home?'

'No, she isn't and anyway—' Conway's red face had now turned magenta. But further objection on his part was cut off by a tap of heels, heralding Marla's return. With her was a sturdy, middle-aged woman in a flour-dusty apron.

'I'm Prue Wilcox!' she said briskly. 'Mrs Lewis says you have some questions. I can't think what about.'

Markby explained about murder and repeated his questions.

'I've seen nothing but I can help you about the keys. At least, I can show you where they were and ought to be. On a hook in the old butler's pantry. They shouldn't have been moved. There'd be no reason.'

'Let's go and see, then?' Markby suggested.

Marla Lewis stayed behind. Matthew accompanied them. They entered the area in use by the family through a fairly newly installed baize door. On the other side of this, the temperature dropped abruptly several degrees. If there was central heating here, it was switched off. But Markby couldn't see any radiators.

The kitchen was reassuringly warm. Evidence of the pastry-making from which Prue had been called was on the table. She led them to a large, walk-in pantry with a stone floor and pointed.

'There, all in place, two of them.'

The keys were large, ornate affairs, antiques in their own right. Markby took a small plastic bag from his Barbour pocket. 'You don't mind if I borrow these?'

They watched as he carefully unhooked the keys with the aid of a handy toasting-fork, and dropped them in the bag. He noticed a tell-tale smear on one of them. It did seem likely that someone in the house had used it at the mausoleum.

'Who has access to them?'

'Everyone in the house,' Prue said. 'And Mutchings, I suppose. He comes in here sometimes. But I don't know whether he knows about the keys or what they open. One can't tell with Mutchings what he does understand.'

'What he chooses to!' said Matthew sourly.

Markby recalled the wild figure. 'Mutchings is the pigman, I take it? I encountered him on my way here, the pigs, too. Sprightly little beasts. I didn't recognise the breed.'

'Tamworths,' said Matthew. 'The ones you saw are only half-grown. We've been more than necessarily successful in breeding them. We eventually get rid of them on to other breeders and fanciers. Tamworths do have their admirers, even if I'm not one! The herd was established by Sir Rupert Devaux, my wife's grand-father. That is the main reason for keeping them at all, together with creating work for Mutchings. He's the last of a family which worked for the Devaux for generations and my wife feels we have an obligation towards him. He lives in a cottage in the park.' Matthew saw that his visitor was about to ask a question and forestalled it. 'Nowhere near the mausoleum. On the other side of the grounds, where the pig-sties are. Personally, I feel no obligation towards Mutchings at all, since any work he does around the place is generally bungled.'

'He does his best!' Prue defended the absentee. 'And he's very good with the pigs. That's why they do so well.'

'I told you,' Matthew said, irritated. 'If I had my way, all the noisy little brutes would be pork chops and Mutchings would be causing chaos on someone else's land! If anyone else would have him!'

There were lines of inquiry here, certainly, but a strong suggestion that they were going to prove tortuous and probably ultimately lead nowhere. Markby took his leave of them. 'Thank you for now. I'll be in touch. You won't forget to ask your wife?'

'Ask her what?' Prue snapped.

'It's okay, Prue, I'll explain.' Conway cast Markby a hunted look.

'She mustn't be worried or upset!' Prue stood her ground, her flour-spattered form defiant. 'You're not to go telling her things about the mausoleum. You'd only frighten her, poor soul, and she couldn't tell you anything. She never goes out of the house! Dr Barnes will tell you the same!'

'I hope', said Markby, 'that we won't worry anyone unduly.'

Before the house, Markby paused by his car to look up at the crumbling façade. So Mutchings was the last of his line, just as Adeline Conway *née* Devaux was the last of hers. There was a sense of inexorable fate here, of things coming to an end. Mutchings and his charges seemed to have disappeared. The grounds were extensive and they could be anywhere. Nor did anything he'd learned about the man so far suggest he'd prove a reliable witness, certainly not one who could be produced in a court of law. Nevertheless Markby, with a sigh, set out in search of him. He ought to be able to find the pigs.

In fact he found Mutchings first. He came on a motley collection of buildings comprising the pig-sties and, as had been described, a cottage. As Markby approached, Mutchings appeared in the open doorway.

'What you doin' here? I thought you got business up at the house!'

'I've finished it for the time being. I'd like a word with you.'

'Tis private property!' said Mutchings, stretching out his gangling arms to encompass the area of cottage and sties. 'If you wants to go wandering round here, you has to ask Mr Conway.'

'I'm a police officer,' said Markby firmly. 'And I'd like to talk to you about the burial chapel. Do you ever go over there to check on it, see if there's any damage? Or show it to visitors?'

Mutchings appeared frightened. 'I never go anywhere near it! I've heard 'em moving about in there, them old Devaux! They call out to me, but I never answer! They'd grab hold of me and drag me down with 'em, into the tomb!'

'When did you hear them, Mutchings? What time of day was that?'

The pigman looked vague. 'Evenings, when I've been rounding up the pigs. Sometimes they do stray over that way.'

'Ever seen lights near the vault? A car parked there?'

Mutchings was beginning to look confused. 'Can't recall! I run away from that place fast! I don't hang about there!'

'So you've never unlocked the door to it? Never borrowed the key and lent it to someone else?'

'I never go near it!' Mutchings' arms flailed. 'I keep away! I don't know about no key! I gotta feed them pigs! I got work!' He turned his back and made off.

Markby let him go and returned to the front of the house and his car. Something purple moved on the portico, catching his eye, and Marla Lewis stepped out from behind a pillar and stood looking down at him from the top of the flight of steps. She must have been waiting there for him and obviously had been anxious not to be seen by anyone else. She came clattering down towards him on her stilt heels with her arms held out to either side for balance. The stiff breeze ruffled her platinum hair where it hung loose behind the Alice band. He wondered whether it was bleached. Probably not entirely, given her pale eyes and complexion, perhaps just helped along a little. He wondered whether he was about to be helped, just a little.

'I just think you should know,' she said, dispensing with any unnecessary preamble, 'that she's crazy.'

'She?' Markby divined the answer but was curious to know what prompted the confidence. Marla was not the sort of woman who divulged information without some purpose of her own.

'Adeline. The whole Devaux line, crazy as coots! That's why they don't want you to talk to her. Mind you, it wouldn't help you, if you did. You wouldn't know if what she said was true or something she imagined in that scrambled head. She wanders about the house at night like Lady Macbeth. I don't know whether Matthew knows that. He knows she's sick and ought to be in a suitable hospital. But it's difficult in the circumstances . . .' Markby glanced expressively up at the portico.

'You mean, she owns this house?'

'Owns everything but not a red cent of actual cash. That's why she married Matthew. Save the family home. Now he can't throw her out of her own house. Prue looks after her. She has nursing experience.'

Markby asked thoughtfully, 'If she died, would Conway inherit the house?' The question was prompted by his own dislike of the unkept air of it all, and wondering if Matthew had a free hand, if he'd fix it up.

But Marla was shaking her head. 'No, it goes to the kid. There's a daughter.' Her lipsticked mouth twisted in a dry smile. 'Superbrat.'

'I see, well, thank you, Mrs Lewis.'

'You're welcome,' she said and turned away.

Driving towards the gate, he wondered what relevance this had, if any. Belatedly, he remembered to look out for the pigs. Just before he rattled over the cattle grid he looked in his windscreen mirror and saw them.

They flashed into the narrow oblong of reflected reality, a vivid, comic and oddly disturbing image. Mutchings, waving a bucket of, presumably, feed, raced across the drive. Hot on his heels galloped the herd, squealing its demands. Mutchings, with a final ungainly gesture, vanished through the gap in the box hedges, pigs in pursuit. Markby wondered whether it was some game he played with his charges.

As he cautiously negotiated the cattle grid, he suspected that Mrs Conway was not the only one round here whose mental state was other than quite normal.

'Are you sure you wouldn't like something to eat?' Meredith asked.

'Honestly, no. Barney Crouch fed me rather well and I haven't recovered. You go ahead, if you're hungry.'

'Me, no. I had lunch in town with your new sergeant. And I've been painting all afternoon. The smell sort of kills your appetite.'

They were slumped before Meredith's television in her tiny sitting room, but neither was watching it. It was warm and late and they were both tired. Markby's legs were stretched out towards the gas fire and Meredith sat sideways on the sofa beside him, resting her back on his shoulder, with her feet on the cushions.

'How did you get on with Turner?' he asked.

'Very well. She's nice. She's got a sense of humour which I like.'

'Has she? She seems an awfully intense sort of young woman to me. But she did a pretty good job today with the Wills.' He shifted on the sofa and changed the conversational tack. 'How's the painting going?'

'Finished the walls. I'll tackle the skirting tomorrow. I've got to go back to work Monday. I'll be quite pleased to, I think!'

'You did well to finish the walls today all on your own.'

Meredith grimaced. 'I did have some help for a while. I think it was help!' She explained about Katie and was surprised when he sat forward with a jerk, so that she almost fell sideways off the sofa.

'Conway? Katie Conway? I was at Park House today. That's an extraordinary household!'

'Is it? I got the impression life there was far from peaceful. Katie has troubles and she brought them to me, or tried to. I suppose I asked for it, speaking to the youth club, telling tales of my derring-do in foreign climes. Teach me a lesson! In future I shall hide my light under the nearest bushel!'

'They keep pigs,' said Markby. 'Not commercially or even as a genuine hobby but as a sort of tradition. Funnily enough, I've been racking my brains trying to remember all I can about Park House, and I do recall my father telling me, years ago, about a private zoo or menagerie which was housed in the grounds. As people went past the place they could hear the animals and if they didn't know about the zoo, it could give them quite a shock, especially at night. Imagine yourself walking down the road in the twilight and hearing a lion roar nearby in the gloom.'

'Did they keep lions?'

'I've no idea what they kept.' He frowned. 'But passers-by can still get a nasty shock these days, like old Barney and his experience at the mausoleum! It's an odd set-up and I'd like to know more. What did Katie tell you?'

Meredith repeated Katie's story. 'I don't know if her father is playing around or who Marla is. And I don't know what's wrong with Mrs Conway.'

'Marla is Conway's p.a. Very glamorous and efficient, I imagine. She probably has designs on the boss. She'd clearly love to get Mrs Conway out of the house and into a clinic of some sort. I gather the illness is a nervous one, and neither her husband nor a sort of nurse cum housekeeper they have, wanted me to interview the lady. Marla Lewis told me privately that Adeline Conway is crazy. But Marla, as I say, is not a disinterested party. I think she'd like to spread the word that Adeline should be removed for her own safety.'

'And Marla's convenience. Hmn. Poor little Katie, she does have troubles, then, and I'm beginning to feel twinges of guilt. Perhaps I should have heard her out. But I really couldn't have done anything. She seemed to think I could walk in over there and give Adeline and Matthew Conway a lecture. I wouldn't be surprised if she doesn't have another go with talking me into it. She's a determined young lady, for all her cherubic appearance.'

'Don't forget that on her mother's side Katie comes from a long line of wealthy eccentrics who indulged their every whim, from private mausoleums to pigs in the shrubbery! One day she'll be the châtelaine of Park House! Marla Lewis described her to me as superbrat.'

'She isn't as bad as that!' Meredith said indignantly. 'I don't like the sound of Marla! Although, in fairness, I'm sure that if Katie doesn't like her father's p.a., she lets it be known. If Marla wants to make sure of Matthew Conway, it's not only Adeline she'll have to get out of the way!'

Chapter Ten

HELEN TURNER had been less successful than Markby that late Saturday afternoon. Having seen the Wills escorted home, she had gone out to the flats where Nikki lived. They were fairly new but cheaply constructed and already shabby. Paintwork peeled and there had been some kind of plumbing disaster which had left a long water stain on the outer wall by the main door. That was unlocked and, entering, Helen found an elderly virago laden with two bulging shopping-bags, about to let herself into a ground-floor flat.

'Arnold,' said this lady. 'That's the family you want. Nikki Arnold. And a right little tearaway she is! Plays her pop music all hours disturbing the whole block. I told her about it and I got an earful of language I couldn't repeat! I doubt she's more'n fifteen! Baggage! But then, with a mother like that, I suppose it's no wonder! Upstairs, Flat Three. But you won't find 'em, not on a Saturday. Lord knows where they get to but Saturdays they're out. It's the only peaceful time I get. They're right above my head!' She pointed at the ceiling. 'You try tomorrow, about twelve. Not earlier, because they don't get up till about eleven. Then they put that music on. I wish they'd move!'

Helen checked at Flat Three and got no reply. So, the next day, Sunday, at twelve, saw her re-entering the flats. She was well aware that Mrs Pride was trusting to see her back by one 'because of the joint'. The evening meal arrangement did not appear to apply to Sundays, when Mrs Pride believed in sitting down to a proper meal at one. What's more, that funny old chap Barney Crouch was coming to eat with them again. Helen had already marked him down as Mrs Pride's admirer, although admiration for her cooking might be the greater lure. Barney, however, had a fund of amusing theatrical stories, some of which he was prevented from telling in full by Mrs Pride, who seemed to think Helen would be shocked. As if she still had it in her to be shocked! Helen grimaced.

However, the Arnolds were in today, and out of bed, because Helen could hear the pop music from the bottom of the staircase. She rang the bell of Flat Three twice, at length. It was a few minutes and she was about to ring again, in case they couldn't hear with all that din, before a female voice shouted, 'Hang on! It's the door!' There was a protesting creak and groan and the flat door was dragged laboriously open.

A blast of heat struck Helen full in the face, dusty air rising from overworking radiators, and permeated by the mixed smells of ashtrays, cheap perfume, curry and fried food. A pneumatic, somewhat raddled redhead wearing turquoise leggings and a white sweatshirt decorated with an appliqué picture of a puppy, materialised in the doorspace and fixed Helen with eyes like green ice.

'Hullo, dear . . .' she said hoarsely. 'What's your beef, then? The music? Kid's enjoying herself, all right?'

There was a pause.

'Bleeding law,' she said resignedly. 'I shoulda expected it. That old misery downstairs, I bet, been complaining. I can't help it if the walls are as thin as paper!'

'No, Mrs Arnold. It's something else.' Helen held out her ID. 'I came yesterday but you were out.'

'I don't,' said Mrs Arnold, dismissing the card with a glance of contempt, 'know nothing about nothing. Why should I? Yesterday we all went to the cinema, me, Nikki and a gentleman friend of mine. Afterwards he took us for a Chinese. We had a lovely time and we got witnesses. Not illegal to have a bit of fun on a Sat'day, is it, now?' Then, with a change of manner, she stood back hospitably and said, 'Well, come in then, if you're coming!'

Helen stepped into the untidy little hall. Mrs Arnold shut the front door by putting her shoulder to it and giving a hefty shove. 'It's never been the same since another friend of mine kicked it in last Christmas. He'd had one or two. What is it, then?'

'Actually, it's Nikki I want to talk to.'

Mrs Arnold's eyes became chips of green ice again. 'She's done nothing! You leave her alone!'

'I want to ask her about a friend of hers. It's very important.'

Mrs Arnold chewed her scarlet lower lip so that lipstick stained her top teeth. 'Nik!' she screeched without warning.

The music blared on. Mrs Arnold pounded on her daughter's bedroom door. 'Nik! Turn that bloody row off! We can't hear ourselves think out here! Come out! There's a policewoman to see you, plain clothes!'

The music was abruptly switched off. The door opened and a young girl edged out into the hall. She was a junior version of her mother, even to the sweatshirt with a puppy motif. (Another friend of Mrs Arnold's, thought Helen, had doubtless got hold of a consignment of those, no questions asked!) She noticed that Nikki looked frightened and smiled reassuringly.

'I haven't done anything!' Nikki mumbled.

''Course you haven't, darling!' crooned her mother hoarsely. ''Course she hasn't!' she repeated fiercely to Helen Turner.

'It's about Lynne Wills, Nikki. You know she's dead?'

Nikki's face turned whiter. Mrs Arnold advised, 'Poor little mare. They was talking about it last night. Her people had to go and look at the body. You'd think the police would find some other way! I hope you catch him! Wanna cup of coffee?'

Somehow, during this conversation, they'd progressed down the hall to the even more untidy sitting room, littered with unwashed mugs and general débris. Helen declined the offer and sat down on the cleanest of the available seats. Nikki sat on the sofa, after pushing aside a heap of clothing and magazines. Mrs Arnold lit a cigarette and perched on the arm.

'I can't tell you anything,' Nikki said almost inaudibly. 'I didn't see Lynne last Thursday. I rang up her house and told her I couldn't go out with her.'

'I know. But you were her friend, weren't you? You usually went out together? What did you do, when you went out?'

'The usual. Went to the Social Club sometimes if there was a gig. Hung round with our mates.'

'Go to local pubs?'

'She only ever had orange juice!' croaked Mrs Arnold. 'My Nikki don't touch alcohol, right, Nik?'

'Yes, that's right,' said Nikki unconvincingly.

'Do you know if Lynne planned to meet anyone that evening?'

Nikki's clenched fists beat on her knees and in a burst of

passion, she shouted, 'I don't know! I told you I didn't!'

'There, there,' said her mother. 'See? She can't help you.'

To talk to Nikki it was going to be necessary to detach her from her mother. 'Which school do you go to?' Helen asked casually.

Nikki looked wary. 'Bamford Community College.'

Plays truant! thought Helen. She got up. 'I'm sorry about your friend, Nikki. It's a nasty shock for you.'

'For us all!' said Mrs Arnold through a cloud of smoke. 'Young girls aren't safe! Those men who prey on them oughta be fixed, like they fix tomcats, that's my opinion.'

As Mrs Arnold prepared to wrestle open the recalcitrant front door, Helen asked, 'Is Mr Arnold still living at home?'

''Course he isn't!' puffed his wife. 'We were only kids when we married, I was sixteen! Only lasted a year. He wasn't Nikki's dad. He shoved off, too. Men do, don't they? Never hang around long enough to pay the bills! I kept my married name, though, because it's a sight better than the one I was born with!'

'Oh, what was that?' asked Helen, mildly curious.

'Mutchings!' The door flew open and catapulted Mrs Arnold into Helen's arms. 'Sorry, dear! It catches you unawares like that! Yes, I was born a Mutchings. Funny old name, isn't it?'

'Got any spare change?'

The speaker was a young girl, pasty-faced and sharp-eyed, but reasonably clean and well-dressed and without any of that look of neglect which marks those who have genuinely hit the bottom of the barrel.

Meredith, whom the girl had accosted at the entry to the London Underground, identified the professional beggar and shook her head. The girl moved on competently to importune someone else. Meredith was left to cope with a thoroughly British feeling of guilt.

Knowing one is in the right doesn't always help. To have been asked for help by anyone and to have refused it left a niggling sense of unease. No one, no young person certainly, ought to be begging for a living. Certainly not in our affluent society. Meredith, who on her travels about the world had seen unimaginable poverty, felt aggrieved and confused. Somewhere along the line that young girl had lost something more important in the long run than innocence. She'd lost self-respect, and she didn't even realise it.

Or am I, thought Meredith as she barged her way on to an already over-crowded tube train, just over-dramatising? It was Monday morning and raining and in this damp commuter throng life was no bowl of cherries for anyone.

The train doors tried to close but were impeded by some object. They sprang open again. A communal ripple of annoyance ran around the carriage as a few more seconds was added to their discomfort. 'Stand clear of the doors!' yelled a disembodied voice. They all shuffled around, each glared at the next as if it was that person's fault. The doors managed to close at the second attempt and they rocked and rattled away in their stuffy capsule. The start of another week.

What really bothered her, apart from being crushed against the metal pole at the end of the line of seats, was that the begging girl had recalled Katie Conway. Not, for goodness sake, because of any resemblance or because Katie was in any financial distress, but because Katie too had asked for help and Meredith had refused it. Again, she knew she had been right to do so, and again, it didn't help. The refusal haunted her conscience. Helen Turner's words hadn't made things any easier. Someone had to listen to the young. 'But it doesn't have to be me!' she thought mutinously. Which was, of course, uncomfortably akin to 'Am I my brother's keeper?' Today was self-flagellation day, all right.

When she came up above ground the rain was pouring down and there was another beggar on the pavement at the Underground entrance. A boy this time, hollow-eyed and malnourished, his unkempt long hair clinging wetly to his thin face, his baggy old overcoat hanging around his spindly frame and his feet shod inadequately in worn-out trainers. Meredith, by now having reasoned herself into a feeling of responsibility for the world's wrongs, gave him a couple of coins.

'Cheers!' he said with a surprisingly happy grin.

But it didn't make her feel any less guilty. Because now she went on her way convinced that by her miserly largesse she had contributed to supporting an undoubted drug habit.

Some days you just can't win.

On Monday morning, while Meredith was being carried down an escalator to the bowels of the London Underground, Markby and Sergeant Turner met over cooling cups of coffee to compare notes in the former's office.

'My visit to Park House raised a lot of questions in my mind, but not many answers. It did turn up the keys!' Markby sighed. 'Bridges did a rush job on them but couldn't get a decent print or even part print.' He glanced at his notes. 'Either because of the ornamental nature of the metalwork or because the handler wore gloves against the cold. I dare say Forensics will tell us in due course that the smear is a common, cheap kind of oil, readily available for household use on hinges or locks. We'll have to await the report on that and on the blood and hair. Mrs Wills has confirmed that the necklet belonged to her daughter.'

'I tracked down Lynne's friend, Nikki Arnold,' said Helen. 'You should see that place, it's a shambles! I spoke to Mrs Arnold and Nikki but I'll have to get the mother out of the way. I'm sure Nikki knows a great deal but my fear is that by the time I get to question her, she'll have been told by her mother to keep quiet. I don't mean by that that Mrs Arnold shares Nikki's knowledge, but she isn't the sort to talk to the police or let her daughter do so. She seems to live off benefit and a number of menfriends.'

Markby tapped his fingers on the desk. 'As far as interviewing Nikki alone, she's under age and we're supposed to have an adult friend or relative present. You might arrange just to bump into her in the street. She's our only real lead and we don't have time on our side.'

'I'm well aware of that, sir. I'll manage something. Eventually I think I can win Mrs Arnold's confidence, partly because I'm a woman. Men have never treated Mrs Arnold well. Her husband left her as did Nikki's father. She's hung on to her married name only because it's preferable to her maiden one.' Helen grinned. 'She told me what it was and it was a new one to me! Mutchings. Is that a common name around here?'

'Mutchings!' Markby gave her a startled look followed by a low whistle. 'Well, Sergeant Turner, it looks as though you might have learned rather more than you thought! Mutchings isn't a common name hereabouts to my knowledge, but I *have* come across it very recently. It's the name of the pigman at Park House! The Arnold woman can't know that we're interested in the mausoleum or she wouldn't have given any hint that she might be connected with the Park House estate in any way.'

'I don't think word had got round about our interest in the

mausoleum by Sunday. She knew the Wills had identified their daughter. But she was away from Bamford all Saturday and possibly hadn't heard all the gossip. She probably knows by now. If so, she'll be unlikely to volunteer any more information. Damn!' concluded Helen crossly. 'I wish I'd known about the pigman then!'

'You didn't, and it can't be helped. The Mutchings were employed by the Devaux for generations! I doubt there's much went on in Park House or its grounds that wasn't common knowledge to every member of that family. Mrs Arnold will certainly know of the mausoleum's existence and she may have told her daughter about the place. Nikki could have told Lynne. All speculation, of course. But yes, cultivate the Arnolds by all means. They may have a lot to tell us!' He smiled at her. 'And well done, sergeant!'

It wasn't Sergeant Turner's way to let grass grow under her feet when it came to pursuing inquiries. At half past three that Monday afternoon as the schools were coming out for the day, she was standing at the main gate of Bamford Community College. It was dry but chilly and Helen rubbed her hands together for warmth as she hoped that Nikki hadn't chosen today to play truant and would appear before long.

It looked as if the older pupils were coming now. A motley gaggle of youths and girls approached noisily. Nikki, she was relieved to see, trailed along by herself in the rear. In her school uniform she looked a little younger and far more vulnerable than she had done on Sunday. Her red hair was plaited into a single long pigtail which hung down her back and her school skirt, surely, was far shorter than regulations required.

Turner stepped forward. 'Nikki? Remember me?'

Nikki jumped. 'You following me around or something?' she demanded aggressively. 'I told you yesterday, I don't know what Lynne did that day!'

She attempted to march past, but Helen fell into step with her. 'Your mum wouldn't be related to the Mutchings family who live in a cottage in the grounds of Park House?' she asked conversationally.

Nikki cast her a wary look. 'There's no Mutchings family there now!' Scorn touched her voice. 'Only my mum's Uncle Winston and he's loopy!' She put her index finger to her temple and made a circular motion. 'Off his trolley. We never go near him! He looks after the pigs up there.'

'I expect your mother went up there when she was a girl.'

'Suppose so. What's it to you?'

'Did your mother ever tell you about the mausoleum in the grounds?'

'No. What is it, anyway?'

'A sort of chapel where the Devaux family members are buried.'

'Don't know nothing about that!' said Nikki instantly.

'Are you sure?'

Nikki stopped and stamped her foot, her cheeks scarlet and her green eyes snapping icily just like her mother's. 'You stay away from me and my mum! You had no right coming to our home like that! All this, it's nothing to do with us, right?'

She broke into a run and, weaving in and out of her school-friends, was lost in the crowd.

'Little madam!' muttered Helen involuntarily. 'And lying through her teeth!'

She followed slowly in the wake of the vanished Nikki. Suddenly there was a cacophony of shrieks and cheers ahead. Hastening towards it, Helen saw that it came from a milling crowd. Clearly a fight had broken out. She began to run.

A mixed circle of youths and girls had formed, yelling encouragement and abuse. Above it all could be distinguished gasps, thuds and screams from the middle of the mêlée. Helen forced her way through, grabbing at arms and shoulders and hauling spectators out of the way. They seemed to her to be exhibiting the naked bloodlust of the mob which had accompanied the tumbrils of the guillotine and their youth only made it worse. Then, when she at last managed to get to the inner circle, she beheld an extraordinary sight.

The fight was not between two boys or even two girls, a not unusual thing. It was between a boy and a girl and the boy was getting the worst of it. He was pinned to the ground, kicking, swearing and trying in vain to fend off Nikki Arnold, who knelt on his chest, pummelling him with both fists and shrieking, 'Don't you ever call me a dirty slag again, Paul Harris!' She accompanied these words with a wide-ranging variety of pornographic and scatological detail which called forth roars of laughter from the onlookers.

'Nikki!' yelled Helen, charging forward. She wrapped both arms around the girl and hauled her off her prostrate victim.

'You let go of me, you filthy copper!' yelled Nikki, kicking backwards and catching Helen a painful blow on the shin.

'Not on your life!' Helen promised through gritted teeth.

The crowd, seeing it was about to be deprived of its entertainment, began to jeer and threatened to interfere. The discomfited victim, on the other hand, his face scratched and mouth bloodied, took the opportunity to scramble to his feet and make off, despite howls of derision from his contemporaries.

At the corner of the street he paused long enough to turn and yell, 'You'll end up like your mate, you will, Nikki Arnold!'

'Oo-aah!!' roared the crowd, surging around Helen and the struggling Nikki.

'I'm a police officer!' bellowed Helen above the din.

That did it. They melted away like snow in the sunshine.

'What's all this about, Nikki?' Helen released her captive who whirled, red of face, panting and defiant, to face her.

'What did you bloody have to interfere for? He called me filthy names and I had him right where I wanted him! I hadn't finished with him!'

'Why did he call you names?' demanded Helen crisply.

'Because he's a shit, that's why! I didn't start it. He called me a slag!'

'Why?' repeated Helen remorselessly.

Nikki's eyes blazed and her reply echoed her earlier language.

'Don't talk like that to me! If the boys here have so low an opinion of you, perhaps it's because of something you've done?'

'It's nothing to do with you!' said Nikki sulkily. 'I can take care of myself! It's supposed to be a free country, isn't it? I can do what I like!'

'Er – what's going on?' broke in a diffident voice.

Helen turned to see a nervous young man with a beard and tweed jacket.

'I'm a teacher!' he said unnecessarily.

Helen opened her mouth to explain. Nikki, profiting by the distraction, bolted away down the road.

'Oh—!' Helen almost borrowed one of Nikki's colourful

phrases, but managed to stop herself in time. She turned to the bearded man. 'Paul Harris. Where does he live?'

The Harris family lived in a flat above a charity shop. The street-level entrance was opened by a thin-faced young man with greasy hair. He glanced at Helen's ID.

'What d'you want him for? I'm his brother.'

'I want to talk to him about a fight at school.'

'Cor!' He looked disgusted. 'Cops worrying about kids having a scrap now, are they? Got nothing else to do? Here, our Paul got the worst of that. She kicked him in the mouth and chipped one of his front teeth! You want to have a go at her, not at him. You come and see what the little tart done!'

The flat was supplied with cheap curtains , carpet and furniture, much of it looking as if it had been bought in the shop beneath. It did, however, boast a wealth of expensive electrical equipment. Helen could see television, video-recorder, stereo and compact disc player.

'Mum's at work,' said Paul's brother. 'My name's Dom. Paul's washing the blood out of his mouth in the bathroom. I'll get him.'

While he was gone, Helen opened a door and peered through. It was the kitchen. A packet of economy brand hamburgers lay defrosting itself on a table by a tin of baked beans. To cook this simple fare, however, there was not only a fat-spotted gas cooker but a smart new microwave oven.

She turned as Dom came back. 'I was just going to cook up our tea,' he said, nodding towards the kitchen scene. 'But I don't know if he can eat it now, not with his mouth. Show her, Paul.'

A smaller, slighter form emerged from behind Dom. Paul pushed up his swollen top lip with a finger and mumbled something. The front tooth was chipped all right. Paul took his hand from his mouth and said more clearly, 'She started it!'

'Letting yourself get duffed up by a girl!' said Dom in disgust.

'She jumped me! She went crazy!'

'All right!' Helen interrupted. 'It's not the fight itself I've come about. It's the fact that you called Nikki certain names. You called her a slag, she says.'

'Why shouldn't he?' asked Dom pugnaciously. 'S'all true!'

'Is it?' she turned her attention to him.

'Course it is! Everyone knows! I've seen that Nikki working

the pubs – and the other one, the one who got herself killed! Mostly weekends you'd see 'em, but sometimes mid-week. They're famous for it!'

'You know this for a fact, do you?'

'I told you, I've seen them!' Dom insisted. Then his expression grew suspicious. 'Here, don't look at me like that! I only saw them, I never paid either of them!' He paused and smirked. 'I don't never pay for it!'

'Were just those two girls involved?'

He frowned. 'Sometimes others but I don't know their names. They sort of come and go, but Nikki and the other one, Lynne, they were regulars, if you see what I mean. There was another girl used to come in with them, quite a while back. I could've fancied her. But she don't come any more. Lynne I never would've fancied and that Nikki, I'd have to be desperate, which I ain't – yet!' Another smirk.

'Which pubs?' Helen asked sharply. 'Where did you see them?'

'All over the place. Royal George, Silver Bells. They used to try it on at the Social Club until the manager – the old chap – not this new one, he told them to hop it.'

Helen sighed. The pattern was becoming all too clear. She glanced around the drab flat again with its wealth of expensive gimmickry. Some things, however, were less clear.

'Are you in employment?' she asked Dom.

He looked indignant. 'Yes, I am! I've got a regular job! What d'you want to know for?'

'Someone seems to earn quite good money.' She indicated the nearest piece of electronic wizardry.

Dom leaned forward. 'Well, that's mine, paid for, see? It's up to me what I spend my money on. Our mum, she's working too. That pays for food and such.'

He probably contributed next to nothing to the domestic bills. Helen asked sharply, 'What do you do?'

'Office cleaning. The company I work for does all kinds of businesses round here. It's a pretty good thing.'

Helen frowned. 'Your company wouldn't by any chance clean the office suite at Park House?'

'Yeah,' said Dom carelessly. Then his face lit up. 'There's a smashing bit of skirt works there!'

'Ever been inside the house itself, the part the family lives in?'

He hunched his thin shoulders. 'No . . . Wouldn't mind having a look round. But no chance. That secretary, the one with the great legs, she watches the cleaning teams all the time we're working, and we watch her!' Dom chuckled.

'We may want to talk to you again,' said Helen which cut short his merriment. She turned to his younger brother who sat with a grimy handkerchief to his mouth. 'Paul, I suggest you make an appointment to see the school dentist about that chipped tooth, okay?'

'We're dealing with a pair of schoolgirls on the game, all right,' Helen said despondently to Markby later. 'Amateur stuff for pocket money. We'll never get evidence. Dom only told me because he wanted to defend Paul's part in the scrap with Nikki. Otherwise no one is going to admit knowing anything about it. But talking of Dom, there's a lot of expensive hi-fi and other equipment in that flat, though every sign of a low standard of living otherwise. Dom, by the way, works for the cleaning firm which services the office suite at Park House. He swears he's never been in the domestic part of the house. He says a secretary, from his description Marla Lewis, watches the team all the time it's working in the office.'

'So this Dom is into a racket of some sort. It could be a lead and it could send us haring off in the wrong direction. I would imagine that Marla Lewis made sure Conway got full value from that cleaning firm and wouldn't give one of them a chance to go sneaking off into the house. But we'll have to check. Now, as regards this girl, Nikki Arnold. She's obviously in moral danger. We could inform social services. They might want to apply for a care order.'

'No!'

He looked up in surprise. Her cheeks were flushed and her eyes sparkled with emotion.

'Sorry, sir,' she said awkwardly. 'But I honestly believe that could be about the worst thing we could do. Mrs Arnold isn't a brilliant mum, but she is a devoted one. The affection's mutual. It's a real little family unit, however imperfect. If we tried to take Nikki away it would be a disaster. She'd never forgive us and never co-operate. And she is fifteen, a bit older than Lynne. If social services put her in a children's home, she'd just run away. At the best she'd end up in a hostel and we all know what goes on in those places! More likely she'd finish up sleeping rough. She'd almost certainly turn to street-walking for cash.'

Markby slapped his hand on a pile of files in exasperation. 'I admit that when Barney Crouch first said to me that he believed Lynne was picking up men for money, I was doubtful because of her age. From what you've now told me, I agree we have to suspect the worst! I'm appalled by the idea. Who wouldn't be? These are schoolkids, after all. I certainly don't like to think it's been going on in Bamford, right under our noses, and no one's noticed!'

'None of us likes the idea, sir. But I want to help Nikki. I want to prevent her from moving on from what she's doing now – if she's doing it – to full-time prostitution. It's only a step, but she probably doesn't realise it.'

'You're really taking an interest in this girl, aren't you?' Markby shook his head. 'A personal interest can sometimes lead to muddled decisions. However we feel, we have to keep clear heads and try and make balanced judgements.'

Helen folded her hands together tightly. 'The first division I worked in included a notorious red-light district, around some docks. Nearly all our work was vice-related in some way, directly or indirectly. It really shook me to see how young the girls were. Nearly all of them used to tell us they were only doing it temporarily. Some had even lied to their families, saying they had regular nightwork in hospitals or factories. There were young married women working there who had lied to their husbands about what they did to earn extra money. Some of them liked to pretend that what they were doing was a public service, almost social work! Most of them believed that when they'd had enough, or it got too risky, or when a "proper job" came along, they could just walk away. A few had already learned to their cost that they couldn't and the others soon did.'

The muscles of her pale face tightened. 'They got beaten up by the punters, beaten up by the pimps, hooked on drugs, inveigled into pornographic movie-making and forced into indescribable acts which they probably couldn't have gone through if they weren't drugged up to the eyes. All that without mention of the possibility of disease. Every so often we took the body of one of them out of the dock.

'We all know there are high-class hookers and expensive brothels working the top of the market. Very few girls get to work those. Yes, you're right. I do want to stop that happening to Nikki. She's a pretty girl now. I'd hate to see her in twenty years time if things go on the way they've begun.'

Markby was silent for a moment. 'Very well, I'll give you a free hand for the time being. Not least, I have to admit, because we need any information that girl can give us and I don't want social workers spiriting her away. And while you're concentrating on the Arnolds, I think I'll pay another visit to Mr and Mrs Reeves!'

Chapter Eleven

MARKBY GOT his opportunity to check Turner's information regarding Dom Harris earlier than he anticipated.

He was on his way to The Silver Bells the following morning just after breakfast-time and had chosen to walk there. As he made his way along the pavements, still slippery with overnight frost, he passed a newsagents' shop and out of it, into his path, stepped Marla Lewis, carrying a bundle of newspapers and magazines. She was clad in knee-high white boots and an amazing coat of pale-blue artificial fur. With her long fair hair and pale complexion, she looked like a walking icicle. But this morning, the icicle was thawing.

'Well,' she lowered long mascara-ed lashes. 'The chief inspector! My, you're an early bird!'

'So are you,' said Markby, feeling foolish.

'I was on the school run!' She grimaced and seeing he didn't immediately understand, explained. 'The parents who pay for private schooling round here also pay for a mini-bus to pick up their kids and take them round their various schools. It leaves from the middle of town and every morning the little darlings are ferried in to the departure point by devoted parents. But, in Katie's case, by whoever is free. I drew the short straw again today. At least it gives me the chance to call and pick up the papers.'

'You really don't like that child, do you?' Markby had pulled himself together and went on the offensive.

'No. And she doesn't like me. I'm many things, Chief Inspector, but not a hypocrite! I speak my mind, That's why I say Adeline's crazy when everyone else is saying she's nervous. The kid is a spoiled brat.'

'Other people seem to find Katie rather charming.'

The eyelashes flickered again. 'I'm not other people. You track down the mystery of the chapel key yet?'

'No. But perhaps you can help with something. I understand there's an office-cleaning firm which deals with Park House.'

'Sure. Every Monday morning early.' The pale eyes watched him warily. She didn't know where this was leading.

'You supervise them?'

'Sure. Like a hawk, Chief Inspector! Matt pays good money for what they do. Anyway, I don't want them messing with any papers or files.'

'So one of them couldn't, for example, slip round to the kitchen at the house? To fetch something? Water? A cup of coffee?'

Carmine lips twisted. 'I don't give them time to drink coffee! If they want to do that, they can do it in their own time and off the premises! And if they wanted anything like that, they wouldn't need to go to Prue's kitchen. There's a little kitchen in the office suite. You know, where I made tea for you and Matt when you called the other day? Are you thinking one of them could slip into Prue's kitchen and borrow the key?'

'I was,' Markby admitted.

'Forget it. I make sure they all leave as soon as they're done.'

'Why so particular?' he asked curiously.

She leaned towards him, the pale eyes mocking. 'Business information, Chief Inspector, is worth money! Competitors might just like to get a look at contracts and so forth. I don't give anyone a chance to snoop!'

'Watch me!' said Markby drily.

'Hey! Is that an invitation?'

A bunch of keys jangled at him. Blue coat and white boots clattered past towards a parked car. Markby realised to his annoyance that, despite the chilly morning, he felt uncomfortably warm.

At The Silver Bells the cold morning hadn't prevented the doors being propped open to let out overnight stale air. Through it came the noise of a vacuum-cleaner and the rattle of bottles. The Reeves were busy making ready for opening time later on. Daphne was cleaning and her husband restocking the bar.

'Oh, hullo, Chief Inspector!' said the landlord with a rather hangdog expression, as Markby walked in. He left the bar and went to close the street door behind the newcomer.

Markby wondered whether he was worried that someone would notice that the police had returned to the pub. Daphne had switched off the vacuum-cleaner and fixed the visitor apprehensively with her slightly prominent blue eyes.

'Surprised to see me back, Mr Reeves? Or not, perhaps.'

'Old Barney no help to you then?' said Reeves in a glum voice.

'As a distraction, no. As an informant, quite interesting. But that wasn't what you intended, was it? That Barney should actually be able to tell me something. The idea was to send me away with something to keep me happy, but really I'd be scurrying down a blind alley! Please don't bother to protest. But you were wrong to dismiss Crouch as an old soak who didn't notice anything. He saw quite a lot.'

Reeves shot the top bolt across the door. 'You can't blame me! No offence, but who wants the Old Bill hanging round their place? It puts the punters off.'

'Perhaps we could discuss the punters, as you call them.'

Daphne moved to the bar, picked up a cloth and stood twisting it between her hands.

'Why don't we all sit down?' Markby took a seat at a table and, after a moment's hesitation during which they exchanged glances, the Reeves joined him. Sitting side by side across the beer-stained surface from him, they reminded him forcibly of Mr and Mrs Wills. The memory hardened his heart and his resolve.

'This is a country town but the same sort of thing goes on here as anywhere else,' he began. 'Human nature doesn't vary, does it, Mr Reeves? No one's perfect and everyone has their little secret shame. Tell me about the girls who've been coming into the pub, the dead girl and her friends.'

'We get a lot of youngsters,' Reeves said sullenly. 'They're just customers.'

'Perhaps some of them have been drumming up a little custom on their own account?'

'Don't know what you mean, squire.' Reeves' deepset little eyes stared fixedly at Markby.

'Don't you, indeed? I think you do.'

Daphne gave a little squeak. Her husband gave her a sidelong glare. Markby turned his attention to her. 'Yes, Mrs Reeves?'

'I never liked it,' she whispered.

Reeves broke in loudly. 'We don't know anything went on!'

'But it didn't look right, Terry! I told you lots of times!' She turned back to Markby. 'That night – when the girl you're asking about left here with a feller – well, she'd left before with men, different men. And there were a coupla other girls used to come in with her and it was always the same thing. I spoke several times to Terry about it, but he said, well, it wasn't doing any harm and it wasn't any of our business!'

'Look!' Reeves leaned across the table and spread out his hand, palm upwards. 'It wasn't like they were working the pub regular! I know a professional tart when I see one and I wouldn't have allowed that sort of thing, not for a minute! Those girls, they were just amateurs, making pocket money. I can't control my customers' morals! People go to pubs to meet other people! Make friends, and okay, pick up men or women or what they fancy! I wouldn't have let the pub be used by professionals, but those girls, they were local kids and what could I do? I can't turn out everyone I think's a bit dodgy!'

'In fact you can, within the law!' said Markby crisply. 'It's up to you to control your pub! If you think someone is a trouble-maker, you can certainly ask him or her to leave!'

'They didn't cause me no trouble!' Reeves howled. 'This is a new business! Bamford's full of other pubs! I can't start turning people away! I want to bring 'em in! Above all, I don't want to make any enemies! Suppose I'd said to that kid, "Hop it because I think you're on the game!" I could have had her old man round here the next day threatening to do me over or sue me! Even if I'd been right, I couldn't have proved it. And supposing I'd been wrong, what then? Word would've gone round and all her friends would have taken offence. I'd have been as good as blacklisted by half the youngsters in town!' He stopped, frowned and jabbed a stubby finger at Markby. 'Here! You're not going to suggest I got a pay-off from any of them, are you? Because I didn't and you can't show otherwise!'

'Oh no!' Daphne whispered. 'Oh, Terry wouldn't have done anything like that. It's like he said, Mr Markby. We didn't like the look of it, but we couldn't do anything. We're newcomers and we can't go offending people! We didn't know for sure what those girls were doing! It just looked that way! We couldn't go accusing them without proof! You're a policeman, you know that!'

'See here,' Reeves' tone became persuasive. 'When we'd got a chance to build the business up a bit, got a regular clientèle, then I was going to do something about it! Then I'd have been able to tell them to clear out! Daph and me, we've got ambitions for this place! But in the short term, see, we got to earn the money to pay for all the improvements and make a living! Everyone's money is good! If they come in here, buy their drinks, maybe buy a few bar meals, don't get rowdy or start picking fights, that's all we can ask. What else they do is their private business. Nothing to do with either of us!'

Markby sighed. What the Reeves had done was turn a blind eye for the sake of short-term expediency. The sad thing was that Reeves was undoubtedly telling the truth. He and his wife did have ambitions for The Silver Bells. In due course, once they'd got established, they would have felt they could be more discerning about the custom. But events had overtaken them.

'You should have told me before,' he said. 'I'll send someone round to take your statements. And if there is anything – anything else at all! – then tell us at once! It's important that we identify the girls concerned. After all,' he got to his feet, 'as a result of the activities you allowed them to pursue here, one of them met a violent death. She was fourteen years old, Mr Reeves, and I suggest you pay far greater attention to the age of youngsters drinking here than you have done so far! I'm obliged to accept that you didn't realise she was under-age in view of the way she was dressed and made up. But if I find that you've served one more drink to one more under-age customer, believe me, I'll have your licence!'

Reeves, perhaps surprisingly, said 'Yes, sir!'

Daphne began to weep quietly. Markby was sorry for her but angry with her, too, because the weakness of her attitude had encouraged the wrongness of her husband's, and she had to share the blame.

As he left, he heard the first shrill and growled exchanges of a quarrel. Sharing the blame was something neither of them intended. They were vociferously placing it squarely on one another.

That same Tuesday, at four in the afternoon, the mini-bus which brought the pupils from the area's private schools, drew up in the Market Square and decanted its cargo.

They scattered singly and in twos and three, calling out fare-wells to one another. Katie Conway set off alone. There was no regular arrangement for taking her from the town centre to Park House at the end of the day, unlike the morning 'school run' of which Marla Lewis had told Markby. It was generally understood that Katie spent some time in Bamford after getting off the bus and, when she was ready, either phoned home to see if anyone were free to come and collect her or took a local taxi. No bus went along the Cherton road.

It was cold and getting a little foggy. The air felt dank and caught in her throat as she hurried along. It was with relief that she pushed through the door of a small café and was bathed in the warm air of its well-lit interior. It was attached to a local bakery and always smelled of new bread and sticky buns.

She looked round. In a corner, Josh Sanderson raised an arm. 'Over here, Kate!'

She joined him and dropped down into a seat, putting her document wallet of school papers on the check tablecloth. 'I can't stop long. Watch my things, I'll just go and get a milkshake.'

She was back from the counter with a tall glass of strawberry coloured milk in a few minutes.

'The police came to our house on Saturday.' She paused after delivering this bombshell to draw a length of pink liquid up a straw and push back her hair which threatened to fall into the glass. 'I wish they hadn't. It's upset everyone! First of all there was just one man, a chief inspector. He went round to the office and talked to Daddy and the horrible Marla, and after that, to Prue. He wanted to talk to Mummy too, but Daddy wouldn't let him. I wasn't there then. When I got in, they, Daddy and Prue, were being very furtive and Prue kept saying to me that "it was nothing for me to worry about!" which was just maddening. They were both very worried about my mother.

'Anyway, after Daddy had telephoned Dr Barnes, he shut him-self up in the office for the rest of the day with Marla the Man-eater. You'd think he wouldn't choose to work at weekends. It's as if he's trying to avoid us. I hope it's not because he wants to be with her. It would be nice if the police came and arrested her. I'm sure she's capable of anything!' Katie concluded vengefully.

'So did they get to talk to you?' Josh asked impatiently.

'Later on. An awfully efficient, humourless woman detective

turned up in the evening. She also wanted to talk to Mummy, but Dr Barnes had sent over a certificate by then, saying Mummy wasn't up to it! The policewoman argued a bit, but she had to make do with me. You could see she was pretty put out by then. She asked me if I'd used the keys to the mausoleum and if I'd seen lights over there at night.'

'Had you?'

She leaned forward, knocking against the glass and making the lurid pink contents slop. Her pale little face was set and her full lower lip jutted pugnaciously. 'No! I don't know why they wanted to come bothering us! Especially the way they keep on wanting to see Mummy! I hope Dr Barnes goes on writing note after note saying they can't! And I still don't know what's supposed to have happened or why they came in the first place! No one explains anything to me! You'd think I was a child!'

'As it happens,' Josh said smugly. 'I know why they came. Someone told Aunt Celia. That girl who was found murdered—'

Katie paled. 'That's nothing to do with us!'

'Hang on. They think she might have been killed in your family burial place, that chapel.'

'The mausoleum? No, they're wrong!'

'All right, all right, perhaps they are!' She looked so agitated that he hastened to soothe her. 'I expect they chase down all sorts of clues which turn out duds.' She still sat staring at him so he pointed to her bulging document wallet. 'Lot of homework?'

She relaxed and sighed. 'Yes, loads of it. It's the English course work. Honestly, I shan't be sorry to see the back of that when I leave in the summer!'

'Have you spoken to your mother again about not going to France? You said you would.' He looked reproachfully at her.

She pulled an apologetic grimace. 'I know I did, but I've got to choose the right moment. Daddy's on my side but my mother's not well. I told you. She gets upset.'

Josh's thin face flushed red. He leaned over the table. 'I think she does that on purpose, just to make you do what she wants or to get her own way! Every time you disagree with her, she turns on the hysterics and you give in! Your father's no help because he won't argue with her, either!'

Katie's face set stubbornly. 'Mummy *is* ill! The doctor comes regularly. It's all to do with when I was born and she was depressed afterwards and didn't get over it. You don't know anything about it, Josh!'

'Sometimes other people see more than family members do! You don't see it because you're too close. You're sixteen and she's had years to get over her depression! She doesn't want to! I think you're making an excuse of it, too! You're as bad as she is! You really do want to go to France but you don't want to own up. You keep putting off telling her you won't go, so that in the end you will!'

'That's all nonsense!' Katie's temper flared. 'I am not going to stay here and listen to you criticising my mother and me! No one tells me what I'm going to do, and that includes you, Josh Sanderson!'

She grabbed her document wallet and stormed out, leaving her milkshake unfinished on the table and although he called after her, she didn't look back.

The streetlights were on but the fog had, if anything, lessened. Katie made her way to the taxi rank. It was empty. She sighed and glanced at the public telephone box across the road. She could call Prue, but she was probably busy about now, getting Adeline up from her afternoon nap. There was nothing for it but to wait until a taxi returned. It couldn't be long.

It was cold standing by the deserted rank and her spirits were still ruffled from her squabble with Josh and the awareness that he was right to some extent. She *was* putting off the final confrontation with her mother. Her father, for all he kept saying she wouldn't have to go to Paris if she didn't want to, wouldn't, when it came to it, be any support. He was afraid of upsetting his wife and always gave way to her wishes in the end. Rebellion surged up inside her. It wasn't fair! And she wasn't going to hang about here getting frozen waiting for a stupid taxi, either! She'd walk home! She'd often done it in the summer and it wasn't so very far!

Katie set off resolutely. Walking through town was no problem. But by the time she reached The Silver Bells it had grown very dark. Once past the new houses, she was alone on the country road with no pavements and the outstretched arms of ancient trees looming over her. She tried humming to encourage herself, but her voice sounded so feeble in the surrounding silence that she gave it up. She clasped her document wallet to her chest, gaining a kind of comfort from its mundane familiarity. Her footsteps crunched beneath her which made her think that if there was anything out there, it could hear her! All kinds of odd noises rustled in the undergrowth. The lights of Bamford were far behind her and ahead was a long, empty, gloomy and seemingly endless tree-lined tunnel. It must be at least another mile to home. She'd been really silly to try and walk it at this time of year.

Unfairly, she blamed Josh for her own bad decision. He had made her cross and at a time when everything seemed to conspire against her. Surely it had only been gossip, that story about the police believing the murder had taken place in the mausoleum? When she got home, she'd make Prue tell her what had been going on and what that policeman had really wanted. To think Josh had the nerve to accuse her of only pretending not to want to go to France! It was the foulest betrayal on the part of someone she'd believed her friend. Betrayal and blame. She had been betrayed and she was getting the blame! Life was so unfair!

And it was so cold and miserable out here on this isolated road. Why was it that everything was going so badly? Katie marched along, angry and anxious and above all, alone.

Chapter Twelve

'IT'S NICE, your having a brother-in-law who's such a good cook,' said Meredith later that evening. She settled back into the passenger seat. 'But if Paul fed me regularly, I'd be enormous! I hope you don't mind leaving so early? It's just that Bamford railway station in the early winter morning is only bearable if I've had my sleep.'

'I've got work too!' Alan reminded her. 'And my sister is a partner in a busy legal practice.' He glanced at the clock on the instrument panel. It was just after eleven.

'The murder of that girl, Lynne? Are you making any progress?'

'Some. It's opened up an unpleasant can of worms, I'm afraid. But we'll sort it out.' You can be sure of that! he thought resolutely. If we can't protect the youngsters in this town, we're failing badly in our job! He turned out of the Market Square and into the High Street.

Bamford was busy about this time of night. Pubs and clubs had emptied. People, mostly young, walked homeward along the pavements or stood gossiping in small groups. The fast food van was doing good business. He could smell its pungent odours even within the car. There didn't appear to be any trouble anywhere. Yet, as Markby cast a professional eye over the scene, he did see something which caused him to slow down and mutter to himself.

'What is it?' Meredith asked him.

'Up ahead. See that car? He's pulled up by the kerb, right by that crowd of kids.'

She looked. A large, dark-coloured car had stopped by a small gang of young people. The driver appeared to be leaning across the empty passenger seat to call something through the open window. As she watched, two of the youngsters, a boy and a girl, detached themselves from their friends and approached the car. The others looked on warily. The boy shook his head. The girl called out to their companions who also gave a negative response. The car drove on slowly.

'I'll just follow him for a bit, see what he does,' Markby said. 'If you don't mind.'

'Of course not. What do you think he's up to?'

'Hmn, perhaps we'll see this time. He's stopping again.'

The brake lights of the car in front glowed red. This time he'd pulled up by a couple of girls.

'Right, time to ask him!' Markby said with sudden decision. He overtook the parked car, pulled up ahead of it and was out of his car and bearing down on the other one, before Meredith had time to blink.

Neither the other driver nor the girls realised Markby was there until he joined them. The girls saw him first and promptly set off along the pavement. Before the driver had time to make off, Markby was leaning down by his window.

'Good evening, sir! I'm a police officer and I wonder – good Lord! Mr Conway!'

'Chief Inspector!' Conway's startled face, livid in the street lights, peered up at him. He fumbled with his seat-belt and got out of his car. 'See here, I'm sorry if that looked damn odd. I'm not kerb-crawling! I'm looking for my daughter! She hasn't come home from school. Naturally my wife and I are worried. I thought I'd just drive into Bamford and ask some of the young people around if they'd seen her. I mean, she shouldn't be with them and they probably don't even know her, but where is she? Sitting at home by the phone, I was going out of my mind. I had to do something!' His voice rose in protest. 'It's not like her, Markby! She always lets us know if she's going to be late and she's always in from school by six-thirty. We dine every evening at seven and she knows it!'

'How old is she?' Markby eyed him thoughtfully.

'Sixteen.' Conway drew himself up. 'But she's a very sensible child!'

Not exactly a child, thought Markby. Aloud he said, 'Teenagers can be thoughtless.'

'I've told you, not Katie! Besides, you know very well that a young girl was murdered only the other day, on my property according to you! Of course I'm concerned when Katie fails to show up!'

Markby murmured, half to himself. 'Pubs are out, Social Club too, probably.'

'She doesn't go to pubs!' Conway snapped. 'And I've been to the Social Club. There was nothing on there this evening to attract young people and none had been in.'

'How about her schoolfriends?'

'I phoned the one she has stayed over with occasionally at night, to go to a party or to work together on some school project. She hadn't been there and as far as anyone knows, she got the school bus to Bamford as usual. She does stay in the town sometimes for an hour, shopping or at the library. But everything closes around six.'

Markby glanced up and down the street. It didn't sound, from what Conway said of his daughter, that she was the sort of girl to have got into the kind of trouble Lynne Wills had found. But his experience of teenagers was that the best of them could be thoughtless and forgetful at times. Matthew Conway, however, was a man he did not want to upset, so it might not be wise to say so.

Trying to be tactful, he suggested, 'Why don't you go home now and I'll phone in to Bamford station and ask that they radio the patrol cars to keep an eye open for her? How would you describe her?'

'She's about five-three with long, red-brown hair, dark auburn you'd call it, I suppose. She'll be wearing her school uniform, grey skirt and pullover. Other than that, she wears hideous great lace-up black shoes and a baggy dark coat she bought at a church jumble sale. Don't ask me why! She only has to ask and she can have any clothes she wants!' Conway concluded fretfully.

'Fashion!' said Markby wisely. 'My eldest niece is into what's called, I believe, "grunge"! I'm sure she'll turn up, and when she does, call Bamford police and let them know so that the patrol cars can cross her off their lists! Don't worry. She's probably on her way home now, blissfully unaware of all the upset she's causing.!'

He watched Conway drive off and returned to the waiting Meredith.

'Looking for his daughter. You know young Katie. Do you think she'd be likely to go off and not let her parents know? She's not come home from school.'

'I couldn't say.' Meredith frowned. 'She might be just staking a claim to independence. She did hint to me she'd done one or two things in the past which would have upset her parents, if they'd known. Perhaps she's doing it again and making sure they know this time? It's all to do with a trip to Paris she doesn't want to make. She could be trying to get attention. It would be naughty of her, but I feel sorry for her.'

'Her father insists she's very sensible.'

'I'd say basically sensible, but inexperienced. She's had a pretty protected life, I fancy. Perhaps a bit young for her age in some ways. She does go out in the evening and likes the usual teenage things. I know because I met her with young Josh Sanderson, going to hear a rock band. Perhaps she's with him?'

'Sanderson,' muttered Markby, scribbling the name in a notebook. 'If she's not turned up by morning, I'll suggest Conway gets in touch with him. I shouldn't think it's a police matter. Teenage rebellion, as you say, or even worse, teen love!'

And Matthew Conway, he thought ruefully, won't like that!

Markby had dismissed the matter firmly from his mind after that. Of course Conway was understandably worried, but the girl was not the type to pick up, or let herself be picked up by, a total stranger. If there was a family row going on about a trip to France, Katie might well be making a bid for attention or trying to manipulate her parents in some way. The young could be quite ruthless at times.

However, the problem was back on his hands the following morning. Arriving at Bamford station, he was waylaid by Matthew Conway as he walked in the door.

'There you are!' Conway surged up, bristling with anger. He had dark circles under his eyes and was unshaven. Markby judged, rightly as it turned out, that he'd sat up all night waiting for his daughter.

'Look, there's not a sign of her! I keep telling your chaps, she doesn't do this sort of thing! Of course she goes out with friends or to the youth club, or to parties! But never, never without making proper arrangements! If she's going to be away all night, she tells us the name of the friend she's staying over with. If she stays in Bamford for a while after getting off the school bus, she's still home in time for dinner, seven sharp!'

'How does she get home?' Markby asked, remembering Park House's lonely situation and trying to quell his sense of unease, a seldom-wrong instinct that this wouldn't prove a storm in a teacup.

Conway explained, adding impatiently, 'I checked with the taxi drivers, last night and this morning! They don't remember her and most of them know her! This is a small town! Katie takes taxis home often! There's no bus along the Cherton road and the taxi ride costs under £2! Look, Chief Inspector!' Matthew put out a hand. 'I know missing youngsters are routine. I know how busy you are with this murder. But please, can you at least ask that all the men on the beat look out for her? I can't stress too often that she doesn't behave this way!'

'Come into my office!' Markby said abruptly.

Sergeant Turner was already there and looked inquiringly at the caller.

'This is Mr Conway from Park House, Sergeant. His daughter, Katie, who's sixteen, didn't come home last night. This is out of character and in the circumstances...' Markby gave her a direct look.

She understood. Evidence suggested one fourteen-year-old had already met a violent end in the grounds of Park House and now a sixteen-year-old had failed to return there. On the face of it, there was unlikely to be any connection between Katie Conway and Lynne Wills. But it couldn't be overlooked.

Markby was recalling the name of Josh Sanderson, written in his notebook. He asked, 'You have checked her friends? Young Sanderson, for instance? He might have seen her yesterday.'

'Oh, Josh... I'd forgotten him,' Conway said. 'I think she sometimes meets him after school, but she wouldn't—' His face reddened. 'She wouldn't have spent the night with him!'

'Sixteen can be a very emotional age,' Markby murmured.

'Not Katie!' Conway thundered. He made an effort to control himself. 'Anyway, Josh lives with an aunt. She wouldn't allow any hanky-panky of that sort. Very strict, old-fashioned sort of woman.'

Markby glanced at his watch. 'I suggest you contact this boy,

Josh, and, ah, also take a good look round your grounds. If you draw a blank, let us know. Now, as you're here, Mr Conway, perhaps I could ask you whether you've found time to ask your wife—'

Conway roared, 'Of course I haven't! Damn it all, I'm worried about our daughter and so is she! She's hysterical! You can't imagine what it's like at home! It's all Prue can do to cope! We had to call the doctor to Adeline this morning! How can I go asking her about the mausoleum? She doesn't know yet about your police inquiries!'

But there Matthew was wrong. As he opened the front door on his return to Park House, his wife flew out of the drawing room and seized the lapels of his coat. Her face white and distorted, she screamed, 'What have the police been doing over there by the Devaux vault! Where's Katie? Why haven't you found her? Why are they here? What's happened? She's had an accident and you're not telling me, Matthew—'

Prue appeared and tried to pull her away, but she clung to him like a limpet, screaming her questions. He felt panic engulf him. This screeching creature had made him her prisoner. He struck out, trying to free himself and she gave a great wail. In the same instant needles of excruciating pain shot across his shoulders making him yell out. Something else was attacking him, he was being assailed from all sides, but the new attacker, whatever it was, was behind him. He couldn't see it and hadn't a notion what it could be. His panic now completely blind, Matthew scrabbled with his hand twisted up behind his back and his fingers encountered fur. Sam had leapt up on his back and hung there, his long sharp claws penetrating even his thick overcoat. The realisation what it was both relieved his instinctive horror and made him swear vigorously.

'Get the creature off me! The bloody thing's gone crazy!'

Prue ran to help. The cat dropped to the floor and raced to the corner where it crouched, emerald eyes blazing and tail swishing to and fro. Its long black fur bristling, it resembled some malevolent hobgoblin.

Adeline had collapsed, sobbing, her energy spent. Prue was able to detach her, too, and Matthew was freed at last, hot, angry ashamed and frightened. His back was smarting. He ought to put iodine or something on his punctured skin. But he stood no chance of getting any sympathy here.

Prue was comforting Adeline, patting her back and crooning, 'There, there!' as if to a baby.

'Didn't the doctor give her something to calm her?' Matthew asked, exasperated.

'She wouldn't take anything! Besides,' Prue explained over Adeline's head, 'she's so het up it would take a massive dose to settle her! Dr Barnes was unwilling, given the amount of medication she's already on, to increase the dosage.'

Matthew hid his face in his hands and breathed deeply, seeking some measure of control. It was the last straw, When this was over and Katie had come home—

His heart gave a little lurch and he told himself fiercely that of course she would be found, and soon! She'd probably just walk in here at any moment and everything would be all right. So, when it was over, and Katie safely back, Adeline would have to – to go away somewhere, just for a while. She would never agree to go of her own free will, but if necessary, he'd apply for a committal order. Barnes would back it up. Barnes must know none of them could go on like this!

'Listen, Addy,' he said soothingly to his wife's heaving back. 'Those police cars are nothing to do with Katie. I promise.'

She tore herself from Prue's embrace, and whirled to face him. 'So what are they doing there? You're lying about this as you lie about everything! D'you think I'm fooled, that I don't always know? That I don't know about you and that woman, for example? You lie about that, why should I believe you about anything?'

'There's no woman!' he shouted, losing his temper again. He met Prue's stern gaze and tried to speak steadily. 'Addy! You're imagining things. Those police cars over by the mausoleum are there because someone has broken in there. Vandals. I didn't want to tell you, upset you about it. There isn't any damage or anything. The police are just looking round. It's not to do with Katie.'

'They've been there since Saturday! You all treat me as if I were a simpleton! I'm not blind or stupid! And I'm not surprised about the vandals! You never go round the estate checking on anything! A property this size is a responsibility and you've never shown the slightest interest! I can't take care of it!'

'You won't let me do anything!' He was losing his grip on his entire self-control. 'You veto everything I suggest about the estate!'

'I know things go on!' she continued bitterly. 'I've seen it for myself!'

'What?' he asked sharply.

Prue put her arm round Adeline. 'Now, dear. You'd do best to come upstairs and lie down for a bit.'

'Wait a minute!' Matthew interrupted. 'What have you seen, Addy?'

She looked sullen and also, he was appalled to see, cunning. It was an unpleasant expression on her face and he didn't recall ever seeing it before. He suddenly felt very afraid, as if the chaos which afflicted her brain were perhaps far greater than even he had ever imagined. What went on in that head of hers? Since Friday night, when he'd seen her wandering about in her night-dress, he'd felt a kind of foreboding. He didn't know quite what of, but Katie's disappearance had come almost as if expected, as if some disaster which had long hovered over them were about to break.

'Lights!' she said suddenly in a loud, clear voice which rang in the hall. 'Car headlights stopping, over there, by the vault. They come at night! I didn't tell you. You'd only say I imagined it! But I don't imagine things!' The last words were expressed almost viciously.

Matthew sighed and offered up a string of silent curses. He was going to have to tell that fellow, Markby, about this, and he'd want to question Adeline.

'I think,' Prue said loudly, 'she ought to go upstairs!'

He nodded. Prue could cope. He couldn't. The cat hissed at him, showing gleaming white incisors and a curled pink tongue. Matthew skirted it cautiously and went into the drawing room. He threw himself down in an armchair, still in his overcoat.

'You need some sleep.'

He looked up. Marla stood in the doorway, watching him. 'I heard the noise from the office suite,' she went on. 'What's wrong with the cat? It flew past me like a bat out of hell!'

'Marla,' he said hoarsely. 'I want you to do something for me. That boy Katie sees, young Sanderson, will you find him and ask

him if he knows where she's been all night? I know I should do
it, but I might lose my temper, if – if—'

'Sure,' she said. 'Don't worry about it. I can handle it.'

'She surely wouldn't, wouldn't have stayed with him? She's just
a child!' His eyes begged her for reassurance.

'We all grow up, Matt!' she said in a quiet voice. 'Sooner or
later! Even your little girl. But I'll see it's all sorted out. No one
will know.'

'Thanks, Marla. Oh, and tell Mutchings to take a look round
the park. She could have – fallen, broken a leg or something.'

It sounded preposterous but these things happened. Though
why she should be wandering around the park after dark, he
couldn't think. But that was the trouble, right now he couldn't
think. His brain seemed jammed.

Marla walked over to him and put a hand on his shoulder.
Her painted mouth was twisted in a wry grimace, but the gesture
was sympathetic. 'I know where the boyfriend lives. If I can't
find him there, I'll check his school. And Mutchings will search.
He wanders round the park all day with those pigs. He wouldn't
miss anything. It's going to be okay, Matt, just leave it with me!'

He leaned back, resting his head, and heaved a sigh. From
behind Marla, Adeline's protesting voice came down the staircase,
followed by Prue Wilcox's firm, soothing tones. He closed his
eyes, wishing he could close his ears.

'You're going to have to do something, Matt,' Marla said.
'Someone is going to have to do something about Adeline. She's
a danger to herself.'

He said, 'I know. When this is settled, Marla. When Katie
comes back.'

Barney Crouch shut his front door and set off up the hill towards
Bamford. He disliked shopping for groceries but sooner or later,
the food ran out and he had to. He'd eaten twice with Doris
Pride recently and he wasn't going to let it become a habit!
Although Doris was a first-rate cook, a real light hand with
pastry, and made Yorkshire puddings which floated off the plate.
Doris was a good woman but that was the problem. Barney had
no wish to be reformed.

Carrying his shopping-bag, he toiled up the steep slope and
found himself opposite the mausoleum. The police vehicles which

had still been there that morning had now, at three in the afternoon, left. Plastic tape cordoned off the area and there was a police notice warning the public to keep away. It was a very nasty business and he didn't like being reminded of it. On impulse, he climbed the stile and set off towards the town across the fields.

He often walked that way in the summer, but generally not in winter. The ground was hard and bumpy and the going difficult. There were a few sheep in the far distance but otherwise no sign of life, other than the crows. Harbingers of ill-luck, crows. He hated them. In those far-off days when gibbets stood at crossroads and malefactors hung from them in chains, carrion crows picked the corpses clean. Passing travellers or country people, averting their eyes from the gruesome sight, would hear the birds cawing to one another, and their great black wings flapping. Life was supposed to be more civilised now. But, of course, thought Barney, it wasn't. There was just a tendency to hide nastiness away.

'Look at those damn birds!' muttered Barney. Ahead of him, the crows were circling above a hedge. 'If I had a gun, I'd come out and take potshots at 'em! Give me the creeps!'

Two more of them flew overhead, cawing raucously. One perched on a bare tree branch, sentry-like. Despite his dislike of the creatures, Barney became curious to know what attracted them over there. It might be a dead sheep. He'd just take a look and if it were so, he'd ring up and let the farmer know when he got back.

'Go on, you brutes!' he shouted at the crows, turning his steps towards the hedge. He clapped his hands together and waved his bag, and when neither had any effect, picked up a clod of frozen earth and hurled it at them. They rose in the air in a flurry of black wings and hoarse cries of protest. But they didn't go far, only just up into the trees where they perched, waiting.

Barney didn't like it. It was probably just a dead animal. Even a small one, like a rabbit, would attract them. But the sinister way they watched him from up there in the trees and all the old evil associations they recalled made him approach the spot cautiously.

He couldn't smell anything. If it was a dead sheep, it hadn't been dead long. He couldn't see anything on the ground. It must be down in the ditch. He picked up a piece of stick and used it to part the long dead grasses and nettles. The stick caught in something. He raised it as far as he could. The end of it came into view and tangled around it, the reason he couldn't free it. Long, glossy, reddish-brown hair.

'Oh no,' Barney whispered, 'Oh, no, no, no . . .'

Chapter Thirteen

MARKBY TURNED his car into the drive of Park House with heavy heart. It was late afternoon, the light fading, and a damp mist has arisen to cling to the skirts of the house. So beautiful was the old place, even in its dilapidated state, and so eloquently did it symbolise the sad, fragile family unit within it, that he wondered if, when the dreadful blow he'd come to deliver fell, house and inhabitants together would survive it.

In his head echoed the voice of Barney Crouch, shaking with emotion. 'I knew her face, Markby, recognised it straight off! Seen her many a time of a summer's day, going in and out of the main gates. Young Katie Conway. Such a pretty little thing.' Then Barney had added almost inaudibly. 'Foul, Markby, a foul, foul deed in a dark world!'

The chief inspector climbed the steps to the tall carved double doors and tugged at the bell-pull, hearing it jangle faintly within. This time someone answered promptly. Prue Wilcox opened the door and, as soon as she saw his face, her own round, plain features drained of colour.

'It's bad news, isn't it?'

'Yes, Mrs Wilcox, I'm afraid it is.' There was a moment of time standing still, the house, its contents, Prue's frozen face. He asked, 'Is Mr Conway at home?'

She opened her mouth to answer but before she could, a man's voice said huskily, 'I'm here . . .' and Conway emerged from the drawing room, his face also a sickly grey. 'Tell me!' he ordered.

'I'm afraid we've found a body, Mr Conway.' There was no way to soften the blunt announcement or take away anything from its cruelty. Conway winced and Prue Wilcox, with a moan, sagged at the knees. Markby grabbed her arm and guided her to a chair in the hall.

'I'm all right,' she whispered. 'Where, where did you . . .?'

'In the fields between here and Bamford. Someone came across her by chance. He recognised her. But we'll need a formal identification, even so. I'm sorry.'

'You're wrong!' Matthew Conway's voice rose unsteadily. 'You, and this person who found – found it, must be wrong! Who would hurt my little girl?'

'We don't know, Mr Conway, not yet.' To his own ears, Markby's voice sounded stiff and formal. He wanted to show his own emotion but he knew he couldn't weaken before them. He had to be strong and inspire them with his strength.

Prue and Matthew stared at one another in silence, communicating by some telepathy. 'It will kill her,' Prue said. She turned her head to Markby. 'Mrs Conway, poor lady. When Katie was born, I came here to nurse the new-born and the mother during her lying-in. I was to stay three months. But Adeline suffered severe post-natal depression and she didn't pull out of it. So I stayed on to look after her. I've looked after her all these years. She – she has no means of coping with this blow, Mr Markby.'

Matthew Conway drew a long, deep breath. 'I'll come with you now, Chief Inspector, to make this identification. Prue, don't say anything to Adeline yet. After all, it might be a mistake.' The hopeless way he spoke these words showed he didn't believe it. 'But I'd be obliged if you'd just wait a few moments, Markby. I need to pull myself together, adjust to the idea of seeing Katie— Is, is she mutilated?'

Markby shook his head. 'No. I'll wait outside. Take your time.'

He went back to his car. Standing by it in the twilight was an ungainly but familiar figure, Winston Mutchings. His arms hung by his sides, twitching from time to time with their own independent nervous energy. As Markby came down the steps, the pigman lurched towards him.

'What you doin' back again? Mr Conway, he can't find his daughter. I looked all over the park like they told me to, but I never found her. You're a p'liceman. You found her?'

'Yes,' Markby said. 'I'm afraid Miss Conway is dead, Mutchings.'

'Don't be daft, of course she isn't!' retorted Mutchings simply.

The confidence with which he dismissed the news shook Markby's own certainty. The chief inspector's gaze moved towards the distant trees at the boundary of the grounds, shielding the mausoleum. They were indistinguishable one from another in the gathering gloom and mist, just a dark barrier.

'Have you heard the voices calling from the chapel again, Mutchings? Since we last spoke?'

Mutchings' features, in the half-light, appeared twisted in terror. He certainly sounded scared. 'No! I keep away! There's been things happening there! P'lice has been there. You oughta know that! Not that they got any right. It's private property.'

'We had Mr Conway's permission. Have you any idea what sort of things might happen there, Mutchings? Suppose you had to hazard a guess, what would you say?'

Mutchings came closer. He whispered hoarsely, 'I reckon I knows! Miz Wilcox, she told me someone unlocked the chapel door. They shouldn't have done that. One of them old Devaux has got out and has been wandering! They're not like other folk, the Devaux. Other folk when they're buried, they rot. Dust to dust, like the vicar says. But not Devaux. They stay whole.'

'Have you seen this – this figure wandering? This Devaux?'

Mutchings shook his head. 'No, I only seen her, even though she ain't dead yet.'

'Whom have you seen?' Markby held his breath.

'Miss Adeline. Sometimes, of a night, I get up and walk up to the house. I go round outside and makes sure all the windows are shut and no one's gone and got in. A couple of times I've looked in a window, when there's been moonlight, and seen Miss Adeline walking round the rooms downstairs in her nightie. She don't see me.'

The somnambulism of which Marla had told him. Markby had a vision of Adeline roaming through the rooms and the gaping face of Mutchings pressed against the outside of the window.

Mutchings appeared to regret having confided his tale to Markby. He rolled his eyes whitely and jumped back. 'But I don't believe what you told me about Miss Conway! She can't be dead. There's no reason for it! What would she be dead for?'

With that, he lurched away into the dusk, leaving Markby wondering whether the pigman's last remarks had been the foolish argument of a simpleton or, on the contrary, a shrewdly direct question. It was possible to deduce a motive for the death of Lynne Wills. But Katie Conway?

Behind him the house door opened and Matthew came down the steps, wearing his overcoat.

'I'm ready. Let's get on with it. I want to get it over with quickly!'

As they drew away from the house towards the gates, Markby could sense the pent-up emotion in the man beside him. He didn't know what Conway would do when he saw Katie. Markby himself, who had in addition seen Lynne Wills, knew that he was angry. A parent is distraught, but a policeman is filled with a numb rage to which he cannot give voice.

Then Conway spoke, echoing Markby's thoughts. 'Who's doing this? Two young girls! What kind of a monster is he?'

'So who is he?' demanded Superintendent Norris. 'Why haven't we got a lead on him?'

'We have, of a sort. Lynne Wills was seen leaving The Silver Bells with a man. We're looking for him, of course, but the witnesses, such as they are, are so vague as to his description there's almost nothing to go on. It could be almost anyone, especially as he may well have shaved off the moustache by now. I've circulated such meagre details as there are and notified the local press. I am, of course, hopeful that we shall pull him in eventually and then get samples for DNA testing which will establish a link with the dead girl. But, if positive, it will only prove that he had sex with her. To make a murder charge stick, we'll need something else, evidence that he moved the body, for example.

'As for Katie, we've no lead yet, I admit, and we don't know—' Markby's voice rose and he met Norris's flinty gaze steadily, '— that we're looking for the same man. These two deaths may not be connected.'

Norris snapped, 'Come on! It's highly unlikely, surely, that we're looking for more than one murderer? In a rural area like yours? How many homicidal maniacs have you got lurking about the bushes?'

'We don't know he's a maniac, either,' Markby pointed out. 'The more I think about it, the more I'm convinced we're looking for two different murderers. Lynne Wills's death probably resulted from a quarrel of a business nature. That can't be said of Katie Conway. She went to a different school to Lynne, she had different friends and I can't imagine Katie hanging around the pubs!'

'The autopsy report!' said Norris with a malevolent glint in his eye.

'Yes, I know. But it wasn't recent. There was no sign of any interference of a sexual nature before the fatal attack.'

All the same, the evidence of Fuller's post-mortem examination had proved a surprise.

'She wasn't a virgin, by the way,' Fuller had said casually. 'There's no sign of recent sexual activity. Certainly none connected with the attack. I suppose, these days, it's no surprise that they're tempted to experiment with sex at a young age. As a parent myself it's a worry. They're subject to so much peer pressure and mischievous influences. But this girl, you tell me, was a convent school pupil and of very good family. I'm surprised.'

Markby too had been surprised. Whether the fact had any relevance to his investigations, he didn't know.

'The press are linking the deaths,' Norris was saying.

Markby made an uncomplimentary remark about the press.

Norris replied with unusual sympathy of manner, 'I absolutely agree. But we can't stop speculation. People hear so much about serial killers these days, they think one lurks round every corner. We must stop panic in the community. I shall be making a statement and when I talk to camera, you'd better be present! We'll have to field some very rough questions!' Without any warning, Norris then asked, 'How are you getting on with Turner?'

'Fine, thanks. A very good officer.'

Norris lowered his voice. 'Glad to hear you say so. She's been marked out for fast-track promotion, you know!' An extraordinary expression, half-knowing and half-smug, crossed his face. 'Got to give the women their chance!'

There was no answer to that and Markby didn't attempt one.

Thanks to Meredith, he did at least have a name to go on, that of Josh Sanderson. The next morning, Markby set out to talk to him. He tried Bamford Community College first, on the assumption that Josh would be a pupil. He was, but hadn't turned up that day. The headmaster and the form teacher both insisted Josh was an exemplary pupil. They were startled that the police should want to see him and clearly feared for the school's reputation. Despite Markby's assurances that this was all part of a routine check, he couldn't prevent suspicion lodging in both men's minds. To his annoyance and regret, before his eyes, Josh was transformed from prize pupil to embarrassment.

Markby left them, armed with Josh's home address and the information that the boy lived with a widowed aunt whose name was Mrs Parry.

She opened the door to him. She was about forty-eight, thin, with an anxious expression, perhaps the result of thick-lensed spectacles which caused her to peer uncertainly at the visitor.

'Oh, a chief inspector . . .' she said. 'Oh, dear . . .'

'It's all right, Mrs Parry. I just want a word with Josh. We're tracing Katie Conway's last movements. I understand she was a friend.'

Mrs Parry gripped her hands together. 'It's such a terrible thing to have happened! Josh is very upset and couldn't go to school. He's a sensitive boy. She was a sweet little girl.'

'She came her to the house often?' Markby glanced round the hall in which they stood. It was aggressively tidy, a display of polished frugality. It was as if Mrs Parry wanted to say to callers, 'My house doesn't have modern gadgets or expensive furnishings, but it's clean!'

'A few times, calling for Josh, but not recently.' Mrs Parry hesitated. 'Before you see Josh, could I have a word with you in private? In here . . .' She was moving towards a door.

He followed her into a neat, threadbare sitting room which brought the old-fashioned word 'parlour' to mind. Markby strongly suspected it was kept mothballed for selected special occasions. There was no heating and the air felt damp. A pair of cheap green glass vases stood on the chimney shelf together with two or three framed photographs. Otherwise there was no effort at decoration, no flowers or ornaments and certainly nothing so decadent as an ashtray. He felt depression steal over him as he wondered what the rest of the house was like. He felt sorry for the boy, although he hadn't met him yet.

Mrs Parry invited him to sit down and seated herself opposite, her knees pressed together, and bolt upright. She had evidently decided it was confession time.

'I want to get something off my chest, Chief Inspector, because I feel I should.'

She had, poor woman, very little chest as far as anyone could tell beneath her clumsily knitted beige jumper. She was a curiously sexless creature. Markby glanced at the photographs above the cheerless hearth. In one of them, a young woman stood by a stolid young man in an ill-fitting suit. Both wore carnations, he in his buttonhole and she as a corsage on a dowdy two-piece costume. She was holding a small bunch of flowers and he supposed it was the Parry's wedding picture. It didn't suggest the day had been marked by any explosion of joyous celebration.

'Josh is my sister's boy,' she was saying and he returned his attention courteously to her. 'My sister, she wasn't married when he was born!'

These words came out in a burst like rifle-fire. The world outside might have grown more tolerant in such matters, but Mrs Parry clung to a more traditional view. 'She tried to look after the baby at first, but she couldn't manage it and keep a regular job. My husband and I had no children, so she gave Josh to us to bring up. He isn't my own, but I've always looked on him as if he were. He was less than a year old when he first came here.'

'Where's his mother now?' Markby asked.

She shook her head. 'We don't know. We last heard from her about three years ago. She'd met someone, a new man, and was going to live abroad with him. I think it was in Italy. We've always told people that Josh's parents lived abroad and that was why he lived with us. It seemed best to offer an explanation, and it is very nearly true!'

There was a pathetic defiance in her manner, a desperate seeking for that respectability so clearly begged by the abnormally tidy surroundings. But now there was a policeman in her parlour! Poor Mrs Parry was fighting the biggest respectability battle of her life.

'But you will understand, Chief Inspector, that when Josh first brought Katherine Conway to meet me, I had very mixed feelings. In fact, I disapproved of the friendship!' She saw his raised eyebrows and hurried on, 'Oh, not the girl's fault! She was a very nicely spoken, well-mannered girl. But the family, you see, so different to us in every way! Well-to-do, successful, living in that big house and Mrs Conway was a Devaux!'

Markby thought of Park House, its falling plaster, ramshackle grounds and the cat's cradle of frustrated emotions within its walls.

'You feared the Conways might disapprove of Josh?'

She didn't like it being phrased like that. She flushed and bridled. 'Josh is a very polite, conscientious, clever boy! It's just that – his birth, you see. And of course, I haven't that sort of money. I hoped Josh's friendship with the Conway girl would be a little growing-up romance, first love, you know . . .' The words seemed incongruous on her pallid lips and she blushed deeply as though conscious of it. 'I thought they'd outgrow it. I certainly hoped and prayed they would! I think, in fact they would have done. But I did worry sometimes, in case they didn't. She was only sixteen and Josh isn't quite seventeen. But time flies, and in a few years' time . . .'

'I understand,' said Markby.

Her face was still very red. She leaned forward and declared vehemently, 'And then that woman came here! A brazen, painted hussy if ever I saw one! Conway sent her. He didn't even have the common decency to come himself! He sent that trollop!'

'Would we be speaking of Mrs Lewis, Mr Conway's personal assistant?' Markby hazarded.

She sniffed. 'That's what she called herself! She came yesterday, asking about Katie, whether Josh had seen her the evening she went missing, whether—' Mrs Parry was working herself up. Her flat chest was doing its best to heave and her eyes, behind the pebble lenses, gleamed with suppressed fury. 'She suggested, she implied, she had the impudence to ask – Oh, I can't bring myself to speak the words! But you understand me, Chief Inspector! She had the gall to suggest immorality had taken place beneath my roof! Under my roof, in my home!'

Markby wondered what had bothered her the most. The suggestion of illicit frolics or the fact that the misbehaviour might have taken place in the austere surroundings she called home.

'I sent her away with a flea in her ear!' said Mrs Parry fiercely. 'I told her Josh had not been brought up to behave like that! He did see Katie that evening, but only for a short while very early on. They had a cup of tea in a café. That's all!'

'That's what I want to talk to Josh about,' said Markby. It wasn't the only thing and, given Mrs Parry's views on morality, asking Josh the other thing was going to be tricky. He risked being sent on his way, as Marla Lewis had been, with a flea in his ear!

'You must excuse my getting so worked up,' she was saying more calmly, 'but it was what I always feared.'

'Misbehaviour?'

'No! Josh isn't that sort of boy! No, I always feared some sort of trouble with the Conways! Because of them being who they are, and we being who we are! Not that this isn't a very respectable household. In fact,' she finished on a note of triumph, 'having seen that personal assistant with her peroxided hair and skirt way above her knees, I wouldn't be surprised if we're not a far more respectable household than the Conways, for all their money!'

'I think,' said Markby, suddenly deciding that he didn't like Mrs Parry, 'I'd like to talk to Josh now, if I may.'

She stood up. 'I'll send him in. Would you like a cup of tea?'

'That would be very kind of you, Mrs Parry.' Thank goodness he was to be given at least a few minutes to talk to the boy without this dragon in attendance.

Josh sidled in looking pale and apprehensive, and rather as if he'd been crying.

'I'm sorry, Josh,' said Markby sympathetically.

'I want you to find him!' Josh's voice was low and filled with emotion. It threatened to break under the strain. 'I want you to find who did that to Katie!'

'So do I. And I will. But I need help, all the help I can get.'

Josh took the chair vacated by his aunt. 'How did she die? They didn't say in the local paper how, only where she was found.'

'Her neck was broken.'

An efficient blow had been Fuller's opinion. A quite professional one, perhaps made by someone who had at some time practised one of the martial arts. A lot of people did these days. It was quite a popular hobby. Most of them, of course, would never use their knowledge in order to kill. Markby didn't tell Josh any of this. The boy was of a spindly built that didn't suggest that athletic pastimes of any sort were of interest to him. He waited.

'I don't understand why,' Josh said. 'It seems stupid.'

The words echoed Mutchings' scornful 'There's no reason for it!'

'I understand you saw her early that evening?'

'Yes. We met in The Black Cat café, after she had got off the school bus. We often did. We just talked.'

'How long did she stay?'

Josh looked unhappy. 'Not long. We, we had an argument. It wasn't much. It was about her going to France. She walked off in a bit of a huff. But she had a lot of homework, anyway, so she couldn't stay long.'

Markby frowned. 'Did she have it with her, the homework?'

The boy nodded. 'She put it on the table. She carried everything in a green leather document wallet. It was bulging and the zip was partly undone because she'd put too much in it.'

'Damn . . .' Markby murmured. No such document wallet nor any school papers had been found by the body. They'd have to search the area again. Nor had Conway remarked on the loss. But his grief at the far greater loss of his daughter might well have driven it from his mind. But the document case had to be somewhere.

'Do you think it likely that she would have tried to walk home, Josh, across those fields?'

'Not in winter. She did it sometimes in summer. I wouldn't have let her do it in the dark! Not on her own, anyway. I'd have gone with her. I thought, when she left, she was going over to the taxi-rank as she usually did. Sometimes she rang home. Why didn't she tell me if she meant to walk it?'

The boy was getting steadily more distressed. Outside the door china rattled. The tea, and Markby hadn't yet got to the most personal question of all. The door opened and Mrs Parry edged in with a tray. Josh got up to help her.

Markby sought for a reason to send the woman away again. Remembering the tea-tray brought in by Marla Lewis, he asked, 'I don't suppose you have any lemon? I'm on a diet, no milk. I'm so sorry to trouble you.'

'Oh, no trouble. It's in the fridge, I'll fetch it.'

His ploy had worked. He leaned forward. 'Josh, I have to ask you this, and I'll do it quickly before your aunt gets back. You know there was a post-mortem examination of Katie's body, don't you? One of the things it showed up was that she wasn't a virgin. That doesn't mean a sex attacker killed her! It just means—'

Josh's face was white. 'I know what it means! It isn't true! Katie wasn't like that sort of girl!'

'I'm sorry, Josh, but it's a fact. You're saying, are you, that it wasn't you?'

'Not me, not anyone! It isn't true!' Josh leapt up, fists clenched. 'You're as bad as that horrible woman Katie's father sent here! You're all the same! I'm not going to answer any more of your filthy questions! You're just trying to make Katie out to be something she wasn't! And you're lying, you're all lying!'

'Josh!' Mrs Parry stood in the doorway, shocked. The boy pushed his way past her and could be heard running up the stairs. A door slammed above their heads.

'I don't know what to say . . .' Mrs Parry looked bewildered. 'He's never behaved like that before!'

'He's upset,' Markby said. 'I'm sorry, it's my fault. An investigation of this sort disturbs people's lives in so many ways. I hope he'll get over it.'

She turned pebble lenses on him and held out her hand. Nestling in the palm was a small, yellow plastic grenade with a green screw stopper at one end.

'I brought you the lemon,' she said.

Chapter Fourteen

'BAMFORD'S GOT itself on the television, then,' said Mrs Pride. 'I can only say I wish it was for some other reason! I did think, when Miss Rissington found the Wills' girl's body, that nothing would shock me any more. But now poor Katie. I can hardly take it in. The sheer wickedness of it! That man who's doing it, he's a fiend. They ought to bring back the hanging. When they catch him, they'll only lock him up for a few years and then let him out to do it again. Oh, isn't that your friend, Mr Markby, Meredith? Who's the other chap? The one who looks so stiff. He looks as if he'd got a pretty good opinion of himself too, I'd say!'

'Superintendent Norris,' Meredith said to Mrs Pride's broad beam as her next-door neighbour stooped to turn off the set.

It was Friday and she had come home on an earlier train, only to be waylaid by Mrs Pride at her front door.

'It's Barney,' Mrs Pride had confided conspiratorially. 'I've got him with me and he's in a terrible state. My police lady isn't going to be in for supper tonight. Would you like to come instead? I think, you see, Barney needs company! He's always better with people around.'

But for once, Barney wasn't better for company. He had sat at the table, doing little justice to Mrs Pride's cooking, and continued to keep an introspective silence from the corner of the sofa. He broke it at last, as the television went blank, to observe, 'It's upset me, too, Doris. I don't know about the Rissington female, but *I* found Katie's body and *I'll* never get over it!'

'It's upset Alan, too,' said Meredith. 'You could see that from the way he behaved on TV. He doesn't like answering press questions.'

'Another cup of tea?' Mrs Pride picked up a teapot shaped like

Anne Hathaway's cottage and began to dispense this panacea.

'My police lady,' she went on proprietorially, 'she's working late today, as I told you. She did say she'd eat at the canteen. I can't think that will have been as good as my shepherd's pie!'

'Excellent shepherd's pie, Doris,' said Barney in response to the hint. 'But I couldn't seem to fancy it. Don't take offence.'

'I haven't taken offence, Barney, but not eating doesn't help anyone! It leaves the brain without any fuel!' She sighed. 'I suppose things are worse over at Park House! Can't imagine how awful it must be. I hear poor Mrs Conway's not doing at all well, not since they broke the news. Dr Barnes has been over there nearly all the time! They do say,' she lowered her voice, 'that she'll have to go away for a bit, you know, to a clinic. But then, she won't be the first Devaux to have done that.'

This enigmatic statement roused signs of interest in both her visitors.

'Batty, were they?' asked Barney. 'It seemed to me they were, when I was researching them years ago. Meant to write a play about 'em,' he explained to Meredith.

'No, they were not batty!' said Mrs Pride indignantly. 'They were just all very highly strung! They're all gone, of course, except for poor Miss Adeline. There, hark at me! Calling her Miss Adeline and she's been Mrs Conway for years! I remember her parents, Sir Reginald and his wife, very well. I can even remember, when I was a girl, old Sir Rupert, Miss Adeline's grandfather! Now, he was a character, no mistake. He had a lot of animals around the place, not just those pigs. Those woolly things from South America, llamas, he had a pair of them. Oh, and some ugly little wild ponies with big heads and back ends more like donkeys. They had some dreadful unpronounceable name!'

'Przevalski's wild horse?' asked Meredith with interest.

'Couldn't say, dear! The ponies and the llamas, they've been gone a long time. The pigs are still there, which gives Winston Mutchings a job. Don't know what he'd do if he didn't have that! He's not backward, Winston, but there are limits, if you see what I mean, to what he can do.'

She pushed a plate of shortbread at them but finding no takers, heaved a sigh and began to drink her own tea rather noisily.

'They married cousins!' said Barney unexpectedly. 'Generations

146

of cousins, all intermarrying! That's what went wrong with the Devaux! They did it to keep the land and money in the family. But you'd have thought, having an interest in breeding livestock, they'd have known better!'

'What a way to talk about it!' Mrs Pride reproached him in shocked tones. 'Miss Adeline was very nervous as a girl, I admit. She had a governess because she couldn't go to school. Now her father, Sir Reginald, he used to go away to Switzerland every now and again for his health, so I dare say she got it from him.'

Barney and Meredith exchanged glances. Barney raised a hand to tap his forehead but, fearing censure, changed his mind.

'Old Sir Rupert,' reminisced Mrs Pride. 'He had a very tricky temper, liable to flare up at any time over nothing. It would have got him into trouble, I dare say, if he hadn't been a magistrate himself!'

'What you are saying, Doris,' said Barney, 'is that there's one law for the rich and another for the poor! The poor are batty and the rich are highly strung. Wonder if Conway knew what he was taking on when he married Adeline? Doubt it. Sort of thing you keep quiet about, tainted blood, isn't it?'

'Nerves,' said Mrs Pride majestically, 'run in families! But not, I'm glad to say, in mine! I'm not going to sit here talking about it any more!'

That put an effective end to that line of conversation. But it had served the purpose in rousing Crouch from his lethargy. He thumped his fist on the coffee table, making the thatched roof-lid of Anne Hathaway's cottage rattle.

'No, confound it, neither am I! I'm going to do something about it! That first girl, Lynne whatsit, I saw her leave the pub with a man! I'd know that man again! He won't go back to The Silver Bells, but I'll stake my last penny he'll turn up at some other pub in the neighbourhood!'

'Dozens of them!' said Mrs Pride disapprovingly. 'Even you can't go round them all, Barney!'

'Oh yes, I can!' he retorted. 'I'll take 'em one night at a time. I'll sit in a corner with my pint all evening, watching! Sooner or later, I'll run into him again!' He began to struggle out of his seat. 'I can start tonight. Time to get in a couple of pints!'

'It's an excuse to go pub-crawling!' declared Mrs Pride. 'You could go round and round for months and never bump into him,

Barney Crouch! And in the meantime, you'll have turned yourself into an alcoholic wreck, worse than what you are now!'

'I am not an alcoholic, Doris Pride! I'm a man who enjoys a quiet drink! I can make a pint, well, two pints, last an evening!'

'Not without someone watching over you, you couldn't! And you needn't think I'll come round the pubs with you!' she retaliated.

'I will,' said Meredith. 'Not every night, perhaps. But I don't mind coming round the pubs with you some nights, Barney. It might be handy if there were two of us. If you saw him, you could follow him and I could phone the police. Only let me off tonight. It's a bit late to start.'

'I never heard anything like it!' cried Mrs Pride, clasping Anne Hathaway's cottage to her ample bosom. 'What ever would the chief inspector say, Meredith?'

'Oh, Alan needn't know!' said Meredith airily. 'He's far too busy with his investigations to worry what I'm doing!'

But she had other things to occupy her, too. The kitchen was painted and lacked only the elusive Welsh dresser to make it complete. On Saturday morning, after breakfast, Meredith moved her step-ladder, tins and brushes to the narrow hallway and surveyed it gloomily, wishing something would happen to prevent her getting to work on its walls.

Her apathy was rooted in the fact that last weekend Katie Conway had been here, enthusiastically spreading paint around the kitchen. Now the smell of the paint and the sight of her step-ladder and rags brought poor Katie to mind so vividly that Meredith felt she could almost see her doughty little form in the sloppy pullover, the yellow paint smeared on her nose and hairline.

The bell rang. She turned her head and saw, through the frosted glass, a large dark outline.

'Hullo, Meredith,' said Father Holland. 'Am I calling at a bad time?'

'No, come in!' She heard the relief in her voice and was impelled to explain.

'Yes, Katie . . .' He sighed. 'Actually, I haven't come to take your mind off her, Meredith. I rather wanted to talk about her, that is, I wanted to ask your help.'

They edged into Meredith's tiny sitting room where Father

Holland subsided on to the sofa, more or less filling it, and clasped his hands on his knees.

'This has been a terrible shock. The youth club is going to feel it dreadfully. The parents are all upset and afraid to let the youngsters out of an evening. It does seem as if we have a maniac on the loose! If, of course, it is just one man . . .'

'I expect Josh is in a bad way.' Meredith remembered the earnest young helper.

'Very much so. To make it worse, I understand that, well, the post mortem turned up an unpalatable fact, difficult for the family to accept and surprising me, I admit. It seems she, ah, wasn't *virgo intacta*. Naturally, the family want to know who . . .'

'And they think Josh was her lover? Well, they were both very young. They might have been silly but it's not the end of the world!' Meredith said indignantly.

'Matthew Conway,' Father Holland said, 'doesn't see it like that! But it's Mrs Conway I've come about. You see, the church runs a bereavement support group. We have a small number of trained counsellors who visit the recently bereaved at home. It helps people, we find, to know that someone cares, is thinking about them. Bereavement often brings a great sense of loneliness, even in the midst of friends and family. The problem is that the flu has laid low two members of the group and another two are away and the remaining one is an elderly man . . .' Father Holland gave Meredith a beseeching look and said, in a perhaps unfortunate turn of phrase, 'I need a woman.'

'You're asking me?' Meredith gasped. 'To visit the Conways?'

'Specifically Mrs Conway. Now, I know you aren't one of our bereavement counsellors! But you were, weren't you, a consul abroad at one time? You must have had to deal with people in distress, accident victims, that sort of thing?'

'Yes,' she agreed unwillingly. 'Even with the relatives of people who'd died while on holiday. But I don't know that it makes me the best person to visit Park House.'

'I think it makes you a very good person, Meredith. You have professional experience, you'd met Katie, and I know you're a sensitive person.'

'Most people find me a bit off-hand! I think I'm pretty tough!'

'Sensitive people often are. Defence mechanism!' he said bluntly. 'Look, I'm the first to admit it's presumptuous of me to ask you. It's a difficult task and made much worse by Mrs Conway's mental state.' He opened up his clasped hands as if he allowed something trapped within them to escape. 'She's unhinged!' he said.

'I gathered from Katie that she was ill... and other people have told me that there's a family trait of – nervousness.'

'She's a poor, sad soul!' Father Holland leaned forward earnestly. 'But I think she would trust you, Meredith! She desperately needs support. She needs someone to talk to who isn't a member of that household!'

Meredith bit her lip. 'She isn't – wasn't – the only one. Katie needed someone, too. She came to me, last Saturday. She asked me to go and talk to her parents. I refused. Now you're here with a similar request. It's as if, as if I'm meant to go. Perhaps I should have gone when Katie asked me. I think, now, she was probably a very confused young woman.'

'Part of the trouble,' said Father Holland sadly, 'is that for both Conways, Katie wasn't a young woman, but a little girl. She would always have been their little girl. I don't think either Matthew or Adeline could ever have accepted the fact that she was growing up.'

There was a chill wind blowing across the crumbling portico of Park House when Meredith got there. It picked up débris and bowled it around the pillars. The curtains at the lower front windows were all drawn in a traditional sign of mourning. It was with great apprehension that she tugged at the bell-pull.

A sturdy, capable-looking woman opened the door. Meredith explained her purpose. The woman looked her up and down.

'You had better come in. I'm Prue Wilcox, the housekeeper. Father Holland did telephone us about you. It's good of you to come.'

'I don't know if I can be of any help!' Meredith told her.

'You knew – you knew Katherine, didn't you?'

The full version of the name caused Meredith to hesitate. 'Oh Katie! Yes, I knew her but only slightly. I met her when I spoke to the youth club and she called at my house once.'

'She was a beautiful child.' Mrs Wilcox glanced at the staircase. 'Mrs Conway is lying down upstairs. You should understand that she's of a very nervous disposition. There is – there is one fact about the post mortem that she must never know.'

'Yes, I understand. Father Holland explained that, too.'

Mrs Wilcox shrugged her shoulders wearily. 'I suppose it was that boy, Sanderson. Although he denies it. But Katie wasn't flighty! There couldn't have been anyone else.'

'I've done things which would have shocked my parents, if they'd known . . .' Katie's voice echoed in Meredith's head. Poor, mixed-up kid. Trying desperately to make her own voice heard and to grow up despite parents determined to see her as a child. Had she seen experiments with sex as the answer and been ashamed, afterwards, to confess?

She followed Prue Wilcox up the wide staircase. Prue tapped at a door and opened it. 'You've a visitor, Adeline dear, from Father Holland. It's a Miss Meredith Mitchell.' She turned back to whisper, 'Go on in. It's all right!'

Meredith supposed, from what Prue had told her, that Adeline might be in bed. But she was fully dressed and standing on the far side of the room, staring out of the window. There was a cat on the windowsill, a monster of a feline. Adeline's long, white fingers caressed its jet-black fur absently. It watched the visitor approach with unwinking green eyes.

Mrs Conway turned her head towards the door. Meredith was struck both by her emaciation and by the dramatic beauty of her ravaged face, dominated by eyes still showing the horror of the recent news.

'My daughter talked about you,' Adeline greeted her. Her voice had a clear, high, childish timbre. 'You spoke to that youth club. I never wanted Katie to go there.'

It wasn't an encouraging beginning. 'I'm so sorry for your loss,' Meredith said. 'She was a charming and intelligent girl.'

'She was a Devaux!' Adeline's voice took on a nerve-jangling sharpness and the cat flattened its ears. 'She wasn't a Conway, there was nothing of the Conways in her! She was my daughter, a Devaux!'

This was going to prove a difficult visit. Meredith looked round the room seeking something which might prove a conversational bridge, defusing some of the tension in the atmosphere. Lying on a chair was some half-finished embroidery in a tambour frame.

'That's very pretty,' she said. 'I wish I had some skill like that. I'm all thumbs when it comes to needlework.'

Adeline glanced at the work. 'My mother taught me. She was a fine needlewoman. I tried to teach Katie when she was younger. She had no patience. I gave way to her on that. I gave way on everything. Now I'm paying the price. I should have stood firm, insisted on a good boarding school, stopped her going into Bamford—' She closed her eyes briefly. 'It's all too late now.'

'It's not your fault,' Meredith said gently. 'You wanted to protect your child but you couldn't live her life for her. What happened was a dreadful tragedy. But it could have happened anywhere.'

'It didn't happen anywhere, it happened here!' Adeline stared at her coldly. Then she relaxed slightly and beckoned with a long, bony hand, the light catching her rings. Meredith moved closer and the cat jumped down and stalked away.

'Do you see over there?' Adeline pointed across the park towards some trees. Above them two pepperpot shapes could be seen.

The mausoleum, thought Meredith. Perhaps not the jolliest sight from your bedroom window, the resting place of your ancestors greeting you every morning with grim reminder.

But Adeline's voice held pride. 'That's the family tomb.'

'So I understand . . .' Meredith's voice trailed off uncertainly. She wasn't sure how much Adeline knew and she ought to have asked Prue for more details before meeting Mrs Conway.

'Something's been going on over there,' said Adeline. 'I don't know what. It's no use my asking. They all lie to me. Nothing but lies, that's all I hear! But I'm not stupid. I've seen the lights.'

'What lights?' Meredith asked more sharply than she intended.

'At night. About the time I go to bed. Sometimes a little later. I've seen lights over there. They move. Perhaps it's a car. If it is, it oughtn't to be there because that's our land, part of the park even though it's on the other side of a wall. Matthew takes no care of the place. He never checks. He leaves everything to poor loyal Mutchings.'

'Can you remember which nights you saw them, Adeline?' Meredith prompted.

But Adeline only turned her head towards her with a sad smile. 'Of course not, my dear. One day, one night, is like another to me. I never go out, you see. I don't leave this house. Here I'm safe. It's my house and they can't harm me while I'm here.

But if I ever left, I'd never come back. That's why they want me to leave.'

'They?'

'Matthew and – that woman. But they'll never get rid of me!' Adeline's voice held an almost vitriolic resolve. Perhaps she was aware of it, because she gave herself a little shake and pointed out of the window again, towards the distant mausoleum.

'Until my grandfather's time, all the Devaux were laid to rest there.'

She could tell Alan what Adeline had said about lights, but to question her further now would be useless. Nor could Adeline's testimony be considered reliable. The mausoleum, however, seemed to obsess her.

Meredith asked, 'Isn't it quite a small building? To hold them all, I mean.'

'Oh, they're not all above ground in the chapel. There was a vault beneath it where the coffins were put. Only a very few, the more famous family members, have tombs in the chapel above. But by my grandfather's time the vault beneath was almost full and there was an offensive smell. It was investigated and some of the early coffins were found to be damaged. They were made of lead which is very soft. In other caskets, still sealed, body-fluids had become trapped. Did you know that the body makes alcohol after death? In the right circumstances a corpse can be preserved in extraordinary completeness. They opened up the coffin of my great-grandfather because my grandfather was curious to see what had happened in that. They found him pickled as you might say, together with his grave-clothes. And, believe it or not, false teeth. My grandfather said he still looked remarkably as he had done in life.'

Meredith shivered but Adeline seemed very matter-of-fact about such grisly details. 'They sealed up the opened coffin again and my grandfather had the vault filled in. They tipped rubble into it, right up to its ceiling and then the entrance was cemented over. But the Devaux are still there, underneath all that pile of stones and bricks. All the coffins are still down there with their contents.'

Adeline turned a fierce, glittering gaze on her. 'And I should be buried there, because I'm the last, true Devaux. And Katie, because she is my daughter, should be laid to rest there, in the chapel. But Matthew, my husband, refuses!'

'I understand how you feel,' Meredith said cautiously. 'But perhaps it would be better—'

Adeline cut her short with a gesture. 'You don't understand. How could you? Matthew doesn't understand, not even Prue does. No one does. The Devaux *are* Park House! We can't be separated! Some of us, like my great-grandfather, don't even putrefy! We stay here for ever!'

There was a long pause. Then Adeline continued, 'The police have been over there. Matthew says vandals broke into the chapel. But I suppose he's telling me more lies. He does, you know.'

Clearly she knew nothing of the possibility of Lynne Wills' murder having taken place there. Conway had believed it dangerous to tell her. For all her unhealthy morbidness of temperament when it came to the past and family history, Adeline shunned real life and the events of the present day. To cope with Katie's death, she had relegated the fact to that web of family history which obsessed her. So long as Katie remained a Devaux and could, if Adeline had her way, be laid to rest with all the others, the pattern remained intact. But if the pattern were broken . . . what then?

The problem when it came to conversation – quite aside from its unexpected twists and turns – was that Meredith didn't know which facts Adeline knew, which had been kept from her or what kind of story had been invented to appease her curiosity. Add to that the fact that she obviously harboured the deepest mistrust of her husband, based on real or imagined wrongs, and the whole proceeding became a minefield. Meredith decided to go along with the vandal story. It even offered a useful argument.

'Places like that do attract vandals, I'd afraid. So I expect Mr Conway doesn't feel that it would be the best place for, for Katie.'

'When did he ever know what was best for Katie? Only I knew that! But he continually thwarted me! Her school, he insisted on the convent because it was a day-school. But it meant she spent her free time in Bamford mixing in who knows what company! I wanted to send her away to Paris, but he was against that too!'

'Perhaps,' Meredith ventured, 'Katie had made up her own mind about Paris.'

The words fell into a pit of non-response. 'I'm very tired,' Adeleine said suddenly, turning away from the window. 'It's very kind of you to come and see me. People don't visit me. Matthew tells them all I'm crazy. It's not true, but he'd like it to be, so that he could get rid of me. But I'll never leave here! Never!' There was a powerful underlying resolve in her words. But then her manner changed. To Meredith's surprise a wistful smile crossed Adeline's thin features. 'You must come again, my dear. Do come again.' She reached out a hand in a gracious gesture.

Meredith took it and burst out impulsively, 'Of course I will!'

The cat sat sentry-like by the door to supervise Meredith's departure. She bent to touch its head but it only glared at her with emerald eyes and beat its plumed tail on the carpet.

'Guarding your mistress, puss?' Meredith murmured.

She descended the staircase slowly, taking her time to look about her. This must once have been a little jewel of a house. It lacked the stately grandeur of more famous residences, but everything here had been designed with care and a desire for harmony. This had been a family home. The portraits which hung on the walls were all of Devaux. None of them was by a first-rate artist, only by competent hands, so that the sitters looked wooden and details, such as the lace they wore, were clumsily rendered. Yet this very second-rateness made them more accessible and somehow real. There was dust up there in the stucco and hairline cracks in all the plaster. The staircarpet beneath her feet was worn in places to its threads. The house was like a beloved child now orphaned and neglected. Although, at this time, it was the owners who were bereaved.

Someone waited for Meredith in the hall below. A tall blonde in a dark-blue, long-sleeved dress, her slender waist accentuated by a wide suede belt, was assessing her with cool grey eyes. As Meredith reached the bottom step, the blonde moved forward and held out a manicured hand.

'Miss Mitchell? I'm Marla Lewis, Mr Conway's personal assistant. Mr Conway asks me to say how grateful he is to you for taking the trouble to come. He would normally have met you himself, but you'll understand, he's feeling pretty stressed out at the moment.'

Meredith briefly shook the red-tipped fingers. 'I understand. Please tell him I'm happy to do anything I can to help. You're an American?' Alan hadn't told her that little fact about the redoubtable Marla whom Meredith now eyed with some curiosity.

'As a matter of fact, I was born in Canada. But my mother took me to the States when I was a child and I was raised and went to school there.' These words were reeled off in a staccato indicating that the speaker didn't like personal questions. 'How did you find Adeline?'

'Coping very well in the circumstances, all things considered.'

The blonde almost smiled. 'All things considered? That's a nice way of putting it. Did she tell you about her crazy idea to bury her daughter in that mausoleum?'

'She did. It's impossible, obviously. But Adeline seems to have a strong sense of family tradition.'

'She has that all right!'

Meredith, disliking the way Marla seemed to infer that Adeline's sense of tradition was somehow a sign of her mental instability, decided to take up the cudgels on Mrs Conway's behalf. She indicated the family portraits on the staircase wall.

'I always find it touching when one family has lived for generations in a house which they built for themselves so long ago. Adeline now seems unwilling to leave the house at all. That's not quite normal, I agree, but I can understand how the feeling came about. It's a distortion of a quite natural attachment.'

'Nothing here,' the blonde said curtly, 'is quite natural, believe me!' She caught Meredith's eye and must have realised that some expression of a more sympathetic attitude was called for. 'We're all very upset about Katie's death. It's a really terrible thing. But nothing lasts for ever, does it? Not even the Devaux family. May be it's not tradition that's needed here. It's a complete change!'

She turned and led the way to the front door. 'Well, it's been nice meeting with you, Meredith. Mind how you go now as you drive out. The pigs are on the loose out there some place.'

'Oh yes, I'd rather like to see the pigs.'

'Would you? I'd happily shoot them!'

The door shut firmly behind Meredith as she walked down the steps to her car. There she paused with her hand on the door to glance back at the curtained windows, sensing that someone watched her, making sure, perhaps, that she left the premises.

Meredith drove slowly towards the gates. It was impossible now to leave here without a visit to that strange building which contrived to dominate the lives of those at the house in such an unhappy way.

She found it easily by driving a couple of hundred yards down the main road. There were the clump of trees, pair of mossy gateposts and path, described to her by Alan. Meredith drew in and switched off the engine.

It was very quiet under the trees. The ground was churned up as a legacy of recent activity but the intrusion of the police had been but a blip in the two-hundred-year history of the chapel. The building itself, when she reached it, seemed forlorn, the more so, because it was so ornate. All dressed up and nowhere to go, she thought in wry amusement. A large new padlock secured the door so she was disappointed in her hope to explore inside it. Meredith prowled round outside, stopping more than once to glance behind her when a rustle in the trees caught her ear. The spot had such an unnerving atmosphere it was difficult not to let one's imagination run away. She also fancied there was an unpleasant smell. But that really was imagination, she told herself firmly, springing from Adeline's grisly tale of the filling in of the underground crypt. If there was anything, it resulted from damp mortar and rotting leafmould.

Evidence for Adeline's story existed, however, in a bramble-grown pile of rubble by one wall. That must have been left over when the workmen finished their grim task some half-century ago. Just at the foot of it was the entrance to a tunnel scraped out by some animal. Fragments of bone, rabbit bone most likely from the size of the pieces, littered the entry. A fox's earth? Some of the unpleasant odour seemed to ooze up from that.

Meredith climbed up the rubble mound with difficulty, negotiating trailing bramble sprays and tall nettles. When she stood on the top she could just reach a dusty window. She pressed her nose against it.

Another face stared back at her from within. Meredith gave a startled cry and nearly toppled from her insecure perch. Then she realised that it was the stone bust of some long departed family worthy which gazed at her with sightless eyes in a stern face framed by mutton-chop whiskers. There was a whole row of them, lined up in niches in the further wall.

She scrambled down, dusting her hands and made her way back to her car. This was not the sort of place to loiter. It had been, in all, a disturbing afternoon and most disturbing of all was the nagging conviction that Adeline Conway was somehow in danger.

Chapter Fifteen

NOT SURPRISINGLY, the visit to Park House had driven the arrangement with Barney right out of Meredith's head. When she answered the door on Saturday evening to find him standing on the step, she was temporarily taken aback.

'All ready to go sleuthing?' Barney rubbed his hands together enthusiastically. 'I've made a list of all the pubs in the neighbourhood and when we've done those, we can cast the net further afield. He's probably got a car. I haven't, but you have, haven't you? We can try the village pubs next.'

'Barney . . .' Meredith began. She broke off and gazed at him helplessly. There was nothing she felt less like doing at this precise moment than sitting in strange pubs on the remote chance that they might see Lynne's manfriend. But Barney looked full of zest, and he had obviously taken great pains to spruce himself up fit to escort a lady. His hair and beard were combed and an ancient tie knotted around his neck. It was impossible to let him down.

'Give me ten minutes to get ready,' she said, relenting. 'I was at Park House this afternoon so I'm a little behind schedule. I am rather tired. I can't promise to spend more than an hour this evening, at any rate, scouring Bamford. And, you know, perhaps you really ought to be taking Sergeant Turner with you, not me!'

Barney laid a gnarled finger alongside his nose. 'Keep it in the family!' he said mysteriously. 'Just in case it don't work!'

The hour turned into nearly three. Barney was a cheerful, garrulous companion and time passed easily. But the thought of spending an unknown number of evenings like this made Meredith realise that her original offer had been rash. There was no doubting Barney's dedication to the task. If Mrs Pride thought all this was an excuse for an extended pub crawl, she was wrong. Well, nearly wrong.

They began at The Bunch of Grapes and proceeded to The White Hart and thence to The Lord Nelson. It was when time was called at this last hostelry, that Meredith looked at her watch and saw with horror how late it was. She had resolutely stuck to tomato juice all evening and felt a little nauseous. To make things worse, they hadn't seen anyone Barney thought remotely resembled the man they sought.

Barney drained his glass. 'An unprofitable evening, but we won't give up, my dear! We'll try The Royal George and The Fisherman's Arms tomorrow.'

It might have been unprofitable in the detection department, but since Meredith had paid for the majority of the drinks that evening, it hadn't been altogether unprofitable for Mr Crouch personally.

'No, Barney, not me, not tomorrow! I've got to be on Bamford rail station early on Monday morning. Give me a call during the week.'

'Fair enough,' said Barney, slightly disappointed. 'I'll keep going on my own. I've got a gut feeling about this!'

'So've I!' muttered Meredith, wishing she hadn't had that last packet of chicken tikka-flavoured crisps.

Meredith went home, fell into bed and passed out. She was awoken on Sunday morning by the doorbell. Turning over on the pillows, she reached for the clock and groaned. It was after eleven. She hoped it wasn't Barney, come to suggest a swift noggin at twelve, in case the mysterious man could be run to earth at a different time of day. She struggled out of bed and threw open the window. Alan Markby stood below in the tiny tiled forecourt, shading his eyes with his hand as he peered up at her.

'Sorry if I woke you! I thought you might like to go out to lunch somewhere!' he called.

'I'll be down in a sec!' Meredith fumbled with her dressing-gown and ran barefoot downstairs to let him in.

'I didn't mean to sleep so late.' She ran her hands through her thick brown hair so that it stuck out like a bush. 'I'll put the coffee on.'

'I'll do it,' he said. 'Go and get yourself dressed.' He reached out and tweaked a lock of the unruly hair. 'Go on, scram! You look like Mad Meg!'

She wrinkled her nose at that, so he stopped and kissed it.

'Coffee!' she reminded him.

'All right, all right . . .'

A little later, over coffee, he told her about Nikki Arnold, and she told him about her visit to Park House.

'I should have reported back to Father Holland, I suppose. But he'll be busy today. I'll call him tomorrow evening, when I get in from work. Or I might even take a couple of days off this week to finish the painting. I do have a few days' leave owing.'

'I ought to speak to that boy Sanderson again tomorrow,' Markby said without enthusiasm.

'You don't really think he had anything to do with Katie's death?' Meredith protested. 'He seemed so fond of her.'

'It wouldn't be the first time a girl was murdered by a jilted lover. By his own admission, he saw her on the evening she died and they squabbled. We only have his word for it that it wasn't a serious dispute. He says he thought she'd gone to the taxi-rank. But no taxi driver remembers her that evening and it does begin to look as if she tried to walk home.'

'It would have been getting very dark by then, surely? Park House is an isolated spot and the road's lonely.'

'The boy says she sometimes walked it in summer, nonetheless. Had he known she intended walking it in winter, he would have tried to dissuade her, and failing that, he would have accompanied her. How do I know he didn't do just that? Failed to talk her out of it and began to walk her home. Then, on the way, they renewed their quarrel. It's a plausible scenario and there's only one main objection. The nature of the blow which killed her. I can't see Josh striking with such ruthless efficiency.' Markby gestured with his hand held out stiffly on a horizontal plane. 'Something like that.'

'Don't!' Meredith said sharply. 'Things are bad enough! Do you know Adeline Conway wants to inter Katie in the Devaux mausoleum?'

Markby groaned. 'Someone will have to talk her out of that!' He frowned. 'Do you know what bothers me most? The girl's document wallet. Josh says, and I've checked this with Prue

Wilcox, that it was green leather and she took it to school every day. He says it was packed with homework on that evening, so full it couldn't be zipped up properly. We've searched the whole area twice where she was found. Not a sign. So, where is it?' He stretched his legs and sighed.

'It's getting to you, Alan, isn't it?' she said quietly.

He shrugged. 'Two murders like this in a small community touch everyone's lives. Nobody is sure any more about anything. They're frightened to walk down familiar streets or let the children out to play. Once the spirit of trust is broken it's never fully repaired. Even when it's all over, and the culprit is nailed, things will never be quite the same again.'

'We don't have to go out to lunch. I'm sure I can rustle up something. I've got a bottle of wine.' Meredith paused, wondering whether to tell him of her expedition in the company of Barney Crouch. A fine waste of time that had turned out to be. She decided not to bother.

'Any luck with the Welsh-dresser hunt, by the way?' Markby drew in his feet and sat up.

'No. There must be one somewhere. But traditional kitchens are all the rage now, so I keep being told. Welsh dressers are snapped up.'

'Why don't you give the landlady of The Silver Bells a call? They've pulled out the old kitchens there and you never know. It's an off-chance, I admit, so don't build your hopes up!'

'That's a good idea! I'll give her a call tomorrow!'

'Speak to the wife. The husband is a real fish out of water down here. I could, given the information we've got now, close that pub down, but they haven't been here long and they've no previous convictions, so I'm giving them a chance to put their house in order, literally. They've worked hard and really want to make a go of it.'

'They could do without the sort of trouble Lynne Wills brought them, then,' Meredith observed.

'Teach him to keep a sharp eye open for the youngsters in his pub!' said Markby unsympathetically. 'Where's that wine?'

Two inquiries, which might or might not be linked, complicated life no end, Markby thought on Monday morning. But it wasn't just that which made him feel so dissatisfied. Spending Sunday with Meredith was always enjoyable, but the start of a new week and the inevitable going of their separate ways again, always underlined the *ad hoc* nature of their relationship. He supposed it was as permanent as it was ever going to get. But a corner of his mind still refused to accept that. It was like an unsolved case, staying on file and nagging at the memory. It wanted tidying up, to be put in order. He sighed loudly.

'Superintendent still think we're looking for one man?' Helen Turner asked, misinterpreting the sigh. Markby had, some ten minutes earlier, been speaking to Norris on the phone.

'What? Oh, yes, well, he's being hard to dissuade, put it that way. I don't know. If there were a link, it would appear to be that wretched mausoleum, if only because it's on Devaux property! But we don't know that Katie ever went near the place!'

'The mausoleum door was opened by someone who got hold of the key and was then able to return it to its hook in the pantry,' Helen said. 'It has to be someone in that house, sir, as I see it.'

'Or Dom Harris, despite Marla's assurances? Is someone checking on that fellow? All those electrical goods, surely at least some of them have to be hot? Or there's Mutchings, we mustn't overlook him just because he's not the brightest. It's that which might make him easily persuaded. The Arnolds, they're the link. If anyone knows who supplied the key, young Nikki does, depend on it! In fact, we're going to have to tackle all the youngsters again. I'll take the boy, Sanderson. You seem to have gained the confidence of Mrs Arnold. Have another go at talking to her. If you can get her on your side, she could get her daughter to talk.'

Helen grimaced. Nevertheless lunch-time saw her at the Arnolds' flat. Someone was home because she could hear the radio or television. She leaned on the bell-push until a noise like a large mouse scrabbling told her that someone wrestled with the recalcitrant door. It flew open and Mrs Arnold appeared in a cerise satin robe and pink feathery mule slippers. Her red hair cascaded in tangled hanks about her face and she clasped a cigarette and a coffee mug in either hand.

'Oh, it's you,' she said. 'Come in, dear. I had a late night and I'm a bit behind.'

Helen followed her to the untidy sitting room where the TV set blared from one corner, showing a cartoon.

'Can we have the television off?' she asked loudly.

'What?' shouted Mrs Arnold.

'The tele—' Helen decided action was called for. She switched the set off.

'It's a bit of company,' said Mrs Arnold. 'I'll fetch you a cuppa.' She disappeared into the adjacent room whence she could be heard clattering utensils. Helen decided not to look into the kitchen.

Mrs Arnold reappeared, her robe trailing. It had fallen open to reveal a black nylon nightdress. 'There you go!' she handed over a steaming mug affably, before collapsing on to the sofa, where she made ineffectual attempts to gather the robe together. 'My Nikki's at school,' she puffed. 'If you were looking for her.'

'Actually, I am looking for her and I've been to school. She hasn't put in an appearance today.'

Mrs Arnold gazed at her over the rim of her mug. Her eyes were ringed with smudged mascara. 'She went off to school this morning. I heard her. She shouted "Goodbye, Mum!"'

'But she didn't go to school, Mrs Arnold. And the school tells me it's not unknown for her to play truant.'

'Play hookey?' Nikki's mother blew a disbelieving cloud of smoke towards the visitor. 'They never said anything to me about that!'

'The school has written to you twice this term, Mrs Arnold, asking you to come in for a case conference about Nikki.'

Mrs Arnold glanced dubiously at a stack of mail behind a pottery owl on the wall unit. 'Might be in with that lot. I haven't got round to it all yet.'

'You don't know where Nikki might have gone?'

'Thought she'd gone to school,' said Mrs Arnold simply. 'Are you sure about this?'

'I think, Mrs Arnold,' Helen said, 'there are a few other things about Nikki you might not be aware of.'

She explained and waited for the reaction. It came in a string of colourful language and concluded with Mrs Arnold saying vigorously, 'I don't believe it! That Lynne Wills, perhaps! But my Nikki, pick up fellers in pubs? Of course she wouldn't! She's not that daft! Here—' Her black-smudged eyelids narrowed. 'You got proof of this?'

'We have strong grounds for suspicion. I think you ought to

ask her about it. And don't let her put you off.'

Mrs Arnold's belligerence evaporated and became a lachry-mose self-pity. She blinked wetly, smudging yet more mascara. 'It's not easy, bringing up a kid on your own, you know!'

'I do realise that.' Helen tried to sound sympathetic. She liked Mrs Arnold. The poor woman's life had no doubt been an unmiti-gated disaster from start to finish, with the single bright light of Nikki.

'I've done my best! I give her a lovely home!' She indicated the chaos around them. There was indeed a ramshackle cosiness about it.

'You say her father abandoned you both? Does he, or did he ever, pay any maintenance towards Nikki's keep? Because if he hasn't, now the law's being tightened up with regard to defaulters, we might be able to track him down and make him pay up.'

She was shaking her head. 'No idea where he is! Don't want to know, either! I don't want him back in my life or Nikki's! We've managed all right without him, me and Nik, up till now! We'll carry on. Thanks, all the same.'

Muddle-headed Mrs Arnold might be, and hopeless about the home, but there was something both touching and heroic in her defiance. Her loyalty to Nikki was unquestionable.

Helen leaned forward. 'Look, perhaps I oughtn't to say this, but I don't want to see social services brought into this—'

Mrs Arnold looked frightened. 'Nor more do I, dear! They came once before, years ago when Nikki was little. I had a real job to get rid of them. They mean well, I suppose, but she was only a young girl who came ... Look, if Nikki's not going to school, I'll see she does, promise! I'll walk there with her myself, right up to the gate! How about that? And about the pubs, I'll tell her off well and truly about that! But she's nearly sixteen, you know. I was married at sixteen. She'll be leaving school in the summer.'

'What kind of job does she hope to get?'

Mrs Arnold looked vague. 'She likes animals. P'rhaps she could work down the pet shop.'

It led neatly to Helen's next question. 'You said you were born a Mutchings. I understand you're related to Winston Mutchings, the pigman at Park House?'

165

Mrs Arnold gave a raucous laugh. 'Poor old Uncle Winston! I haven't set eyes on him in years! When Aunt Florrie was alive, I used to go and visit their cottage. But she's been gone ten years or more. Florrie used to clean in the big house. I suppose Uncle Winston manages all right for himself on his own.'

'So you know the grounds of Park House? The mausoleum, the burial vault, for example?'

'Spooky old spot, that!' Mrs Arnold's plump shoulders quivered. 'I was never inside it. Climbed up and looked through a window once. I saw a lot of stone heads in niches. Give you the real creeps.'

'Perhaps you told Nikki about it?'

Mrs Arnold shrugged and the cerise gown fell off to reveal her in all her black nylon lace glory. 'May have done, dear. Kids like that sort of thing, don't they? I used to like all those old horror films with the vampires and that when I was her age. I always fancied that actor who played Dracula. I've always thought,' mused Mrs Arnold gathering up the robe and wriggling her toes in the pink feather mules, 'that I'd have liked a really distinguished-looking man around me.' She looked perplexed. 'But I never seem to meet any.'

The idea that a Welsh dresser might just conceivably be stacked up with rubbish removed during renovations at The Silver Bells preyed on Meredith's mind all night. As a result she took the drastic step of phoning The Silver Bells early on Monday morning before leaving for work.

Daphne answered the phone and listened as Meredith first apologised for calling so early and then tentatively broached the matter of kitchens.

'Don't worry about it being early, love,' said Daphne's voice. 'We're up at crack of dawn here! Welsh dresser?'

'Or anything in the style of a kitchen dresser. Do you know the kind of thing I mean?'

'Oh, yes. There was one. Horrible old thing. It's out back in the barn. We took it out with the rest.' Daphne paused. 'You a dealer?'

Meredith, hardly able to believe that a dresser was within her grasp, exclaimed, 'No! But I'll pay a reasonable price.'

'You won't want it when you see it!' said the landlady sapiently.

'No one would! Only, if you're a dealer, it's best I tell you so now and save you a wasted trip out.'

'I'm not a dealer! A friend of mine told me you had taken out your old kitchens, Alan Markby. He's—'

'Oh, Mr Markby!' Daphne's voice brightened. 'He did tell me he had a friend who was doing up a kitchen. Well, you can come round any time and look at the old dresser. But honestly, it's junk.'

'I'll be round as soon as I can!' Meredith promised.

After all, she thought hopefully, one man's junk is another man's antique.

Chapter Sixteen

As FOR Markby himself, having seen Sergeant Turner set off about her daily tasks, he had turned his thoughts to Josh Sanderson. He was well aware of the headmaster's unfavourable reaction the last time he'd shown up at Bamford Community College. Markby grimaced. It wouldn't be fair on Josh to reinforce the man's prejudices. He would wait until after three-thirty and hope to catch Josh at his aunt's house on his return from school.

Life being what it was and murder, however dreadful, having to take its place in the scheme of things, Markby turned his attention to outstanding matters unconnected with the inquiry into the two girls' deaths. When these were cleared up, it was almost twelve.

Markby tapped his fingers on the desk in a rapid tattoo. How about the old first question when tackling a case of murder, *cui bono*? Who benefits? Always supposing Katie's death were not an act of mindless violence, then someone did. Neither of her parents nor Prue would. What had Meredith said? If Marla wanted to make sure of Matthew Conway, it wasn't only Adeline who had to be got out of the way. Time to talk to the lady again. Even svelte Mrs Lewis must nibble at a diet cracker and press her carmine lips on the rim of a cup of black coffee, or even eat an apple.

Markby allowed himself a brief fantasy of those perfect white teeth biting into the crisp apple flesh. Why did it conjure up vampires? Apple. Eve. Serpent. Evil. Now then! he reproved himself. This is no time for word games! Let's keep a little logic in this. Why did Americans always have such good teeth? Why did the thought of interviewing Marla Lewis make him so apprehensive?

* * *

169

Marla opened the door at the side of the house which led to the office suite. Framed in it, she looked Markby up and down as if he'd called selling bootlaces.

'Hi!' she said casually. 'You want to talk to Matt again? Can't you go a little easy on him? It's really difficult for him to adjust to this. Anyway, it's lunch-time. Don't you eat?'

'No,' said Markby ungraciously. 'I'm a policeman. I grab unsuitable snacks at unsuitable hours and suffer indigestion. I'll probably end up with an ulcer. The public expects that for its taxes. I want to talk to you and I thought you might be free now.'

Her pale eyes flickered over him. 'Sure. Come in.'

She stood back and he brushed against her as he entered the office suite. She was wearing some perfume or other. The place was very quiet.

'Matt's eating with Adeline and Prue in the main house,' she said, divining his thought. 'And then he's taking the afternoon off. So if you want to talk here, we won't be disturbed. Or would you rather we went up to my apartment?'

'Here will do!' he said hastily.

He hadn't been far wrong about the lunch. There was a tray on her desk with three rye crispbreads and a tub of cottage cheese.

'I'll fix you tea. Milk, right? Sit there!' A red nail pointed at a futuristic chair which looked as if it had been designed like those prison cells, once in the Tower of London, called 'little ease' because they allowed the unfortunate captive no comfort whatever he did. 'And don't touch a thing!' she added in a minatory tone. She'd make a fine prison wardress, too!

She slammed a filing drawer shut on her way out to emphasise the privacy of the office contents. She was quick making the tea. But it didn't take long to pour hot water on to a teabag.

Markby, jiggling the bag up and down on its string, observed mildly, 'I don't have a warrant. I'm not empowered to search.'

'Snoop and search,' she said, 'are different!' She picked up one of the crispbreads and snapped it efficiently into equal halves between her scarlet talons. 'You might have planted a bug.'

'A listening device!' Markby blinked. 'I'm ordinary CID, not MI5!'

'Oh come on, you're not ordinary!' She bit into the crispbread, pale eyes laughing at him over it. 'So ask, Chief Inspector!'

He did. 'How are Mrs Conway and Mrs Wilcox coping today?'

'Adeline is nuttier than ever. Prue is being British. The stiff upper lip. The thin Red Line, whatever. My, how you do disapprove of me! You think I'm hard-hearted Hannah, right?'

'Got it in one!' said Markby, deciding to pay her back in coin.

She smiled. 'I like you. I really do. Don't look so scared. I'm really a pussy-cat.' (A lioness! thought Markby.) 'I just talk tough. I'm sorry for them all, truly. Well, for Matt mostly. For Prue next. It's no use being sorry for Adeline. She's way past all that. She ought to be in a sanatorium, being looked after.'

'On the day Katie died,' Markby went on, ignoring that, 'can you take me through the routine in this house, as you experienced it?'

She frowned. 'Let's see. Was I on the school run that day?'

'So you told me at the time. I met you coming from the newsagent's, remember?'

'So you did.' She paused. 'Then I came back here and it was a normal day. Normal in this office, anyway. All day. In the evening the kid didn't come home, but I didn't know anything about that until late.'

'How late?'

'Oh, around ten to ten-thirty. I went up to my apartment after I finished here, around six. I showered, fixed myself dinner, did the usual things. I think I washed my hair. Around ten-fifteen, let's say, I heard Adeline screeching. That's not unusual, but the time was. She's usually in bed by ten. I went out on the upper landing and looked over the rail to see what was wrong. She was down below in the hall and Prue was trying to calm her. There was no sign of Matt. So I went down and asked Prue what the hell was going on. She told me Katie hadn't come home and Matt had just left to drive out to Bamford and look for her.'

Markby nodded, wondering if she knew he could check that bit. 'What did you think might have happened to Katie?'

She was silent for a moment. 'I thought she was with the boyfriend. Did you talk to him?'

'Yes. What time did Mr Conway come back?'

'I'm not sure. Just before midnight, I think. I went right back upstairs after I spoke with Prue. I can't help her with Addy.'

'So between six and ten-fifteen at night, when for a few minutes you were talking to Mrs Wilcox, you were in your apartment at the top of the house alone?'

Her eyes were no longer smiling but like burnished steel. 'That's right!'

'You didn't talk to anyone at any other time during the evening?'

'Yes. I talked to my mother.'

'Your mother!' Markby almost fell off the uncomfortable chair. 'She's staying in your flat? You said you were alone up there!'

'Of course she isn't! She's in New Jersey! Telephone, Chief Inspector! I phoned her around eight-thirty British time, three-thirty in the afternoon over there. We spoke for around ten minutes. It's expensive and I can't stay on the line longer.' She gave a little hiss of exasperation. 'What's wrong? Did you think that girls like me don't have mothers?'

It was a quarter to four and Josh Sanderson was walking quickly away from the school gates. He picked his way through the scattered crowd, alone in the way the habitual loner is, not just temporarily without company, but with the indefinable air of one who, like Kipling's cat, walks by himself.

One or two of his contemporaries glanced at him, because they knew about Katie, but no one spoke to him. It was as if his presence embarrassed them. Normally, they would have ignored him. They had always treated him as beneath contempt. He was no use at sports, no good at playing comedian (always an accepted alternative to athletic prowess), and never had anything to offer by way of earthy gossip. He was just a clever, bookish, silent dreamer, who went around with a toffy-nosed girl from the convent school.

But that girl was dead now, just as Lynne Wills, whom they'd all known, was dead. Since Katie's murder, and especially because on the day after it a senior copper had come to school to ask for Josh by name, they could no longer ignore his presence. But neither did they know what to do about it. They mirrored that wider unease which Markby had described to Meredith. Brash youths who would have dismissed Josh as of no importance, now wondered whether, after all, he was what he'd always seemed to be. Or whether it was possible that their shallow, snap judgements had been wrong.

Josh knew what was in their minds but he didn't care. He didn't care about anything now. Katie had been the only person who had meant anything to him, and Katie was gone. The aching void couldn't be filled. He had once dreamed that, if he worked hard and managed to get a university place, he might, at some future date, have a proper career, in law or something, which even the Conways couldn't scorn. Then he and Katie could be together for ever, The plan to send her to Paris had terrified him because it would have removed her from his world before he could achieve his aims. She would have returned changed, no longer interested in his provincial talk and unsophisticated ways. As it was, she'd slipped out of his life, anyway. For neither of them, now, was there any future.

He didn't want to go home. Aunt Celia, for all she kept saying how tragic it was, could not hide her secret satisfaction that Katie had gone. He ought to love Aunt Celia because she'd always been good to him. But he didn't. He couldn't love his absent mother, because he didn't know her. He'd given all his love to one person only.

Josh turned his steps towards the town park. In summer he and Katie had sometimes sat on the bench in the children's play area, to gossip and watch the little ones at play. In wintertime, the park keeper closed the gates at early twilight and no one bothered to go there after school. If he went there now, it was because he could be with Katie again, and no one would disturb him.

The play area was deserted. Ignoring the sign which forbade use of the equipment to children over twelve years of age, Josh sat on the roundabout, propelling it with his feet, stood on the swings sending them swooping back and forth, and even squeezed into the space rocket and bounced it until it creaked alarmingly on its rusty springs. Then, because the park keeper would be making his rounds soon and descend on him in fury, he clambered out and began to walk towards the gates.

It was then he sensed he wasn't alone and, at the same time, heard a scuff of a foot behind him. He turned, expecting the wrathful park keeper, but it was another dark figure that emerged from behind some bushes, grasped his shoulder and exclaimed, 'Got you! I've been wanting a word with you!'

Josh gasped and wriggled, trying to free himself from the painful hold the other had on him. 'What do you want?'

'I think you know!' Matthew Conway released the boy at last, giving him a vicious shove which sent him staggering backwards. 'You were messing with my daughter!'

In the gloom, Josh felt his face burn and the anger well up in him. 'I didn't and it's all a lie! I don't believe what the police say! It's not true!'

'It's true and you, of all people, know it! She was a sweet, trusting child, and she had to make a friend of you, you lecherous little brute! I ought to beat the living daylights out of you!'

The anger in Josh burst out, overwhelming him. He flew at Matthew Conway, fists clenched, and began to strike a furious battery of blows. They didn't hurt Matthew, but they took him by surprise so that for a moment or two he just stood there, accepting the rain of punches. Then he swore vigorously and gripped Josh by the scruff of his neck, shaking him as a terrier shakes a rat.

'Right! You asked for it!' He drew back his raised arm.

Josh screwed up his eyes and hunched his shoulders against the expected attack. But it didn't come. Instead, another voice ordered, 'All right, that's enough, Conway! Let him go!'

Josh felt himself released. He opened his eyes and saw, in the twilight, that another man had joined them. It was the chief inspector, Markby. He had come sprinting across the grass and was panting.

'Josh? Are you all right?'

'Yes,' Josh mumbled, rubbing his sore neck.

'Then just go over by the main gates and wait for me there. I want a word with Mr Conway.'

When Josh had moved out of earshot, the two men faced one another in the gathering gloom.

'He seduced my daughter!' Conway said thickly.

'You don't know that for a fact and the boy denies it!' was Markby's crisp reply. 'I appreciate your distress, Conway, but I want to make a couple of things clear to you. Nothing which has happened gives you permission to carry out an assault on Josh Sanderson or anyone else, or to take the law into your own hands in any way! Is that understood? I don't care for the way you go about things. I didn't like you prowling the streets by car at night, accosting youngsters, when your daughter went missing, although I understand your motive. I dislike even more your stalking that young man, following him into a deserted park, waylaying him and attacking him!'

'He attacked me!' Conway blustered. 'He went berserk!'

'You grabbed him first. I saw it from over there. The boy was scared. Think yourself lucky you're not being charged! I think you should go home, Mr Conway, and stay there. Good night!'

Conway pushed his way past him and strode out of the park, passing by the hovering figure of Josh without a word or a glance.

Markby rejoined Josh at the gates. 'I'll walk you to your home, Josh. The keeper will be locking up at any moment here. I wanted to see you, anyway. I called round at your house, after school. I felt going to the school might upset the headmaster again. Your aunt said you might have gone to any of the places you used to go with Katie. She mentioned the café and the park. I checked the café, but I very nearly didn't bother with the park because it was getting dark. Fortunately, I decided just to look in!'

Josh mumbled, 'He thinks Katie and I, you know, that we did *that*! You think it too, so does Aunt Celia. But we didn't!'

'Okay, Josh, I believe you. I understand how much her death hurts you, and I don't want to make the hurt worse. But I have to ask questions if I'm to find her killer. Did she have any other boyfriends? Before you came along, perhaps?'

'No!' Josh shouted. Vehemently he went on, 'He acts as though he cares about her! But they didn't care! They neither of them did!'

'Who are "they", Josh?'

'Her parents! Her mother acts crazy, but I don't believe she's as crazy as she makes out! Her father runs around with another woman! They just used Katie to get at one another! She was a sort of weapon they could beat one another with! You don't use people you love like that! Or you don't love them, if you do!'

'When people are very unhappy, they often don't think straight. They hurt the ones they love. I'm sure Mr and Mrs Conway loved Katie dearly, even though they caused her a lot of distress. In the same way, I'm sure Katie loved her parents. But she told Miss Mitchell that she'd done things which would have upset them, had they known. Do you know what those things were?'

'No!' The boy hesitated. 'But last year—'

'Go on!' Markby prompted.

'I can't tell you anything particular. Last year, things were bad for her at home. She got depressed and went through a sort of funny spell. She avoided everyone, even me. She stopped coming to the youth club for several weeks. I thought she'd found other friends. But then she started coming back to the club and we were friends again, so it was all right.'

'You didn't ask her where she'd been? Who'd she been seeing in the meantime?'

In the yellow glare of a street light, Josh shook his head, his spectacles glinting. 'I didn't ask her anything because I was afraid she'd be angry and go off again. She was back, we were together and that's all that mattered. I don't care if you can't understand that.'

'Oh, I understand it, Josh,' Markby said.

He understood it only too well. What this boy was talking of was the real price of loving.

'I don't think you'll get any more trouble from Mr Conway,' he said aloud. 'But if you do, let me know at once.'

He watched young Sanderson walk off along the evening pavements, towards the cheerless, loveless house of his aunt. They could hunt down Katie's killer, but for Josh it would make no difference. As he'd told Meredith, the scars murder left couldn't be erased.

'Are you asleep Adeline?'

Prue Wilcox tiptoed towards the bed. Adeline Conway, fully dressed, lay on her side, her head resting on one crooked arm. Her discarded slippers lay on the floor. Her eyes were closed and she breathed evenly. The sun was going down and the room dimly lit.

Prue heaved a deep sigh of relief. She hated to admit it to herself, and never would have done so to anyone else, but running the house and looking after Adeline was all getting a little too much for her. She wasn't young any more. But now that there was the terrible tragedy of Katie's death, how could she abandon the Conways, even for the shortest time? She had so been hoping for a little break, a holiday. Her sister in Cornwall was always writing and suggesting a visit. She had planned to suggest to Matthew that a temporary nurse be brought in for a week or two. But not now. It was impossible now.

Prue crept away and, as her charge was safely asleep, took herself off to her room for forty winks on her own account. Silence fell over Park House.

In the room she'd quitted, however, Adeline Conway stirred and opened her eyes. 'Prue?'

Sam the cat, curled up on the bed, opened one emerald eye and closed it again, as Adeline sat up, rubbed her eyes and looked around her. It must be evening, she thought. Only a sombre greyness could be discerned through the window. She swung her legs to the floor and felt for her slippers. Peering in the mirror, she frowned at her shadow-veiled reflection as if unsure of its identity. She touched her face and hair with exploring fingers and the reflection did the same. She, then, was that pale, thin woman with the haunted eyes. That's what she looked like. When others looked at her, that was what they saw.

It occurred to Adeline to wonder how old she was, because somehow she'd lost track of birthdays the last few years. She tried to work it out. Katie was sixteen. So that meant that she, Adeline, was thirty-eight.

She stared doubtfully at the reflection. It looked a lot older than thirty-eight. And there was something about Katie, something she couldn't remember. It was there, in her mind, but something blotted it out as if it lay behind a mental wall. Looking around her here, she knew who she was, where she was – and then she couldn't think back because the wall was in the way. Whatever was on the other side of it, it was very bad. She didn't want to think about it, remember it. Better to leave the wall there to shield her.

She went out into the hall. It was very quiet everywhere. Just the clock ticked in the entry below. She listened at Prue's door. There were faint, rhythmic snores. Prue was asleep. Matthew was—

Now where was Matthew? He was in his office, that's where. She would go and tell Matthew that they would have tea. It must be tea-time. Below her, the clock struck four, confirming it. She was vaguely aware that the clock was wrong, had been for years, but it didn't matter. She would fetch Matthew and they'd have tea. If Katie came in, she would have tea too. The thought of her daughter made her uneasy again. There was something...

She walked carefully downstairs, holding on to the banister.

Matthew's office suite lay on the other side of that green door. Adeline eyed it fearfully. She had never been beyond it. But that's where Matthew was and possibly Katie, too. With unheard-of bravery, she put out a hand and turned the handle.

The door swung open on well-oiled hinges. Adeline walked through with the wonder of a modern-day Alice. Why, it was so clean and bright here! And so warm! She was in a short, narrow corridor, painted white and lit by bright neon strips in the ceiling. There was a blue-grey carpet on the floor. A door to the right, open, showed an empty, darkened office with a large, Victorian desk. She recalled that desk. It had been her father's. Matthew must have moved it here.

But he wasn't there. There was someone in a room to the left. Not the first door, the second one at the end of the corridor. What was behind the first? She opened it curiously and saw, with surprise, a modern kitchenette, tea things, a kettle, a biscuit tin. Why, they could have tea down here!

She moved on towards the second door. The sound of typing came from behind it. Adeline opened it noiselessly and caught her breath.

It was a large, brilliant room with a desk, filing cabinets, some machinery the purpose of which she didn't understand and a young woman, sitting at a typewriter with her back to her. The woman had long, straight, blonde hair.

Adeline approached her softly across the blue carpet. The typist tapped on, unaware. Adeline could smell perfume. She could see the woman's hands, tapping away, with long red finger-nails. Loudly, she demanded, 'Who are you?'

The typist gave a suppressed shriek and whirled around. Her chair allowed her to do that, Adeline noticed. It was on a sort of spindle, like an old-fashioned piano stool. And this woman was good-looking in a brittle way, not pale and thin like the woman in the mirror, but young and healthy.

'Addy?' this strange woman stood up. 'What the hell— You startled me! What are you doing here?' She peered at the newcomer. 'Addy, are you okay? You look – where's Prue?' Her voice rose sharply.

Adeline said, 'Prue's asleep. I want my husband. Where is he?'

'He went into town. Why don't you go back to your part of the house, and I'll go and find Prue?' The blonde edged round Adeline and began to move towards the door.

Adeline began to be irritated by her. 'I came to have tea. We can have tea here. I saw the tea things in the kitchen.'

'Heck,' muttered the other. 'She's flipped! I knew it!' She raised her voice. 'Come on, Adeline. Let me take you back to your own part of the house.'

Adeline's thin features stiffened. 'It's all my house! Not part of it! All of it! I can go wherever I want! It all belongs to me!' Intelligence gleamed in her deepset eyes. 'I know who you are!'

'Take it easy, Addy!' Her opponent put out a hand.

Adeline's head shot forward like a snake's at the end of her long, thin neck. 'Where's Matthew? Where's my husband? What have you done with him? Where's my daughter?'

'Sure, it's all your house. But you'd much rather have tea in your own drawing room, wouldn't you? The fire's lit in there. Much cosier. Matthew will come there, just as soon as he gets back from town.' She hesitated, then turned and moved towards the door. 'Come on, Adeline.'

Adeline's eyes flickered around the room and her gaze landed on a large metal punch on the desk. Her thin hand reached out.

The blonde had reached the door and, by chance, looked back to see if Adeline were following. Adeline leapt towards her, her arm raised on high, grasping the punch.

Her face distorted and lips drawn back, she screeched. 'I know who you are! You're the one who wants my house and my husband! But you won't have them, either of them! They're mine and you won't take them away from me! I won't let you!'

She saw the horror on the painted face and alarm leap into the pale eyes. The blonde threw up both hands and tried to grasp her assailant's wrists. But Adeline laughed aloud because the gesture was so futile. She felt so strong, stronger than she'd ever felt. Her arms were like steel and she wrenched them free contemptuously.

The force of the movement caused the other to totter on her high heels and stagger back. Adeline struck out and the punch connected with the woman's temple. She saw the red blood running down the hated face, saw vision blur in the pale eyes, and with a thrill of triumph running through her own veins, Adeline stood over Marla as she toppled sideways and collapsed at her feet, a dark sticky patch staining the blue-grey carpet.

Matthew Conway was driving back from his encounter with Josh and Markby. He felt angry, with them and with himself, conscious that he'd mishandled the affair and gained nothing except the chief inspector's suspicion.

The urge to face the youth had been too great, the seething rage in him too fierce to ignore. He'd tracked Josh from the school gate to the park and, hidden behind the bushes, watched as the wretched boy played – played! – on the swings and toy rocket. A great gangling youngster of that age, just fooling around behind the park keeper's back, as if he hadn't a care in the world! Katie lay dead. God only knew what part that boy had in her death! But it was of so little import to the little bastard that he horsed around on children's play equipment while Matthew, bereaved, wretched and furious, watched uncomprehendingly. The boy was a monster!

Even now he felt himself turn hot and cold at the thought of it. He should have wrung the blighter's neck, done it straight away before Markby turned up to interfere. Damn Markby! He'd shown more sympathy for the boy than for Matthew himself, the dead girl's father!

Matthew turned into the drive. It was nearly dark. Mutchings would have penned the pigs for the night so he hadn't to watch out for them. He pressed his foot on the accelerator and then, almost immediately, was forced to brake. The car swerved violently, left the drive, bumped over the grass and stopped. He threw open the door.

'Prue! What the devil—?'

Prue was running towards him, waving her arms. 'Adeline's in the grounds, Matthew! Mutchings is looking for her. I thought she was asleep and I just went to take a nap. Thank God I woke up and checked on her when I did. I had to call the ambulance!'

His heart seemed to freeze. He croaked, 'Why? What's happened to her?'

'Not to her, to Marla! She attacked Marla!'

It took them an hour in the darkness to find Adeline. They scoured the park with torches, calling to one another and to the missing woman. Matthew was on the point of telephoning the police when they came across her, shivering with cold and hiding in the bushes by the wall which divided the rest of the park from the mausoleum.

'Of all the damn places!' he said wearily to Prue.

At least, once discovered, she hadn't been difficult to coax out. Prue had been able to lead her indoors. Dr Barnes was sent for and gave Adeline a sedative. Afterwards, there had been a brief, fraught interview in the drawing room.

'The time's come for her to be hospitalised,' the doctor said, not unsympathetically but firmly. 'She's blanking out Katie's death. She's woozy and confused with the drugs and I can't keep her sedated. When her head clears, she'll remember what happened to Katie. Then I don't know what she'll do. She could harm herself, Matthew. Or if not herself, then someone else.'

They hadn't told him about Marla, only that Adeline had run out into the night and hidden in the grounds. But the uncontrollable twitch Matthew felt run across his features might have given the game away. If the doctor found out, he'd insist on the hospital, send for them to take Adeline here and now. Wasn't that what he'd wanted? Yet now the moment had come, Matthew was terrified at the prospect.

However, the doctor was too intent on speaking his own mind to have noticed Matthew's agitation. 'I know a private clinic. It's comfortable, discreet and extremely successful with nervous cases. Perhaps after a month or two there—'

'Later!' Matthew blurted. 'Not now, I can't talk about it now! We'll take care of her, Prue and I!'

It was only after the doctor had left that Matthew could get back in his car and drive to the Cottage Hospital to see what had happened to Marla. He prayed he wouldn't find her seriously injured, and that she wasn't spreading the tale all over Bamford.

To his immense relief she was not badly hurt. He found her sitting in Casualty's waiting room, with a large plaster on the side of her head, and in a spitting temper.

'Where the hell have you been, Matt? I've been here hours! They wanted to keep me in overnight in case I had concussion. Stay here? All night? I told them, not a chance! So they patched me up and dumped me out here! My head is going like a drum. Everyone stares at me. I tried to call the house and no one answers! Your wife is as crazy as a loon—'

'Hush!' He made desperate efforts to silence her. 'Not here! People can hear! What did you tell them?'

He looked round him in hunted fashion and met the gaze of

a red-faced elderly woman, well wrapped up in an overcoat despite the warmth of the waiting room. Her bulbous blue eyes fixed him unwaveringly. Matthew turned his back to her.

Marla was staring at him too, with contempt. 'Oh, don't be afraid. I told them I slipped and hit my head on the filing cabinet. I didn't tell them she came creeping up on me and tried to crack my head open with something she grabbed off my desk! Matt, she's dangerous! I always said it and now, perhaps, you'll believe me! She's got to go away!'

'It's only the shock over Katie!' he pleaded. 'I couldn't come earlier because we had to find her. She'd run out into the grounds. Then Barnes came. It's the trauma and the extra medication she's been taking. Don't make a fuss, Marla. I'll make it up to you . . .'

'How?' Her pale eyes fixed him speculatively.

'You can go up to London, buy yourself a whole new outfit, anything you want, and charge it to me. Go to the beautician's and have the whole works—'

'Oh, great, with a big purple bruise on my head and three stitches in the gash? If it leaves a scar, I'll sue!'

'For pity's sake, if it's money, we can settle it!' he cried out, forgetting he was in a public place.

She was silent for a moment. 'Yes, sure, if it's money! But I don't want money, Matt! You know what I want!'

'I can't promise anything!' he muttered. He took her elbow and began to propel her towards the exit, anxious to get them both out of this place.

As the doors swung closed behind them, a nurse approached the red-faced woman in the overcoat.

'Someone will see you now, Miss Rissington. Would you like to come this way?'

Chapter Seventeen

MEREDITH DESCENDED from the early evening train on to an already gloomy platform at Bamford station. The brightly lit carriages drew away, disappearing into the night and leaving a sense of desolation behind them. The wind blew chilly round her face and ankles and she shivered despite her lined Aquascutum raincoat. That expensive item had proved a wise investment. She'd had it for years and it still managed to look respectable despite, during that time, being sat on, crushed on public transport and rolled up and stuffed into a variety of cases and bags, even, on a few occasions when she'd been delayed at airports and continental railway termini, slept under.

Other passengers who had quitted the train here hurried past her and disappeared into the carpark. There were sounds of engines being started up. She lived near enough to her house to walk there, but tonight she wished she had the car.

She was already alone. There were no station staff to be seen. The newspaper kiosk and snack shop were closed. An empty polystyrene coffee cup bowled along the edge of the platform and flipped over on to the track. Just outside, a solitary taxi waited at the rank. The driver opened his door and leaned out when he saw her but she called out, 'No thanks!' and gripping her briefcase, set off across the deserted yard towards town.

It wasn't, after all, late, for goodness sake! Only half past six. But at this time of year, that meant night had already fallen. The shops were all shut and the last home-going shopworkers waited at the bus-stops. At least she wouldn't have to make this dispiriting walk again for the rest of the week. She'd had leave entitlement due and elected to take a few days. There'd be no excuse for not finishing the painting or doing all other outstanding odd tasks.

Of which, thought Meredith ruefully, the first was to get in touch with Father Holland and report on her visit to Adeline Conway. She could have phoned him. But she needed to talk to him face to face. She wanted to explain her fears about Adeline, although perhaps explain was too optimistic a word. She couldn't even explain them to herself. She wanted to try and convey her own sense of unease. Someone had to move to help Adeline quickly and in some practical way, of that she was sure. Yet she couldn't say whence the danger came, possibly from Adeline herself. Meredith could sense that within the unfortunate woman's fragile shell intolerable pressures were building; she threatened to self-destruct, like a volcano. None of this could adequately be explained across the disembodied medium of a telephone line.

Meredith hesitated at the street corner. She could go and see Father Holland now, before going home. She'd get it all said and ease her mind of the responsibility and then, with luck, be able to relax for the rest of the evening.

The church and its adjacent vicarage lay at the end of a short, wide cul-de-sac, not so much a road as a piece of medieval Bamford which had survived all redevelopment. Beneath the asphalt road surface lay the paving stones of the original Bamford marketplace, so Father Holland had told her. Later, as the town expanded, a new market square had been built and the focus of the town's life moved half a mile to the west.

'You can't move a church,' he'd pointed out. 'You can move houses and people, but the church stays fixed where it is, even if it is inconvenient to reach and lost in the middle of fields. In the fourteenth century,' he'd added, stamping the motor-cyclist's boots he wore with his cassock, 'this was where it was all at!'

And this was where she now found herself. It was very quiet all around. The ground to the left was occupied by the churchyard with its rustling pine-trees. The church lay straight ahead, its steeple rising black against the dark blue of the sky. Bats, which had quitted their steeple home, wheeled and darted above the graves. Occasionally one swooped low over her, almost skimming her hair. They were a problem in Bamford church and the subject of much heated correspondence in the local press. They were protected by law and couldn't be evicted. But their droppings were causing a problem in the steeple rafters and there had been complaints about the fusty odour. There was a light on in the church porch and another gleaming softly from within. No one had yet locked up for the night.

Meredith opened the creaking vicarage gate to the right and walked up to the front door. All the house lights were on downstairs but much ringing of the bell produced no response. Tentatively she tried the door which the vicar tended to leave unfastened during the day. It was locked now, either because darkness had fallen or because the vicar had gone out, leaving the house lit for security. The lights in the church might mean he was there.

Meredith retraced her steps and approached the church porch, the mass of the building brooding silently over her. She opened its heavy oak inner door by means of the great wrought-iron ring which operated the cumbersome latch, and peered in.

A mixed odour of candlewax and brass polish, dust in ancient hangings and the inevitable bat-smell greeted her. Pillars, pews, font, reclining tomb effigies, magazine stand, all emerged from semi-darkness. The one light shone up at the chancel. It picked up the curve of the Gothic vault and the commemorative wall plaques above tenebrous choir stalls. There was no light in the vestry and no sign of the vicar. She was about to pull the door closed and leave when her ear caught a faint sound.

Someone else was here. Now Meredith saw a small, dark figure crouched in a front pew and veiled by the shadow of a stout pillar. The figure's head was bent and whoever it was appeared to be praying. Again Meredith made to withdraw out of respect for another's devotions. Then the figure gave a distinct snuffle. The suppliant was crying and sounded both female and very young.

Meredith stepped down into the church and made her way to the spot. A young girl knelt with her head on her clasped hands. Only her hair could be seen, gleaming red like warm embers in the chancel light. To say either 'Are you all right?' when a person obviously is not, or 'Is anything wrong?' when it clearly is, are both fatuous, Meredith knew. But she said them both, because it was the established formula in such situations and she couldn't think of a better.

The girl raised her head. Her face was a pale oval framed by the loose curls of red hair. Her chubby prettiness was distorted by anguish. It was the face of a child with the eyes of a woman, a living Murillo, a Mary Magdalene for our time. Meredith thought she could guess who this was.

She took a seat on the pew beside the girl and said quietly, 'Hullo. My name's Meredith Mitchell. I've given a talk to the church youth club but I don't think you were there.'

The girl shook her head. She scrambled from her kneeling position and sat on the pew bench, pushing her untidy red curls away from her face. 'I don't go to the club no more,' she said huskily. 'I used to, couple of years ago. Then I sort of went off religion.'

'Oh, I see.' Meredith waited.

In the poor light she fancied she saw the girl flush. 'I mean, I know I'm here now ... but—'

'But you're in a mess,' Meredith supplied. 'And you don't know what to do? Right?'

'Yeah ...' Red curls nodded vigorously.

'You're not Nikki Arnold, by any chance?'

She saw suspicion flash into the girl's eyes. 'Here!' she said indignantly. 'How'd you know that?'

'Well, I'm a friend of Chief Inspector Markby who's investigating Lynne Wills' death. Is it because of Lynne you're here? She was your friend, wasn't she?'

Nikki crossed her arms and hugged herself as though she were cold but possibly it was only a gesture intended to comfort herself. 'Yes, we were really good mates. It's horrible, thinking she's dead. Sort of strange, too. I mean, sometimes it doesn't seem real, like she can't be dead. I've got some music tapes at home she lent me. I couldn't play them now. It'd be like she was there, watching me. Suppose I ought to go round to their house and give them back, but I can't. Her mum and dad, they'd start asking questions like that policewoman.'

'Nikki,' Meredith said gently. 'Do you know who might have killed your friend?'

The girl's eyes widened in astonishment. 'No, of course I don't!'

'But you'd like him to be found, wouldn't you? And there are things you know which you haven't told anyone, aren't there? Everything helps, every little bit of information. All pieced together, it will mean the man who killed Lynne is caught.'

Nikki looked down at her hands, twisting them together. Her

nails were bitten. 'That policewoman!' she said with surprising venom. 'She's no right coming to our place and talking to my mum like that! She went telling my mum tales about me! She's made it all out worse'n it is. Mum's been going on to me something rotten ever since! I've always got on really well with my mum. We've been friends! That policewoman's messed it all up!'

'No, Nikki,' Meredith said quietly, 'You messed things up. But now you've got a chance to put them right. You're lucky. Usually when we make a mess of things, we don't have that chance, believe me.'

There was a long silence. Then somewhere up in the roof a wooden beam gave a snapping noise.

'It was only fun,' Nikki said sullenly. 'And we made a bit of money, so what? Everything costs a lot. My mum hasn't got any money so I had to get it somewhere else. I'd have got a part-time job but you can't get them now in Bamford. Every time a shop puts a card in the window, twenty other people have got there before you. Lynne and me, we weren't slags! We just, you know, if there was a fellow we fancied or if he looked like he'd pay up . . . we, you know. There weren't a lot of 'em! My mum keeps yelling at me to tell her how many blokes there were! I can't remember, but there weren't many!'

There was a kind of ignorant innocence about her self-justification which was profoundly depressing. She didn't see what she and her friend had been doing as prostitution, just a way of earning a little pocket money. A part-time job, like any other. If Nikki could have earned the money helping out in local stores on a Saturday, she'd have done so. The recession had dried up the supply of such work so they'd earned it another way. The casual amorality was both shocking and frightening. It would be impossible to explain to Nikki where she'd gone wrong, because she genuinely couldn't see that she had. As for the risks inherent in such a practice, that had only become apparent to Nikki now, with Lynne's death. Even so, she did not really seem to make the connection. Meredith felt herself gripped by that helplessness with which social and charity workers are so familiar.

'You picked men up,' she said. 'And you took them to the Devaux family vault. What was wrong with using their cars?'

Nikki gave her a patient look. 'They could've shoved us out the door and driven off with paying! I mean, in a car, you're like, trapped. So we got them out of their cars, all right?'

'Well, yes. But the vault, wasn't it a grim spot to choose?'

Nikki's face lit up. 'Yes! It was really bad!'

Meredith blinked. She and Nikki were on opposite sides of a cultural and language divide here. It was the very eeriness of the vault which had made it so desirable, lending it an aura of eroticism, the sexual fascination of the vampire legend. As for 'bad', as used by Nikki that clearly meant 'good'.

'Just like a horror video! Some of the fellers, they didn't like it much, but most of them got a real buzz outa it. They went running round making ghost noises and standing on the tombs pretending to be Dracula! Some of them were a real laugh!' Nikki's enthusiasm faded. 'Only we didn't mean for it to turn real. I mean, for Lynne...'

Meredith felt a surge of anger. Not towards Nikki, but towards a popular culture which had so corrupted two young minds.

'But how did you get into it? You must have had the key at some point. Did the pigman give it to you?'

'Old Uncle Winston?' Nikki gave an unexpected giggle. 'Catch him going anywhere near! He did, one time, when we was in there, Lynne and me, just looking about. We climbed on a sort of shelf and saw him through the window, chasing after those pigs! So we made moaning noises. He heard us and went running off, waving his arms and scared stiff!'

'So who did give you the key?'

Nikki looked defiant and clamped her lips together.

'I think I can guess,' Meredith said, 'I think I know who but I don't know why. Katie Conway gave you the key, didn't she?'

Nikki raised her head and stared at Meredith insolently. 'So what! It was her house, her key! Her family place where they all got buried! Why shouldn't she give us the key?'

'It's why she should do it that interests me!' Meredith said. 'Where did you meet Katie, Nikki? And what hold did you have over her that persuaded her to lend you the key to the Devaux vault?'

Nikki looked sullen. 'It was Dom's idea...'

Helen Turner was sitting in front of Mrs Pride's television set with a cup of tea, when Meredith ushered in Nikki Arnold. She looked up in surprise and exclaimed, 'What on earth—?'

'Here's Nikki,' said Meredith briskly. 'She's got an awful lot to tell you, Helen. She wants to get it off her chest, don't you, Nik?'

'Yeah, all right,' said Nikki, sitting on the edge of Mrs Pride's armchair and casting a bright, appraising glance around the neat sitting room, perhaps contrasting it with the shambles of her mother's home. Having unburdened herself to Meredith, her normal self-assurance seemed to have returned. 'Can I have a cup of tea?'

'Course you can!' said Mrs Pride happily. 'I'll put the kettle on again! And I know what else you'd like, dear! You'd like a bit of my angel cake!'

Helen's eyes met Meredith's with an indescribable expression. 'Yes, well, I'll leave you to it!' Meredith said. 'I haven't been home yet.'

'Not staying for tea and cake?' Mrs Pride offered hopefully.

'Really. I've got a couple of lamb chops sitting in the fridge, and,' Meredith added honestly, 'I'm whacked!'

But when she did get indoors, having left Nikki comfortably ensconced with a cup of tea in one hand and large slice of cake in the other, it was to find that the evening's revelations weren't yet over.

She had no sooner set about preparing her own modest supper when the phone rang. She glanced at her watch. It was now gone eight. She picked up the receiver and asked cautiously, 'Hullo?'

'Meredith!' came Barney Crouch's voice excitedly. 'Where've you been? You've got to come at once!'

'Barney! I can't, I've only just got home—'

'I'm in the bar at The Crossed Keys!' Barney's words rolled over hers. 'Come straight away and bring your car!'

The phone went dead. Meredith went out into the kitchen and switched off the grill. It was going to be a long evening and without even a piece of Mrs Pride's angel cake to sustain her.

Chapter Eighteen

MEREDITH KNEW The Crossed Keys well. It was a small and unsophisticated hotel on the Market Square; before she'd bought her house she had stayed there. The 'lounge bar', as it liked to be known, was primarily intended for residents and passing business trade, together with such few locals as disliked the hurly-burly of the usual pub atmosphere. There was no piped music at The Crossed Keys. No bar billiards or snooker room, no bar meals. If you wanted to eat, you had to go to the dining room, and signs of hilarity would have resulted in an immediate request to leave.

The lounge bar had the appearance of a room full of sale items. There were mismatched easy chairs in browns and dark greens, motley bric-à-brac, pictures indistinguishable beneath dark layers of varnish and a bookcase of dusty volumes which no one ever borrowed. Barney, who looked quite at home here, was slumped in the corner of a horsehair-stuffed chesterfield, nursing a whisky glass. As Meredith entered and glanced round, he caught her eye and engaged in a series of exaggerated winks, nods and waggles of his beard which threatened to dislocate his jaw.

'Barney!' said Meredith as she joined him, 'I hope you don't think you're being discreet! If you keep twitching and rolling your eyes like that, people will think you've got the DTs.'

'He's here!' Barney growled.

'What? Where?' Meredith's head snapped round. 'Which one?'

'No!' Barney's voice grew agonised. 'Talk about me being blooming obvious! Don't stare like that!'

'I'm not. I don't know whom I'm supposed to be staring at!'

'Over there at the bar, smallish stocky fellow with a moustache

191

and the tweed jacket. There, just ordered himself another. Stay here, I'll get you a drink. I'll go and stand next to him so you'll be sure which one I mean. Are you still on the tomato juice?'

'I'll have a bitter lemon straight, if possible, and a packet of crisps or peanuts, please. I haven't had any supper, Barney!'

Meredith hunted in her purse. Barney accepted the money with dignity and approached the bar. There was something of the era of the black and white cinema about his whole manner, a stagy furtiveness and a distinct suggestion that suitable music ought to be playing atmospherically in the background. Not surprisingly, the man with the moustache gave him a curious look.

'Don't think he's spotted me!' said Barney on his return, setting the bitter lemon and a packet of cheese and onion crisps on the table and scrupulously adding her change in a neat pile of coins. 'He doesn't realise I've been watching him. I've got a knack for this sort of thing, y'know.'

There was no reply to this modestly made but clearly inaccurate claim. Meredith said, 'Thanks for getting the crisps. All right if I eat them now? We're not going to have to bolt out of here, are we?'

'No, not yet, not now he's ordered himself another drink. But he's been here best part of an hour and he could move at any time. That's when we follow him! You did bring the car?' Barney sounded anxious.

'Um, yes . . .' Meredith crunched on the crisps. 'You are sure you've got the right man, Barney? This could turn out very embarrassing.'

'That's him! Stake my life on it!' Barney paused. 'Life, yes. That's what he'll get for what he did!'

'We don't actually know he's done anything!'

'I saw him leaving with that girl! Why is he hiding out in this damn-awful pub? No one would do that unless he was forced to!'

'Then we ought to ring Alan Markby and get him over here.'

'All in good time!' said Barney.

She glanced at him suspiciously, guessing that he felt he was just getting into his stride and was unwilling to relinquish the thrill of the chase.

'Have you been tracking him round the bars since I last saw you?'

'I haven't missed a moment of opening hours!' said Barney

proudly. 'I've been in every pub for miles around. I was beginning to think he'd bolted and I came here tonight as a last resort. I mean, who drinks here by choice? Just look at the place! You'd think there'd been a funeral! But then he walked in. I thought, you silly old bugger, Barney! I should have realised he'd choose a place like this. A clientèle that's all ships passing in the night. Here today, gone tomorrow. Ask no questions, don't care about any answers. I'll wager he's been drinking here since that night at The Silver Bells, afraid to show his face anywhere else!'

Meredith was beginning to think that a mixture of cheese and onion crisps and bitter lemon on an empty stomach was unfortunate. 'I'm going to phone Alan!' she said firmly.

Barney grasped her wrist as she made to rise. 'No, you can't! No time! He's leaving!'

Their quarry drained his glass and set it down with an air of finality. He bid the lugubrious barman farewell and walked briskly towards the exit.

'Look natural!' ordered Barney as they dived after him. 'Sorry, ladies first!' They had wedged themselves together in the door-space. 'This is the tricky bit! He's making for the carpark!'

'I'm not sure we can follow him at this time of night without giving the game away. There aren't so many cars about and the headlights—'

'There he goes!' Barney's voice cracked in excitement. 'Look, there! Come on, we'll lose him!'

A hatchback was drawing out of the carpark and signalling left. The street lighting bleached out its colour which might have been red but now appeared dull yellowish-grey. Barney was making inarticulate cries of distress. Meredith bundled him into the front passenger seat and scuttled round to the driver's side.

'This isn't going to be easy! Fasten your safety belt!' she gasped as she scrambled in.

The lack of traffic at this hour at least made it easy to pick up the rear lights of the hatchback ahead of them.

'Turning left again,' muttered Barney. 'Could be going out to the new housing estate.'

But the car ahead kept going until it had left the fringes of the town and struck out into open countryside. They were now driving down an unlit country road, both sets of headlights cutting swathes of light through the blackness.

'He must know we're behind him!' Meredith said. 'And it must look odd.'

'So what? Why should he think we're following him? It's a public road. Watch out. He's slowing down!'

The headlights of the car in front had picked up a group of houses on one side of the road. The driver slowed and turned into the gateway of the end house and stopped.

'Drive straight past, slow and steady, so's I can try and get his licence number!' Barney instructed.

Meredith grimaced. 'I can't help wishing you were at the wheel, not me!'

They slid past the stationary car. As they did, there was a sudden glare of light. The driver had opened his door and was getting out. They saw him clearly. He looked towards them and they were past.

'Got it!' said Barney triumphantly. 'Think so, anyway, not sure about the last number.'

'He got a good look at us!'

'Not a chance,' said the confident Barney. 'He was in the light and we were in the dark. Anyway, our headlights would have blinded him. Hang on, there's a signpost. That was Claypits Lane. Okay, now you can drive back to Bamford and we'll get hold of your chief inspector.'

'I just hope you're right about all this, Barney!'

'This is the address, Claypits Lane, if your informants are right about it, sir!' The police driver spoke over his shoulder to his back-seat passenger.

'Okay, pull in here. We'll walk down to the house. No point in giving chummy advance notice of our arrival!'

The driver took the car up on to the grass verge, hard under a hedge, and switched off the engine. 'Want me to come along, sir?' he asked hopefully.

'Yes, you might as well. Although I don't anticipate he'll give any trouble.'

The slam of the car doors echoed across open land. It was just after seven in the morning, still not fully light at this time of year. The police car had cut dark tracks into the frost which silvered the verge. A dank mist clung to the fields and obscured trees which were just beginning to emerge from the gloom into the dawning day. Despite his overcoat, Markby felt the chill air bite into him.

The driver rubbed his hands together. 'Bit nippy!' he observed.

Markby grinned and they set off up the lane. The houses were about fifty yards further on. They looked as if they might have been built by someone who had found himself with a spare piece of land and anticipated the explosion of housing demand which had marked the Seventies. Markby opened the gate of the end house and they walked up the drive. There was a light at an upstairs window which looked like that of a bathroom and another at the side of the house downstairs.

'He's home,' said the driver. 'Think he's your man, sir?'

'According to a not altogether reliable witness! We'll need a lot more evidence than an identification by Barney Crouch! Try the garage door, Wilson. If that's the kitchen light, he can't see the garage from there.'

It was an up-and-over door and swung up easily with only a slight creak. A red hatchback was parked inside. The garage was a model of tidiness, tools neatly affixed to hooks, tins and bottles stacked on a shelf. This, thought Markby, was the garage of a man who, if he set himself to clean out a car, would do it thoroughly. He eyed the hatchback. Nevertheless, when stripped down by the forensic boys, it would yield something. If it were indeed the car that had transported Lynne Wills' body. And there were the tyres which, if they hadn't been changed, could be matched to the tracks by the mausoleum and at the playing field. There might even be traces of leaf mould from that around the Devaux vault.

'That's the numberplate Crouch gave,' the constable beside him said nervously. He was a young fellow and it wasn't every day he got to accompany a chief inspector, possibly to make a significant arrest.

'All right!' Markby said. 'Let's hear what he's got to say before one of his neighbours looks out, sees us poking about here and phones the police!'

The man opened the door holding a pint bottle of milk in his free hand. He blinked and looked from one to the other of them.

'Mr Geoffrey Garton?' Markby produced his card. 'Could I have a word?'

'What about?' Garton stood foursquare in the doorway, blocking their entry. 'Bit early, isn't it?'

He was in his mid-forties and getting paunchy. His hair was thinning and the moustache had possibly been grown to compensate. His colour looked a little high. There could be several reasons for that. He was a drinker? He was alarmed at the sight of them? He was running a fever? He had a heart condition? Markby hoped it wasn't the last.

'Perhaps we could talk more easily indoors, Mr Garton? Is your wife here?'

'Wife? Haven't got one, she left three or four years ago.' Garton moved aside and gestured with the milk bottle towards the rear of the house. 'I was just about to get my breakfast. Come in the kitchen. It's the warmest spot. I don't bother much with heating the rest of the house. I'm out all day.'

The hallway was cold, nearly as cold as that of Park House. There was a stuffy overnight smell. Garton's kitchen was spartan. His breakfast, one cup, one bowl, one spoon, surrounded by a packet of cornflakes, sliced bread in a plastic bag and a pot of supermarket jam, looked pathetic. Markby thought of Barney's lavish spread. Then he thought of his own breakfast table and realised, with a grimace, that it looked very like this one: that of a single man, making shift for himself with the least expenditure of effort.

The parallel was uncomfortable. He heard himself ask sharply, 'Where do you work, Mr Garton?'

'At Norton's cash-and-carry. I'm responsible for stock and re-orders. Look, what's all this about? Nothing wrong at the store, is there? We haven't had a break-in?' Garton glanced at his watch. 'I don't like to be late for work.'

'Is that your car in the garage?'

'Yes! And it's not been in any accident!' Garton sounded more assured. He'd been rattled when he first saw them, but now he hoped this was all going to be about a traffic offence of some kind.

'And were you driving it on the night of—' Markby consulted his notebook, not because he'd forgotten the date of Lynne's murder but because the sight of the notebook impressed some people.

Garton glanced at the little book anxiously. 'Yes, yes, I suppose so! I can't recall that date off-hand.'

'It was a Thursday. What do you usually do on a Thursday evening?'

'I generally, well, it depends! If there's something on telly, I stay here, get my supper and watch the box.'

'Go to the pub?'

'Sometimes,' Garton said unwillingly.

'A witness claims to have seen you on the night in question in The Silver Bells, Bamford. Is that possible?'

'I suppose it's possible but I couldn't say for sure!' Garton snapped. 'I don't remember!' His tongue passed over his lower lip. 'Why the hell should I? It was just an evening like any other! Perhaps I did go out for a drink, but I don't recall which pub. I haven't got a regular.'

'Have you ever seen this girl?'

The photo was one Lynne's parents had given the police. It had been taken a few months earlier by her school photographer. In her uniform, without make-up, her hair neatly brushed and tied in a ponytail, she looked her age and no more, her smile bright and optimistic.

Garton's hand shook as he returned it. 'No! I don't know her!'

Markby put notebook and photo away. 'We'd like to take a look at your car. Have you any objections? We'll only keep it for the day.'

'A whole day? What am I supposed to do without it?' Garton looked panic-stricken. 'What do you want if for?'

'I'd like our forensics branch to check it over, Mr Garton.'

He knew he had his man. He'd known it as soon as Garton opened the door. But he had to be able to prove it. Garton's expression was ludicrously transparent. He was wondering whether the thorough cleaning he'd given the vehicle had been enough.

'All right,' he said reluctantly.

'And you'll be asked to give samples of body fluids!'

Garton's face turned grey. 'I'll refuse! It's a bloody infringement of my civil rights!'

'No, it isn't and, actually, no, you can't,' Markby said mildly.

Garton glowered. 'You wait! I'll be getting on to my solicitor about this!'

He hadn't cleaned it well enough. Traces of blood, skin and hair were turned up and he'd forgotten the tyres. Thanks to DNA testing it was possible to identify the semen traces on the body of the dead girl and on her clothing as originating from Garton. He'd even made the simple mistake of pinching out the flame of the candle-stub at the mausoleum with his fingers, leaving clear prints in the soft wax.

Later, faced with such a mountain of evidence, Garton presented a dejected, pathetic figure, occasionally rising to bursts of self-justification, mostly bewailing his bad luck.

'I didn't know she was that young! She didn't look like that picture of yours the night I met her! I swear I thought she was at least eighteen and so would you have! It was all her idea! She was a real little bitch. She picked me up and had me drive us out to some deserted chapel. The place gave me the creeps! I asked her why'd she wanted us to go there. We could've used the car. But she insisted. A joke, she said it was. A joke! I began to think, then, she was weird. But we agreed a price and I paid her, fair and square. Then she tried to get more money out of me! She claimed she was under age and I'd get into trouble. She was a little blackmailer, that's what she was! Not that I believed her. I told you, she looked older! I lost my temper. Just being in that place with all those tombs had upset me! I grabbed her and we struggled a bit and she fell. It was an accident! I wasn't out to kill her! I didn't even mean to hurt her, just make her realise she'd picked the wrong man to play her tricks on. I wanted to give her a bit of a fright. But then I got the fright, didn't I? When I saw she was dead, that is. I was scared out of my wits. I just bundled her into the car and dumped her out on the playing field because I thought, well, it would put you off the scent.'

'What about the other girl?' Markby asked.

Garton stared at him with bulging, bloodshot eyes. 'What other girl? Hey! You don't mean the Conway kid? You're not pinning that one on me! I never set eyes on her in my life! I read about her death in the local press. I know they were trying to connect it up with – with the Wills girl, but I had nothing to do with it, right? I know who the Conways are! I'd never have gone near Matt Conway's daughter! I'd be crazy!' Garton paused to draw breath. 'I want my solicitor now.'

'Certainly,' Markby said. 'He'd better be here when you're charged with the murder of Lynne Theresa Wills.'

Chapter Nineteen

'WHAT SELFISH creatures we are,' Barney mused. 'The thing I feel most deeply is a sense of relief that what I heard that night at the mausoleum was only Garton dragging the poor kid's body along, and not some ancient Devaux getting up from the tomb for a stroll! Selfish and daft, that's what!'

'And don't you think,' Alan Markby asked him, 'that for you and Meredith to go chasing around pubs seeking out Garton was just a bit selfish and daft, as you put it?'

'We found him for you!' Meredith said defensively from her station at the cooker. A hot chocolate smell was filling the air from the saucepan as she jiggled it over the hob.

'And only by the purest good luck didn't tip him off! You should have called me from The Crossed Keys! For crying out loud, Barney! If you remembered him so well, why didn't you give us a better description at the start? You and the Reeves were so vague that we couldn't even get enough to give a police artist a chance to make a sketch!'

Barney looked embarrassed. 'Markby, I'll make a confession to you. I've had a life-long aversion to getting embroiled in the cogwheels of officialdom. I did tell you I saw the girl leave with the fellow. I didn't fail in my duty! And quite frankly, I was less clear about him then than later. I'd had a hell of a fright at the mausoleum, remember!' He paused, sheepishly. 'Chiefly, I suppose, I was scared I'd have to attend some kind of identity parade, point at some wretch, fill out some kind of form, oh, I don't know! I did know I wasn't certain enough of him to do that, point him out at a parade. So I thought, best to keep quiet, I'd done my bit. But then, when Katie died, I knew how wrong I was.'

'So why didn't you come back to me and explain all that? I'd have understood!' Markby exclaimed in frustration. 'Half the country feels the way you do. More of 'em, probably. No one likes to get drawn into official inquiries. I know they're either scared of repercussions from the villains or just want to avoid the police. God knows why! Nearly all the people who feel that way are utterly respectable citizens!'

'I'm sorry!' Barney said stubbornly. 'I regret it, but I did it and I can't undo it. There!' He greeted the arrival of the cocoa with unnecessary effusion. 'Ah, cocoa! Bless you, dear girl. I haven't had a mug of that since I don't know when!' He pushed the three waiting mugs forward.

Meredith filled them carefully and joined the other two at her kitchen table. She fancied Alan was gazing at her reproachfully. He was prepared to excuse Barney's amateur sleuthing and rambling excuses on the grounds that Barney was unreliable, anyway, and his brains were pickled in Scotch. She, Meredith, he clearly felt ought to have known better. On reflection, she also felt she ought to have known better. But she wasn't going to admit it. 'I did take Nikki straight to Helen Turner,' she pointed out.

'Yes and thank you,' he conceded. 'That was a good piece of work.'

She propped her chin on her hands, elbows on the table, and contemplated the steam curling from her cocoa mug. 'I won't get in your way again. I'm going to finish my decorating. That's what I've taken time off for. And I'm going over to The Silver Bells to take a look at the Welsh dresser the landlady has kindly offered me.'

'Nor shall I trouble you again,' said Barney nobly. 'Doris Pride won't let me.'

'This is all very encouraging!' said Markby sardonically. 'Of course I'm grateful to you both. But police work is best left to us coppers, you know. That's what they pay us for.'

'We do take the point!' Meredith sipped cautiously at the hot drink. 'But before I do anything else, I must go and see Adeline Conway. She invited me and I promised I'd go. She's so lonely.'

'Tricky,' said Markby. 'Especially in view of developments.'

Barney slurped noisily in his mug and said ominously, 'You never know, with a kink in the bloodline, how it's going to take 'em! Watch yourself!'

'Adeline's very frail. I don't think she could do any harm.'

'I wouldn't bet good money on it!' Seeing how the other two looked at him, Barney rattled the spoon in his cocoa mug and went on somewhat diffidently. 'Now I'm not meddling, Markby, not again. This is just gossip and normally I don't listen to what women say. Not even Doris Pride. But she did mention something which, well, stuck in my head, as it were.'

'Barney!' Alan Markby said sharply, 'If you've heard anything relevant to inquiries, let's have it!'

'I don't know that it is relevant! Probably isn't. Sure it isn't, in fact. But anyhow, one of Doris's good women – well, you know her, Markby. Name of Rissington. She found young Lynne's body. Well, when the woman Rissington was a girl, she had a run-in with TB. It left her chesty. Mind you, to look at her, you'd never think it! But every so often, they take an X-ray, down at the Cottage Hospital. X-ray department shares a waiting room with Casualty. The other afternoon, latish, Rissington was sitting down there waiting her turn for the radiographer, when who should stagger in, supported by a couple of eager ambulance men, but that delectable secretary of Matthew Conway's!'

'Marla!' Markby exclaimed. 'When was this?'

'Monday, I fancy. You'll have to check with Rissington. The fair Marla wasn't so easy on the eye as usual. She had a lump the size of a tennis ball on her forehead which was turning nicely yellow and purple, and she was using the sort of language Rissington reckoned she hadn't heard since her father, the admiral, died. Marla was telling anyone who'd listen that she'd fallen and hit her head on a cupboard. To top it all, she jumped the queue for radiography and went in ahead of Miss Rissington because it was thought she might have a depressed fracture. Apparently she didn't, because she reappeared, patched up with a plaster, and still cussing like an old salt! I only pass this on for what it's worth and because Meredith proposes going over to Park House. You'd better watch out in case Adeline Conway starts to foam at the mouth, dear girl, that's all!'

'It's the atmosphere in that house I dread, not anything poor Adeline might do,' Meredith said. 'It was unnerving before, but now they'll know the truth about Katie! At least, Matthew and Prue will know. They won't, can't, tell Adeline. Poor little Katie, how unhappy she must have been. Little wonder she went off the rails last year!'

'Turner tried to interview Adeline, bearing in mind what you told us,' Markby pushed his mug away disconsolately. 'Hopeless task. Adeline's full of pills and doesn't know the time of day, let alone what's going on.'

'But I don't know what's going on either!' protested Barney plaintively. 'Come on, I gave you my information! What did young Katie get up to last year? Why did she give the key of the mausoleum to the other girls? Didn't she want to know what they wanted it for?'

Meredith glanced at Markby. 'For a time last year Katie decided to rebel. She broke off her friendship with Josh and stopped going to the youth club. She deliberately took up with the most unsuitable friends she could find and they turned out to be Lynne Wills and Nikki Arnold. They took her with them into pubs, where she'd never set foot before. They taught her to drink and experiment with soft drugs and finally taught her the oldest trade of them all!'

'Katie?' Barney exclaimed. 'I never saw her in The Bells—' He broke off. 'Hang on though . . . There was a whole time last year when I was laid up with the damn aches and pains. I didn't get out to the pub or anywhere else for a couple of months. Doris did all my shopping. Good woman, Doris. But I couldn't get her to bring in any beer. That must have been the time Katie was going around with the other two.'

'If you had been active socially then and seen her in the pubs, what would you have done, Barney?' Markby asked him.

Barney looked confused. 'Don't know. You mean, would I have tipped the wink to anyone, the Conways, or your chaps in blue? I'll be honest. I'd have been shocked but I'd have kept quiet. I don't like to draw attention to myself, you see, and the Conways would have kicked up a devil of a fuss.' He sighed. 'Better that than what happened. But we don't like to cause trouble, do we? Especially for ourselves.'

'Terry Reeves and Daphne didn't,' said Meredith. 'Well, anyhow, Katie spent those vital few weeks going around with Lynne and Nikki, and lying to her parents about visiting a convent friend or going to the youth club. She didn't need money and she didn't do it for the kicks. She did it because it was the worst she could do. She wanted to punish her parents, but she only punished herself.'

Markby said abruptly, 'Why no one at Park House realised

that something was very wrong beats me! One doesn't expect Adeline to notice anything, but Matthew or Prue Wilcox should have seen it.'

'Prue's wrapped up in Adeline and Matthew's wrapped up in his own problems!' Meredith said firmly. 'Her parents accepted that she was at the club or with her schoolfriend. They didn't check. Why should they? Ironically it was because she had always been so reliable that they didn't imagine anything had changed. They could never have believed Katie would lie to them.'

'She always looked so unspoiled and innocent,' Barney said sadly.

'She was a decent kid and had enough sense to realise the mess she'd got into. She broke with Nikki and Lynne and went back to Josh and the youth club. But it's more difficult to cut loose from bad company than get into it. Which is where the unlovely Dom comes on the scene.'

'He denies any involvement,' Markby said glumly. 'And we can't prove otherwise. It's his word against Nikki's. He has a passion for horror films and all manner of necrophilia. The flat's full of videos. All the electronic gadgetry in that place was bought and paid for. We checked. The mother of that family works her fingers to the bone to provide the necessities of life and Dom spends his money on whatever new gimmick takes his fancy. Father's no longer around. Dom's the only client Nikki has so far named and that's because she wanted to shift the blame for use of the chapel on to him.'

'He'd had a look at the chapel from the outside after one of his stints as an office cleaner at the house. It was just the thing to appeal to him and he had the idea to use the place for a nocturnal lovenest,' Meredith explained. 'The two girls took it up with enthusiasm. Nikki's mother had also told her tales about the mausoleum. They decided to take other men there. Getting the key was easy. Lynne had a blackmailer's instincts all right. Katie was easily made to lend them the key against a threat that they would tell the Conways what she had been doing during the brief time she had been under the two girls' influence. Katie insisted the key was returned because she was afraid Prue might notice it was missing. But no one ever checked the chapel, once the door had been unlocked it stayed that way. But then Lynne was killed there . . . and we're back to the noises you heard,

Barney! It gave you a fright, but just think, if you hadn't been there and heard or seen the light in the mausoleum . . .'

'I suppose,' Barney said wistfully, 'you really must rule out Garton as Katie's murderer? He's owned up to killing Lynne. Couldn't he have killed Katie too?'

He sat up straight with a jerk. 'Got it! He saw Katie walking along the road and stopped her, thinking she was still in the business. She told him she wasn't any longer but he refused to believe her. He lost his temper as he must have done with young Lynne, there was a scrap and he killed her. There! That's what must have happened!'

Markby stared at him thoughtfully. 'It'd be convenient and Norris would be very happy, Barney. But I'm afraid it's not on.'

'Why not?' argued Barney. 'It seems clear enough to me.'

'Because Garton has an alibi for the day of Katie's death.'

'Oh drat!' said Barney disconsolately. 'Are you sure?'

'He can give chapter and verse. He was on a business trip to Nottingham. He left at eight in the morning and didn't get back till nearly ten at night. He has petrol receipts, names and times of meetings with people in Nottingham and a receipt from the restaurant in the motorway service area where he stopped on the way back. That receipt is timed. No, he didn't kill Katie.'

'But someone did . . .' Meredith pointed out.

Barney put down his cocoa mug and said seriously, 'You know Markby, it wasn't me!'

They looked at him, Meredith astonished and Markby a little quizzical.

'I mean, I know I found her but it's never occurred to me until this minute that you might think I did it!'

'I didn't say I did,' Markby told him.

'Yes, but look here,' Barney said in some agitation. 'You haven't bally well said you don't!'

There was a downpour during the night. When Matthew Conway came down to breakfast, which he always ate with Prue in the kitchen, he found an early morning visitor.

Mutchings was awkwardly ensconced on a wooden chair, both gnarled hands clasping a mug of tea. He'd left his boots in the porch and his large, flat feet in crudely darned socks rested, heels together and toes turned out, on the stone-flagged floor like a pair of flounders. His wet hair clung to his scalp and in an untidy fringe over his brow from beneath which his eyes peered out, filled with unease at unfamiliar surroundings. In the kitchen warmth his damp clothing emitted a feral animal odour.

He got up as Matthew came in. 'Morning, sir! Miz Wilcox said I could wait here till you come!'

From the stove where she was busy with sizzling bacon and eggs, Prue called, 'Mutchings has come to report some storm damage.'

'You'll have to tell me while I eat,' said Matthew, taking his accustomed seat and shifting it further from the pigman.

Prue dished up his breakfast expertly and then turned her attention to Mutchings. 'Are your hands clean, Winston? I've made you a bacon sandwich.' She indicated two doorsteps of bread.

'Right you are, Miz Wilcox!' Mutchings' lugubrious expression brightened. He stared down at his upturned palms. 'They're all right.'

'No they're not. Go and wash them!'

As Mutchings lumbered obediently to the sink, Matthew twitched an exasperated eyebrow at Prue.

'He worries,' she said in a low voice. 'He was here first thing wanting to tell you. He can't cope when there's any change.' She flushed as the import of her words struck her.

'How well can any of us cope?' Matthew asked. He began to eat, thinking, 'Here I am, stuffing myself with bacon and eggs and preparing to listen to Mutchings' nonsense, just as if nothing had happened. As if Katie—'

His eyes went to the empty place where once his daughter had sat to share breakfast with them.

Prue had noticed. 'I don't expect Mutchings' news will amount to much!' she said loudly.

'Oh no, sir!' called Mutchings indistinctly through a mouthful of bread and bacon. 'Pigs is all right. I got the little buggers shut up till you've been down and looked at the wall.'

'What wall?' Matthew snapped.

'Over by pig-sties. Rain washed out the bank and the stones has fallen. I blocked it up temp'ry. But it'll need rebuilding. If you was to get in a load of new stones, I'd fix a dandy new bit of wall.'

'I'll come as soon as I've finished. If you've blocked up the gap, you'd better let the piglets out or they'll be squealing.' Matthew threw down his knife and fork. 'Repairs! New stones! For what, Prue, for what?' He raised agonised eyes to her face.

She shook her head. 'I don't know, Matt. I don't know.'

Adeline had breakfasted on a tray in her room as usual, picking at the toast and drinking half a cup of tea. Then she got up without waiting for Prue to come, dressed and went downstairs.

Prue was on her knees before the drawing-room hearth. 'Down already, dear? I've just got the fire going.' She eyed her charge. 'Will you be all right for a while? I've got to go into Bamford and do a bit of shopping and Matthew has gone to inspect a damaged wall.'

'Of course I shall be all right,' said Adeline in her clear, high voice. 'It's my home. No one can harm me while I'm here.'

'That's right, dear.' Prue bit her lip. 'I won't be gone long!'

Adeline sat down and picked up her embroidery. She cut off a length of silk and carefully split it so that she worked with three threads. Sam, who had been out for his morning stroll, came in and settled down before the fire to clean his wet paws. Adeline began to stitch, the needle going in and out with deft precision. It was soothing to watch the work grow, the flowers now completed and the green fronds of the leaves spreading across the cloth. The fire crackled. In and out went the needle. Sam contorted himself into a spiral to reach his back.

Click. Adeline raised her head and Sam stopped washing himself.

'What are you doing here?' Adeline asked coldly.

From the doorway Marla Lewis said, 'Prue asked me to keep an eye on you.'

'I don't want you near me!'

'Don't worry, Addy. It's mutual!' Marla had not advanced any further into the room and kept one hand prudently on the door-handle. 'I'm just looking in to check, okay?'

'I told you, I don't want you here and I don't want you checking on me! You don't need to. This is my house!' Adeline put down the needlework and stared with hostile eyes at the other woman. Then she gave a small, triumphant smile. 'And you'll never get me out of it!'

Marla looked spiteful. 'Don't be so sure, Addy! They don't tell you everything!'

Suspicion, never far from Adeline's mind, returned with a jab of physical pain. 'What do you mean?'

'You're sick, Addy. So they don't tell you things. Like what Dr Barnes really thinks ought to be done with you. Like what the police were really doing over by that creepy mausoleum.' Marla's pale eyes glowed. 'There was a kid murdered over there, Addy.'

'What child?' Blood drained from Adeline's face.

'Not Katie. Another one. There's things you don't know about your sweet little daughter, too!'

Adeline's fingers closed on the scissors. 'Don't you dare to mention her name! You're lying to me.'

'Wrong, Addy. They lie to you. I don't. Shall I tell you why they lie?' Marla was watching the scissors and was poised ready for instant flight. 'Matt, Prue, the doctor, all of them think if you knew the truth it would push you over the edge. But I think you went over that edge long ago, Adeline. You're as crazy as they come and any day now the guys in the white coats are going to come and collect you. Telling you the truth isn't going to make one iota of difference!'

'What truth?' Adeline's voice cracked. She stared at Marla, her eyes wide with fear. 'Tell me!'

'Oh, you want to hear it? Okay, here it is . . .'

Meredith too had stayed awake, listening to the force of the gale beat against the window, her mind running on Adeline. She also got up to face the havoc wrought by the storm.

Débris had been brought down from treetops and tiles from roofs. Gullies and drains were blocked. Above the kitchen window, the gutter overflowed in a steady stream of brackish water. Meredith borrowed a ladder from Mrs Pride and climbed up unsteadily to clean it out. She didn't like heights and she didn't like ladders and she didn't like putting her hand into nameless mess. This, she thought ruefully, is all part of the joy of home-ownership!

When she'd got it done, she cleaned herself up and set off for Park House. As she rattled across the cattle-grid and drove slowly up the water-logged drive between dripping ranks of overgrown hedging, the pale sun shone on the crumbling façade of the house and made wet pillars and plaster gleam. Meredith parked and climbed the steps leading up the front door with care. They were littered with dead leaves and twigs and very slippery. There was a distant burst of squealing. Alan had described the Tamworth piglet herd to her, but she had never encountered it. It seemed today she might have that chance. It sounded as though Mutchings had just released them into the grounds from overnight confinement in their piggery. They were raucously celebrating their freedom.

She was surprised to find that the front door to the house stood ajar. Meredith pushed it cautiously and called out, 'Hullo? Anyone home?' Receiving no reply, she walked into the hall and called out again more loudly but to no effect.

The place seemed deserted. After a moment's hesitation, she turned the handle of the drawing-room. 'Adeline?'

There was a hiss and a flash of black fur shot past her legs like a rocket. Meredith gave a squeak of alarm. The cat had been shut in the room and, released, bounded across the hall and out through the open front door. Unease touched her. Who had shut the animal in? Adeline herself? Why? And where was she?

Meredith looked around the drawing room. Someone had earlier tidied it and lit the fire in the hearth. The only untidy note was struck by an empty needlework bag which lay on the hearth-rug. The fire smouldered and crackled dully, sending out gusts of acrid smoke which made her wrinkle her nose. Coal did not have that effect.

Meredith crouched before the grate. Something had been cut into strips and thrown into the fire. She used a poker to hook fluttering, half-consumed shreds from destruction. The charred length of dangling linen still showed purple daisies and green leaves. With a spasm of alarm, she recognised Adeline's embroidery. Had Adeline herself committed this wanton act of destruction or someone else?

There was a sound from the door and a heavy step. A man's voice exclaimed, 'Addy? Is that you?'

Meredith jumped up and turned to face Matthew Conway in some confusion. 'I'm so sorry. I'm Meredith Mitchell. I was looking for Adeline. The front door was open when I came. I opened this door and let the cat out. It was shut in and there's no sign of your wife.'

Matthew had come further into the room. His disappointment was clear. 'Oh damn, I thought you were Addy. I'm sorry, I don't mean to sound rude.' He cast her a curious look. 'What are you doing with that?'

Meredith realised belatedly that she was still holding the poker. 'Oh, there was something smouldering on the fire and I—' She pulled a face. 'Confession's good for the soul. I wanted to know what it was and hooked it out. It was a piece of embroidery.'

'Addy's needlework?' A note of panic entered the man's voice. He strode past her, scooped up the bag on the hearthrug and shook it. Scissors and an empty tambour frame fell out. 'Hell! What's she done now? She must have burned all the silks as well!' He threw the needlework pouch down and looked wildly around him before fixing Meredith with a desperate expression. 'I've been looking for her too. I can't find her anywhere! Prue had to go into Bamford and I said I'd keep an eye on Addy. But she's given us the slip. Marla's hunting round upstairs. You say the front door was open? Don't say she's run out into the grounds again! It's soaking wet underfoot!'

He was making for the door. His alarm had infected Meredith, adding to the initial unease she had felt, and she hurried after him.

Matthew, conscious she was behind him, was speaking to her in disjointed bursts. 'It's the medication – She gets woozy – She doesn't know what she's doing – She isn't dangerous! – She's obsessed with the house, her family name and now, since Katie—'

They had exited abruptly through the front door and were descending the slippery steps to the drive with incautious haste. Meredith skidded and jumped the last two down to the gravel.

'I'll go one way,' she offered, 'and you go the other and we'll meet up again at the back of the house.'

'Thanks!' he said hoarsely. 'I'm very grateful. She has no reason to hurt you. So if you find her, just persuade her back indoors.'

His words puzzled Meredith. If Adeline weren't dangerous, why refer to such a possibility? Marla had been seen in Casualty with a large bruise. Was Barney right?

But there was no time to inquire into that now. They turned away from one another to start out on their separate routes. But before the plan could be put into execution, a shout halted them. Meredith looked round.

An ungainly form which could only be Winston Mutchings was lurching towards them. The pigman's heavy boots squelched across the turf. Both arms were held high above his head signalling some indecipherable semaphore, and his face was distorted into a gargoyle grotesqueness.

'Mr Conway, you gotta come! You gotta come at once, sir! Tis the pigs!'

'I can't be bothered with the wretched brutes now, Mutchings!' Matthew snapped.

He made to stride off but Mutchings gripped his sleeve, detaining him. 'You gotta come, sir!' He began to tug his employer along. 'Tis Miss Adeline, see? The pigs has found her!'

'Oh, my God!'

Matthew began to run. Meredith, with a tingle of horror running up her spine, plunged after him. Mutchings leading the way, they stumbled in a clumsy procession across the wet grass towards the Devaux mausoleum, its pepperpot turrets rising from the clump of dark, dripping trees.

The squealing of the piglets was now near at hand and Meredith could see the animals at last. They were milling about by the fence which divided the grounds from the mausoleum. She had never seen pigs so agitated. They raced to and fro, churning up the soft earth with their sharp trotters, squeaking and shrieking to one another and all the time, circling something which lay on the ground. Occasionally one of them would approach whatever it was with lowered snout and then, with a wild squeal, turn on its plump hindquarters and scuttle away.

'Get out of the way, you brutes!' Matthew was yelling. 'Mutchings, for God's sake, drive the blasted animals off!'

Mutchings was doing his best, but his whistling and shouting was to little avail. The piglets ignored him, darting under his feet and doubling back and splitting up when he tried to herd them. Matthew began to grab passing piglets and physically drag them aside but Mutchings shouted, 'You be careful, sir! Them can give you a powerful nasty bite!'

Meredith had made her way through the chaos to the central focus of it. Adeline Conway lay in a pathetic huddle on the ground by the fence. She was on her side, her head propped on one arm and her face turned upwards. Her sightless eyes stared up at the branches above from which droplets fell to spot her

210

face and neck like tears. Yet it struck Meredith that she looked strangely peaceful. She didn't know how long Adeline had been there. Her clothes were already taking up moisture from the ground, her light shoes mud-caked and sodden, ankles and legs splashed with streaked earth. All round, the ground had been churned into a mire by the pounding, scrabbling trotters of the piglets and the rooting of their inquisitive snouts. Even as she watched, one of them escaped Mutchings and galloped up to snuffle at Adeline's hair.

'Get away, get away from her!' Matthew shrieked. He scooped up a clod of earth and hurled it at the piglet which squealed indignantly and bounded away.

Mutchings had found a fallen branch and by brandishing it was managing to drive the animals off. Matthew crouched over his wife's body. He reached down and lifted her gently into his arms. Adeline's head fell back, her mouth gaping, her arms hanging loosely by her sides.

Matthew cradled her to his chest and began to rock them both back and forth. 'Addy, Addy . . .'

'She's a goner . . .'

Meredith spun round with a cry. Mutchings, still gripping the branch, had come up behind her. He rolled his eyes whitely towards the trees and the half-hidden mausoleum.

'They got her, them old Devaux! They've taken her off! She's with them now!'

Chapter Twenty

'HEART FAILURE, brought on by stress and shock,' Meredith said. 'That's what the doctor believes. Physically she was very weak, even before Katie's death. It was all too much.'

'She died of grief, that's what!' said Mrs Pride firmly. 'Broken-hearted, poor soul.'

'It does seem as if she just gave up. Her mind was very confused. We can only speculate as to why she destroyed her needle-work. Just because she wasn't going to finish it? I don't know. Perhaps she just felt everything else was destroyed and there was no future for her. She hadn't been out of the main gates for years and even though she wanted to get to the mausoleum, she couldn't bring herself to do it. So she cut across the grounds to the nearest point to the mausoleum which could be reached without going out to the road, lay down by her ancestors and died.'

'Grief!' repeated Mrs Pride. 'It turns heads, does grief. They do say as they'll bury Miss Adeline and her daughter together, though not in that nasty mausoleum. Only they'll have to wait a bit until they get permission to bury little Katie. I do wish they'd hurry up and find the fellow as killed her. They seem sure it's not this chap they've got for killing Lynne Wills. Whoever it was, he's responsible for both Miss Adeline's death and Katie's and a wicked devil he is!'

'Matthew Conway must be going through a dreadful time. Though it must have been very difficult living with Adeline all these years, he still loved her very much in his heart.'

Mrs Pride gave a disbelieving snort.

'You didn't see him!' Meredith protested. 'He was distraught when we found the body. He just crouched there in the mud nursing her. We couldn't get him to put her down.'

Mrs Pride leaned across the teapot. 'Bad conscience!' she declared. 'I'm not an uncharitable woman. I'll believe the best of anyone. But if Matthew Conway is cut up over his wife's death, it's because he knows he treated her wrong, there! It's on his conscience and won't let him rest easy.' Majestic and serene in judgement, she tipped up Anne Hathaway's cottage and a steady stream of tea splashed into the cup. 'Serve him right!'

She passed a cup to Meredith and went on, 'So you think you might be able to get your Welsh dresser, then, from the pub?'

Meredith adjusted to the abrupt change of subject. 'I'm certainly going along there to take a look at it. Not that I particularly feel like going today, but if I leave it too long, the Reeves may get rid of it.'

'Take a very good look at it!' counselled Mrs Pride. 'There's a lot of woodworm in old stuff. Of course you know what you want, dear, but I wouldn't give any of it houseroom! Don't forget, if you want it brought over to your place, my nephew, Dean, has got a van and he'll be pleased to fetch it for you.'

Meredith arrived at The Silver Bells in early afternoon to be met by an unexpected scene of chaos. A fire engine was parked before the pub together with, a little further down the road, a white van which declared itself to be from the Water Board. Hoses snaked across the pavement and disappeared down an open cellar flap. Large puddles of water were everywhere. A chalked notice on a board propped against a telegraph pole apologised to customers for the pub being closed and promised to open that evening. It seemed, in the light of the evidence, an optimistic undertaking.

On the other hand, there was not, as far as Meredith could see, any sign of fire. The thatch, the most likely seat of it, was intact. There was no smell of burning or floating scraps of ash. She approached a fireman in uniform who was stooped over the open cellar, hands on knees, staring into the depths below.

'Fire?' he said, looking up. 'Not a fire, love, flood. We've been pumping out.' He pointed downwards. 'Cellar was awash, barrels floating around all over the place. If there's water in the beer tonight, at least they'll know where it came from!'

This, presumably, was a joke. There was a shout from below and a second fireman's head popped out at Meredith's feet.

'You can roll those hoses up, Tom, it's not coming in any more.'
A Water Board official in a yellow oilskin jacket appeared.
'It'll be the watertable risen. We can't trace any leak in the pipes.
These old places . . .' He cast a dismissive glance at The Silver
Bells. 'They've always been liable to flood, specially where there
are cellars.'

Meredith left them to their professional deliberations and put
her head through the open pub door. A dishevelled, harassed
blonde appeared carrying a bucket and mop.

'We're closed! Gotta flood in the cellars! It was all that rain.'

'I'm sorry I've come at such a bad moment,' Meredith apologised. 'It's about the Welsh dresser—'

The blonde's face brightened momentarily. 'Oh, you're the
chief inspector's friend. It's out back in the barn. Just go and help
yourself. There's only the one like it out there. You're welcome to
it if you want it, only you'll have to arrange to move it yourself.'

'I've got that fixed up. How much—'

The blonde waved the bucket at her. 'We don't want any
money, just take it! Terry's only going to chop it up and burn it
when he gets round to it. I reckon it's a horrible old thing myself.
I wouldn't have it in my kitchen!'

From somewhere a man's voice bellowed, 'Daph! What're
you doing?'

'I've got to go,' said Mrs Reeves. 'You should see that cellar.
It's a right mess. I just hope the insurance is going to pay up.
Poor Terry, he's going mad! We just didn't need this! 'Scuse me!'

She vanished. Meredith went outside again. The fire crew was
about to depart. The Water Board men were discussing a series
of paint marks on the pavement. From below in the cellars came
a crash of heavy objects and vigorous swearing.

Meredith made her way round to the back of the building
where she found extensive stone-built outhouses. It looked as if
The Silver Bells had once been a coaching inn. She dragged open
one of the heavy wooden doors and peered in. The old barn, as
Daphne had called it, was more likely an old coach-house. It was
stacked high with junk. At one end, wooden stairs led up to a
part-floor above in the rafters, laden with more items. Down at
ground level, most things appeared to have come from refurbish-
ment of the pub. There was an old fridge, tables and chairs, a
massive wrought-iron Victorian kitchen range, a more modern,

but antiquated and oil-splashed, cooker, assorted cupboards and the Welsh dresser.

It stood at the foot of the stairs. Though very knocked about and dirty, it showed no sign of the dreaded woodworm and appeared sound in every other way. Meredith tugged at the dis-coloured brass handles of its central drawer. It had three drawers in a row and, beneath and to either side, small cupboards. The whole balanced on curved legs. The drawer was stiff and came out reluctantly revealing itself to be a knife compartment lined with stained and worn green baize. She rattled it. It could be lifted out. With an effort, Meredith shoved the drawer back in again. Part of the problem was caused by the ill-fitting knife boxes which would have either to be refitted or removed.

She ran a hand over the surface of the wood. It was warm, smooth as satin and polished by the touch of countless fingers. This fine old piece, unless she was mistaken, was upwards of a hundred years old. It might even be twice that. It had probably been made by a local craftsman and stood for its entire life in the kitchens of what had then been an inn on a lonely road. And now Terry Reeves proposed to chop it up and burn it! Meredith felt genuine shock, followed by a pang of conscience. She ought to go back and try to explain to Daphne that what she was cheerfully giving away was actually worth quite a bit of money or would be, when restored. Even in its present condition, any antique dealer's eyes would gleam at the sight of it.

But Terry and Daphne were far too busy with the damage in the cellars and the resultant loss of business to want to be both-ered about a piece of despised old furniture. Nor was its age likely to impress them. To their way of thinking, the age of the dresser counted against it. But if she delayed removing the piece until business were usual again at the pub, she might return to find Terry had consigned it to the flames. The safest course of action was to remove it as quickly as possible and return at some later date and offer again to pay for it.

Meredith went home and asked Mrs Pride if Dean could go and fetch the dresser without delay as its days were numbered.

'I'll get on to him straight away!' Mrs Pride promised.

She was as good as her word. That same evening there was a ring at the door. Meredith opened it to find a large young man in jeans and, despite the inclement weather, a sleeveless tee-shirt. Bright ginger hair tumbled to his shoulders and his bare arms were covered in tattoos.

'Hullo!' he said cheerfully. 'I've got a kitchen cupboard for you!' He jerked a thumb over his shoulder at a battered white van parked under the street lamp. A second hirsute, brawny figure lounged against it.

'A Welsh dresser, you mean?' Meredith asked anxiously, hoping he hadn't brought the wrong thing.

'Yeah, one of them things with four legs, shelves up top and drawers down the bottom. Fetched it from the pub because Auntie Doris said you needed it in a hurry. Want it brought in?'

'Oh, please! You've, er, got help?' She peered at the other figure.

'Sure, got my mate.'

Dean's mate detached himself from the side of the van. The dresser was unloaded and with some difficulty manoeuvred down the narrow hallway to Meredith's kitchen. In the barn it had looked quite small. In her tiny kitchen it looked formidably large. What little space was now left was filled by Dean and his mate who stood with folded arms and quizzical expressions, surveying the newcomer.

'It wants a bit of a clean up,' said Dean's mate whose wrists, like a Roman gladiator's, were adorned with metal-studded leather bands. 'You'll have to strip all that down. And you'll need to keep it away from your central heating or that old wood will split clean down the grain.' He wasn't the encouraging kind.

'I'll get advice,' said Meredith. 'And I haven't got central heating.'

'Rather you than me,' said Jeremiah.

'By the way, did you tell either of the Reeves you were taking the dresser?'

'No, they were busy down the cellars. They've had a flood at The Bells,' Dean told her. 'It ain't half left a mess. We just went round the back and loaded the old cupboard up.'

'I suppose that's all right . . .' She pressed beer money into their massive paws, thanked them, and ushered them out.

Back in the kitchen with the dresser it was obvious that she had taken on quite a task. The dresser was very dirty and to strip all its surfaces of a century or more of accumulated grease and grime was going to take hours of hard work. Meredith crawled about on the floor to look underneath it and then returned her attention to the drawers. The two at either end slid in and out quite well, it was the middle one that stuck.

She jerked it open again. It was the loose knife compartment. It didn't lie flat and every time the drawer was open, caught on the upper framework. She grasped it and eased the whole thing out.

No wonder it didn't fit. Someone had jammed some papers underneath. For a brief, very brief moment she felt a thrill of discovery. But then she saw that the papers were new, not old. Not an exciting historical find, but just some hand-written sheets on lined paper. She picked them up.

'Macbeth is thought to be an unlucky play and it is theatrical superstition never to refer to it by name. It is always called The Scottish Play and if anyone in the theatre forgets and says the name aloud, other actors . . .'

Meredith turned the sheet over. This was a school essay, written in a round, young hand. She put the sheets on the kitchen table and after a moment's deliberation, went to where Mrs Pride's old pink overall still hung on the back of the door. Meredith rooted in the pocket and took out the scrap of paper on which Katie had written her parents' name and her home phone number.

For a while she sat at the table with Katie's note in her hand, staring at the essay. It didn't make sense, it couldn't. And yet, it did. It did if she just stopped thinking about the Conways and all their troubles, and turned her mind to the difficulties encountered by others.

A little later, Meredith, Alan Markby and Helen Turner sat round the table examining the sheets of paper.

'It looks like the kid's homework, all right,' said Helen

Markby picked up Katie's note which Meredith had found in the pink overall. 'We'll need a proper handwriting expert on it. Or Conway might be able to identify his daughter's work or, come to that, a teacher at her school. The English teacher who presumably set Macbeth as a subject, for example.'

He looked up at Meredith. 'Don't say anything about this to anyone. Anyone at all! We'll get the handwriting identified first thing in the morning.'

'What do you think about my theory?' Meredith asked.

'I think your theory is very interesting, but theories don't put cases in court.' He gathered up the sheets of Katie's essay. 'You've done your bit, Meredith, okay? Don't, please, be tempted to pursue your investigations any further.'

'Of course not!' she said. 'I told you the other evening, all I want to do is finish decorating the house.'

'Yes, but I know you, and I know you always have to go and find things out for yourself! Above all, don't touch the dresser any more and don't tell anyone about your find. It's very import-ant that no one knows we have this.' He waved the slim wedge of paper at her.

'Won't you going up to London tomorrow, anyway?' Helen asked, seeking to defuse the indignation on Meredith's face.

'No, I took the rest of this week off. I was going to do so much and now, well, tomorrow is already Friday and I haven't done a thing.'

Unexpectedly Alan smiled at her. 'I don't know, you seem to have accomplished quite a lot!'

Helen Turner glanced at him, at Meredith and then back to her chief. 'If you don't need me any more, I'll start this on its way.' She took charge of the sheets of essay.

When she had gone, the other two sat in silence. 'I ought to be going too,' he said at last. 'Tomorrow is going to prove a long day.'

'Will you take him in?' Meredith asked in a controlled voice.

'That would be premature. The finding of Katie's essay is a strong lead but not conclusive proof. Besides which, the hand-writing has to be confirmed. Above all, I don't want him to panic. We have a fair idea of what happens when he panics.' He saw Meredith give an involuntary shiver. 'It might be better in the circumstances if you did leave Bamford for the day. Couldn't you go up to London after all?'

'They're not expecting me at the office.'

'Does it matter? Couldn't you just roll in anyway? Or go and do some shopping or something? I'd much prefer you to be out of the way.'

Her hazel eyes held his gaze with uncomfortable directness. 'Is that just the policeman talking?'

'Let's say it gives me one less thing to worry about.'

'I've told you repeatedly, I won't interfere. You don't have to worry about me!'

'But I do, don't I?'

'Then don't!' That came out more sharply than intended and the silence which followed was more fraught than before.

'This is an old argument now, isn't it? And we're going to rehash it all over again,' Markby said. 'It doesn't have to be this way.'

'I'm not going to rehash it.'

'I want to marry you.'

'I know. I've explained it before. I'm deeply honoured – and that's not just a phrase, I mean it. But I think we should stay as we are.' She saw the muscles round his mouth tighten obstinately. 'I'm sorry, Alan! But you know that's how I feel!'

'Yes, you make that clear enough.' He was angry now. Not the shouting, arm-waving kind of anger but the bottled-up kind which is always so much more difficult to confront or defuse.

She wanted to say she was sorry again, because she was sorry, but she sensed that she couldn't say it. Just at the moment it would only make things worse. Meredith watched him prepare to leave.

As he struggled into his coat, he said, 'Remember what I said. Go out for the day tomorrow! That's official police advice. You don't have to listen to it just because I said it. It's going to be a tricky operation and I don't want any unnecessary complications.'

He didn't wait for her but let himself out of the front door which shut behind him with a very final-sounding click.

Meredith locked up for the night. There was a stiff wind blowing but no sign of any more rain. She went back to the kitchen and looked at the dresser. Alan had said not to touch it any more, but she picked up the knife compartment and returned it to the drawer, sliding the whole lot shut. For all its newly painted cosiness, the kitchen, the whole of the little house, seemed to echo with unwished emptiness. Perhaps it would be best to do as he said and go out for the day tomorrow, go up to London. She was, in more ways than one, on her own. But that was the way she'd always wanted it, wasn't it?

Chapter Twenty-One

'I TRIED!' was what she said to Alan afterwards and it was the truth. She did try. Meredith got up early and went down to the railway station to catch the London train, rueing the surrender of a day's leave but consoling herself that it was all in a good cause. From that moment on, things started to go wrong.

It struck her that the waiting room and platform all looked strangely deserted. Where were the usual fellow commuters, wan of face and short of temper, clustered singly and in little groups, briefcases and newspapers at the ready? Her heart sank. This was going to prove one of those days.

'Landslip!' said the booking clerk. 'Can't blame British Rail for that. It was all the rain we had. Chunks of mud have fallen from the embankment a mile up the line. It's made the track unsafe. The engineers are working on it now.'

'So how am I supposed to get to London?'

'From the next station up the line, Abbots Weston. The track's fine from there on.'

'To Abbots Weston is normally a twenty-minute train journey. How do I get there to catch the train?'

'By special free bus. BR laid it on to take the passengers from Bamford to Abbots Weston.'

Meredith looked out at the deserted yard. 'So where is this bus?'

'Oh, it left ten minutes ago. We put out a message on local radio telling passengers what time to be here to pick it up. The driver has to allow time in early morning traffic to get to Abbots Weston in time to connect with the train leaving there.'

'I didn't listen to local radio this morning.'

'That's a pity,' he said. 'There'll be another bus at twenty to

221

eleven and normal rail service from eight o'clock tonight, expected time. But not until tomorrow, if they run into more problems.'

'Thank you!' said Meredith, meaning 'Forget it!'

She walked home again, stopping off on the way to buy a newspaper and a packet of biscuits. If she had to go out for the day 'on official police advice', all she could do was to take the car and drive to some point on the map which looked as though it might be interesting.

She had the car keys in her bag so she opened up the garage before going indoors, and backed the car out to stand in front of the house. Then she went indoors to change out of her city gear. She dropped her bag and newspaper on the telephone table in the hall, the keys beside them, and hung up her raincoat. It was then, as she turned towards the foot of the stairs, that she heard a noise.

It came from behind the closed kitchen door at the far end of the narrow hall. It sounded like something being dropped. Meredith froze.

There were straightforward explanations. Above the draining board several kitchen implements hung on hooks attached to the tiled wall by plastic suction caps. From time to time, one of them fell off taking with it a ladle or slice and landed with a clatter on the stainless steel sink unit. Or it could be Alan, who had a key to the front door and had decided to return and examine the dresser again. Or Mrs Pride, who had a key to the back door for emergencies and often brought round bulky items of mail which had arrived when Meredith was away. It was arranged with the postman that packets which couldn't be pushed through the letter-box were left in the care of the next-door neighbour.

Meredith looked at her wristwatch. She had been gone from the house a mere three-quarters of an hour and it hardly seemed likely that anyone could have forced a way in meantime.

On reflection the most likely explanation was a hook and its burden falling from the wall. The trouble was, her nerves were on edge because of yesterday's discovery and Alan's instructions. Cautiously Meredith turned the handle of the kitchen door. The hinges creaked as it opened in a way she hadn't noticed before and if anyone were in there, he or she could hardly fail to have heard. But of course, there was no one there! she thought resolutely as she pushed the door open.

She was wrong.

Terry Reeves was standing by the Welsh dresser and staring at her pugnaciously. Behind him, the back door was ajar and rattled in the through-draught.

'What're you doing here?' he demanded. 'You're supposed to have gone up to the smoke, to work! I saw you leave.'

'The rain's washed the track out between here and Abbots Weston,' Meredith said. 'And I missed the connecting bus.'

'Bloody rain!' said Reeves. 'Caused a helluva mess in my cellar!'

The conversation was threatening to become surreal. Meredith introduced logic into it. 'I'm here because it's my house! What are you doing here? How did you get in?'

Reeves jerked his head towards the open back door. 'A doddle to get that open. You oughta get a proper safety lock on that. Amateur could get in that way.'

'You're not an amateur!' Meredith said, making another determined effort to escape from what felt increasingly like a Buñuel film.

Reeves paused. 'No,' he said in a different voice. 'No, I'm not. You're right there, love.'

The endearment came across both as an insult and a challenge. This was not surreal at all. It was real and very nasty.

Meredith asked, she hoped normally, 'So what do you want?' Don't panic, she told herself. Just keep calm and hope he keeps calm. He doesn't, with luck, want more trouble than he's already in.

Reeves seemed to be thinking along the same lines. He took his time before answering, running his tongue over his upper lip. He glanced at the dresser. 'I didn't realise Daph had given you that. I had a bit of a shock last night when I went out back and saw it was gone.'

'I offered to pay for it. Do you, er, want it back?'

'Load of junk!' said Reeves morosely. 'Course I don't want it, didn't think anyone would want that old cupboard!'

'Well, actually, it's worth something. I'm quite happy to give you a fair price. It's very old.' Things were slipping back into Buñuel territory again.

'Yeah, like I said, old. A load of junk. What d'you want it for?' His voice rose on an aggrieved note.

'I wanted an antique dresser. I've looked all over the place for one and it was very kind of your wife to offer it.'

She could almost see Reeves' brain working. His furrowed brow made his eyebrows meet above his flattened nose. She wondered if at some time he'd been a boxer.

'I come round here,' Reeves began carefully, 'because I left something in one of the drawers. You wasn't at home and I didn't want to bother you later, so I let myself in.' He looked straight at her.

The subtext was clear. He didn't for one moment expect her to believe such a preposterous tale. He'd already admitted he'd waited to see her leave that morning before breaking in. But he was offering them both a way out of a situation neither wanted to be in, a trade-off. Let me off the hook, accept my story, he was saying, and you won't get hurt! His deepset little eyes watched her face to see if she'd understood and whether she'd play along.

Meredith was perfectly willing to accept the absurd compromise in principle. Unfortunately for them both, there was one small problem. What he was looking for was no longer there.

'I see,' she said in the same careful tone he'd used. 'I understand, of course. But I'm afraid that if you're looking for the wad of old papers under the knife compartment, I threw it out. They made the drawer stick.'

There was a hiss of breath from Reeves. His eyes were like pebbles of granite. 'Where did you throw them?'

'Well, when I say "throw", I ought to have said "burned". I burned a lot of old papers in the back yard last night. I had a bit of a clear out. I just tossed the – the ones from the dresser on top of the others.'

'I don't believe you!' Reeves said softly.

'All right.' Meredith felt a curious sense of relief. The strain of the Buñuelesque dialogue was proving too much to sustain. 'No, actually, the police have them.'

'Stupid mare!' Reeves shouted at her viciously. He stepped sideways, away from the piece of furniture it was now vain for him to search. The movement placing him near the stove.

Katie had stood in that very spot to make the coffee. Suddenly Meredith had a reprise of her former experience, seeing Katie quite clearly in the sloppy pullover and Mrs Pride's pink overall, yellow paint smeared on her nose and hairline. The image, shocking in its reality, smiled and held out a mug and then abruptly faded.

'What on earth for?' Meredith burst out. 'Why Katie? What harm could the poor kid have done you?'

Her vehemence clearly took Reeves aback. 'It wasn't my fault!' He mumbled and then rallied, his voice harshening. 'Harm? Do you know what those wretched little tarts were using my pub for? Do you know how hard Daph and I have worked in that place? Have you any idea what it means to have the police hanging round the place, showing the customers pictures of corpses and asking everyone what they'd seen? It was ruining us!'

'Yes, I do know! I also know about the girls. But Katie hadn't been in your pub since last year!'

'Doesn't matter!' Reeves grew sullen. 'I had that copper friend of yours, Markby, come round preaching away to me and Daph about letting the girls use the pub for pick-ups. I told him, I hadn't wanted no trouble. But he went all pi on me! Ruddy cops! Then, after he left, Daph started giving me ear-ache. She went on and on! "She'd told me so. We should've told the police at the time. We should've stopped those girls coming in." ' His voice reverted to its normal gruff tone. 'I should've done this, that and I don't know what else! All my bleedin' fault, and that's what everyone was telling me!'

He moved towards her and automatically, Meredith took a step back. 'It wasn't my fault one of them girls got herself killed, was it? It was nothing to do with me! But the way I felt by the time Markby and Daph had finished with me, I'd have wrung the necks of the lot of 'em! But that doesn't mean I went out looking for one of them!'

He shook his head. 'It was just by chance I met up with her. I was driving along the old Cherton road. I was on my way to collect some bar snacks from the cash and carry on that new trading estate over at Westerfield. The headlights picked up a young girl walking along the road. I just looked in the mirror as I drove past and would you believe it? It was one of them, those girls who used to come in my pub and carry on her tricks! All right, may be it was last year she came. But last year, this year, what's it matter? She was one of them and I remembered her!' Reeves paused and added reflectively. 'She was the sort you'd remember, she was. Sort of innocent looking!' He snorted. 'Innocent! She was just like all the others! So, anyway, I stopped and offered her a lift.'

'She wasn't just like all the others!' Meredith said tightly.

Reeves was beginning to sweat, pearls forming on his low brow. 'I only wanted to talk to her, right? I wanted to tell her, make her understand, how much trouble she and her mates had caused me and Daph! That's all I wanted, to make her understand!' He thrust forward his bulldog jaw. 'But she started shouting and kicking up a fuss. I lost my temper and I hit out.' He scowled. 'Didn't mean to kill the silly little tart, just wanted to shut her up. But then I saw I'd shut her up permanent! I dumped her body in a field. I never saw her writing case in the dark. She must've dropped it in the van when she was hitting out at me. Course, I had to go on to Westerfield and get the bar snacks or Daph would have been asking questions. But it all made me late back to the pub. I got there just on opening time and Daph was jumping up and down anyway. I parked the van in the yard and when I opened the door and the light came on, I saw that zipped writing case lying there. Daph was yelling out at me to come indoors, bring in the snacks, open up the bar, do a dozen things all at once! I was in a real state. I wanted to hide the writing case for the time being. I couldn't get the whole thing in the dresser, so I took out the papers and shoved them under that inner drawer and the case I put somewhere else. I meant to get rid of them both, but it's been one thing after another! I just never had a bloody chance!' He was shouting now. 'And then, to top it all, Daph went and gave you the flipping dresser and you took it away!'

He stopped speaking, his words leaving an audible echo. As it faded there was another sound. The front doorbell rang.

'Who is it?' Reeves growled.

'I don't know!' Meredith made a hesitant move towards the door.

Reeves put his hand inside his leather jacket. 'You just stop where you are!'

She saw the gun, then, which he'd been carrying in his jacket. She gasped, 'Where did you get that?'

'Souvenir!' Reeves said briefly. 'Falklands!'

He had, of course, been in the army. Alan had told her that in passing. The blow that had killed Katie had come from a man trained in unarmed combat. She remembered Alan demonstrating it. Yet neither of them had thought of Reeves then. Even though, Meredith recalled bitterly, she herself had spoken at the time of the Reeves duo being able to do without the kind of problems caused by Lynne and her friends in The Silver Bells. She and Alan had held all the pieces of the puzzle that Sunday morning, and just hadn't put them together.

Reeves gestured with the revolver. 'Go and find out. Don't open the door. Just ask! Remember, I'm right behind you, so is this!' The snout of the revolver jerked again.

They moved together, Indian file, down the narrow hall. A dark shape was outlined against the frosted glass panel of the door.

'Who is it?' Meredith called in response to a painful jab in the ribs.

'Police!'

'Just a minute!' She turned her head over her shoulder. 'What now?'

'Ask what they want!'

Meredith repeated the request.

'We'd like a word. Can you open the door, please?'

'I'm – it's not convenient!' Another painful jab in the ribs. 'Can you come back later?'

The dark shape on the other side of the door moved away and was replaced by another.

'Meredith!' Alan's voice, just not able to control an edge of anxiety. 'Can you open the door?'

He'd understood! she thought with relief, even though it made the situation no less dangerous to her. The police must have been to The Silver Bells, found Reeves gone and got the truth out of Daphne! Reeves was breathing noisily by her ear. She could feel his breath.

'Is Reeves there?'

'Yes!' she shouted before Reeves could prevent her.

He swore and the revolver was pushed hard against her spine. Despite herself, Meredith yelped.

'Are you all right?' Alan's voice gained in urgency. 'Meredith! Reeves! Do you hear me?'

'I hear you!' Reeves bellowed. 'And you just listen to me! Then no one's going to get hurt! Not your girlfriend here, not no one, right? I've got a gun – ' To Meredith he added, 'You tell him!'

'It's true!' Meredith called. 'He's got a gun. It's a revolver he got in the Falklands—'

'That's enough!' Reeves ordered. 'I didn't say give him a bleedin' lecture!'

He gripped her arm and edged them both into the sitting room where, pressed against the wall, he twitched aside the net curtain in the bay window. 'That your car out front there?' She nodded. 'Got the keys on you?'

'On the hall table.'

Reeves propelled her back to the hall and scooped up the keys. 'You still out there, Markby? You pull all your men back! Your girlfriend and me, we're going for a drive!'

'Where?' demanded Meredith. 'You can't get away—'

'I told you to shut up!' Reeves was in no mood for sweet reason. 'Your girl is going to open the door, Markby, and we're both coming out! I got the gun right here in her back and it'll blow a hole clean through her if you try and interfere, okay?'

'All right, we understand,' said Alan's voice.

'Get those coppers back, then!'

There was a pause during which feet could be heard scraping on the road outside. Reeves grasped Meredith's arm again and pushed her ahead of him back into the sitting room to take another look from behind the curtain.

'Okay, lady! Just do as I tell you. We stay nice and close together, right? I don't want any fancy police-marksman thinking he can pick me off!'

'They're probably not armed!' said Meredith hoarsely.

'If they've been to the pub, Daph will've told them I got the gun. She's no good at keeping her trap shut, Daph. Like all ruddy women, they gotta yap all the time! They'll have picked up a coupla armed men before they came here, you bet your life!' Reeves gave an unlovely grin. 'And it is your life, don't you forget it! Don't go trying to do something clever!'

They retreated to the hall again. Reeves signalled to her to open the door.

Meredith tried to put the words 'blow a hole clean through her' out of her mind, but they were as disagreeably lodged there as the gun in her spine. The stretch of road appeared empty, but on the other side, a lace curtain moved.

'Coppers are in that house over there!' Reeves breathed by

her ear. There was a curious complicity between them now. They were in this together.

'It's probably only a neighbour watching!' she whispered back.

'Shut up! Go on, move!'

He was efficient. He kept her shielding him as they crossed the pavement. The passenger side was nearest. Reeves unlocked the door, pushed her through to the driver's seat and followed her in, slamming the door after them in a one swift movement.

'You drive!' he ordered as she untangled her legs from the gear stick.

'Which way?'

He frowned. 'Go down to the bottom and turn right, follow the one-way system out to the main road!'

The car coughed and, just for the purpose, started up first time which it didn't always do. Meredith, gripping the wheel, looked desperately up the street for signs of life. Reeves reached across and put the revolver to her head. 'Just so's they can see I mean business!' he explained.

'You're obscuring my view of the road!'

'You're not taking your flippin' test! I'll tell you anything you need to know. Just drive!'

They proceeded to the bottom of the road and then, as he'd directed, made to turn right into the one-way system. Except that round the corner, a police car blocked the way.

Reeves swore. 'Turn left!'

'That's no entry!' Meredith protested. 'It's all part of the one-way system! If I go left I'll go against the traffic flow!'

'I said, go left!'

Meredith drove unhappily the wrong way down the long narrow lane, one of the oldest of Bamford's streets. It was empty of traffic at the moment. Perhaps the police were stopping cars from entering the area. Meredith thought inconsequentially that Mrs Farthing of the ladies circle lived in one of the ancient stone cottages bordering the lane to either side.

'Put your foot down!' Reeves ordered.

The needle crept round the speedometer and then it happened. Not another car, but the majestic form of Mrs Pride on her bicycle appeared before them. She was pedalling along, blissfully unaware of anything untoward, straight towards them.

Suddenly Mrs Pride saw the car coming towards her. She wobbled violently but here the lane was at its narrowest and there was nowhere she could go. Meredith's reaction was instinctive and took no heed of Reeves or the weapon he held to her head. She slammed on the brakes. The car screeched and bucked and spun in the narrow confines, the wing on Reeves' side striking the nearest wall with a sickening crunch. Meredith flung up her arms to shield her face. At the same time, there was a deafening explosion.

Chapter Twenty-Two

'MY CAR's a write-off!' said Meredith glumly.

'Just be thankful you weren't written off!' Alan Markby retorted.

Meredith gingerly raised her hands to the polystyrene collar which Bamford Cottage Hospital had fitted to take the strain off her injured neck. 'I know it could be worse, but a chipped vertebra is no fun. I can't turn my head without using my hands. I must look like one of those ventriloquist's dolls! My spine feels like a lot of beads strung on a very loose string and my shoulders are very, very sore!'

'I wasn't being unsympathetic. Here, let me give you a hand . . .' They had reached his car. Meredith shuffled into the front passenger seat in a series of crab-like movements.

'I'm not complaining really,' she admitted as they drove out of the carpark of the medical centre where the doctor had just checked on her progress. 'I got off cheap at the price. I thought Reeves had shot me! I'm still a bit deaf on that side from the noise of the explosion! Doctor says that's temporary. Hope he's right!'

'Look at it this way. You had a straight choice. You hit the wall and put yourself in a neck-collar. If you hadn't, Reeves' arm wouldn't have been knocked down and he wouldn't have shot himself. He might indeed at some stage have shot you. He nearly bled to death, you know. People don't realise how dangerous a thigh wound can be. It certainly took the fight out of him. As we ran up, he was shouting out to us to call an ambulance! Didn't give a damn about anything else.'

'Mmn, I find it hard to rustle up any sympathy for Reeves. The person I do feel quite worried about is poor Mrs Pride. She's not a young woman to come off her bike like that. She was coming back from a mercy visit to her friend Mrs Farthing, who's had flu, and now she's laid up as well! Her leg is black and blue, an awful sight, and she's cracked a bone in her forearm. Between us we shall present a truly impressive sight, me in my collar and she with her arm in a sling and her leg propped up on a pile of cushions! And her bicycle has joined my car on the out-of-action list! Barney's looking after her.' Meredith paused. 'Nothing like a nice moan.'

'Get it off your chest, as they say! Feel better now?'

'No.'

'Well, sympathy is one thing. Allowing you to wallow in your misery is another! Next time I tell you to go out for the day, go! Isn't that Prue Wilcox over there on the pavement? She looks very determined.'

Meredith managed to roll her eyes sideways without moving her damaged neck. Prue was striding along swinging her arms, very much as though she were on the parade ground. Markby drew over to the kerb, tapped on the horn, and leaned across Meredith to press the button which operated the window. It slid down with a soft purr.

'Oh, Meredith!' said Prue, approaching to stoop by the opening. 'How are you today? I hope you're feeling better. I was meaning to stop by your house and see you.'

'I'm just a bit stiff and sore. The main thing is, they got Reeves.'

'How are things at Park House?' Markby asked. 'I was a little surprised to hear Conway has inherited it. I – er – rather got the impression Adeline wanted to avoid that!'

Prue shook her head sadly. 'My dear chief inspector! The whole thing is a sad example of the pitfalls of making a will so simple that it doesn't cover the unforeseen! Adeline's will left the house to Katie outright. She thought that took care of Matthew! But she had failed to include a clause to cover the event of Katie predeceasing her. I suppose Adeline thought that couldn't happen. She herself was in frail health and Katie was as fit as a fiddle. Certainly the solicitor was remiss in not explaining to her just what would happen if Katie died first, as a child, leaving no issue. When Katie did die poor Adeline was in no state to remember to make a new will and Matthew, you can be sure, didn't remind her! Because you see, there is no one else, no more Devaux relatives who can claim on the estate and so Matthew, as surviving spouse, gets Park House, after all!' Prue sniffed. 'I shall be leaving next week.'

'A holiday? You certainly deserve one.'

'No. I'm going to live with my sister in Cornwall. I shall never come back here, never!' Prue said fiercely.

'However will Matthew Conway manage without you?' Meredith exclaimed.

'Very well, no doubt. He intends to remarry! There is poor Adeline, hardly cold, and he's planning to replace her. It's not merely unfeeling. It's indecent! But I can't say I'm surprised. Adeline always said that if anything happened to her, Matthew would marry again at once. You were at the funeral, weren't you, Mr Markby? I couldn't stay behind and talk to anyone afterwards. I already knew what Matthew meant to do and seeing him standing there, receiving people's condolences and shaking hands, I just couldn't bear it.'

'I'm sorry I wasn't up to the funeral,' Meredith said. 'It does seem all wrong that Marla will be the mistress of Park House.'

A grim smile crossed Prue Wilxcox's homely features. 'Oh no, that's one small satisfaction I've got, at least! It's not Marla he means to marry!'

'What?' Markby and Meredith shouted together and Meredith forgot herself so far as to turn her head and gave a squawk of pain.

'No. He deceived us all on that one. Marla too! He's had a lady friend in London all along. He kept very quiet about her because, if you please, he wanted to protect her reputation! Hah!' Prue gave vent to a loud cry of disbelief causing passers-by to look startled and hurry their steps. 'He let everyone, including Marla herself, believe that she'd be the next Mrs Conway. Oh, I know it was treating her badly but I have to say it was no more than she deserved! I shall never know why poor Adeline went out to die like that—'

Prue stopped, her voice choking. 'I'm sure Marla had something to do with it. She was all alone with Adeline just before it happened. But there, I can't prove it. At least she's not profited by it. If she thought whatever she did would get her Park House, she was wrong. She's left already, by the way. There was a dreadful scene before she stormed upstairs, packed her bags and flounced out!'

'I can imagine it,' Markby remarked. 'I'm surprised there

wasn't another murder! Sorry, Prue!' he added quickly.

'Well, I had no intention of staying, whatever happened. It would all have been too painful to be in the house without Adeline and little Katie. You'd think in the circumstances Matthew would at least try to honour what Adeline saw as honour-bound commitments, but do you know what he's done?'

Prue began to work herself up again. 'He's sold the pigs! Every one! So now poor Mutchings is out of a job and what will he do? He's not a young man and he only knows about pigs. I took him to the Job Centre earlier today to sign on. There's very little chance he'll get other work, although they did say something about street cleaning. I also had to take him to a solicitor and find out about his rights as a tenant to the cottage. It's the only home he's ever had. But I don't think Matthew will find it easy to put Mutchings out. Poor Winston is in a dreadful state. His world had fallen apart. The pigs were his life and his entire family history is tied to Park House. To think that Matthew could be so cruel!'

'I would have thought Conway could have made Mutchings gardener,' said Markby, thinking of the untrimmed hedges which lined the approach to Park House.

'He doesn't want Winston around the place. The sight of him makes Matthew uneasy. He deserves to be uneasy!' said Prue fiercely.

'Mrs Pride said Matthew had a bad conscience.' Meredith sighed. 'It does seem as though so many innocent people suffered in all this. Or if they weren't exactly innocent, they weren't the worst offenders. There's Daphne Reeves who is a nice woman who just happened to marry a thug. Mutchings, of course, and poor young Josh Sanderson.'

'That's the way it goes,' said Alan, beside her.

Prue straightened up. 'I'll still try and come and see you before I leave, Meredith. 'I'm just off to see if I can buy a cat basket. I'm taking Sam, Adeline's cat, with me to Cornwall. I hope he'll settle. One hears of cats making their way back to their old homes over hundreds of miles. But he knows Adeline is gone. He roams around the place looking so miserable. But he's taken to sleeping on my bed so I think he'll be all right, and my sister likes cats.'

With that, she strode briskly away.

'You said, didn't you, that after a crime like murder in a community, nothing could ever be the same again,' Meredith remarked sadly.

'I did. Nor can it. But things repair themselves somehow. Maybe Conway will relent and let Mutchings stay on as gardener, especially if he's unable to get him out of the cottage. Prue will settle with her sister and the cat with Prue. Josh is the one I'm most worried about. Nor should I like to be in Matthew Conway's shoes! People here believe in observing the outward niceties. If he brings a new wife down from London so soon, neither he nor she will find life easy.'

'I still feel sorry for him,' Meredith said slowly. 'I saw him grieving over Adeline's body. Only Mutchings and I did that. I know Matthew was heart-broken. Besides Adeline, he's lost Katie and has had to face the news of how she behaved last year and the trouble she got into – no, I won't condemn Matthew. He has to rebuild his life.'

'Isn't that what we all try to do ? Build some sort of life for ourselves?'

She glanced at his face. She knew what he was thinking but this wasn't the time to start the old argument again. One day at a time, as someone somewhere had said.

The next two weeks passed in some confusion. Prue called as promised and bade a final farewell. Sam, it seemed, had accepted the basket bought for his conveyance and taken to sleeping in it. The transfer to Cornwall promised well.

'How is Matthew managing?' Meredith ventured to ask.

I have no idea!' said Prue icily. '*She* has been down! *She* has had the effrontery to measure up for new curtains! I couldn't bring myself to speak to her!'

She was obviously Matthew's intended new wife. Meredith didn't pursue the subject.

'Goodbye, Meredith dear!' said Prue, kissing her cheek. 'I know Adeline took to you when you called, which was so nice. She was such a lonely person.'

The Silver Bells had closed up, with Reeves in custody and Daphne departed to stay with relatives. Mrs Pride's leg was not doing so well, but mending slowly in Barney's care.

Meredith's neck had mended too and now that she was able

to dispense with the collar and move about without stabs of agony, she set out to do something she wanted very much to do, take flowers to the joint grave of Adeline and Katie Conway.

They lay together in the 'new cemetery', an adjunct to the old and overflowing Bamford churchyard. This new burial ground lacked the higgledy-piggledy informality of the old graveyard. Its plots lay in regimented rows and all its headstones were shining white and identical. Trees had been planted to break up the uniformity and provide some shelter or shade according to season. Approaching with her floral spray in its cellophane wrapping, Meredith came upon Matthew Conway himself, standing by a conifer sapling, his coat collar turned up against the wind and his hands in his pockets.

He appeared quite lost in thought. She hadn't seen him since the day of Adeline's death and she hesitated to disturb him now, but he turned his head.

'Miss Mitchell?'

'Hullo, Matthew. How are you?' She held out her burden. 'I wasn't able to come to the funeral so I brought some flowers today.'

'Thank you.' Matthew took his hands from his pockets. 'How are you? You were quite badly injured, I understand.'

'Not badly. Just awkwardly. I'm okay again, thanks.' She looked around. 'I've brought a jug to put the flowers in. There must be some water somewhere.'

'There's a tap over there, by that hut.'

Meredith fetched the water and arranged her flowers self-consciously as he watched. When she'd finished, she stepped back and studied the effect. She was unable, when she'd done that, to prevent herself reading the inscription on the temporary wooden cross awaiting the marble headstone.

Matthew's eyes were also fixed on the inscription. 'Adeline would have wished to lie in the mausoleum, but that was out of the question. One tries to observe the wishes of the departed, of course. However, Adeline's wishes, like everything else she said or thought, were – outlandish.'

'She was ill,' Meredith said gently.

'I know that. I coped with that for many years! I don't enjoy a very good opinion locally, do I?' Matthew asked disconcertingly. 'Do you share in the general disapproval?'

236

'No, why should I?'

'I'm getting married again, at Christmas. That's shocked everyone.'

'You have to make a new life for yourself,' she told him.

He smiled wryly at her. 'Thank you. You're the first person who's had a kind word. Of course, people expressed sympathy at my loss! But they were less keen to express understanding for my attempt to, as you say, make a new life. I didn't behave very well by Marla, I know. I do regret that. But I wanted to protect my – my fiancée.'

Meredith was silent.

'I wanted to protect them, too.' Matthew raised a hand to point at the headstone. 'I didn't do it very well. In fact, I failed.'

It was difficult to know how to respond to the bitterness in his voice. Meredith tried tentatively, 'How – how does your fiancée look forward to living at Park House?'

'Oh, she'll really make something of it! Adeline wouldn't have a thing done. But Fiona is an interior designer by training.'

'That's nice,' said Meredith uncertainly.

'And she's keen to keep a horse. She's always been a dedicated horsewoman but unable to keep a horse of her own in town. So I'm having the stables refurbished.' Matthew gave her another wry smile. 'And since it seems I can't get Mutchings out of his cottage, I've engaged him as stableman.'

'That is good!' said Meredith with more fervour.

But Matthew hadn't been deflected from his earlier train of thought. His gaze had returned to the wooden cross. 'You think, because you love people and you want to protect them, look after them, that you'll be able to do it. And then you find that you can't. Prue had some hard words for me before we left.' He shrugged. 'I dare say they were true. I failed Katie. I should have realised something was wrong last year. I should have known that the way things were between Adeline and me must have made the poor child wretched. I shall never forgive myself for being wrapped up in my own wretchedness, for being so selfish!'

'It's natural that you should think this way now,' Meredith sought to comfort him. 'After a death, it's usual to feel guilt. But sometimes things just get, well, out of hand. We can't be every-where, see everything. I expect Prue was upset when she spoke to you. She was very fond of Adeline.'

'And she wanted to see me suffer!' he said harshly. 'She thought, she told me so, that I'd got away with it! Those were her words. But do you realise, Miss Mitchell, that now I look at every man I see in Bamford and wonder if he was one of those who paid my daughter for sex?'

'Don't!' Meredith burst out. 'Don't think like that!'

'How else am I to think? You see, I'll never know who or how many... So don't let anyone tell you, Miss Mitchell, that I'm not being punished. Because I am... and will go on being so, with endless questions I'll never be able to answer.'

He turned away abruptly and began to stride away between the neat rectangles of chippings.

At that moment a car back-fired by the church. Rooks flew up cawing furiously. Matthew stopped, half-turned towards Meredith with a surprised expression and opened his mouth to speak. But instead of words, a pink froth appeared on his lips before he pitched forward on to his face.

Chapter Twenty-Three

MEREDITH'S FIRST thought was that he'd suffered some kind of seizure, possibly a cerebral shock. She ran towards him and then, as she knelt over him, she saw a small neat hole in the back of his coat between his shoulder-blades. A thick dark liquid began to ooze out of it and spread in a slow stain into the material. Matthew's frozen features, turned sideways, still registered surprise, eyes and mouth both open. He seemed to wish to speak, if only he could, and express his shock at what had happened to him.

But he couldn't because, as Meredith realised even without benefit of medical opinion, he was dead. It had not been a car she'd heard, but a shot.

She had barely had time to register the fact before the second shot came. It sped over her head and splattered against a headstone. Marble chips flew in all directions.

It was definitely time to get out of here. Whoever was firing clearly meant to prevent her rendering any first aid to Matthew. Not that any first aid could have helped him. But the assassin was taking precautions. The immediate problem was where, not knowing the location of the killer, Meredith could find cover.

Expediency led her to dive for the nearest headstone and crouch behind it. She felt rather as a rabbit must do in the middle of a cornfield when the harvesters have cleared all but this one small patch. Any minute now, the terriers will be sent in to flush out the game to be picked off with ease out there on the open stubble by the men with the guns.

Meredith shouted, 'He's dead!' because that presumably was what the killer wanted to know. There was no reason, surely, why whoever it was should want to kill her, Meredith. The second shot had been intended to frighten her.

And she ought to feel frightened, very frightened. But perversely, just at this moment as the wind caught her words and lost them in the air above the cemetery, Meredith felt angry and unfairly victimised. This was the second time in a couple of weeks she'd been menaced with a gun. At least she'd known where Reeves was. This time the killer was out of sight and the first thing to do was locate just where the threat came from.

The cemetery was as silent, in an appropriate phrase, as the grave. All the birds had fled. From where she crouched she couldn't see anyone moving or part of another person sticking out from behind a headstone such as her own chosen shelter. The whole area seemed utterly deserted. But the space between her own shoulder-blades was tingling uncomfortably with the knowledge that it wasn't. She could see the dead man's hand, stretched out, reminding her that the gunman was an accurate shot.

She peered apprehensively around the headstone which sheltered her. It was new and at the foot of it lay a withered funeral wreath. 'Lynne, beloved daughter ...' read faded lettering on the card still attached to the floral tribute. She had no time to dwell on this sad coincidence now. Across the new cemetery, over the wall and in the middle of the churchyard beyond, stood the church. The original shot had seemed to come from there. The building was left open during the day because Father Holland believed people should have access to their local place of worship. Meredith raised her eyes. The church steeple took the form of a spire on a tower base. At the point where the spire rose from the roof there was a parapet running all round it, accessible from inside the supporting tower. There was a permanently locked door to the tower at ground level outside the building, but another, inside the church, which was frequently open. As she stared up at the parapet, she fancied she saw something move and then a gleam as if light reflected from a polished surface. The gunman was up there and had an uninterrupted view of everything down here on the ground. He could pick off anyone at will.

It was a nasty thought. If this wasn't the time to panic it would be difficult to think of a better time. Meredith fought to stay calm and reason it out. She tried to put herself in the murderer's shoes. The killer, having achieved the intention in disposing of Matthew, would now seek escape. Someone else might have heard the shot and come to investigate. The killer might not have any more ammunition or, if he did, had no reason to waste any more on Meredith who, so long as she cowered behind the slab of marble, was rendered harmless. And she knew now he didn't want to kill her because from up on his lofty perch he could have picked her off easily, the headstone offering no protection.

All the same, it was hard not to feel a sitting target. The small clump of immature trees around the tap from which she'd earlier fetched water for her flowers offered better cover and there was also the little groundsman's hut to which Matthew had drawn her attention. Meredith turned her wrist to see the watch-face and counted the second hand as it moved round its full circle. Then she scrambled out from behind her refuge and, scurrying like an ungainly spider from headstone to headstone, reached the hut. It was padlocked and no use to her, but the trees offered a relative sanctuary.

There had been no further shots. She could see the parapet but no longer any sign of life up there. The rooks too, thought the coast was clear, and were beginning to return, circling above the spire. If there was a figure with a gun up there, they would see it. They didn't. The killer had made off, satisfied that the victim was dead.

In automatic confirmation of this thought, Meredith looked back and saw Matthew still sprawled in the open. She edged cautiously out of the trees. Silence. Up on the parapet, nothing. A bird rustled in the tree behind her, making her jump. Doubled over uncomfortably she made for the gate which joined the 'new' cemetery to the old churchyard which, with its ancient trees, offered excellent cover and was, in any case, the way out.

No one took a pot shot at her on the way. Meredith straightened up painfully. She had a crick in her back, her recently injured neck was beginning to ache again, her heart throbbed painfully and she wanted desperately to go to the loo. But there was no sign of any danger now and the most powerful urge of all was to check out her deductions and see the spot from which the sniper had taken aim. Then she'd go and report what had happened. The outer door of the church porch stood open. She made for it, hugging the wall. In the porch, she opened the inner door and peered inside. The interior seemed empty and, as she had suspected, the little door giving access to the tower was held open by a long hook attached to a bracket in the wall.

Meredith crossed to it and stuck her head through, looking up the spiral stairs. She listened. Nothing, only that deadness of sound which betokens absence of human presence. Still cautious, but knowing she was protected from view by the twist of the stair around the central pillar, she began to climb the worn stone steps. At intervals slits in the outer wall allowed in a little light to aid the climber and a glimpse of the world outside to let him know how high up he'd got. The stench of bat droppings was getting worse and more noxious, making her feel sick, a feeling encouraged by the apparently never-ending clockwise twist of the narrow stairway. She paused and leaned against the cold stone wall and listened again. But she was sure now there was no longer anyone up there.

At the top of the stair Meredith emerged into the tiny raftered room beneath the spire. Above her head there was a rustling and squeaking. Looking up, she saw tiny dark shapes hanging among the woodwork, wrapped in their wings, peering at her with cross little fox-like faces.

The tiny door which led out on to the parapet stood ajar. Propped against it was a hunting rifle. The killer, having no wish to be encumbered on the precipitous descent of the spiral stair or be stopped later in possession of it, had clearly facilitated escape by abandoning the weapon.

Avoiding it, Meredith stepped out on to the narrow walkway. At once the wind seized at her clothes. She hadn't allowed for the strength of it up here or the bitter cold. She felt very insecure. The masonry of the parapet wall looked neither high enough nor structurally sound enough. Behind her the spire was inclined at a sharp angle away from her so that she couldn't lean back against it as she could have done against a flat wall. The ground below appeared to rise and fall as vertigo began to close in. For all the cold, she had begun to sweat. Matthew's body lay in a pathetic tiny huddle over in the distance and his outstretched hand seemed to beckon. The wind continued to do its bit, tugging at her. It was all too obvious from up here how inadequate had been her attempt to shelter behind the headstone. The killer, had he so wished, could have targeted her at leisure. Or she, thought Meredith. Because, after all, the most likely killer this time was a woman. Marla Lewis. Hell hath no fury like a woman scorned.

She edged her way back through the door into the tower room. The bats squeaked irritably again. Meredith began to descend the spiral stair to the church below. Halfway down she heard the door at the bottom of the stair slam and a key turn in its ancient lock. *

Meredith hurtled recklessly down the remaining stairs. Solid oak barred her way. She rattled at it in vain. She was trapped. Distantly she heard the roar of a car engine.

Meredith sat down on a stone step and propped her chin in her hands. What now? It seemed likely that the killer had been escaping across the churchyard and seen Meredith approach. He – or Marla, if it were Marla – had followed her back inside, waited until Meredith was at the top of the stair and simply shut her in, containing the nuisance.

Frustrated, Meredith got up and hammered on the door but to no avail, only bruising her hands. She would have to wait until someone came to collect a magazine or see to flowers, or Father Holland came to lock up at night. It was extremely cold in here and, besides, the crime was still unreported and the perpetrator of it making an unhindered escape. Meredith lamented in vain not having gone to raise the alarm first and left exploring the tower till later. She'd been an idiot.

Slowly she reclimbed the stair at the top. The bats were really annoyed now. One or two flew down and circled her head before darting back to the roof space. Meredith steeled herself and edged out on to the narrow parapet again. She made her way round the base of the spire, doing her best not to look over the rim, until she reached the further side from where, holding tightly to the parapet edge, she could see the main path up to the church. Beyond that she could glimpse the roof of the vicarage above its garden wall. There was no one down there. The only company she had was a gargoyle water spout in the shape of a dragon's head. Its mouth gaped in an unseemly grin as if it relished her predicament.

Meredith sank down and squatted on her heels behind the rim where she couldn't see the ground and wondered if there was anything up here she could throw or wave. At that moment she heard the roar of a motorcycle.

Forgetting her fears, she got up quickly and leaned out over the stone rim. Yes, it was Father Holland, dismounting from his Yamaha. Now he was walking up the path to the church. But then something seemed to occur to him, because he stopped, turned and to her dismay, began to walk back again.

Melanie howled his name. The wind caught her words and whisked them away. She did the only thing she could think of. She took off her shoe and hurled it from the parapet. It crashed to the pavement before the church. Father Holland turned curiously and looked up. Meredith waved frantically. Father Holland politely waved back. Meredith took off her other shoe and dropped that over the edge. Father Holland watched it fall, puzzled. Perhaps he thought she conducted Galileo-like experiments with gravity. It was unlikely he could identify the figure above from where he stood and may just have thought he had a lunatic on his tower. At any rate, he went into the church to investigate.

Heedless of her former vertigo, Meredith hurtled barefoot back round the parapet to the tiny door, through the bat-room to the accompaniment of more outraged squeaks and flutterings, and down the spiral stair.

As she reached the bottom, the oak door was unlocked and opened. Father Holland put his bearded face round the pillar.

'Oh, hullo, Meredith? Get yourself locked in with the bats?'

'The gun,' said Alan Markby, picking up the bottle of wine, 'almost certainly came from Park House. The trouble with these old country homes is that they often have a couple of sporting guns lying around and the owners overlook them. Matthew never went out shooting. When we contacted Prue in Cornwall she said there should be two guns belonging to Adeline's father, locked up in a gun cupboard. We discovered the cupboard forced and found only one gun. There were no fingerprints on the gun left on the tower and none on the gun cupboard.'

'She wiped them off. She wore gloves.'

'Ah, you mean Marla, do you?' He poured them both another glass.

'Of course I mean her! Look at her motive! She believes Matthew jilted her and cheated her of being mistress of Park House! Prue heard them have a dreadful quarrel!'

'Yes, but she didn't hear any actual murder threat. We know Marla left Park House over two weeks ago. She'd been living in a borrowed flat in London since then, waiting to fly home. The police actually took her in for questioning at Heathrow Airport, which she didn't much like.'

'And?'

'And she's sitting tight, saying nothing, and has got a very good legal representative who is saying quite a lot. I'm afraid we're going to have to let the lady go with apologies.'

'What!' Meredith almost jumped out of her chair. 'She's responsible for two deaths, if you count Adeline's and I do – to say nothing of taking a pot shot at me! Has she got an alibi?'

'For the time of Matthew's death? No. But then, neither do we have a witness who saw her back in Bamford, let alone near the church, and circumstantial evidence isn't enough. It's for us to prove she did it, not for her to prove she didn't, remember! Perhaps she didn't.'

'Hah!'

'Yes, well, other unexpected lines of inquiry are presenting themselves now that Conway is dead. Lawyers trying to settle his business affairs have access to his files and very interesting they are! It's normal for creditors to be clamouring for their cash or goods at times like this. But the odd thing is that, in the wake of Conway's sudden departure, so many people are coy about coming forward to tell of business dealings. It now begins to look as if he was engaged in the export of prohibited goods to certain troubled areas of the world.'

'Arms?' Meredith exclaimed in astonishment.

'No, computer and other technical equipment without which, of course, much of the military hardware is useless. He always did a lot of business in the Gulf area. Who knows, perhaps he failed to deliver on a deal? Went back on his word? In that part of the world, matters of honour are often settled with a bullet. It'll all come out in the wash, as the saying goes. And if it doesn't, Matthew's killing will remain on our files. We never close an unsolved murder enquiry.

'Investigation of his other activities isn't my department! There are people up in London more competent to take care of it. But if Mrs Lewis has information relevant to breaches of guidelines in dealing with Iraq or others, running away won't save her from being called to give account!'

Meredith glowered over that for a moment or two, before

turning to the matter nearer home. 'So what happens to Park House now?'

'That's going to be the subject of a long legal wrangle. Documents are flying between solicitors at a great rate. Matthew Conway ordered his lawyers to draw up a new will for him, in view of his approaching marriage. But he hadn't signed it. His fiancée is claiming that he made his intent and wishes clear in letters to the lawyers and to her. Along with being naturally distraught, she's reportedly also hopping wild. As you appear to be. Relax. The muscles will all tense up and your neck will start hurting again.'

'How can I? You're just sitting there, calmly telling me that, Sinister Unknowns aside, the most likely suspect for Matthew's murder is about to be released without charge, free to leave the country!'

Markby put his clasped hands on the table. 'That shocks you? Why? Did you think the British copper always got his man or woman? Oh, no, we don't do that.' His eyes met hers and held her gaze. 'Or I don't, anyway, do I?'

'Don't take it so badly!' Helen Turner advised her later. 'I know you've a personal interest in seeing Marla get her come-uppance, but if you were a policewoman, you'd get use to those kinds of frustration. Have you any idea how many times we're sure we can identify a villain, yet we know we're unlikely ever to get him into court?'

'I could never be a policewoman,' said Meredith thoughtfully. 'Don't get me wrong! I'm full of admiration for the dedication with which most police officers do a very messy job. My trouble is, I can't bend my sense of natural justice or the rightness of things to fit in with rules and regulations, or the insensitivity of so much police probing and prying. I've tried to explain all this to Alan many times. I hope he understands. It's one of the things which stops us from ever setting up home together as any kind of unit. I couldn't fit in with the police work. Not his fault. Mine.'

'No one's fault!' said Helen firmly. 'A lot of police marriages bite the dust. Sad fact of life. Take me!' She saw the surprise on Meredith's face and added hastily, 'Oh, I wasn't married! But I was engaged to a fellow copper. Then one day we sat down and talked through what it would really mean if we married and both tried to continue our police careers. We decided it was more than we'd be able to juggle, and one of us would have to find a different job. Then we discovered that neither of us was prepared to give up police work. So that was that. We parted friends, as they say. Although *they*, whoever they are, lie of course! Whoever parts real friends? We parted in a state of armed truce, each entrenched in our respective points of view. Both obstinate, I suppose.' She smiled sadly.

'I'm so sorry,' Meredith told her. 'But you do understand, then. I want Alan and me to stay as we are because in its way, it works. Don't you think that's fair enough?'

'Sure, I do!' said Helen with a wry grin.

'I wish he did!' said Meredith.

'That was very nice, Barney, thank you!' said Mrs Pride as he retrieved the tray from her lap.

'Be back with the tea in just a jiff, Doris!'

'Seems funny, sitting about in front of the fire in my own house, being waited on!' she observed as he made for the kitchen. 'Specially as the leg is really a lot better.'

His voice floated back. 'Nothing funny about it at all! And you rest that leg! That was a very nasty accident you had! The least I can do is return some of the effort you put into looking after me last year when my legs played me up! Legs are tricky things as you get older. Mind you, I could have told Markby to watch out for that fellow Reeves!'

'Could you, indeed? Then why didn't you?'

Barney appeared in the doorway, clasping Anne Hathaway's cottage. 'Because I couldn't have explained exactly what I feared! But I've seen that kind before. I was in the army myself, Korean war. We had all sorts. There were chaps who hated service life, some who didn't mind it and made the best of it, some who quite liked it and a few, always a tricky type, who absolutely loved it! The army was father and mother, wife and lover to them! Everything was neat and tidy, cut and dried. They knew who everyone was and what he was supposed to do and their lives had meaning! Oh, brave as lions, most of them! But Lord knows how they got on once they were demobbed. Civvy life, unlike service life, is too rambling and inefficient for them. It tends, most of the time, to be downright boring, nothing to get the blood pounding, no satisfaction. Things go wrong and they don't know what to do. Mark my words, when that case comes to court, there will be some item of army brass telling the jury what a model soldier Reeves was. Keen as mustard, devoted to duty, utterly reliable with recruits, never a black mark against his name! A man like that is an orphan without his regimental boots and badges!'

He vanished again. Mrs Pride reached for the remote control of the television placed conveniently for her sound hand, and pressed a few buttons. 'Nothing on, never is!' she lamented. 'Though after all the goings-on in Bamford, watching things on the telly isn't going to be the same at all. Too much excitement never does you any good, that's what my mother used to say. I don't think I could cope with any more upsets for a while!'

Barney returned with the tea-tray and took the chair opposite to her. 'You need someone to look after you, Doris. A woman of your age trying to manage all on her own, it's not right.'

'Look who's talking!' said Mrs Pride. 'What have I been telling you for the last I don't know how many years, Barney Crouch? Living down in that out of the way place of yours, walking along that lonely road to the pub every night. If I can't manage on my own, which I don't admit, then you certainly can't! Oh, and I'll have a piece of sponge cake. In the tin with the picture of Windsor Castle on the lid.'

Barney fetched the cake tin. 'I know what you're getting at. It's not that your house isn't very comfortable, Doris. But I – well, I've got used to my place.'

'Murderers lying in wait all over the place out there!' said Mrs Pride with some relish.

'No one's going to murder me!'

'You don't know!' she told him. She shifted her bruised leg on the cushions. 'And I shan't be able to keep cycling out there to see you like I did! Fact is, I doubt I shall ever come again.'

'Doris!'

'How can I? My bike is wrecked. I can't afford a new one. Besides, it's shaken my confidence, falling off like that. I don't know that I'd fancy riding it any more.'

'I suppose,' said Barney sadly, 'that I shall have to give up my house sooner or later.'

'Sooner the better. Before it falls down round your ears!'

'I'd miss you, Doris. I'll own up. I don't know how I'd manage without your visits.' Barney began to look nervous and rattled the lid of the teapot.

Mrs Pride studied her slice of sponge cake.

Barney finally broke the silence. 'Look, I'll sell my place, which will give us a nice little nest egg, and we'll set up here together! What do you say, Doris?'

'I'm not about to start living in sin, not at my time of life! This accident has made me all too aware how near I am to meeting my maker!' the object of his attentions informed him. 'St Peter has got enough written in his book about me without another chapter!'

'All right, then, we'll get married. Seems daft at our age, but if that's what you want, fair enough!'

'That's not much of a proposal!' she objected.

'If I get down on my knees,' said Barney firmly, 'I shan't be able to get up again and you, in your state, couldn't help me! I should be honoured, Doris, if you'd accept me.'

'I'll think about it,' said Mrs Pride. 'Just pop the kettle back on and we'll have another cup of tea.'